THE
ORDEAL
OF
RUNNING
STANDING

Books by Thomas Fall

NOVELS

Prettiest Girl in Town
The Justicer
The Profit and the Loss
The Ordeal of Running Standing

JUVENILES

Eddie No-Name
My Bird Is Romeo
Edge of Manhood
Wild Boy
Canalboat to Freedom
Dandy's Mountain
Goat Boy of Brooklyn
Jim Thorpe

THE
ORDEAL
OF
RUNNING
STANDING

Thomas Fall

The McCall Publishing Company

NEW YORK

Published simultaneously in Canada by
Doubleday Canada Ltd., Toronto.

Library of Congress Catalog Card Number: 76-122124

SBN 8415-0047-9

The McCall Publishing Company
230 Park Avenue, New York, N.Y. 10017

PRINTED IN THE UNITED STATES OF AMERICA

Design by Tere LoPrete

For Jo   again

PART ONE

The Jesus Road

1

O<small>N</small> this fine day in 1898, Pole Bean, Round Face Woman, and Carrot Nose accompanied the goatherd through the Kiowa village. Pole Bean was a spindly white man who explained the Jesus Road and taught the Indians the white man's way. Shaped more like the beans than the poles they grew on, he was tall and bent forward. His white name was the Reverend John Holcombe.

As the trio passed with the goatherd, the boy Running Standing stayed behind the flap of his father's tipi. His half brother, Long Neck, who was older and therefore more experienced in every way, always jeered at him for hiding—but he remained out of sight, wanting to observe Carrot Nose before she observed him.

Carrot Nose was new at the mission school and the boy knew that he would have to contend with her. Not only was she carrot-nosed, her hair was carrot-colored. Tied in a bird's nest at the base of her skull, it was probably very long and would make an impressive scalp lock. After she had gone, he dug his rolled-up blond-woman scalp lock out of the cowhide bag that contained all his possessions. It was a small hank of hair and skin that had once decorated his grandfather's battle shield.

Looking at it occasionally, and handling it, gave him a sense of connection with Kiowa glory. Only the past had glory.

"Carrot Nose will be Pole Bean's number two wife," said
Lives-in-a-Tree, the boy's mother, who had been suspiciously
watching the Jesus people make the rounds.

"No, she will not," said Falling Water, the boy's other-
mother. "You should know that the Jesus Road does not
permit a man two wives."

The boy's two mothers glared at each other. He had noticed
that they glared a lot lately. If the family decided to take the
Jesus Road, one of them would have to be cast out of the
family.

He glanced at Rabbit Hand, his father. Rabbit Hand was
tying the goat he had just been given to a stake in front of
the tipi. After the goat was secured, Rabbit Hand began whetting his knife on a small oilstone that he always carried. When
he had nothing else to do, which was most of the time, he
whetted his knife, testing its edge occasionally with his thumb.
He had something to do now. As soon as he was satisfied with
the knife edge, he would kill the goat.

"If you can believe the white people," he said to his quarreling women, "the Jesus Road allows a man only one wife."
And Running Standing thought of female wolves snarling in
heat as he watched his mothers watch each other.

Falling Water, his other-mother, was older, larger, and
wiser in the ways of the white world. Confident that Rabbit
Hand would in the end choose her, she had recently taken the
Jesus Road and begun urging its acceptance by her husband.
She was ugly and fat, the boy thought; she was part Co-
manche, part Pawnee, very stupid, and maybe even part white.
Her father had given Rabbit Hand a good horse and forty-
seven rabbit skins as inducement to take her.

His real mother, Lives-in-a-Tree, was smaller, younger, and
darker-skinned—a beautiful Kiowa full blood from a low-
caste family in another village. The boy knew that no one in
his father's class of Kiowas would have considered marrying
her under any circumstances had she not been extraordinarily
beautiful. She was also intelligent, which often confused her
husband.

The boy despised himself for caring about his mother's feelings. And he resented his half brother, Long Neck, for laughing at them.

His father sprang suddenly toward the goat, grabbed the
animal's head, twisted it upward, and sawed furiously into its
throat with the knife. Blood spurted and the goat bellowed

and struggled with death. "Hallelujah!" the boy cried aloud. At his cry, and the bellow of the goat, everyone closed in: his half brother; his little half sister, Turkey Eyes, who could only crawl; his two old aunts, and his ancient distant uncle, Weasel Ear. They formed a hungry circle, their mouths hopeful. Long Neck, the boy noticed, nervously stroked the chest of his fighting cock, which he carried with him everywhere. The cock's feathers bristled, perhaps at the scent of blood.

Rabbit Hand rolled the dead goat over in the dust, slit open its belly, reached inside the cavity and tore out the purple fresh liver, which he held up. He tasted it, reached again into the goat and cut out the gall, which he squeezed over the liver. He cut off a piece and chewed judiciously. Deferring to age, he served first the ancient uncle—it would take him a long time to eat because he had no teeth; then he served Long Neck, the half brother; then the boy—who took his piece in trembling hands.

He watched his father, who stood over the goat and ate until the liver was gone before moving away to lick his knife blade and leave the carcass to the women, who rushed in and ate the heart and kidneys before drawing the entrails and beginning the task of skinning and butchering.

The boy then crossed through the tipi village alone and full of meat. The scent of goat tallow lay sweet in the air.

Suddenly his half brother, as belligerent as the gamecock under his arm, appeared at the edge of the village.

"Are you going to the mission?" Long Neck asked.

Running Standing did not answer. He could not understand why his half brother always ridiculed him.

Long Neck threw back his head and laughed. "The Jesus Road did not get me," he said, "but it will get you if you keep going over there."

The boy turned, ignoring Long Neck, and ran in the morning sun across the hot prairie toward the mission house to have a closer look at the new teacher.

"There he is," said Round Face Woman, nudging Carrot Nose into attention. "That is Running Standing. He has been eating raw liver again. Did you ever see such eyes?"

Suddenly the boy needed to blink his eyes but he dared not.

"Don't frighten him," said Pole Bean. Listening to them, the boy resisted an impulse to expand his chest.

"Does he come here often?" asked Carrot Nose.

"Yes, frequently," said Round Face Woman. "He comes closer now than he used to. He is quite like his father, but with more spirit. At least he has the spirit to come and stare at us."

Carrot Nose, watching through the open window, said, "It is positively weird to talk about him as though he were not there. One could almost believe he understands us."

The boy was uneasy. He stared back and tried to make himself look stupid.

"He speaks only Kiowa," said Pole Bean, "but I don't think he ever says very much, even to his own people."

"How old did you say he was?" asked Carrot Nose.

"There's no way to know. He was several years old before we discovered him. His father did not put his name on the tribal rolls until the land allotment was announced. Then he had to, of course, or lose a headright."

The boy was no more than six feet from the window, and he stood on a large round stone to make himself tall enough to see inside. Once the stone had been much farther from the window. Recently he had rolled it nearer, so that he could better see and hear what the Jesus people said about him. He had feared they might move the stone away, but they had not, and he realized that for some reason they had left it there for him to stand on when he came.

"It is generally conceded," Pole Bean explained to Carrot Nose, "that his people, the Kiowa, killed more whites than any other Indians."

The new teacher shuddered and said, "I want to talk to him. Where is the interpreter?"

"Susan Antelope is in the garden. I will bring her." Round Face Woman turned through the door at the front of the little house and made her way around the side toward the vegetable garden that separated the one-room dugout residence from the somewhat larger building that served as mission and schoolhouse.

Susan Antelope was part Kiowa, part Cheyenne, part Mexican, and part white. Her real name was Face-of-Antelope. She could speak at least a little of all the major languages on the reservation. She came from the garden, a lithe, pretty girl of nineteen, unmarried, and as watchful in her way as Running Standing was. He wondered why she had taken the Jesus Road. With her talent for languages she could get along easily. He already knew that Indians usually took the Jesus

Road in desperation. Face-of-Antelope should not be desperate.

"Tell the boy—" Carrot Nose began, then interrupted herself to ask: "What did you say his name was?"

"Running Standing," said the girl. "His grandfather was Spotted Foot, one of the Kiowas imprisoned at Fort Marion. His father is Rabbit Hand, a rather subdued Indian who still keeps his family in the tipi village. They do not trust Indians who live in houses."

Carrot Nose nodded. "I want to talk to him, but first let us pray."

The boy watched her fall to her knees to make a Jesus medicine. Clasping her outstretched hands, she closed her eyes and lifted her face toward the ceiling.

"We beseech Thee, dear Father, Maker of all mysteries, to invest our humble minds and hearts with the knowledge and forbearance required to guide this savage boy into Thy enlightenment. A-men."

Carrot Nose then said to Susan Antelope: "Tell the boy I will be honored if he will come inside and talk to me. Emphasize *honored*. Tell him I need his help in a very important matter. Appeal to his sense of pride, for they are a proud people."

As Susan Antelope devised her message in Kiowa, the boy thought fast. He did not want the whites to know that he understood them. He feared that if he went inside he might accidentally betray himself. And he disliked Carrot Nose for the simple reason that she seemed stupid.

He did not answer Susan Antelope, but whirled off the stone instead and ran toward the river as fast as he could. He climbed onto a rocky ledge at the river's edge, clasped his hands before him, raised his eyes toward the hot windy sky, and said in his own language:

"O Great Spirit, please bring back our buffalo and take the Jesus people away from our lands."

Then he struck out over the dry prairie toward his village.

His home of rain-stained, sagging canvas stood at the lower end of the tipi village oval, near the Cheyenne-Arapaho border. Other Kiowas in other Kiowa villages had begun living in houses made of cottonwood boards, but Running Standing's people were the remnants of intractable families, the bitter-enders who could be comfortable only in tipis. They still seriously danced around a fire, believed in their Grandmother

Gods, mourned the ending of their Sun Dances, and turned to their owl prophet for omens.

He found his father sitting in the dust outside the tipi, still savoring the goat liver. Rabbit Hand was tall for a Kiowa. His high cheekbones cast shadows down his face at noon. His hair braids hung in front of his shoulders to a point near his knees. He was always naked above the waist except during the coldest weather or when he went to the agency; he always wore shoes and a shirt to the agency. He had never yet gone to Pole Bean's mission, but the boy feared he would wear a shirt and probably even cut his hair if he ever did.

"Carrot Nose is no different from the others," he told his father.

Rabbit Hand looked up and said, "Running Standing, why do you keep going there?"

"They talk about me. I want to hear what they say."

"Do you really understand their lingo?"

"Some of it. I can say 'Hallelujah!' " the boy said, and he laughed as he bundled up the skins he had been saving to take to market. "That is their happy cry. Hallelujah."

"What are you going to do with those skins?"

"Trade them in Cloud Chief for a knife and oilstone like yours. On the next issue day, I will make the kill for you."

Laughter behind him came from his half brother, who had emerged from the tipi carrying his rooster. Like their father, Long Neck was naked to the waist, but he wore no braids. He had cut his hair four years ago when he attended the mission school for a few days and continued now to wear it short. Each day he was at the school, he had jumped out the window and perched himself on a pile of boards where he flapped his arms and crowed for a while before going home. He was proud of the fact that the Jesus people had soon given up on him. He now carried a rooster everywhere he went.

"Running Standing might kill a goat," he jeered, "but never a steer, and certainly never a bull!"

Long Neck had once killed a bull with his father's knife. The Indian Agency had tried to encourage livestock raising on the reservation, but the young boys had stalked and shot the breeding stock, and Long Neck had bravely attacked and killed the only bull.

"Do not speak that way," said Rabbit Hand. He rose suddenly and hit Long Neck a· sharp blow with his fist. Long Neck fell backward into the dust and his rooster flew squawking to the ground. "All you learned at the white Jesus school," Rabbit Hand told him, "was to make fun of your young brother. It is not the Indian way. I do not like it."

Long Neck scrambled to his feet, collected his rooster, and disappeared around the side of the tipi.

Deeply disturbed, but pretending not to be, Rabbit Hand turned back to Running Standing and asked, "How many skins do you have?"

"Ten beaver, four skunk, twenty-one squirrel."

"Do not trade them for an oilstone and a knife. Make the store man give you money first, and then buy what you want. That way you may have some money left over."

"Why will I?" the boy asked.

"Getting more than they give is the white man's way. They call it *business*. They do not even consider it dishonest."

The boy felt shrewd. Armed with new knowledge, he slung the bundle over his back, headed toward the prairie, and ran all the way to town.

2

FIVE miles across the Kiowa border, in Cheyenne-Arapaho country, lay the town of Cloud Chief, near the Washita River. On the Kiowa side of the border the short-grass prairie was dotted as far as the eye could see with cattle belonging to white cowmen, a few of whom paid small grazing fees to the Indians while the others simply poached the abundant grass at will. Over on the Cheyenne-Arapaho side, the reservation had been broken up and allotted in small acreages to individuals of those tribes; over there, the land not allotted had been opened to white homesteading, most of it claimed by farmers from Ohio, Indiana, Missouri, the deep South, and from Germany and Scandinavia. The Indians, who had always roamed and lived on buffalo and detested vegetables, now had most of the rich river-bottom land that would grow cotton, corn, and produce; and the white farmers, who needed only a plot of fertile ground and some seed, now found themselves plowing up good grassland in the hope of growing fields of wheat . . . or something.

With his skins tied in a bundle on his back, the boy ran. His father and Long Neck had taught him to run great distances. For their pride, and for his own, he had once run twelve miles. Long Neck could run twenty miles, but nowadays, if you ran twenty miles, all you could do was turn around and run home again.

As he ran, breathing deeply, the boy thought about the school he must avoid—the airless, closed-in house of cottonwood boards where pale white women taught the white lingo to Indian children by day: where people gathered at night to shout and praise the Jesus Road, swooning, sometimes, without even chewing peyote. He shuddered to think of it. They were probably the bloodiest people who ever lived, these whites; they had even killed their own Jesus.

As he approached Cloud Chief, Long Neck overtook him. They ran alongside each other for a while, the rooster riding comfortably under Long Neck's arm. "I decided to come and help you," he said.

"I do not need your help," said Running Standing.

"Then I will not help you," said Long Neck, laughing.

"Why do you laugh at me?"

"Because the Jesus people will get you."

"They won't."

"Are you brave enough to go into their school and not let them put you on the Jesus Road? I went there," he bragged, "and touched them . . . and walked away safely. They have not even tried to get me back."

Now the boy understood that his half brother was counting coup. In the glory days, no braver act could be performed by a warrior than to walk near enough to an enemy to touch his chest and determine whether fear made his heart beat fast.

"Falling Water thinks the Jesus Road is good," said the boy, believing his half brother would be impressed by the point of view of his own mother.

But Long Neck simply snorted. "Falling Water is stupid," he said.

"Lives-in-a-Tree does not like the Jesus Road."

"She is also stupid. She thinks she will be cast out of the family if our father takes the Jesus Road. That is why she does not like it."

"What will become of her if she is cast out?"

A bitter smile traveled the full length of Long Neck's face as he ran. "Don't you know that Lives-in-a-Tree has been secretly going to meet Wolf's Tongue on the bank of Owl Creek?"

"I . . . do not understand," said the boy.

"Because you are unwise and very young. Lives-in-a-Tree hopes Wolf's Tongue will take her in with him if she is cast out."

The boy was shocked. He hefted the bundle of skins higher onto his shoulder and lengthened his stride. "What do they do when they meet on the bank of the creek?" he asked.

"They laugh together and sometimes they roll on the ground."

"Does Rabbit Hand know about this?"

"No—Rabbit Hand is stupid, too."

"But he is our father."

"All our elders are stupid. Do not pay any attention to them, Running Standing."

"Does Falling Water know?"

"Nobody knows. Lives-in-a-Tree is very sly. Even Weasel Ear does not know, and he talks with old women from all the villages."

"How do you know about it, Long Neck?"

"I saw a look in her eye one afternoon. It made me suspicious. I followed her and watched them." Again he laughed hilariously.

The boy was silent. He thought hard about what he had just learned. He ran with Long Neck on the prairie, occasionally leaping over piles of bleached buffalo bones. Wolf's Tongue was a scar-faced Kiowa with no family. He had once tried to be a medicine man but had been unmasked as a fake.

As the boy reflected on the new information about his mother, he noticed that Long Neck had tucked his rooster higher under his arm and was slowly pulling ahead. Once more he lengthened his own stride but could not quite catch up.

"Why have all our elders become stupid?" he shouted ahead to Long Neck.

"The Jesus Road has got them!" Long Neck said.

"Not Lives-in-a-Tree," said the boy.

"Rabbit Hand would choose your mother over mine, but she does not know it. Fear makes her heart beat fast. She will end up living in Wolf's Tongue's cave. Everyone will despise her."

"Why do you think Rabbit Hand would choose her if he took the Jesus Road?"

Long Neck stretched out his stride in a sudden new burst of easy speed. His legs were long and he pulled ahead fast, laughing over his shoulder as though the question was stupid beyond belief.

"Why do you ridicule me?" the boy shouted. "We are brothers and yet you ridicule me wherever we go!"

Long Neck said nothing. Soon he was far enough ahead to appear to have come to town alone instead of with his younger brother.

Running Standing hoped, as he slowed his pace and reached the edge of town, that Long Neck would not stand around in Cloud Chief laughing at him all afternoon.

Main Street ran from the public watering trough at the east end to the blacksmith shop at the west, housing in between a dozen flourishing businesses behind vertically nailed boards. There were two saloons, two hardwares, two cafés, two general stores, and one of everything else that white people seemed to need, including a real estate office, a post office, a newspaper, and a mysterious printing shop.

Cloud Chief, the County Seat of the Territorial County of Washita—a name derived from the Washita River along which generations of Plains Indians had lived, fought, and died—was a white man's town. Its stores had already begun selling Indian artifacts.

When Running Standing reached the edge of town, he saw an arbor of brush near a large cottonwood tree on the bank above the river. Beside the arbor was a fancy road wagon and a Cheyenne family that had camped to sell watermelons to whites who came along the main road. It was a splendid wagon and he paused nearby to admire it . . . and to wonder.

His presence caused the Cheyennes to speak among themselves. He could understand only enough to know that they were talking about him. A young girl his own age spoke to him in white lingo.

"Come over and visit us," she said. "Do you understand me?" She was very pretty. Her long black braids were tied with red and white twine. She wore a yellow buckskin dress

with a brown apron of store goods over it and a string of
beads made of bleached chinaberry seeds.

He was reluctant to let anyone know that he understood
the lingo, but he wanted to visit these Cheyennes and find out
where they got their wagon. Very few Indians had such magnificent wagons.

"Kiowa," he said, pointing to himself.

"I do not speak Kiowa well," she replied. "Do you understand me? Come closer to us. What are you carrying on your
shoulders?" Her brown glistening eyes looked cautiously out
of an otherwise wholly placid face. Her elders stood beside
the wagon, perhaps amused or perhaps not, waiting to see
what he would do.

"I understand you," he said at last and walked toward
them. He unslung the bundle of skins from his back and
walked around the big orange and black wagon, rubbing his
hands over the iron-rimmed wheels.

One of the men was whittling on a stick with a knife similar
to Rabbit Hand's. He spoke briefly to the girl in Cheyenne,
then to the boy in white lingo.

"My young friend, what are you going to sell in Cloud
Chief?"

The boy unrolled his skins and spread them out for inspection. The Cheyennes all admired the drying and scraping
he had done.

"I am going to buy a knife," he told them, "like that one."
He glanced at the knife with which the girl's father was
whittling.

The man held up the knife for inspection and said, "I will
give it to you." He stepped forward and held it out with a
huge smile.

The boy took it, tested its edge with his thumb. He was
very proud. He noticed that the Cheyenne women still admired his skins. He gathered them up quickly and presented
them to the girl's father.

The large, square-jawed Indian accepted them gratefully.
Then he rolled the biggest watermelon out of the arbor and
gave it to the boy, who smiled, cut it open with his new knife,
and began eating it in large chunks.

"You have blood on your face," said the girl. "We heard
that your people were issued some goats this morning."

"What is your name?" the boy asked.

"Crosses-the-River."

"Do you go to school?"

"I go to Red Moon School. They call me Sara Cross at the school. What is your name?"

"Running Standing," he said, staring at her, beginning to realize what she was.

"We don't eat raw liver anymore," she said.

"Because you are Jesus Indians," he told her with rising disgust.

"Yes," she admitted. She did not seem in the least ashamed.

"Is your father Chief Killer?" he asked straight out.

"Yes. My father is Killer Cross." Now she seemed proud. And the chief held himself erect, still smiling.

The boy stood up, wiped the blade clean, closed the knife, and placed it on the wheel of the wagon. He rolled up the skins, slung them over his shoulder, and went on into town. He did not even look back at the awesome road wagon, for he knew that these Cheyennes had managed to get it by becoming Jesus Indians and he wanted no part of them. Anyone who would take the Jesus Road to get a wagon was beneath contempt, he thought . . . and this explained the mystery of Killer Cross.

Killer was one of the most famous Indians in the area. It had been widely told down in the Kiowa villages that Chief Killer of the Cheyennes had suddenly taken the Jesus Road so hard one afternoon that he jumped onto the platform at a brush arbor meeting and made a Jesus medicine in the Cheyenne tongue.

Chief Killer had been no more than a minor chief before he took the Jesus Road, for in the glory days he had been barely old enough to lead a raid or two. But now that the whites liked him so much, he was important to all his people. His family had been given the name Cross on the Indian rolls when the girl's name was changed at the school from Crosses-the-River to Sara Cross.

Thinking about them, the boy could not control his urge to stomp the ground as he went toward Main Street to sell his wares.

Near the watering trough a group of whites and Indians had gathered in a noisy circle around a gamecock fight. Hearing his half brother's voice urging his rooster on, the boy skirted the crowd and hurried down the street. Since there were two general stores, he decided to practice the shrewdness he had learned from his father.

He sold his skins at one store, receiving two dollars, then put the money into his pocket and went to the other store to look for a knife and an oilstone. Not wanting the storekeeper to know immediately what he wished to buy, he searched up and down the aisle, appraising everything he saw, enjoying the odors of gingersnaps and cheese and tar soap and coffee and tea. And there, beneath a glass countertop, was a display of knives, stones, razors, and shears—glittering and beautiful. He saw the knife he wanted but quickly passed it by, hoping not to alert the storekeeper to his precise desire. He did not pass quickly enough.

"You like-em knife?" The storekeeper reached beneath the glass and drew out the knife, offering it up for him to handle.

He took it, turning it over and over, testing its edge. His glance flicked to an oilstone and immediately the storekeeper handed it to him also.

"Speak-em white lingo?" the man asked. "Got-em two dollars, boy?"

He stared at the storekeeper. He had exactly two dollars and feared that he was being swindled. What power did white men have that told them precisely how much money you had in your pocket? Despite his half brother's belief that Rabbit Hand was stupid, the boy was impressed with the accuracy of his father's prediction. He was perfectly willing to give up his two dollars for the knife and stone—there was nothing else he wanted—but he feared losing face if he returned to his tipi with no leftover money. On the other hand, he could not bargain with the storekeeper without admitting that he understood white lingo—a revelation he had vowed never to make to a white man as long as he lived.

He placed the knife and stone on the glass counter and backed away, stalling for time to decide what to do. Finding himself now beside the gingersnap barrel, he took one and put it into his mouth.

"Hey, don't do that," the storekeeper said. "Those snaps are not free samples. They are for sale." Then he asked, with a tone of suspicion, "You got-em any money, boy? Any wampum?" He rubbed his forefinger and thumb together.

The boy then knew the white man's power was less than perfect. If it told him how much you got for skins, it failed to reveal whether you had already spent any of it.

Now he noticed a rack containing many long strings of glass beads. One string was especially colorful, with rich shades of purple. Frequently, just after sunset, if his mother was standing in shadows, her face around the eyes was exactly that color. He wanted the beads for her.

To convince the storekeeper he understood nothing, he took another gingersnap from the barrel and popped it into his mouth. And while the man screamed at him, he removed the purple beads from the rack and put them alongside the stone and knife on the glass. The storekeeper's interest was immediately renewed.

"I'll be glad when you Indians learn to speak white lingo," he muttered. "Maybe there's somebody outside can talk to you. What are you—Arapaho, Caddo, Wichita?"

The boy stood silently beside the counter, fingering the money in his pocket and concentrating on the pile of merchandise he coveted. The storekeeper went to the front and searched the street for assistance, returning presently with the Cheyenne girl, Crosses-the-River, and her father, Killer Cross.

"He does not speak white lingo, Killer," the storekeeper said. "Maybe you or young Sara can help me. I don't even know what tribe he comes from."

"Him?" the girl's father said. "Him Kiowa. We no speak Kiowa, Charlie."

"I think he wants to buy a knife."

For several moments the girl and her father stared at the boy. Their faces betrayed no flicker of recognition, and he was grateful even though they were Jesus Indians.

The storekeeper said, "Try signs on him, Killer."

Killer Cross looked down and made the signs that said, "This is a friendly white man. You can trust him."

The boy refused to answer, and Killer tried again, this time making the signs that said, "I will help you. I am your friend."

The last Indian on earth the boy wanted for a friend was a Jesus Cheyenne. Again he refused to answer but stared at the storekeeper as blankly as he could.

Killer said, "He no understand signs, Charlie. He must be very backward young Kiowa."

The boy noticed Crosses-the-River's eyes. She was laughing at him silently. She was very pretty and it seemed a shame that such a girl was on the Jesus Road.

Ignoring her, he looked around the store as though searching for something else he wanted. In one sense, he wanted everything he saw, and in another, he wanted only the knife and stone for himself and the purple beads for his mother.

"Killer," said the storekeeper, "can you find out whether he has any money?"

"Oh," said Killer Cross, "he have a little money, Charlie. I don't know how much, but he have a little."

"Are these the things he wants to buy?" asked Crosses-the-River, who had moved over to the glass counter.

"I guess so," said the storekeeper. "He piled them up."

"The beads are beautiful," she remarked, lifting them to put around her own neck with the chinaberry beads.

The boy pushed at her and took the beads from her hand. He wanted to shout: "Those are for my mother—to remember me by when she has to live in a cave with Wolf's Tongue. She will not want them if they have been around the neck of a Jesus Cheyenne!" He said nothing, of course, but put the beads back beside the knife.

"I think this boy no like us, Charlie," said Killer Cross. "He knows we are on the Jesus Road."

"Well, the devil take him," said the storekeeper. "You stay on the Jesus Road, Killer. It is the only road to be on."

Killer Cross smiled hugely. "Me know. We stay," he said.

In frustration, the boy stomped around the store again. As he passed the gingersnap barrel, he grabbed a handful and munched them while the storekeeper screamed.

"He no understand you, Charlie," said Killer. "He very backward boy. But he have a little money and he wants to buy these things. Maybe he thinks you try to cheat him."

"Me no cheat Indians," the storekeeper said, reverting to pidgin English in his excitement.

"No, no, no," said Killer, "but maybe backward boy think so. How much cost this things he want to buy, Charlie? This one?" He picked up the knife and read the pencil mark on the tag attached to it. "One dollar, right Charlie? Me read white money lingo good, no? How much this?" He picked up the stone. Unable to comprehend its indicated price, he showed it to his daughter.

"Fifty cents," she said. "That's one dollar fifty cents. And," she added, examining the sign that said 15 CENTS EACH on the bead rack, "the beads bring it to one dollar sixty-five cents."

Killer Cross then turned to the boy. "Hey, boy, you look here. Reach in pocket like this and pull out money. Like this, see?" He pulled money from his own pocket to demonstrate.

The boy was now captivated by the pretense. Solemnly he dug the two dollars out of his pocket.

"By golly, Killer," said the storekeeper, "you were right. I did not believe he had any money. Let's see . . . you get thirty-five cents change, young fellow. Understand-em change, boy?" He did not seem in the least unhappy to have had his swindle thwarted. Simply pleased to have made his sale, the storekeeper had lost no face at all.

"Want to wear the knife home on your belt?" the storekeeper asked at last. "Bet you do—if I could make you understand me."

As he spoke, the boy thrust his new knife under his belt. He put the oilstone in one pocket and the beads in another. He left the store so excited he forgot to pick up his thirty-five cents change. He didn't need it, anyway, for there was nothing else he wanted.

Outside he hurried across the street toward the edge of town, wondering about the Cheyenne father and daughter from the Jesus Road. He had insulted them at their arbor, and yet they had befriended him in the store. He turned at the sound of running footsteps and saw the girl approaching.

"You left your change on the counter," said Crosses-the-River. She held out her hands.

He took the thirty-five cents. "How did your father know I had money in my pocket?"

"My father carves wood. Little totem poles. He sells them at the other store. We went there just after you sold your skins."

The boy tried to give his thirty-five cents back to her. "You can have it."

"I don't need it," she told him.

"Then give it to your father for helping me."

"Why don't you give it to him yourself?"

They stood looking at each other fiercely for a moment, then burst into laughter. It was wonderful to laugh with this girl, and he wished suddenly that he could roll her on the ground.

"Did you know Charlie was trying to cheat me?" he asked.

"We know he cheats Indians whenever he can. He could not have tried to cheat you if you had spoken to him in white lingo."

"What difference would that make?"

"The articles all had prices on them."

"Because I can talk white lingo does not mean I can read it," he said.

The girl nodded thoughtfully. "Don't you go to school anywhere?"

"No. I go to the mission sometimes and listen, but I do not go to school."

"Why do you hate the Jesus Road?"

"Because it is lined with snakes and full of quicksand."

The girl smiled. "That is what the *old* Indians say."

"It is what I say, and it is true."

"I don't think it is true."

"But you are a Jesus Indian!" he cried, shaking his head. "All right, Crosses-the-River, I will go to your arbor and give the leftover money to your father. All except one piece. I must take home something to prove that I was not cheated."

"If you want to, you may call me Sara instead of Crosses-the-River."

"I like your real name better."

"If you went to school, they would not call you Running Standing."

"What would they call me?"

"They would give you a white-man name. Something like . . . Joe Standing."

"I would kill them with my new knife if they called me that."

"What is your name on the Kiowa roll?"

"Running Standing."

"Didn't they change it?"

"We have not been allotted yet. The Kiowa and Comanche roll is only a tribe roll."

She nodded. "It is the same with Wichita, Caddo, Apache, and Delaware."

"And also Tonkawa," he added. "They are on our reservation too."

"A Tonkawa girl goes to school with me at Red Moon."

"Tonkawas used to eat people," he said.

"But not anymore. Why did you buy the string of purple beads?"

He glared at her. "I won't tell you."

She shrugged. "The Tonkawa girl I know told me her grandfather once ate a whole Cheyenne by himself."

"Why did you ask about the beads?"

"The girl has a string of purple beads and I just happened to think of it."

"How long did it take her grandfather to eat a whole Cheyenne?"

"One day, I think. It might have been a very young Cheyenne. I am not sure."

Suddenly they were laughing again, doubled over, facing each other. And when he looked up, he saw his half brother standing above them, scowling. The rooster tucked under his arm seemed to be scowling, too. Its comb and wattles were bloody, but its eyes were clear.

"I see you are making friends with Jesus Indians," said Long Neck in Kiowa.

"I can if I want to," the boy replied in his own language.

A smile containing evil knowledge came up on Long Neck's face. "The Jesus Road will have you soon, because you have a look that says you want to roll this girl on the ground. Did you know she is Killer Cross's daughter?"

"Leave me alone, Long Neck."

"Does she know that our Sky-Walker has an owl medicine so strong that Jesus Indians can be prayed to death by owl prayer? If Weasel Ear saw you making friends with her, he might ask Sky-Walker to pray Killer Cross to death."

"What is he saying about my father?" the girl asked in white lingo. "Who is he?"

Although annoyed by his brother, the boy was at once fascinated by the idea of such a contest of medicines. An owl prayer pitted directly against a Jesus medicine in a battle to the death should prove something everyone needed to know these days.

He turned to the girl and switched once more to the white lingo. "This is my half brother, Long Neck. He says the owl prophet in our village can make a prayer so strong it could kill a Jesus Cheyenne."

The girl shook her head in wonder. "Do you still believe in owl prayer? I am surprised that your village remains so backward."

Anger shot through him and he stomped around her in a circle. "My half brother and I believe that Sky-Walker can pray Killer Cross to death. Let us go and talk to your father. I will give him my leftover money for helping me. My half brother can challenge him to pray against our owl prophet, and we will find out the truth. We will see which power is the strongest."

The girl whirled away, walking fast, and said over her shoulder, "Come with me." She, too, was stomping the ground. And she was beautiful, he thought, overwhelmed.

There were six members of the Cross family—the father, and the girl, a tall, gentle-faced woman who was probably the mother, two older women who might have been aunts, and a young man about Long Neck's age. According to stories told about them in the Kiowa village, they were all Jesus Indians. When informed of the owl prayer threat against Killer Cross's life, they all talked at once.

At last, perhaps in apprehension, thought Running Standing, the father held up his hand for silence. He stood beside the brush arbor stand and there was no doubt about it: His big square face was troubled.

"We no wish," he said in white lingo, "to quarrel over medicines."

"What did he say?" asked Long Neck in Kiowa.

"He does not want to fight us with medicine."

Long Neck's smile was contemptuous. "Tell him he can prove he believes the Jesus Road only by challenging our owl prophet. Otherwise our people can only laugh at him."

The boy repeated his half brother's statement. Again Killer Cross held up his hand to silence his excited family.

"We are friendly, and you are not. There is no such thing as owl power. Go home to your village and take our good wishes to all our Kiowa brothers. That is all I have to say."

The boy reported to his half brother in Kiowa, and Long Neck said bitterly, "Tell him we think he is afraid."

The boy translated Long Neck's message, then drew the leftover coins from his pocket and held them out. "Thank you for helping me at the store, even though you are afraid to trust your Jesus medicine."

Killer Cross drew himself high. "I do not want your leftover money."

"Then I will give it to Crosses-the-River." He offered the coins to her. She took them and with a blazing motion flung them into the grass. She threw so hard her chinaberry beads broke and sprinkled into the dust.

Long Neck laughed at her. Running Standing did not laugh
but had to restrain an impulse to help her pick up the scattered beads before he departed.

3

Two distinct branches of Kiowa medicine had always been
practiced by specialists who functioned under the exclu-
sive influence of the Ten Grandmothers—the principal Kiowa
gods. Buffalo doctors in the various clans cured the sick and
healed the wounded with whistles, rattles, dances, and chants;
and owl doctors in the villages ministered to Kiowa fears with
prophecies derived from owl prayer.

The Ten Grandmothers evolved from an ancient legend
about a maiden who, while chasing a porcupine, once climbed
so high in a tree that she penetrated the dome of the sky—
where the porcupine, suddenly revealed as the sun itself,
promptly took her for his wife and fathered her child, whom
they named Sun Boy. The new mother was warned by her
husband never to look down at the earth through the holes
that were occasionally made in the sky by celestial buffalo
pulling up roots. Curiosity, however, at last got the better of
her; while strolling one day with her young son in search of
berries, she peered through a hole and immediately became
nostalgic for her former life on earth. Disobeying her husband, she let herself down through the hole on a long rope,
carrying Sun Boy in her arms.

In a rage, the husband dropped a huge stone through the
hole, hitting his wife on the head and killing her instantly.
The child, Sun Boy, wandered the earth, playing alone, until
one day he threw into the air a gaming hoop, which came
down on his head, splitting him in half, thus providing him
with a twin brother. Calling themselves the Half Boys and
setting out to rid the world of monsters, one brother was
drowned and the other, mourning his loss, turned himself into
a magical power that, as a final act before physical disappear-

ance, he willed to the Kiowas in the form of ten medicine bundles, forever afterward called *Grandmothers,* so sacred that their contents were known only to the highest hereditary priests, who opened them ceremonially once a year and cleansed them with prayer.

The Ten Grandmothers were custodians of the Kiowas' right to tribal existence and the cleansing had always been the climactic ritual of the annual Kiowa Sun Dance—until recently, when the cavalry from Fort Sill descended upon the Sun Dance encampment and forbade the ceremony. The Grandmothers still existed on the reservation, of course, sacred and unopened in the hands of the Keepers. But the yearly Big Medicine was gone. And without it to renew the spiritual strength of buffalo doctors and owl prophets, the Kiowas were finding all the powers they believed in pitifully weak. Their right to tribal existence was now threatened by the Jesus Road—the white-man medicine that, like peyote, once swallowed, gave you incredible sensations. The trouble with the white medicine was that, unlike peyote, it did not seem to wear off. As it operated inside you as a continuing influence, you soon ceased to care whether you were even a Kiowa.

The fat owl prophet Sky-Walker, because of a recent spectacular success, had become something of a new hope among the dispirited Kiowas in Running Standing's village. All alone, without the help of Grandmother invocation, he had prayed to death a Jesus Osage who, while visiting the tipi of some Kiowa in-laws, had bragged of the time the Osages raided the Kiowa clan near Saddle Mountain. Everyone still remembered the incident; the raiders had taken them by such surprise that defense was impossible. A few Kiowas had escaped down Otter Creek; the rest of the clan had been killed and their heads left in camp buckets as offerings to the Osage gods.

Now, if this Osage visitor had not pretended to travel the Jesus Road while arrogantly counting coup among his in-laws, the rotund Sky-Walker would not have become so angry. But the man was too crude. Sky-Walker jumped to his feet, brought his owl out of his shirt, and began to chant.

"What are you doing?" asked the Osage.

"I am killing you," Sky-Walker told him.

"Killing me? How are you doing it?"

"With owl prayer. My former friend, the sun will break over Rainy Mountain tomorrow morning as wide and bright as an owl's eye in the night. It will shine upon your lifeless body grown stiff in the early wind. This will be your last day upon the Jesus or any other road."

"Do not do this thing!" cried the Osage, thus losing face as he cowered before his doom.

The prophet rubbed his owl and continued chanting as the frightened Osage attempted to run for his life from the tipi village.

The Kiowas later speculated vehemently on whether the Osage might have remained alive if he had disavowed the Jesus Road then and there, but Sky-Walker insisted that it had been too late for disavowal. In any event, his prophecy came true. The Osage was found dead the next morning on a trail that led away from the mountain.

People now listened when Sky-Walker spoke, often going to him for prophecy and exhortation. When asking for omens, they always took him presents to be used as offerings to the owls. Because he insisted that the most effective offering to owls was food and the only method of transmitting it to them was to eat it himself, he had grown so fat he waddled when he walked—the only fat man in Running Standing's village.

The boy listened to his half brother describe to Weasel Ear, their distant uncle, the encounter with the Jesus Cheyennes at the watermelon stand. Long Neck shook his fist and cried, "Killer Cross says there is no such thing as owl power."

Old Weasel Ear rose from the darkness of the tipi as though on fire. "I will go and tell Sky-Walker this thing." The boy saw the new look on his old uncle's face. "If Sky-Walker is afraid of that Cheyenne," he added, "I will borrow his owl and pray Killer Cross to death myself."

Running Standing trembled and his half brother said, "I will go with you to see Sky-Walker."

"No," the old man told him. "You do not speak the owl tongue. I must go alone. I will offer a piece of goat meat to the Grandmother, and then I will take this problem to Sky-Walker himself."

He hurried to the tipi of the Grandmother Keeper with a piece of meat for appeasement, his agitated gait suddenly steadier than it had been in years; then he crossed out of sight to the upper end of the oval to see the prophet.

The family waited. Running Standing stood outside his father's tipi watching his mothers simmer the goat's head in a

pot that hung over a fire. Word of Weasel Ear's visit to the
prophet, and the nature of the problem he took there, spread
rapidly through the village. Men and boys stopped smoking.
Women stopped pounding berries and scraping hides. Girls
stopped carrying water from the creek. Babies, hanging from
lodgepoles in their cradleboards, heard the silence and
listened.

"I do not like this," said Rabbit Hand. "It may not be
right to question someone else's medicine."

"Do not worry," said Falling Water. "Weasel Ear has ap-
peased the Grandmother."

Lives-in-a-Tree shoved the goat's head under with a stick.
"Why do you care what he does?" she asked Rabbit Hand.
"Nobody's medicine is any good. Nothing will happen."

The boy cringed at his mother's agnosticism and decided
not to give her the purple beads. He asked in astonishment,
"You do not believe in owl power or Jesus power either?"

"No," said Lives-in-a-Tree. "There is no power."

"What makes the sun. shine?"

"Nobody knows."

"But in the glory days—"

"The glory days have no meaning, or we would not be
living like this, as prisoners of the whites."

The other-mother, laughing shrilly, glanced at the boy, then
turned her face upward toward the sunset. "Brother Cross
will pray that fat fool Sky-Walker to death. And maybe old
Weasel Ear, too. All of you will learn that there is a Jesus
power!"

"Hush!" cried Rabbit Hand, stomping the dust. Many people from neighboring tipis had now gathered around him. "I
have decided what I am going to do," he announced, and he
was more than angry, the boy knew. He was also frightened.
"If Killer Cross dies, I will trust the owl power and stay on
the Indian road. If Sky-Walker dies, I will go to Pole Bean's
mission and get on the Jesus Road as fast as I can."

A titter of agreement rose around the fire. Most Kiowas
had grown weary of resisting the Jesus Road, however odious
it seemed to them. They had no religion now. Without their
Sun Dance to cleanse the Grandmother bundles, they could
only make offerings of appeasement to them—for a prayer
to an uncleansed bundle would be a blasphemy. Owl power
was all they had, and they needed more.

"Sky-Walker will kill that Cheyenne," someone said in a

voice suggesting that he might be trying to reassure himself as well as those around him.

"If he doesn't, Weasel Ear will. Old Weasel Ear is not afraid of Jesus medicine."

Listening to his elders and sensing disaster if Sky-Walker should decide to turn a matter of such importance over to Weasel Ear, the boy backed away from the crowd around his father and ran toward the owl prophet's tipi.

The sun had sunk below the horizon. Shadows stretched on the prairie, and in them the boy stood for a while among the group of Kiowas waiting near Sky-Walker's flap. He eased closer to listen. Inside, the prophet and his helper were not speaking owl lingo. They were speaking Kiowa.

"Loan me your owl," Weasel Ear was saying. "I will pray him to death myself."

"I will make a chant," said the prophet, "and see if I am spoken to about this thing."

The boy then heard Sky-Walker go into his high-voiced owl tongue. He turned away from the gathering and walked to the rear of the tipi. In deference to summer heat, the canvas sides were rolled up opposite the flap. Lying on his stomach in the grass, he could see inside. He crawled closer in the shadows.

"I do not hear anything," the prophet said at last. "The owls do not speak to me."

The boy was angry. Sky-Walker, who had already prayed a Jesus Osage to death, seemed now to be unsure of his medicine.

"Listen again," Weasel Ear urged.

The boy then did an unforgivable thing. He did it without thinking, or he would never have committed such blasphemy. Forcing his voice into its highest owllike register, he said weirdly into the night: "You must pray that Jesus Cheyenne to death, Sky-Walker, my brother." He was so frightened by the owl sound he had created that he shook all over.

Instantly the prophet and Weasel Ear jumped from the ground, looking at each other.

"They spoke!" cried Weasel Ear. "I heard them myself."

"That is the clearest I have ever heard an owl in my life," said Sky-Walker.

"I may have owl power myself. I heard them."

"The word is clear. Together we must pray that Cheyenne right into the ground."

Running Standing edged backward through the shadows and hurried to his own tipi, where he waited until his old uncle returned with the word. "We are going to kill him," Weasel Ear announced, his voice as light as his step. "I heard the owls myself. We will build a medicine tipi tomorrow."

A cheer went up. Someone threw more wood under the simmering goat's head. When the flame leaped high, the Kiowas danced spontaneously, and far into the night. Long Neck at last took the stick from Lives-in-a-Tree and fished the goat's head out of the pot. He held it over his head and danced an old death dance while hot fat, broth, and goat brains ran down his muscular arms and over his chicken.

By midmorning the whites in Cloud Chief knew that Sky-Walker intended to pray Killer Cross to death. Susan Antelope, the mission interpreter, who had been sent to town for a coal tar elixir, returned to the mission immediately and reported what she had heard. Running Standing was already on the stone outside the window, watching and listening.

"We must stop this somehow," said Round Face Woman. "John, the imagination of the savage mind is beyond belief, isn't it?"

Pole Bean, pale and speculative, lay on the daybed in a robe, suffering a summer cold. At last he said, "You know, Ruth, this might be a good thing. Can't you see the effect it might have on the entire village to watch a heathen prayer fail before their eyes?"

"I quite agree," said Carrot Nose. "Perhaps we could ask Killer Cross to return the challenge openly. He could sit in the medicine tipi while they try to pray him to death, and pray a Christian prayer for love and understanding all the while. It would make a strong impression."

But Susan Antelope told them it would be impossible. "Killer Cross will never do that. He will be afraid."

"But why? He is a Christian."

The girl shook her head. "He does not really believe in Jesus. He wants his children to believe but secretly he does not. I am sure of this. He will be afraid."

Pole Bean stared at his wife. "I am going to talk to him before he commits himself to anything. If he does not already believe in Jesus, he might now convince himself along with many others." Pole Bean took the bottle of black elixir, unscrewed the cap, and drank a few quick swallows.

"John," said his wife, "you must not leave a sick bed."

"God's work cannot wait. Susan, you had better come with me. They may talk Cheyenne among themselves if I am there alone."

He went into the dugout end of their little house to dress.

The boy backed away from the window and struck out across the prairie, reaching Cloud Chief ahead of Pole Bean and Susan Antelope. At the river bank on the outskirts of town he scrambled up through the willows to the cottonwood tree near Killer Cross's watermelon stand. Quietly he climbed the tree and pulled himself out on a limb where he could see and hear. To his surprise, his half brother was there, stroking the rooster under his arm and jeering at the Jesus Cheyennes in Kiowa.

The young Cheyenne who was Long Neck's age stepped forward. His hair was shorter than Long Neck's and he wore a store shirt. He shook both fists and shouted in his own tongue. Long Neck, naked to the waist, expanded his chest and said in Kiowa: "All Jesus Indians are cowards!"

Raging, the Cheyenne struck at the rooster and knocked it squawking from Long Neck's arm. The rooster landed on its feet, stretched its neck high, bristled its feathers, and flew, spurs flailing, at the Cheyenne's face.

Long Neck stepped back and laughed. "Even my chicken can whip a Jesus Indian," he said.

The Cheyenne covered his face against the game rooster's attack. The bird squawked and flew again. The Cheyenne drew a knife from his belt and brandished it. Before Long Neck could grab his bird, it attacked once more—this time impaling itself on the knife.

Blood spurted. The rooster dropped, kicking in death, to the ground.

Flinging blood from his knife, the Cheyenne turned to face Long Neck. They stood eight feet apart, both crouching. Slowly the Cheyenne advanced. Long Neck glanced around, his face stricken with the knowledge that he was helpless before the knife. He backed away, moving directly beneath the boy in the tree.

Running Standing pulled his own knife and dropped it at Long Neck's feet. Astonished, his half brother looked up for an instant, gratefully grabbed the knife out of the dust, shook it at the Cheyenne, went into a crouch of his own . . . and moved forward. Both boys lurched, their knives clicking savagely; and both jumped backward, circling each other—both bloody.

Pole Bean arrived in a clatter of wheels and leaped from the buggy, jumping between the boys before they could charge each other again.

"Help me, Brother Cross!" he shouted. He pushed Long Neck away from the Cheyenne as Killer Cross rushed forward to pull his son toward the road wagon.

From his perch on the tree limb Running Standing watched. Crosses-the-River stared up at him. Her head cocked sideways in the playful manner of a puppy, but her brown eyes flicked anger. She wore a beaverskin ribbon around the crown of her head. Her braids hung glistening in front of her shoulders. Her chinaberry beads, which she had gathered and restrung, hung around her neck, and she fingered them as she watched Pole Bean calm the angry combatants.

Pole Bean was indeed impressive. Because he had braved a knife fight, the Cheyennes would listen to him. Long Neck picked up his dead chicken and leaned against the tree, blood dripping from his hands.

Pole Bean pointed toward Running Standing on the limb and said to Susan Antelope, "Tell him to come down." Then to the Cheyennes he explained in white lingo, "The boy speaks only Kiowa."

The Cheyennes knew, of course, that Running Standing understood the white lingo. They did not betray him, and he was grateful. He climbed down and took his knife from Long Neck, wiping the bloody handle on his pants. Pole Bean asked for water, with which he soaked his handkerchief to clean Long Neck's chest and arms. Then he cleaned the young Cheyenne. All the blood had come from the rooster.

"Tell these Kiowa boys to go home," said Pole Bean to Susan Antelope. "I must talk to Brother Cross."

Susan Antelope spoke to them in Kiowa. "The missionary hopes Chief Killer will go to the medicine tipi and pray against your prophet. Go away and give him a chance to convince the Jesus Cheyennes."

Long Neck nodded grudgingly. "We will go somewhere and eat my chicken," he said.

They walked away from the arbor, down the bank, and around the river bend to a sandbar at the water's edge. Long Neck fashioned a spit over forked sticks, then opened the chicken, flinging away the entrails but keeping the liver and heart, which he ate raw. He could not share these morsels, he said, because they were the vitals of his spiritual brother—the rooster—and he could honor the dead bird only by eating them himself.

They plucked the bird, saving the wing and tail feathers, which they divided evenly. They skewered it on a green willow shoot and Long Neck began roasting it.

"I do not want to eat this chicken," said Running Standing. "I am going to crawl back near the arbor and listen to Pole Bean."

"You don't understand Cheyenne."

"Neither does Pole Bean. They will talk white lingo."

"Then you can tell me what they say when we get home," said Long Neck, pleased to have the entire chicken for himself. He sat on the sand, turning the bird slowly on the spit, as the boy made his way back up the river bank.

Running Standing crawled again through the willows toward the cottonwood tree. Before he reached the tree, Crosses-the-River stepped from behind a pokeberry thicket, startling him.

"Wouldn't your half brother give you any chicken?" She smiled but her brown eyes still shot anger tongues.

"You followed me?" he asked, intrigued.

She nodded. "To tell you that my father will not accept the challenge of your prophet. He no longer believes in the old medicine."

"He is afraid. He does not believe in the Jesus medicine, either."

"He does," she insisted, and she seemed amused by something not quite connected with the Jesus medicine, but perhaps with being a girl. He was not sure. "You see, Joe," she went on, "we are civilized and you are still a stone-age Indian."

"What kind of Indian is that?"

"We brought the stone age unchanged into the present time. Some of us have now taken the road of knowledge. The rest must take it or live in misery."

"I do not understand, Crosses-the-River. What is this stone age you call me?"

"It means the very olden time, Joe. Before the wheel was invented. Think of it. For ages our people moved entire villages over the buffalo range, but they never used wagons because they could not think of the wheel. They dragged everything over the ground."

"We have always had wheels," he said with indignation. "The Kiowa Sun Boy split himself in half by throwing a wheel into the air."

"That is what I mean! We had hoops for playing games and dancing, but we never thought of making a wheel to go after the buffalo."

"And now that we have the white man's wheels," he said triumphantly, "we have no buffalo."

"Oh, Joe!" she sighed.

Now he realized that the word *Joe* was something she had begun calling him.

"What is Joe?"

"After the Kiowa allotment, you will need a name. I think Joe Standing is a very good name."

He grabbed her suddenly and threw her to the ground, understanding in that quick moment that he was old enough to do what all boys tried to do to girls when they got the feeling that until now he had always scorned. Instead of submitting, as he had supposed she might—after which he could for the first time have counted coup among the boys in his village—she kicked him sharply in the stomach, grabbed his knife from his belt, brandished it as she got to her feet. The glinting blade warned him not to try again.

"I may change your name to Sara Wildcat," he told her. "That is a good name for you."

She did not smile. "Don't be a savage, Joe."

"I do not like this thing. Give me my knife."

"I will cut you with it if you touch me."

"Why are you mad at me?"

"I am not," she said.

"I do not understand."

"You are a stone-age Indian, that is why."

"Give me my knife."

Still she brandished it. "Go down to the water. I will throw it to you there."

"Why?"

"Because I do not trust you not to roll me on the ground."

He hesitated, thought about it, and grinned. "I will roll you on the ground later," he said.

"Then I will keep your knife and cut you if I can." She was not smiling.

"Keep the knife," he told her. "I will give it to you. And here are some chicken feathers that you might like. They are from my half brother's rooster." He pulled the feathers from his pocket and gave them to her.

She reached for them warily. They were beautiful in the splotches of morning sun that came through the trees along the river. They were brown, with greenish blue hints, much the color of her eyes underneath the trees.

"Thank you for the feathers, Joe." She put the longest one behind the ribbon around her head.

"I would like to give you these, too," he said, pulling the purple beads from his other pocket.

Again she reached out cautiously, took them, held them up against the sky for a moment, then put them around her neck with the string of chinaberry seeds.

"Thank you, Joe."

"You are welcome," he said and turned immediately down the bank. When he reached the water's edge, he looked back. She stood against the pokeberries with her hand poised in the air. She tossed the knife toward him and it landed in the grass at his feet.

4

RUNNING across the prairie, the boy came upon a small herd of cattle, selected a certain large steer, whirled toward it, leaped upon its neck, and stabbed repeatedly until his knife found the jugular. Even before it stopped kicking, he cut out a piece of liver, which he ate as he continued running toward the Kiowa village—leaving the rest of the carcass where it lay in the sun.

When the white cowmen who were poaching the reservation grass saw buzzards circling and hurried over to investigate, they shook their heads, cursed lividly, and talked to each other for a while about redskins. Their knowledge of the subject, derived from personal experiences, was vast. They had originally come out to this Oklahoma Territory several years ago to slaughter the buffalo for hides and had stayed to invest in the cattle business, now especially profitable when herds were slipped onto the reservation for fattening. Never in their lives had they seen anyone or anything as self-centered and improvident as a goddamn Indian.

The creek near the tipi village ran through a shallow gully eroded among outcropping ledges of red sandstone. Blackjack oak, sprawling elms, tupelo, sumac, and scrubby pines lined its banks. Sky-Walker and Weasel Ear were in the gully cutting pine saplings for tipi poles.

Running Standing lay in a crevice, hidden behind a sumac tangle, watching. As each pole was cut, the old man held it while Sky-Walker skinned off its bark.

Having thrown themselves zealously into the challenge of praying a Jesus Indian to death, both men had stripped themselves of all white adornment. They wore only breechclouts, moccasins, and doeskin hair ties. Sky-Walker's bulbous thighs and breast fat quivered as he worked. Weasel Ear, old and scrawny, was comical in contrast to the corpulent prophet; he was simply a string of meat, thought Running Standing, almost dry enough to pound.

The task of cutting and peeling the poles was painful, for neither man had done any work in a very long time. They both grumbled.

"It is not easy to build a tipi," said Sky-Walker, pausing for breath.

"We should not be doing this," said Weasel Ear. "You are too fat and I am too old."

"You are right, brother, but we must have the poles." The prophet sat down to rest. "Perhaps we should have sent some young boys to cut them for us."

"Yes, we should have done that, brother," said Weasel Ear, pleased with the fraternal connection he had established with the impressive prophet.

"Let us think about this thing before we cut any more poles. We will need all our strength for prayer against that Cheyenne. I am very hot and you are weak and pale. This job would be good experience for young boys."

"Running Standing and Long Neck could do it for us. Perhaps we should return and send them here."

"No . . . no . . ." the boy suddenly wailed in his owl voice from behind the sumac thicket.

The fat man and the old man stopped breathing to listen. Their eyes rolled toward each other, then toward the treetops.

The boy went on in a mournful moan: "Medicine tipi must be built by experienced hands, my brothers. It is no job for boys. *No . . . no . . .*"

The owl voice then said no more.

The prophet turned to his helper. "Did you hear them, brother? They spoke again."

"I heard them," said the old man. "You have great owl power. They speak to you so clear that I can hear them, too. Let's go back to work, brother."

The fat man rose and they resumed their task of skinning the poles.

Satisfied with the progress thus being made on the poles for the medicine tipi, the boy eased away from the sumacs, slipped quietly up the creek to a crossing, and went to his village, pleased also to have rescued himself accidentally from the labor of cutting poles—a job that should have been women's work in the first place.

After the conical framework had been tied together above the buffalo wallow, Sky-Walker and Weasel Ear received many offers of help, all of which they spurned with airs of mystery. Now that the poles were cut and peeled, their admonition from the owls to do it themselves was safely beyond serious threat of violation.

Each tribe on this Oklahoma reservation reacted to the impending duel of medicines in accordance with its own history's investment in the curious present. The Geronimo Apaches did not even hear of the medicine tipi for the simple reason that all of them—seventy families: men, women, and children—were still in prison at Fort Sill, learning under military orders the art of growing potatoes in soil where potatoes had never grown and from soldiers who had never grown them. Nor were the Tonkawas particularly involved. What few of them remained on the reservation were outcasts among the tribes, their former cannibalism having precluded a significant place for them in either white or Indian society: Nobody cared what Tonkawas thought about anything and consequently they did not think about anything.

The remnant of Delawares, with their reputation for having

been made slaves and turned into women by the Iroquois generations ago back East, were equally unmoved by cultural conflicts with the whites. The Wichitas and Caddos, having long considered themselves peaceful Indians, viewed the medicine contest with disdain; they felt that for decades life would have been simpler had the Plains tribes not battled the whites to the bitterest possible end. Already adequate farmers, they needed only a little more time on the Jesus Road to reach tranquillity and they had no interest in sight-seeing detours. The Comanches stayed south of the mountains and paid little attention to life on this northern border.

But the Cheyennes and Arapahos above the Washita—now bona fide landowners identified with double names on the Indian rolls and fast absorbing Christianity—were agitated. They did not want this contest and resented Killer Cross's declaration, at Pole Bean's behest, that he had accepted the challenge.

"I am ready to show my faith in Jesus," he said on Main Street in Cloud Chief. "I will sit face to face with Sky-Walker and pray for his salvation while he prays for my demise."

Demise, of course, was a word Pole Bean had given him. Many of the whites who laughed when they heard him use it would not have known what it meant out of context; but they cheered him on and debated whether it would be safe for them to gather at the buffalo wallow to watch. Some thought it would be perfectly safe, while others feared that if the owl power *should* prevail, those Kiowas might get out of hand and scalp everybody before the cavalry could put them down.

The Jesus Kiowas at Rainy Mountain, doubtful if not embarrassed, tried to ignore the whole thing, but there were no skeptics in Sky-Walker's village. His people were joyous at the prospect before them. They knew what was going to happen and why. The Jesus power would be revealed in all its fraudulence and very soon they would be looking down upon a dead Cheyenne.

Watching it all, and listening, Running Standing felt his sense of power growing with every nuance of agitation and often thought of himself as a secret owl. He wanted an owl of his own, like Sky-Walker's—carefully skinned and treated with tallow, to be kept at all times inside his shirt or in his pocket or under his blanket, to slip his hand into like a glove and bring out suddenly and talk with and listen to for prophecy. Thinking about it, he determined to go along the creek soon in search of an owl, for his destiny was clear. He would become the next owl prophet of his people.

The magnitude of Sky-Walker's devotion to the deadly task before him was dramatized to the entire village when he rejected the use of white-man canvas for his medicine tipi. He insisted on covering the poles with real skins—which proved so difficult to find in sufficient numbers that a few skeptics suspected him of malingering. When the tipi was at last ready, he announced that three days of preliminary prayer would be required to achieve the atmosphere demanded by the owls. And he added pointedly that offerings of food would be accepted in front of the tipi.

Sky-Walker appeared frequently at the flap to receive the offerings. He talked to his owl, which fitted onto his right hand and turned occasionally to face him and to whisper mysteriously into his ear. During the three days, as throngs gathered at the old wallow to witness the battle of medicines, Sky-Walker prayed often and ate continuously. Weasel Ear stayed with him in the tipi but had to bring his own food: He could not eat owl offerings for he was only a prophet's helper.

Killer Cross arrived on the afternoon of the final preparation day. He brought his family in the orange and black road wagon. Many of his friends, including Pole Bean and Round Face Woman, came with him in buggies, wagons, and carts. The boy, watching the Cheyennes make camp above the wallow, noticed Killer Cross's strained countenance. He spoke to the girl the first chance he had. She was wearing both strings of beads—the purple glass ones he had given her and the old chinaberry seeds. But she was not wearing the rooster feather that had come from Long Neck's chicken.

"Hello, Crosses-the-River."

"Hello, Joe."

"My name is Running Standing."

"I call you Joe."

"Are you still afraid of me?"

"Why should I be?"

"I might roll you on the ground."

Her eyes leveled with his. There was no laughter in them, but there was no conspicuous anger, either. "I am not afraid of you when there are so many people around."

"You should have kept my new knife. Then if I met you along the creek sometime, you could protect yourself."

"I will be safe," she told him, lifting the ruffled apron she wore over her dress. There, strung on a beaded belt, was a knife—with a brass knob on the end of its handle, as shiny as an owl's eye. "I borrowed it from my brother. He says he will kill you anytime I want him to."

The boy stared at her. "Where is the feather I gave you?"

"I threw it away. It was your brother's feather. I did not want it."

He was pleased. "I can see fear in your father's face today. I believe he knows he is going to die."

She shrugged impressively and said, "My father will be a hero when this is over."

"What is a hero?"

"Someone who does a very brave thing."

"He is not brave," the boy insisted. "He comes here only because he is afraid of Pole Bean."

She thought about that for several moments. Then, apparently deciding to be honest, she nodded. "Reverend told him Jesus would be mad at him if he did not come and pray against Sky-Walker. I do not like this thing, Joe. Reverend frightened my father, and Sky-Walker frightens him, too."

If she had not been so beautiful, he would have laughed at her. But the admission touched him. "Will you walk with me along the creek?" he asked.

She hesitated, thinking carefully before she spoke. "If you will call me Sara, instead of Crosses-the-River, I will walk with you."

"All right, Sara. I will not call you Crosses-the-River anymore."

She looked up at the sky, toward the west, shading her eyes. "At the beginning of sunset," she told him, "I will walk with you along the creek." Then she hurried away to her family's campsite.

His chest swelled. He waited, breathing heavily. And he hung nearby, impatient with the sun for moving toward the horizon at its normal leisurely pace.

Weasel Ear appeared outside the medicine tipi to announce that Sky-Walker would begin his final prayer at dark and pray nonstop until Killer Cross was dead. Those who believed in owl power cheered loudly, those who didn't laughed, and those who were unsure listened quietly. It did not matter, said Weasel Ear, whether the Jesus Indian even came to the tipi; but if he cared to test his medicine in face-to-face confrontation, he would be welcome to sit on a log that had been provided just outside at right angles to the flap.

Again the believers in owl power cheered, for they realized that the log had been cleverly placed so that Killer Cross could not possibly face the east if he sat on it and that his own prayer would thus be ineffective even if there were some power in the Jesus medicine.

Lest he should be sent gathering firewood, Running Standing ducked out of Weasel Ear's sight and joined his own family encampment at the northern point of the wallow. The sun at last was gradually losing its glare; it now became a red ball hanging motionless above the rim of the prairie distance.

"Where is Lives-in-a-Tree?" he asked his half brother in a low voice.

Long Neck grinned. "She is not here. Do not ask me where she is because"—his grin broadened—"I do not know." He fingered the drying foot of his dead rooster, which he now wore around his neck on a thong. The foot had been cut off just above the spur; when its dangling tendon was manipulated, it would claw the air.

"Did I see you talking to Chief Killer's daughter?" asked Rabbit Hand.

"Yes," said Running Standing. "Her name is Crosses-the-River but I call her Sara Cross. That is her Jesus Road name."

"Why do you use her Jesus name if you do not want to go on the Jesus Road yourself?"

"She is going to walk with me along the creek and I am going to roll her on the ground."

"I did not know you were old enough to roll a girl on the ground."

"I did not either until now."

"Why don't you roll a Kiowa girl on the ground instead?"

"Because she is the one I want."

Rabbit Hand shook his head. "You should be like Long Neck. He does not care who he rolls on the ground." Rabbit Hand then fell into a thoughtful silence.

The boy looked up at the sky. The gap below the sun had closed. Streaks of purple, gray, and green swam above the horizon. He glanced across the wallow at Killer Cross's camp and saw that the girl also watched the sky. And he saw her remove her ruffled apron, drape it over a wheel of her father's wagon, and turn toward the creek. The brass knob on her knife handle gathered brightness from the sunset.

When he caught up with her, he said with a grin, "Hello, Sara Cross." White-lingo names, always difficult to pronounce, sounded foolish.

"Hello, Joe Standing." A tremor of disgust went through him at the sound of the name she had given him.

"I see you brought your knife," he said.

She nodded several times, and as she walked her strings of beads rattled.

"You do not need a knife," he told her, "to walk along the creek."

"I am going to keep it wherever I go."

"For the rest of your life?"

"Only when I am around a stone-age Indian."

"Your brother may need it," he said in dismay.

"I may need it, too."

"Why do you hate the olden time so much?"

"Because we do not live in the olden time. We must be white-men Indians or starve to death. My father does not wish to starve, and neither do I, and neither does my mother."

"The Jesus Road has filled you with so many lies," he said angrily, "that only lizards would crawl out if you were cut open."

She stopped on the ledge of sandstone above the flowing creek and looked up at him. The sunset sky filled her dark eyes, and the trouble he saw there touched him in a way he did not like. He felt tender toward her, when more than anything he wanted his feelings to be as lean and tough as the hamstrings of a big buck. He wanted this girl to think him as wild as a prairie mustang, as dangerous as a buffalo.

He glanced around among the sandstone ledges for a place to throw her down, and even as he did, she moved out of his reach, deftly descending the bank to the sandy edge of the creek.

"Joe," she said, "I may be sent to Carlisle. Why don't you come, too?"

"Carlisle!" he cried, rushing down the bank. "Crosses-the-River, it is bad enough for you to go to Red Moon School!"

"You promised to call me Sara."

"If you go to Carlisle, I do not even want to know your name." He stomped around on the sand and into the edge of the creek, kicking the water furiously. "You know what happens to people who go to Carlisle. They turn into white men."

"Oh, Joe," she cried, "we must all become white. It is only a matter of time. You will become white, too."

"I am going to be the next Kiowa owl prophet," he said.

Now she actually laughed, and sat down on a fallen log. "I will believe you if Sky-Walker kills my father. But if he fails, will you stop believing in owl power?"

"And get on the Jesus Road?" He came out of the water and stood above her.

She moved over to make a place for him on the log. "Reverend says the Jesus power does not kill anyone, Joe. It means people love each other."

"What does love each other mean?"

"To be generous and give to each other instead of taking away."

"But that is the Indian way," he said. "The Jesus people have taken away everything we have."

"Reverend says they took it to teach us the Jesus Road, and now they are beginning to give it back to us. I do not really understand it myself, but at Carlisle they will teach us what it all means."

"How can your father believe the Jesus Road if his prayer has no power to kill anyone?"

"Joe," she said, shaking her head, "he does not truly believe it. He is frightened half to death right now. He believes Sky-Walker is going to kill him."

"Then maybe we should try to stop this thing."

Again she shook her head. "No. Reverend says owl power does not exist. He says my father and Sky-Walker will just pray and pray and pray. Nobody will die."

"If nobody dies, your father will win. He is not trying to kill Sky-Walker."

"He would like to kill Sky-Walker," she said, "but he knows he can't. Reverend promised to have me sent to Carlisle if he will pray against Sky-Walker long enough for everybody to see that owl power is a fake. Reverend could have you sent to Carlisle, too, Joe. If you wanted to go." Her lips trembled.

He moved closer to her, angry with her continued talk of Carlisle and ready to throw her on the ground.

But she moved farther down the log. She broke off a dead

branch, drew the knife from its sheath, and began whittling. She turned to face him, keeping the knife between them.

"What are you whittling?" he asked. "A totem pole to sell at Charlie's store?"

"I warn you, Joe, do not try to roll me on the ground."

"Did you come to the creek only to tell me about Carlisle?"

"Yes, I did. Someday," she said, "I am going to marry a well-educated white Indian, in a church, and come back to live among our people in a big house made of cottonwood boards. A house much bigger than my father's." The thought seemed to have transported her into a sinewy dream. "I will send all my children to school, Joe."

"I am going to have many wives," he told her, expanding his chest—and before he could say more, she sprang from the log, scrambled quickly up the sandstone ledge, her strings of beads rattling, her hair braids flying . . . and disappeared.

He sat alone on the log for a few minutes, and then he walked along the edge of the creek, stomping and kicking the water, listening for owls. He did not hear any.

5

AT dusk Weasel Ear appeared at the flap of the medicine tipi and held up his hands to silence the large gathering.

"Sky-Walker has decided to turn himself into an owl for this important contest," he told them. "Soon he will fly down from the mountains and begin the prayer of death. Is Killer Cross here to face his destiny?"

The tall Cheyenne chief pushed toward the tipi and Running Standing stood beside his half brother, watching.

"Killer is afraid," whispered Long Neck.

"He knows he is going to die," said the boy.

"Yes, he knows. Some Arapahos told me he dug a grave for himself this morning. They say he lay down in the hole to be sure it fitted him because he wants to be comfortable in there. Did you roll his daughter on the ground?"

"She ran away from me."

Long Neck laughed and made a little noise of disgust.

Killer Cross stood before the log at the tipi entrance and shouted: "My friends, I will now pray to Jesus for Sky-Walker's soul." He held his arms toward heaven. "Blessed Jesus, have mercy on my poor heathen brother who calls himself Sky-Walker. Listen to me, Jesus! When a big owl flies down from the mountain, it will only be Sky-Walker. Believe me, Jesus, and don't do nothing to him."

A murmur of approval went up from the Jesus Indians, a shudder from the Jesus whites, and a titter of laughter from the nervous heathens.

Weasel Ear ignited the fire in several places and watched the flames leap. With a malevolent smile, he asked Susan Antelope to inquire whether the Cheyenne wished to sit on the log and wait for death—or to stand by the fire and wait for it.

"I will sit here," said Killer Cross.

He is very brave, thought Running Standing with a new respect.

"They say you dug yourself a grave today," taunted Weasel Ear. "Did you make it big enough?"

Killer listened to the question and decided to ignore it. "Blessed Jesus," he implored the heavens, "do not kill Sky-Walker for his heathen prayer. Do not even kill him for turning himself into an owl. Forgive him, Jesus."

Weasel Ear ducked back inside the tipi, closing the flap after him.

"Don't sit there, Killer," cried someone from the crowd. "Sky-Walker placed that log so you cannot face the east if you sit on it."

"It does not matter which way one faces Jesus," Killer told them. "Have mercy on everybody, Jesus!"

Running Standing stared at the Cheyenne chief. Firelight leaping in his face showed fear. You had to admire him greatly. "I wonder," he said to his half brother, "if he lay on his back in that grave, or on his side."

"On his back, I guess," Long Neck replied. "The Jesus people always fold the hands of the dead across their chests."

"When I die, I want to be buried standing up."

"Not me," Long Neck admitted. "I want to lie on my side and be comfortable."

Inside the tipi Weasel Ear helped Sky-Walker turn himself

into an owl. They had fashioned an owl's head by sewing
together some leftover pieces of buffalo hide. Weasel Ear
fitted it over Sky-Walker's head, fastening it with thongs that
ran under his armpits. Tiny holes through which the prophet
could see were pierced at the bottom of the mask, camouflaged
among the painted stripes of white and gray. Huge eyes and
pointed ears were painted on the grotesque face. Long strings
of hawk feathers were tied down each arm to operate as
wings when he flapped.

"Now you are an owl, brother," said Weasel Ear.

"Give me another peyote button," said the fat prophet. And
his voice, muffled inside the mask, frightened Weasel Ear.

"You sound like a distant owl," he said.

"I am a distant owl."

"Are you sure you want more peyote?"

"Yes; I must fly a long way and pray hard against the
Cheyenne."

Weasel Ear gave him another button and untied one side of
the mask enough for him to get it into his mouth.

"Is the gun loaded, brother?" Sky-Walker asked.

Weasel Ear glanced at the lodgepole in the rear of the tipi
where the gun was hanging. It was an old carbine that had
once been taken from a dead soldier.

"It is loaded, brother."

"Is the dipper ready?"

"It hangs from the same pole."

"Go outside and tell them I am on the mountaintop flapping
my wings."

"Are you leaving now?"

"I am already far away, brother. I am on a green mountain,
high in a tree. I am ready to swoop down upon the Jesus
Cheyenne." Sky-Walker flapped his wings. "Go outside and
tell them I am on my way."

Weasel Ear parted the opening and let himself through.

"Silence!" he said with hands in the air. "Sky-Walker has
turned himself into an owl. He is flying here from the mountain where he has been perched in a tall tree gathering his
strongest power." He pointed toward Killer Cross on the log.
"Look at him! He feels the power already! Soon you will see
the owl swoop down from the mountain!"

The crowd murmured into the hot night. Killer Cross
squirmed on the log as Susan Antelope translated. Firelight
danced over the front of the tipi.

"I hear him!" shouted Weasel Ear at the sound of brushing and thumping inside. "Here he comes!"

The flap opened and the huge owl leaped out, its wings spread as though in flight, chanting weirdly in a voice the boy could only imagine was Sky-Walker's.

The Indians gasped and swept back. The whites who had come from Cloud Chief to gamble and be amused grew silent instantly.

"What is the owl saying?" whispered Long Neck.

"I do not know," said the boy, mesmerized.

"Don't you understand the white lingo?"

"That is owl talk."

For several minutes the owl strutted before the fire, chanting words no one could understand. It swooped toward Killer Cross, backed away and dipped toward the fire—its grotesque shadow projected on the tipi, first large, then small. The prophet's bulbous thighs became streaked below the owl's body as the sweat rolled down. The tempo of the dance increased and the sound of the owl prayer rose into a strident wail.

The boy watched Killer Cross, who, forgetting his own prayer, leaned toward the owl with terror twisting his face.

The owl now picked up a sharp stick that lay near the tipi opening. It danced toward Killer Cross. Pointing at its victim's chest, it whirled round twice; then, with the stick, carefully drew the outline of a man spread-eagled in the dust at the edge of the wallow between the fire and the tipi. It pointed again at Killer Cross on the log and everyone knew that the outline on the ground was Killer's effigy.

With a flourish of its great wings and another wail, the owl drew a heart on the left side of the effigy's chest—a large heart—and swooped toward the Cheyenne to point the stick and chatter at him again.

Killer drew back in horror.

"Pray, Brother Cross!" the boy heard Pole Bean shout above the gasping crowd. "For God's sake, pray!"

But the Cheyenne, near convulsions, did not hear.

The owl swooped around the effigy and into the tipi—emerging suddenly with the dipper concealed in the end of its right wing. It reached into the fire, brought out a dipper of red coals, and poured them slowly into the heart of the effigy.

Killer Cross grabbed his chest and bent forward.

"That owl has got him," Long Neck whispered as the crowd groaned along with the pitiful Cheyenne.

"Yes," said the boy.

"Pray, brother!" cried Pole Bean.

The owl did not pause in its dance. Working fast to pursue its advantage, and wailing its prayer into the night, it swooped inside the tipi once more—to reappear with the carbine in its wings.

The crowd screamed and surged backward. The owl brandished the carbine, quivered mightily, aimed at the glowing coals in the heart of the effigy, and fired. Sparks showered upward with the gun's report, and Killer Cross slumped from the log to the ground.

"He's dead!" said Long Neck.

"Look," said the boy, now watching the strangest gyration he had yet seen the owl perform.

The gigantic bird was jumping up and down with joy, flapping its wings as though it might ascend into the air. "It is going to fly away," said Long Neck.

But it did not fly. It rose mightily, almost off the ground, and then, with a strange cry, slumped and fell beside Killer Cross.

"Damned if they didn't kill each other," cried a white man in the back of the crowd. "I'd 've covered any bet but that one."

The boy stared at the two inert figures, a tremor running through him as he beheld the destructive fruits of such an awesome clash of power. For there could be little doubt that the Jesus prayer was potent. The thought reached him that Killer Cross might even have survived if he had not forgotten to continue praying as the owl got him.

The crowd surged in around the fallen men. Pole Bean yelled for everybody to stand back. "Give them air!" he cried.

"Air won't help those two redskins," said someone in white lingo.

But as the words were spoken, Killer Cross stirred and raised himself to an elbow, blinking into the firelight.

A cheer went up and the Cheyenne stared at the fallen owl beside him. "Did I kill him?" Killer asked, astounded and so badly frightened by his apparent power that he almost fainted again. "I did not mean to kill him, Jesus!" he shouted to the heavens. "I only meant to teach him a lesson and put him on the Jesus Road."

Running Standing's glance flicked from Killer Cross to Pole Bean, Round Face Woman, and Carrot Nose. They were obviously proud of their Indian—and the boy could not blame them. Pole Bean leaned over the dead owl, working its great wings, listening to its heart . . . and shaking his own head.

"He is dead, all right. Have mercy, Lord. Have mercy on his soul, dear Jesus."

And many others joined him in beseeching blessed mercy.

6

THERE was some talk of burying Sky-Walker in the grave Killer Cross had dug for himself, but it was jocose. The hole was long and narrow, whereas to fit the dead prophet it needed to be short and wide; furthermore, in these days a self-respecting Indian could not properly be buried in another Indian's patch of earth.

Killer Cross said he would not mind if Sky-Walker used his grave; the hole would otherwise just go to waste. But he was secretly relieved when Sky-Walker's body was laid to rest on the mountain near the tree from which Weasel Ear had told everyone the owl had flown.

The impact of the prayer contest on the mission was considerable. So many Kiowas and Tonkawas flocked to the Jesus Road that the missionary hastily called a revival meeting and Killer Cross was its hero. As soon as he was over the immediate shock of what he had done—and his vanquished foe's body had been disposed of—Killer agreed to appear in Pole Bean's pulpit. Running Standing listened to them talk about it.

"But you must make it clear to everyone," Pole Bean admonished the victorious Cheyenne, "that you did not work any power over Sky-Walker. It was the power of Jesus working *through* you."

They were sitting around a table in the mission house: Killer Cross; his daughter, Crosses-the-River; his proud son,

Billy, who had once attacked Long Neck with a knife, and the Jesus whites—and the boy stood outside on the stone, watching through the window.

"He almost got me," Killer admitted, "but my power was too strong. I did not know I had that much power, Reverend."

"Jesus was too strong," Pole Bean corrected, showing concern for the minimal extent of the Cheyenne's understanding of what had happened.

Killer's chest expanded and his chin lifted a bit imperiously, but he did not intend to argue with the missionary. "I will tell them from the pulpit how I killed him with my Jesus power," he said simply. Pole Bean and Round Face Woman looked at each other in apprehension.

Crosses-the-River stared at her father and said, "Were you only pretending when you fell off that log?"

Killer angrily shook his head. "I did not fake anything."

"I do not understand why you didn't die," she said.

"He only fainted," Pole Bean told her. "It happens sometimes when people get a shock." Then he explained that a shock meant the violent jarring of the feelings or the mind by unexpected happenings.

"Maybe Sky-Walker fainted," she said. "He did not expect that happening. Maybe they buried him in a fainted condition."

"No, his heart had stopped," said Round Face Woman gently. "He was dead, my dear, don't worry."

"He put his heart out on the ground," said Killer's son Billy with a mischievous grin, "and poured hot coals on it and then shot it dead. He did not know it was his own heart until he killed himself, and then he did not know nothing."

"I killed him!" said the boy's father, banging his fist impatiently on the table.

"No, Jesus killed him," said Crosses-the-River. "You asked Jesus to save his life, but Jesus got mad at him and killed him."

"No, no," said Pole Bean.

"Perhaps his faith in owls killed him," said Round Face Woman, desperate to make the girl understand.

"Then owls *do* have power," said Crosses-the-River, and the boy was thinking the same thing.

Suddenly the Cheyennes began talking to each other in their own language. They were much too excited to remember the words of the white lingo.

"Where is Susan Antelope?" asked Pole Bean. "I need her here at all times."

"I will interpret for you," said Crosses-the-River. "My father's feelings are hurt. You do not believe he killed the owl even though you saw him do it. He says you do not like him anymore because you fear he may have more Jesus power than you have."

"Ruth," said Pole Bean to his wife, "it may not be a good idea to put this man in the pulpit."

"But . . . we have to," said Round Face Woman. "Everyone expects it."

"Yes," said Carrot Nose, who had been quiet until now. "We will lose face with all of them if we don't. Let him testify that he killed the man. We will get many converts, and the process of education will take place later—slowly and naturally."

Killer Cross spoke to his daughter once more in Cheyenne. The girl argued with him for a moment, then shrugged. "He wants to preach about his power," she explained, "and he will build his own pulpit if you do not let him."

"Tell him not to do that, my dear," said Round Face Woman quickly. "We will let him testify in our pulpit."

Killer Cross then noticed the boy outside the window and pointed.

"Don't mind him," said Pole Bean. "He comes here often to look at us. We don't mind."

Crosses-the-River glanced out the window and said, "I wonder why he comes?"

"We are a bit mystified ourselves," said Carrot Nose. "He does not understand a word we say, yet he comes almost every day."

"He should go with me to Carlisle," said the girl.

"He could, if he wanted to."

The girl turned to watch him more closely. She leaned forward, elbows on her knees and chin in her palms. She was trying to puzzle him out, he knew, and a smile struggled to reach his face. But he held it deep inside himself and stared back at her through the window.

The tipi village rattled in a cacophony of agitation. Ever since the failure a few years ago of the Cheyenne Ghost Dance—a religion to which most of the reservation tribes had belonged for a while because it claimed the power to bring back the buffalo and end the white scourge forever—most Kiowas would only snort at the suggestion that a Cheyenne could do anything spectacular. But Killer Cross's demonstration of Jesus power had been spectacular. If he could pray to death an owl prophet who had himself once prayed to death a Jesus Osage, he had to be reckoned with.

Rabbit Hand announced that he was going to the Jesus meeting to hear Killer Cross tell how he had done it. "They say that Face-of-Antelope will be there to tell us what he says."

Rabbit Hand dug his issue shirt and shoes out of his cowhide bag, which hung from one of the tipi poles. He donned them slowly and when he stood up, the boy thought with dismay, he looked like a Wichita farmer instead of a Kiowa fighting man.

"I am going, too," said Long Neck suddenly. "Killer Cross has so much power we had better listen to him, although I do not like his son Billy." Long Neck dug out his own shirt and shoes. He tucked his rooster's claw inside the shirt as he buttoned it.

"How about you, old woman?" Rabbit Hand asked Falling Water.

"I am going," said the boy's other-mother with song in her voice. For many weeks she had been urging the family to go to the mission with her, and now she dressed for the occasion. She draped her most colorful blanket over her shoulders and only her moccasins showed beneath the blanket.

"Aren't you going to wear your white-man shoes?" asked Rabbit Hand.

"Have you forgotten that you sold my shoes to buy your knife?"

Rabbit Hand blinked, remembering. "And you, short woman?" he said to Lives-in-a-Tree. The boy's mother lifted her long fine nose defiantly. Disgust rose in her face but her dark eyes, swimming with fear, told the deeper truth.

"I do not wish to listen to a Jesus Cheyenne," she said.

"He has power," said Rabbit Hand. "We should go and hear him."

"I remember the Ghost Dance. I do not trust any Cheyenne."

"Then put the baby in her cradleboard. We will take her with us."

"She is too small," said Lives-in-a-Tree, but Rabbit Hand glowered until she obeyed. The little girl was promptly placed in the cradleboard and slung onto Falling Water's back.

Rabbit Hand then turned to the boy.

"Will you go with us, Running Standing? You could listen to everything and report to us later whether Face-of-Antelope has told the truth."

"We already know she does not tell the truth," said Lives-in-a-Tree. "She is a part-Cheyenne Jesus Indian who always says what the Jesus Road people want her to say."

"Hush, short woman," said Rabbit Hand, his face livid. He stomped the ground. His issue shoes made a strangely hollow sound and he looked down at them, distracted from his anger, wiggling them one at a time.

"I will also go and listen," said the boy, "but I will not wear my issue shirt. I do not like it."

They set off across the prairie before dusk, ahead of the other Kiowas who were preparing to attend the revival meeting.

Running Standing and his half brother ran alongside each other, holding their arms tight against their chests. Rabbit Hand followed with long but casual strides, alone in his troubled thoughts. Falling Water, with the child on her back, brought up the rear, singing.

"Falling Water sings a lot these days," said Running Standing.

"She believes she is winning," said Long Neck. "Lives-in-a-Tree is stupid."

"How do you know?"

"I asked him last night if he did not intend to choose her after we get on the Jesus Road and he is allowed only one wife in his tipi."

"And he told you?" Running Standing was aghast that his half brother could be so brazen.

"He hit me," said Long Neck. "That is how I know he prefers Lives-in-a-Tree. But Falling Water is smart. She is already on the Jesus Road, waiting for him."

"What will she do if he kicks her out and chooses to keep Lives-in-a-Tree?"

"He can't choose Lives-in-a-Tree now."

"Why can't he?"

"Because she has already rolled on the ground with Wolf's Tongue."

"Does Rabbit Hand know this?"

"Not yet, but I will tell him."

The boy was horrified. He ran silently for a while and then he said, "What will he do when you tell him?"

"He will kick her out and keep Falling Water for his only wife, that is all. In the olden time, he would cut off her nose before he kicked her out, so that everyone would know for the rest of her life what kind of woman she was. Then he would hold a feast for Wolf's Tongue."

"Why would he hold a feast?"

"To honor him for uncovering an unfaithful woman."

"I would kill him instead of honoring him," said the boy with a surge of passion that made his heart pound.

His half brother laughed. "That is because you are about to turn white even though you do not know it. You already have one foot on the Jesus Road."

"No, I have not," said the boy, wondering in agony if Long Neck could possibly be right.

"They say that Cheyenne girl you like is going to Carlisle."

"I do not like her."

Long Neck's laugh was contemptuous. "If you did not like her, she would not be the only girl you wish to roll on the ground. Have you tried any others?" Anger raged in the boy, but he held his tongue and kept running. "Is that not true?" Long Neck persisted. "It is clear to everyone that you like that Jesus girl a lot. There are plenty of other girls you could roll on the ground if you wanted to. But you want a Jesus Road girl, don't you?"

"I do not!"

"After Killer Cross tells how he killed Sky-Walker, everyone will get on the Jesus Road. Even Lives-in-a-Tree and Wolf's Tongue."

"Long Neck, would you ever like to go to Carlisle?"

The boy cringed before his half brother's continued scornful laughter—an eruption of sound so shrill and mocking that no words were necessary to convey what was in his heart.

Running Standing suddenly asked, "Will you get on the Jesus Road with everybody else?"

Long Neck did not hesitate to reply. "I will if the power is there. It would be stupid not to go where the power is."

"Then why do you laugh at me and say that the Jesus Road will get me?"

This proved to be a harder question. Long Neck thought about it, even slowing his pace a bit.

"Well," said the boy, "why do you?"

"We are almost there," said Long Neck as the mission came into view.

"Answer me, Long Neck. I am confused. I do not want to be stupid."

"I will tell you later—"

"Tell me now. I want to know before I listen to Killer Cross."

"I must have time to think about it."

"We can go on past the mission and run down the road toward Cloud Chief for a while."

Long Neck nodded. They reached the mission, running abreast, and went on by. The Jesus whites saw them from the window and watched, profoundly puzzled. It was simply incredible, Carrot Nose remarked, that Kiowa boys would hold foot races at a time like this. Round Face Woman nodded, and Pole Bean reminded them that to the primitive mind physical endurance was sublime.

On the road toward Cloud Chief the boys met many people streaming toward the mission to hear Killer Cross speak from the pulpit—whites as well as Arapahos and Cheyennes.

"Have you thought about it?" the boy finally asked.

"Yes, I have. We can go back now."

They turned abruptly and reversed their direction.

"Well, what is the answer?"

"The Jesus Road is going to get us both."

"Then why do you laugh at me?"

"I do not know," said Long Neck with solemn honesty.

"That is not a very good answer," cried the boy, confused. His half brother, in a burst of speed as they neared the mission again, pulled steadily ahead of him.

7

MORE people than could be accommodated inside came to hear Killer Cross speak from Pole Bean's pulpit. From a short distance away, Running Standing watched the house fill to overflowing. He had never been inside and would now go only close enough to hear through the open door.

But he could see inside. Rabbit Hand and Falling Water sat near the front, serious and silent. The baby peered from her cradleboard that hung with many others from the row of clothes-pegs on the wall opposite the door. Some of the children were asleep, but most of them stared at the crowd. They were grandchildren of the last generation of true Kiowa warriors—children who, if born sooner, might have looked out from the cradleboards upon a war dance against the whites or some enemy tribe instead of a stampede to the Jesus Road. And there was Long Neck, near his father, working the claws of his rooster's foot.

Killer Cross had not yet appeared. His family of Jesus Cheyennes had camped in the yard behind Pole Bean's house. The rear end of the big road wagon was visible from here. Killer's women—including Crosses-the-River—had a fire going near the wagon. Their bedding, tied in bundles, hung from the running gear underneath the wagon where water and milk buckets also hung. They had prepared to spend the night . . . or longer.

When Killer strode toward the mission with Pole Bean, everyone became quiet. Round Face Woman, Carrot Nose, and Face-of-Antelope followed them. Then came the Cheyenne family, single file, with Crosses-the-River bringing up the rear. Running Standing watched her.

"Aren't you going inside?" she asked when she drew near to him.

"I am going to watch from here."

"You always stay at a distance, don't you?"

"Yes, I do," he said.

She was wearing a brown store dress and her two strings of beads. Over her dress was the ruffled apron. He glanced at her waistline to see if she still carried the knife. Noticing his glance, she lifted the apron to reveal it. The brass knob glared at him.

He said, "Your brother will be mad if you lose that knife."

"No, he won't. He gave it to me, to take to Carlisle."

"When are you going to Carlisle?"

"In a few days. My father, the Reverend, and the other missionary over at the Arapahos are going to take several of us in the wagon to the train depot at Rush Springs."

"Reverend Pole Bean?" he asked.

"His name is the Reverend John Holcombe, Joe. You ought to call him that."

He ignored the remark and asked, "Why will you need a knife at Carlisle? Isn't everybody there on the Jesus Road?"

"Some of them may only have one foot on it."

"Does your father still think he has more power than Pole Bean?"

She nodded sadly. "Reverend said a doctor from Fort Sill told him Sky-Walker probably had a heart attack in his excitement. He was too fat from eating all the offerings people brought to the owls."

"Did his heart attack him?"

"The doctor meant that his heart was weak and stopped."

"Your father stopped it," the boy said, "with Jesus power."

The girl shook her head so vigorously that her beads rattled, and she whirled away to enter the mission house. But she got only as far as the door. There were no empty seats inside. So many people had crowded around the doors and windows that she had to return.

"You can watch from here with me," he told her.

She was silent, but she stood beside him.

"How far away is Carlisle?" he asked.

"A long way—in a place called Pennsylvania."

"How long does it take to get there?"

"Many days."

"Have you ever ridden on the train?"

"No, but I saw one at Rush Springs last year."

"They say it runs by itself."

"It burns wood and coal. Smoke and steam make it go."

"I do not believe it."

"You do not believe anything."

"I believe your father killed Sky-Walker."
"Then why do you want to be an owl prophet?"
"I don't anymore. I don't want to be anything."
"Reverend says everybody wants to be something."
"I don't."

Killer Cross's testimony stirred the Kiowas even more than the missionaries had hoped it might. He lifted his chin high, expanded his chest, strode back and forth behind the pulpit, and told them that he felt humble with so much power. Although he was already on the Jesus Road, he admitted that he had not really believed in Jesus until the power had demonstrated itself to him by striking down the owl.

"I was sure that I would die, brothers and sisters," he testified. "I went down to the river bottom and dug my grave, and while I dug that hole, Jesus kept telling me I would not need it, but I dug it. Jesus said, 'There ain't no owl power,' into my ear. But I thought it was Sky-Walker, not Jesus. I thought he wanted to set a trap to get me into that medicine tipi, but I could not be sure, so I dug my grave before I went. And Jesus said to me, when that prophet turned himself into an owl and flew down from the mountain, 'Pray, Brother Cross, for God's sake pray.' I heard it loud and clear, but I did not pray because I thought I was already dead."

Killer paused for Face-of-Antelope to translate for the Kiowas. They gasped and waited.

Killer stared out at them from the pulpit for a long time before continuing:

"The power rose up in me like a cyclone wind. It shouted into my ear, 'You had better have faith in me, brother. Tell me what to do, because that fat owl is going to pour hot coals into your heart any minute.' I told the power, 'I am already dead so it don't matter.' It said to me: 'Even if you are dead, brother, I am not. Jesus power never dies.' And I said to the power, 'Why don't you hide in the fire, and when the owl reaches for some coals, you can run up through his wing and get inside him.' And the power said to me: 'That is what I am going to do, brother.' "

Again the Cheyenne waited for Face-of-Antelope to translate. The boy whispered to Crosses-the-River, "Now do you believe him?"

She did not answer and he was amused. They both turned back to listen as Killer Cross continued:

"Even then"—he was beginning now to shout as Pole Bean sometimes did from the pulpit—"even then, I was not sure. But the power jumped right into the fire and waited until the owl reached for the coals. I saw it slip into the owl's wing and rush up inside him, and it sent me a message: 'I will wait here in his chest, brother. Soon he is going to get a gun and shoot you. Do not be afraid, brother. I will attack his heart the minute he is ready to shoot.' " Killer rocked back on his heels and said finally, "That is what happened. The owl brought the gun from the tipi and tried to shoot me, but the power attacked his heart and made him turn the gun down toward the ground and shoot his own heart. All of you saw that owl put his heart down there on the ground."

Face-of-Antelope translated, the Kiowas gasped, and Killer Cross stepped triumphantly from the pulpit, his face serene.

"Well," said Running Standing, "do you believe him now?"

Crosses-the-River shook her head slowly. "I believe he thinks that it happened that way."

"You told me the doctor from Fort Sill said Sky-Walker's heart had been attacked."

"That does not mean my father's power did it."

"Then what *did* attack his heart?"

"I do not know, Joe. I do not understand a lot of things that are happening. I will find out about them at Carlisle. Why don't you change your mind and go with me?"

He stood beside her but could not answer.

The people in the schoolhouse stood up to sing. Round Face Woman led a hymn that all the Jesus Indians knew. Pole Bean stood at the end of the platform and shook hands with the other Indians who wished to come forward to get on the Jesus Road.

Rabbit Hand rose and Long Neck followed. Falling Water did not rise because she was already a Jesus Indian. Running Standing watched his father and his half brother walk to the end of the platform and shake hands with the missionary and kneel down.

"Aren't you going with them?" asked Crosses-the-River.

"No."

"Why not? You believe my father, don't you?"

"Yes, I believe him."

"Then why don't you want to follow him on the Jesus Road?"

"The owl he killed was a fake. He could not kill a real owl."

"A fake owl?" she asked.

"I was Sky-Walker's owl power," the boy admitted.

"You were? Joe, how could you think that you were Sky-Walker's owl power?"

"Because I hid in the grass and told him in owl talk to pray against your father, and I scared him."

"You spoke to Sky-Walker in owl talk?" Crosses-the-River threw back her head and laughed herself almost into convulsions.

While she laughed, Running Standing spun away and ran past the mission house toward the creek, alone.

He sat at the water's edge for a long time, staring up at the moon through the tops of pecan trees. To the north, at last, he heard the singing of Kiowas trudging back to the tipi village and saw their lantern lights across the prairie. Their song was the hymn they had sung at the mission. Most of them were now on the Jesus Road. His mother and Wolf's Tongue would be among the few stone-age Indians left on the reservation. Soon there would not even be a reservation. Each Indian would be allotted a little plot of land and white people would be given all the rest. In time, there would be a town here somewhere and its stores, as in Cloud Chief, would be white-man stores where nothing could be heard except the white lingo.

He did not like to think about these things, but there was nothing else to think about except owl power—which he knew was a fake.

A real owl hooted from the limb of a nearby tree. He looked up, searching the moonlit treetops. Perhaps he could catch it and put Crosses-the-River's father to a more significant test. Perhaps the Jesus Cheyenne chief could not kill a Kiowa with a real owl.

The owl did not hoot again for a long while, and when it did, the sound seemed far away up the creek. He rose and moved carefully toward it, his eyes vainly searching the moon-bright splotches overhead. Again he waited, hoping not to pass the owl by. But he had apparently frightened it away, for he did not hear it again. Nor did he really care. He could not have caught it at night—and it probably had no power, anyway. Lives-in-a-Tree was right: There was no power anymore.

8

WHEN finally he returned to his village, many fires were burning. A din of excited voices reached his ears as he approached his father's tipi. He could see his half brother and several others of the village gathered before the fire in front of the flap.

"While we were all at the mission," said Long Neck excitedly, "Lives-in-a-Tree ran off with Wolf's Tongue. Rabbit Hand got very mad and went after her."

"Is he going to choose her after all?" the boy asked hopefully. "Is he going to bring her back and put her on the Jesus Road?"

"No. He already found her and cut off her nose."

"Did you tell him—?"

"Yes, I did."

The boy was stunned. "Long Neck—you said he would not do that."

"I said that's what they did to women in the glory days."

"How could he do it? Rabbit Hand is now on the Jesus Road himself!"

"But Lives-in-a-Tree is not. She is a heathen."

"Where is she?"

Long Neck's voice rose into a pitch of near hysteria. "Inside with Falling Water. Go look at her."

The boy's stomach turned over. Tears came before he could control himself. "Is Rabbit Hand inside with her?" he asked.

"No, he is staying out in the woods. He will not come home until Lives-in-a-Tree is gone from his tipi."

"Where will she go?"

"Back to her own people if they will take her." Long Neck's laughter was fierce. "Even Wolf's Tongue will not have her now."

The boy did not go inside that night. He returned to the creek and spent the night on the sand. He slept with his head on a pile of leaves that were caught in a tangle of willow roots and dreamed hideously of noseless owls. When he returned to the village after daybreak, he saw his mother leaving alone. She had a white rag tied around her face and she walked with quick steps, stooped over as though she might fall forward. She carried a small bundle of possessions in her hand.

He followed her through the village to the tipi of the Grandmother Keeper. He circled behind it, crawled close in the grass, and listened as Lives-in-a-Tree made an offering of some dried goat meat to the Grandmother. In return, the old Keeper offered her sanctuary for a few days—but she declined. He gave her his best wishes and told her he was sorry he could not bless her; but, without the Sun Dance to cleanse the Grandmother, that was the best he could do. She said she understood. She would return to her people now. They would take her in because they had always been *dapoms*—or no-accounts—and would not even be surprised by what had happened. Many women in her family history had lost their noses.

She left the Grandmother Keeper's tipi and trudged across the prairie. The boy lay in the grass and watched her go.

The Kiowa women were outraged by Rabbit Hand's cruelty to Lives-in-a-Tree. It had been years since a woman's nose had been cut off.

"They should all lose their noses for doing that thing," Rabbit Hand righteously insisted to a group of his friends. "The old Kiowas handled these things the right way. Women are beginning to get out of hand."

"That is true," nodded Medicine Water, who was, like Rabbit Hand, the son of a now dead warrior. He knew that his grandmother had lost her own nose fifty years earlier. "Women these days do not even like to cut lodgepoles," he said.

Little Moccasin, a young friend of Medicine Water who had once tried but failed to prove himself a medicine man, was in stout agreement. "Will you now make a feast for Wolf's Tongue?" he asked.

"I do not have much to make a feast with," Rabbit Hand admitted. "I have only one small piece of goat leg."

"Perhaps," said Talks-a-Lot, "we could ask for contributions." Although Talks-a-Lot's prestige had declined gravely during the reservation years, he was descended from a principal chief and still had friends. "Many of our men will be happy to help you feast Wolf's Tongue for exposing that woman." They all agreed.

"I could give him my knife and oilstone," said Rabbit Hand. "And my issue shoes."

"I have two beaver skins you can have to give him," said Little Moccasin.

"And I will give you Sky-Walker's gun," Medicine Water added.

"The gun he shot into the heart?"

"Yes, I took it when Killer Cross killed him."

"Wolf's Tongue would like to have that gun, I am sure."

Running Standing lingered nearby and listened to them make plans to honor the man none of them would have associated with before today.

They combed the village for bits of meat and searched the woods along the creek for wild plums and persimmons—a task they were unaccustomed to because normally it was women's work. They gathered wood for a fire and ground little mounds of chicory and sumac leaves to extend their supply of tobacco. The only woman who helped them was Falling Water. Although silent about the whole thing, her face sang happily as she prepared to cook the feast for the men. Getting rid of Lives-in-a-Tree was the greatest event of her life.

The boy watched her and understood her happiness. Once when they were alone beside the pot she had hung over the fire, she glanced at him and said, "Lives-in-a-Tree deserved to lose her nose, my son."

"I am not your son," he said and turned away. He went to the prairie and ran for a while.

As he returned to the village, he saw someone approaching on horseback from the northeast—the direction of Pole Bean's mission—and soon recognized Crosses-the-River, riding fast. He ran to meet her and intercepted her half a mile from his father's tipi.

"I heard what happened to your mother," she said. Horror was on her face. "They are coming to arrest Rabbit Hand."

"Who is coming?"

"The soldiers and the Indian police. They will put him in prison."

"Why will they?"

She was astounded that he would ask such a question. "For the terrible thing he did to your mother."

The boy looked at Crosses-the-River, sitting on the horse with only a blanket for a saddle. In the midmorning light her nose cast a sharp shadow across her cheek and the macabre image of a noseless Crosses-the-River with a white rag over her face came into his mind.

"Did you ride over here to warn him?"

She shook her head. "Even if he tries to hide, they will find him."

"Then why did you come?"

"To give you these." She removed the string of purple beads from her neck and handed them down to him. "I know you bought them for your mother. Give them to her now."

He stared at the beads. "No."

"Why won't you?"

"She has lost her nose."

"Joe!"

"I want you to have them with you at Carlisle," he said, offering them up to her again.

"I don't want your beads," she cried.

"Neither do I!" He flung them in anger as far as he could into the grass.

She sat for a moment longer, considering him. "I am leaving tomorrow morning for the train." She reined the horse around.

"You do not believe in the Jesus Road any more than I do," he said. "You do not fool me, Crosses-the-River. You are going to Carlisle because the white people want you to."

"We may not believe in the Jesus Road, Joe, but we have to get on it. We have no choice." She kicked heels into the horse's ribs and rode away.

He stood watching her for a while and then searched in the grass until he found the beads. The string had broken when they hit the ground, but most of the beads were still on it. He sat down on the prairie to restring the few loose beads he was able to retrieve. At last he tied the string back together, put it into his pocket, and returned to the village, where Rabbit Hand's friends had gathered with Wolf's Tongue for the feast.

The food bubbling in the pot smelled good, but he was not invited to participate. He did not care, for he was not hungry. His half brother was invited to join the feast, however. Long Neck's revelation of Lives-in-a-Tree's assignations with the honored guest had made him a man—and he strutted around the pot as he smoked, suddenly contemporary with his elders, and waited his turn to be served.

The boy stayed at a distance, sitting out in the grass, watching and listening all afternoon. The men talked of the glory time, relating again and again the stories of Kiowa bravery that he had heard all his life. And they recounted other incidents of fallen women. One incident in particular put a shriek into Long Neck's laughter and a proud look on Falling Water's face as she watched her son behaving in such a manly way. It was the story about Three Eyes, who, like Wolf's Tongue, had uncovered during the Medicine Lodge treaty negotiations the adulterous inclinations of Lightning Bolt's three wives. Lightning Bolt, a famed Kiowa warrior, subchief, and diplomat who had married three sisters from Big Tree's clan, searched out his evil wives one at a time that night and bit their noses off. The feast he then provided to honor Three Eyes became the social event of the treaty signing.

The soldiers and the Indian police arrived at sundown to arrest Rabbit Hand. The celebrants were indignant, of course, and haughty; but they could do nothing. Rabbit Hand was placed on an extra horse the police had brought for the purpose of taking him to jail.

Running Standing silently watched his father go. He then went to the creek for a while and sat on a log. Darkness slowly fell over him. He did not admire his father for feasting Wolf's Tongue. He did not admire the sudden manly stature of his half brother. He hated Falling Water, his other-mother; and he could not even think about Lives-in-a-Tree.

The prairie was far into darkness when he decided what he was going to do. He rose, went quietly to the tipi, and took the bag containing his possessions from the lodgepole above his bed. The women and the old man were asleep. Long Neck spoke to him.

"Where are you going?"

"To look for owls."

"You can't find owls at night."

"You can if you know where to look," he said, again slipping out through the flap into the darkness.

He slung the bag over his shoulder and ran at an easy pace across the prairie toward Cloud Chief. When he reached the river, he turned downstream, away from the town, toward Killer Cross's farm in the valley. He passed the grave Killer had dug for himself—still open and yawning in the moonlight —and came at last to the little house of cottonwood boards where the Cross family lived at the edge of the tree-lined river.

He slept in the woods and soon after daylight saw a wagon appear in the yard. In it were missionaries and the students destined for Carlisle. He watched Crosses-the-River, pretty in her buckskin dress and brown apron, bustling about the fire in the yard, serving everybody coffee, biscuits, and meat for breakfast; and he heard them talking, mostly in Cheyenne, about going to school and the long train ride ahead and Pennsylvania and all the happiness one could reach by way of the Jesus Road.

Crosses-the-River's things were loaded finally, and when the wagon pulled away from the house with its merry cargo, the boy slung his bag of belongings over his shoulder and followed it, keeping to the woods. At a bend in the river he hurried ahead and waited near the bridge in a clump of sumacs while the wagon rattled across. With a quick dart toward the tailgate, he swung himself up underneath the wagon bed, clinging to the running gear among the swinging lanterns and buckets.

PART TWO

Crosses-the-River

9

THEY spent six years at Carlisle. The school was conducted in a restored army barracks in the Cumberland Valley in southern Pennsylvania. Girls were taught the essentials of civilized housekeeping: cooking, nursing, and sewing. Boys were taught wagon-making, blacksmithing, tinsmithing, and carpentry. Everyone studied English, history, geography, chemistry, physics, biology, and mathematics. The more enterprising students who wished to earn their own spending money were placed in the Outing System if they signed the following pledge:

I want to go out and work.

If I am sent, I promise to obey my employer and to keep all the rules of the school and not to speak Indian to any other students who may be sent to work with me.

I will attend Sunday school and Church when I am away.

I will not absent myself without permission of my employer and I will not loaf about stores or elsewhere evenings or Sundays.

I will not make a practice of staying for meals when visiting friends.

I will not use tobacco or spirituous liquors in any form.

I will not play cards or gamble, but will save as much money as possible in my account.

I will bathe regularly and do all that I can to please my employer, improve myself, and make the best use of the chance given me.

Signed_____, Pupil

During the six years, Joe worked variously as a gardener's helper, store clerk, and brush cutter for a surveyor. Sara worked four years at Bennacker's Cumberland Valley Dairy Farm near Carlisle, becoming so proficient at bookkeeping and office-managing that the school registry finally hired her away from Bennacker's with steady hours at higher pay.

It became her habit during that last fall to wait for Joe in the late afternoon at the gymnasium door. On a chilly day in November, she sat outside the gym door on a bench underneath an elm tree and listened to unusual cheers inside.

"What's going on?" she asked Johnny Half Bird, a Cherokee, who came through the door.

"Joe is doing flips on the tumbling pad."

Joe had told her, when they watched the clowns from the visiting circus, that he was going to learn, and she had urged him to wait until the football season was over before trying. Even the coach had admonished him—an injured Joe Standing, before the Thanksgiving game, would have been a calamity.

"He shouldn't do that," she said.

"Can't stop him, Sara." Johnny Half Bird grinned, shook his head, and said, "You know Joe. At least," he added significantly, "you ought to."

Johnny's assumption nettled her. She and Joe were of course in love. But they had not become lovers. Sara wanted to give herself to Joe in a Christian way, and would not, in the pagan fashion, be merely rolled on the ground.

She had long since ceased needing her brother's hunting knife for protection. She was basically a Jesus girl, Joe had told her one time, not bitter, but resigned. She would not need that knife anymore; he would not do anything to her that she didn't want him to. When she had stopped wearing the knife at her waist, many students, who knew why she had always worn it, immediately divined a meaning much more tantalizing than the truth. Who would ever have believed that Joe Standing could be stopped short of achieving something he wanted? Tell him to make a touchdown, and somehow he'd do it. Tell him to throw the javelin because the team needed five more points and the regular javelin competitor had a pulled muscle, and he'd throw that pointed stick out of sight. Tell him to run the mile or especially the five-mile marathon, and he'd win your track meet for you. But never, never tell him there was something he could not or should not do.

She stood now by the gymnasium door as Johnny Half Bird went up the path, and waited for Joe to emerge.

"You've been tumbling in there," she said when at last he came through, ebullient. The stop in the shower rooms after football practice always refreshed him, and today the extra fun of tumbling with admirers watching had put a special glow into his bronze face. For there was something daring about what he had done. He had defied the coach, and providence.

"I'll soon be doing the double," he said.

"I heard them cheering," she told him. "But you shouldn't be tumbling now. Coach told you not to. The team will resent you for taking chances on getting hurt before the final game."

He laughed, put his arm around her shoulder—Joe towered over her now; he had shot up to his full height the second year they were here—and guided her down the path. He was tall for a Kiowa, and she was glad, for she had grown rather tall herself.

"Know what they're saying, Sara? Buck Failey, that oil company man, is coming to the game Thursday."

Failey worked for Roscoe Petroleum of Pennsylvania and New York, a company that had announced the intention of fielding a team of professional players to challenge any other company that could field a similar team. It was the wildest possible dream of Joe Standing's life that playing football for money might someday be possible. Coach had said the day of professional football was just around the corner, but Sara was not happy at the prospect. She wanted to return home, and Joe's chance to be employed at professional sports was threatening her own dream.

"If you are going to be scouted Thursday, it's all the more reason not to take a chance on getting hurt," she said. Joe merely laughed.

Kicking Boy, a Pine Ridge Sioux who was the team full-back, shouted across the yard from the administration building that the coach wanted to see Joe in his office right away.

"Somebody must have told on me," Joe said. "Probably the Kick himself. Down deep, that butt-headed Sioux still hates all Kiowas and Cheyennes."

Once more she waited for him, this time on a bench in the main corridor outside the football coach's office. He was inside a long time and returned at last to the corridor not exactly chastened—that was never Joe's mood—but dramatically uncommunicative.

"Well," she asked, "did he bawl you out?"

Joe nodded, his lips pursed in thought, and guided her down the steps toward the dormitories, where he left her.

She stood for a moment and watched him. Joe usually told her just about everything that was on his mind. In fact, he often poured out his feelings, trusting her with every nuance of his attitude toward himself and the life they were entering as educated Indians.

He walked past the men's dorm and disappeared around the far turn toward the railroad tracks. For a moment she considered following, but better thoughts commanded her. Above all, she did not want to anger Joe.

When he did not appear in the dining hall that evening, everyone asked where he was.

Mary Half Bird, with a knowing look, said, "Coach really got on him, didn't he?"

"I don't know."

"He's missed supper several times lately," said a Cochise Apache girl whose white name was Molly Mayberry.

"Hush, Molly," said Tucumcari, a Hopi who was first-string left end and was going to marry Molly next summer after graduation. Tuc always came to Joe's defense. Joe had made a hero of him on the field by occasionally throwing him a pass. The pass play was controversial, but referees were permitting it because it was not covered by the rules one way or the other. Spectators loved it, and Joe had begun to work it effectively with Tuc when other tactics seemed to bog down.

Sara finished eating and left the dining hall. Her roommates at the dorm were an Osage from Kansas named Mary Beth Elk Horn and a Potawatomi from Ohio named Edna Enge. Mary Beth was buxom, spirited, and very popular—a football cheerleader and a fiercely competitive first-string guard on the girls' basketball team. Edna was introspective and ambitious to become a musician; she had already played the organ at forty-six weddings among her fellow students.

"If you ask me," said Mary Beth Elk Horn, "Coach should be grateful to Joe instead of bawling him out. He won't get hurt."

"He's indestructible," said Edna Enge.

The next afternoon Sara waited for him to come out of the gym. She had seen him twice during the day, and he had seemed remote.

"Do you want to tell me what's on your mind?" she said, walking beside him.

"Yes. Let's go downtown and eat supper somewhere."

"At a café?"

"Just like a couple of white folks," he said. "Without a coach or a colonel's wife or anybody herding us around and getting us in and out as though we were incompetents."

"All right. I'll go check out."

"Why do you want to check out? We're not in jail. Let's just go." His words were intense. "Sara, let's get married. Tonight. Let's go somewhere and get started on our own. Not back home . . . but in Harrisburg, maybe."

Frightened that she might anger him and upset some delicate balance, she put her arm through his and walked close to him. "I want to get married in a church, in June, after we have finished school. Just as we have always planned."

"And then go home and help all our people become Jesus people?"

"It isn't ridiculous, Joe."

"Of course it is. There's no way to help our people. We can stay in the East and be interesting freaks and have a better life. Two Indians who speak and understand the white lingo pretty well. Back home, we'll just be two Indians. We'll sink out of sight and you know it."

She was silent, and he asked, "How much money have you got in your account, Sara? I have ninety-one dollars in mine."

"I have six hundred plus," she said.

"I can make five hundred more next Thursday. How would you like that? We could go on a honeymoon and—"

"How could you?"

"By not throwing any passes."

They stopped walking. "From gamblers?" she asked.

"They didn't say who they were."

"Did you tell Coach about this?"

"No. Sara, please leave with me. Now."

"I want you to win the Thanksgiving game and—"

"I'm not going to play in that game."

"Joe, you are!"

"Suppose we get beat. You'd think I threw it."

"Not if you told me you didn't. Joe, you aren't afraid of gamblers."

He turned from her abruptly and walked away.

"Joe," she cried, "aren't we going to have supper somewhere?"

"Forget it," he said. "We'd soon be having a quarrel."

He did not go toward town, nor toward the barracks, but straight across the fields in the direction of the railroad watering tank. The thought reached her that he would wait at the tank until a train came through, swing aboard it, and disappear from her life entirely.

She called to him again. He heard, she knew he did because his stride lengthened.

She watched until he went out of sight down the tracks. Then she returned to the girls' dorm, not sure whether she should have followed him. The one insurmountable problem with Joe was the excess of his moods. If he was happy, he was wildly happy and did exuberant and sometimes embarrassing things; if he was sad, he was desolate; if he was angry, he raged.

"Where have you been?" asked Mary Beth Elk Horn.

"Nowhere."

"I saw you and Joe on the road to town."

"We were just walking."

Mary Beth's eyes stayed on her for several moments, but there was no further questioning. That night was a sleepless nightmare and Sara was a wreck the next morning. Neither of her roommates remarked on how she looked, but they both watched her.

She saw Joe that afternoon as usual, but no mention was made of the incident on the road to town.

Suddenly he said, "Sara, I hope that stupid Tucumcari doesn't drop the ball tomorrow."

"He won't, Joe," she said.

The next afternoon, before the game was five minutes old, Joe tried a pass that missed its mark. Just barely missed, she noticed. And poor Tucumcari ran his heart out trying to catch it.

Horrified, she sat in the grandstand beside Edna Enge. "Don't worry, Sara," said Edna into her ear, "Joe will connect next time."

But he didn't. During the first half he threw two more times—clear over Tuc's head. And Carlisle fell three touchdowns behind.

At half time she pushed through the crowd and ran along the sidelines toward the home-team end zone, where the squad was gathered around the coach for intermission discussion and instruction. Joe saw her and motioned angrily for her to go away. She returned toward her seat, crushed.

As the second half began, she made her way through the grandstand aisle, pausing at the exit for a final glance. Joe had dropped back to throw again. Tucumcari appeared to be breaking into the open, but Joe did not throw. Instead, he tucked the ball under his arm and began running as she had never seen him run before. He surprised everyone, probably even himself, galloping, slashing, and spinning fifty-six yards into the open and across the goal line.

She stayed in the aisle at the wooden ramp and watched. Joe did not throw another pass. He ran on every play, and soon the score was tied. With less than two minutes to go, he performed the trick that would be remembered in years to come. He took the ball, dropped back to pass, rushed forward instead; when he reached the line, instead of slashing through as far as he could, he spun into the air exactly in the manner of the circus clown he'd been practicing to imitate. He did a perfect flip over the pileup and hit the ground on his feet, running with the winning score. The laughter and the cheering could be heard all the way to Dickinson College on the other side of town.

At least half the Indian enrollment waited outside the gym for him to emerge from the shower rooms. And standing among them was Buck Failey, the Roscoe Petroleum Company's athletic scout. He found Sara in the crowd and approached her. "I'm Buck Failey," he said, taking off his hat.

"You are?" Sara said, ridiculously. He was a strong-looking large blond man with an open face and light blue eyes. He smiled easily—almost too easily for you to believe it was genuine.

"And you are Sara Cross, unless I am mistaken."

"I am," she admitted.

"I asked someone to point you out to me. Apparently it's no secret that you and Standing are going to be married next summer."

"In June. It is no secret." She wondered, looking into those blue very-white-man eyes, whether she could trust Buck Failey. She would try to give him a chance.

"Joe tells me you want him to return home rather than play football for money."

This was a surprise. Joe had not mentioned that he had ever spoken to the man. She smiled just enough to cover up any truthful show of feeling and said, "Joe will make up his own mind what to do if the opportunity arises."

"We are prepared to offer him a good position with Roscoe Petroleum, so he will be with us if the professional team develops," Buck Failey went on in a voice that was conversationally charming. She decided to consider trusting him. He had a job to do, and there could be nothing wrong with a man doing his job.

"I am sure he will listen to any offer your company makes, Mr. Failey."

"Call me Buck, please. All my friends do."

"If we become friends, I will, Mr. Failey." The same smile still covered her face.

He laughed. "Good, Miss Cross. I am going to call you Miss Cross as long as you are deciding whether we are friends."

"That will be proper," she told him. "But in June, if we have not yet become friends, you'll have to change it to Mrs. Standing."

"Wonderful," Buck Failey said. "Now, Miss Cross, there is a lady named Mrs. Failey—she hopes that you will someday decide to call her Cora—sitting in a rented rig over by the front entrance. She'll be pleased if you and Mr. Standing accept our invitation to dine with us in downtown Carlisle tonight."

Feeling more farcical than droll, Sara stayed comfortably behind her bland smile, hoping it had not changed, and said, "Thank you, Mr. Failey, but we couldn't possibly. Everyone will be expecting us in the dining hall this evening." Her heart was pounding.

He nodded matter-of-factly and said, "I quite understand. Perhaps after you have had your school celebration, you would join us for dinner. Tomorrow evening."

"Mr. Failey, I couldn't promise anything until I speak with Joe. I was not aware that he even knew you."

The easy smile now left the white man's face. "You were not?" he said.

"Joe told me only that he had heard you would be here today."

Buck Failey, obviously aware that he had stumbled into a conflict, tried to back away. "Would you like me to leave and let you talk to him? I could come see you both tomorrow."

"If you'll tell me how to find you, I will tell Joe," she said. "He'll get in touch with you if he wants to."

By now several students had gathered around them to listen and she was embarrassed. Their looks revealed their opinion. They thought she should make a date with Mr. Failey. Very few Indian students had an opportunity to do anything after graduation except go back home.

"Very well," Buck Failey said. "We'll be at the Carlisle Hotel." He pushed away through the crowd.

At that moment Sara had a premonition that Joe was going to be furious with her for the way she had handled her initial encounter with Buck Failey. For at bottom, Joe would be in torment for having spent half the game trying to lose it and the other half winning it back.

"Now listen to me," he said as soon as they were alone after dinner. "Don't ask any questions. I said I wouldn't throw the game, and I didn't."

"I am not asking questions."

They were standing at the junction of their dormitory paths, and as students passed, they stopped talking.

"Joe," she said tentatively, "what's wrong?"

"Wrong?"

"I don't mean about the game. Now that we are getting close to the end here, you don't want to go home and I don't understand it."

"Who said I didn't?"

"We can't quite seem to talk about it without quarreling. Joe, if it's because of your mother . . . if that's what's bothering you—"

She stopped in mid-sentence. He glared down at her. "If what is bothering me?"

"Please don't be angry, because I love you and I almost

die when you are in torment. Joe, if the idea of seeing her again, since she is noseless—"

He slapped her hard. The blow came so swiftly it must have surprised even him. More dismayed than actually pained, she glanced quickly around to determine whether anyone had seen it. No one was in sight.

She blinked against the tears, knowing that she had at least touched an area of truth, and said, "Joe, I met Mr. Failey this afternoon. He told me that you said we were going to be married in June. I didn't know you even knew him."

He bit his lip and studied her and said finally, "You talked to Buck?"

"While you were in the shower room. He wanted us to dine with him and Mrs. Failey." She laughed, surprised that she could. "Doesn't that sound elegant, Joe? Imagine Indians *dining*. He asked us for tonight, but I told him we wanted to be with our classmates."

"Crosses-the-River," he said, "you have plenty of what the white lingo calls native intelligence, but for some reason— the Jesus Road influence maybe—you are a simpleton."

Her mouth was dry and rage foamed up in the confusion inside her. She had never believed that Joe could hit her, and she knew now that he could and would. She also knew that if he had to, she would let him.

She said simply, "Mr. and Mrs. Failey are at the Carlisle Hotel, waiting to hear from you."

"I'm going there now."

"I'm going, too."

They turned to the main road, and he walked so fast toward Carlisle that she had to run a few steps from time to time to keep up. She did not want to lag behind, for she was conscious of the image they made together on the road.

"Wait for me," she said once. "We look like a couple of Indians, with you so far in front."

He stopped and whirled toward her. "What do you think we are?"

She caught up, grasped his arm, and put her forehead against his chest. "That was supposed to be a joke. I'm not very good at jokes."

Suddenly he put his arms around her and kissed her. "I'm sorry. I really am. Sara, I'm all wound up."

"I know you are, darling. We'll work everything out. You

were marvelous this afternoon after you decided to win the game."

He took her shoulders in his big hard hands, pushed her away from him, and said, "If I had been deliberately throwing over Tuc's head, I could simply have started connecting with those passes."

The realization of her blundering assumption shook her. "Joe, of course. I didn't think of it that way. Tuc wasn't trying, was he?"

Suddenly he shoved her away so hard that she lost her balance and fell in the road.

"Sara . . . I didn't mean to shove you down."

"I know it," she said, scrambling up.

He stood over her darkly, a totem against the moon-brightened sky, and said, "You're wound up, too, whether you know it or not. You're so full of the Jesus Road that you think the worst of people you don't understand. You've become very white, Sara."

She did not answer, and he went on:

"First you thought I was trying to lose the game, and then you thought Tuc was trying to lose it. We were under pressure out there, with Failey watching and gamblers in the grandstand. Our timing was off, and Tuc suggested in the huddle that I start running instead of throwing. Now, Sara, you have got to get some of the Jesus Road out of your system."

He whirled away toward town again, and she followed him. As they reached the edge of Carlisle, he slowed his pace to let her catch up. When they entered the hotel lobby together, she marveled that his attitude could change so quickly from anger to solicitude. He began to treat her as a protected and valuable lady. And despite all that had happened on the road, it felt good.

The clerk told them that Mr. and Mrs. Failey were in the dining room having a late dinner. He sent a message in and Buck Failey appeared almost instantly.

"Good, Joe! Glad you're here. Some game, some game! Come in and have a bite with us. We're nearly through, but we'll get an order in for you two in a hurry."

"We've eaten, Buck," Joe told him easily, "but we could have a cup of coffee, I guess. Couldn't we, Sara?"

"Yes," she said.

And Buck Failey once more turned his big bland easy smile

full upon her. "Hello, Miss Cross. Come into the dining room and meet Mrs. Failey, won't you? Miss Cross and I have decided to be formal with each other until we're sure we can be friends," he explained to Joe.

Joe laughed loudly but Sara knew that he was furious.

The Carlisle Hotel dining room was altogether the nicest eating place she had ever been in. Its entire perimeter was covered with a tufted wainscoting and the electric chandeliers were of solid silver, and the people at all the linen-covered tables were dressed in tailored cheviot and cassimere and taffeta and all-silk messaline.

Cora Failey was blond, tall, thin, and nervously merry. She wore a heavy plain gold wedding band, gold bracelets at each wrist, and a gold pin in the shape of a C at her throat. "It's a pleasure, Miss Cross," she said with a humor-conveying glance at Joe.

"Thank you, Mrs. Failey," Sara said, struggling to produce again her own identity-concealing smile. She sat in the chair Buck Failey pulled out for her. And thankfully realized that Cora Failey's meaningful glance at Joe had been in no way returned.

They had dessert and coffee with the Faileys, and Sara listened to Joe and Buck talk about the prospects of professional football and then about the "real" job waiting at Roscoe Petroleum Company, which was planning to expand into Texas and Louisiana.

Sara could not doubt Failey's sincerity. He was a big open earnest man who had come out of poverty on his own athletic ability. He kept talking about his college days, but never mentioned which college.

"Miss Cross," he added with a sweep of his hand, "will understand that although the amount of money a man can earn at a given time in his life is not his most important consideration, it undeniably weighs heavy in any decision he has to make." The statement ended in an upsweeping inflection, as though it were a question the answer to which was obvious.

"Why will I understand that, Mr. Failey?" she heard herself say. Cora Failey let out a little laugh that was immediately choked off. And Joe frowned.

"Of course she understands," he said to Buck, and Sara sat miserably and ate chiffon pie that was too delicious to ignore.

Presently Cora Failey asked if Sara would like to join her in the powder room. Sara declined. Even though she needed to go, she preferred not to leave herself alone with the braceleted blonde.

She dared not look at Joe, for she knew that everything she did or said was irritating him. At last he made a move to leave. "I'll come talk to you in the morning, Buck. Privately," he added with emphasis.

"Good, Joe. We'll be here until midafternoon, then we are joining Mr. Roscoe on the three-twenty to New York. If you're not busy, maybe you could come down to the depot and meet him. He's a great man, and he'd be pleased if you did."

"I might just do that," Joe said, and Sara noticed the extravagance of his enthusiasm.

On the long walk back from town she tried to hold her tongue until he got the anger out of his system, but there appeared to be no end to his frustration and at last they quarreled.

"You sat there like a simpleton," he said.

"You called me a simpleton before. Do you spend so much time with simpletons that you know exactly how they act?"

"Sara, Buck Failey is a friend of mine. I expect you to treat him as my friend."

"You had not bothered to tell me you knew him, but you think I should be able to read your mind."

"You knew before we got there tonight. It didn't make any difference, apparently."

"What did I do that was so bad?"

"That Miss and Mister stuff, for one thing. And you refused to go to the powder room with Cora."

"I didn't want to be alone with her. But I needed to go and I still do. Excuse me, please." She walked to the ditch at the side of the road, squatted, and relieved herself.

"You shouldn't do that in front of me. You've been taught modesty here at Carlisle."

"I just can't decide whether I'm supposed to be white or Indian around you."

He paused for a moment, and she heard him splashing the road. He said, "Can't you be somewhere in between?"

"Just the other day," she cried, straightening her clothes, "you said we could be a couple of freaks if we stayed in the East instead of a couple of Indians back home. Did you mean

we should be as white as possible or as Indian as possible?
Which?"

"As in-between as possible," he said.

"You are the simpleton, Joe. Nobody can be in-between
anything. We are white educated Indians and we have to live
that way, no matter where we go."

"Then don't pee in ditches anymore."

"Then you stop doing it in the road."

"I will," he shouted and buttoned up his pants. He broke
into a run, leaving her alone, his footsteps growing faint ahead
of her, his dark figure disappearing in the moon-brightened
night.

10

FOR weeks Sara brooded over their quarrel, but Joe appeared determined to ignore the incident completely. She
searched everything he said for remaining signs of anger and,
finding none, could almost believe she had dreamed that terrible night on the road. He loved being the hero of his final
game at Carlisle, and that seemed to sustain him throughout
the winter.

Neither of them mentioned professional football. When
other graduating students spoke of plans for the future, Joe
was silent and managed not to look at her until the subject
changed. But increasing talk of Indian Statehood that spring
gave her hope that his interests might shift toward home
again.

President Roosevelt brought a delegation of chiefs from
Oklahoma Territory to participate in his inaugural parade in
Washington, and six of them visited Carlisle in March. Quanah Parker, the old Comanche, was the most powerful chief
on the Oklahoma reservations, and he impressed the Carlisle
students. His English was quite understandable and everyone
knew he could also speak Spanish, as well as a number of
tribal languages.

"My young friends," he said to a group of athletes gathered around him in the dining hall, "President Teddy is a good friend of mine and he is a good man. He wants Indians to have their own State with their own governor and senators in Congress. It will be good to have an Indian State. You have helped all our people by winning so many football games. You are our very good young people. Learn as much as you can and then come home and help make Sequoyah the best State in the Union."

Joe stepped up to ask when Sequoyah would become a state and Quanah replied that President Teddy thought within two years. "He is my friend and he tells me the truth."

Joe talked of Indian Statehood all afternoon and Sara was excited. She had not seen him show this much interest in anything outside of football in a long time. But old Geronimo destroyed her hope that evening when the students gathered in the auditorium. The once-fierce Apache chief, looking older than the mountains around Fort Sill where he had been a prisoner for nearly twenty years, spoke through an interpreter and said:

"My young friends, I am going to talk to you a few minutes. Listen well to what I say.

"You are all just the same as my own children to me when I look at you. You are here to study and to learn the ways of the white man. Do it well. Obey your father here as you would your own father.

"The Lord made my heart good and I feel good wherever I go. Do as you are told all the time and you won't get hungry. He holds you in His hands and He carries you around like a baby. That is all I have to say to you."

The students cheered dutifully, but later in private conversations many of them voiced the same idea about the old man's speech that Joe expressed.

"He's just another Jesus Indian, Sara. Didn't you listen to him? We're all babies in the arms of Jesus, and if we're good little babies, we'll have plenty to eat. That old scoundrel's brain has turned to mush."

"He's very old, Joe, and he was in prison a long time. Chief Quanah didn't talk that way. He didn't call us babies in the arms of Jesus."

"They say he brings only one of his wives along when he comes to Washington," Joe said, and dismissed the subject of Quanah and Sequoyah State entirely.

In desperation, she talked to her roommates about the problem of her future with Joe.

Mary Beth Elk Horn's view of it was definite. "If Joe wants to play professional football," she said, "you shouldn't object. Who wants to go back home and be an Indian again?"

"I do," Edna answered quickly. "Our people need us. I thought Chief Quanah was wonderful."

"I just don't think we're under that much obligation," Mary Beth insisted. "We have a right to our lives."

"Our people have rights, too—"

"I suppose," Sara said, "that graduating students have to face this problem every spring. All the time I've been here, I never once thought I'd have to decide whether to go home when I finished."

"You'd better remember," Mary Beth warned, "that what the man wants is more important in marriage than what the woman wants. Even though we've been educated, we're still just women. And you know what women are to Indian men."

"I don't agree with you," said Edna Enge, and they talked for an hour about the role they would have to play as women from Carlisle, realizing that education had destroyed any possibility of traditional Indian marriage. Men who had never left the reservation would be afraid of them and would therefore treat them with contempt.

"We have to marry somebody from here, or from Haskell," said Mary Beth at last, "or not marry at all."

"Or marry white men," said Edna stoutly.

"I wouldn't do that," Sara replied.

"You won't have to, but we might," Edna replied. "The reservation men at home certainly won't have us. And many of the educated men here and at Haskell will go right back and take several wives. We'd better understand that before we go home. Personally, I couldn't tolerate extra wives in my house."

"Joe's father had two wives," Sara said. "But he doesn't want two."

"Joe may be different," Edna admitted, "but many of the boys leaving here this summer will go home and take up the old ways. Chief Quanah still has four wives, and a lot of the boys look up to him."

"Well," Mary Beth said pointedly to Sara, "you're a fool if you don't do whatever will make Joe happy. Because in the end he'll do what he wants to, whether you like it or not."

"I believe," Sara said, "that there's a purpose to our lives. We're the first generation of our people to have a larger purpose than just to provide another generation."

"White women," said Edna Enge, "have a lot of power over their men."

"And you know why, don't you?" said Mary Beth Elk Horn. "Their men just can't take sex whenever they feel like it. The woman has to be willing. Can you imagine Chief Quanah—or an old Osage, or a Cheyenne, or a Kiowa— waiting to find out if his woman was willing?"

"Being married to a white man," Edna mused, "might be nice."

"Now don't tell me," Mary Beth objected, "that you'd like to make a man jump through a hoop for sex." She turned to Sara and said bluntly, "If you marry Joe and make him go home against his will, you'll be forcing him to jump through a hoop."

Sara turned away from her roommates and went to the window and pretended to stare into the blackness outside.

Edna said, "You might make a white man jump the hoop, but you'd never be able to do it to an Indian."

"That's nonsense," Mary Beth told her. "Some of our most virile men are already pretty white in that respect."

Sara thought about it for several days. Each time she saw Joe, she sensed increasing tension in him and wondered whether she was already making him jump through a hoop— in anticipation of sex.

On a spring afternoon in early April she asked Joe to go for a walk with her along the creek below North Mountain.

"Let's take a lunch," he said.

"I'll go to the dining room and pack one. And Joe, could you get some wine from Tuc?" Tucumcari had a friend in the valley who made wild huckleberry wine every year, and Tuc usually had a fair supply cached in his footlocker.

Joe lowered his voice. "That's crazy. If they caught us drinking wine, they'd expel us from school."

"Well, today I just feel sort of insubordinate. They won't catch us. We'll be in the woods at the foot of the mountain. Anyway, we had some wine together last Christmas out at Bennacker's party and it didn't destroy us."

"I can get some." He looked down at her through the big smiling grin on his face and said seriously, "Are you planning to get me drunk and then persuade me to do something I wouldn't do sober?"

"You'll find out soon enough. I'll get the food and you get the wine."

He went toward the boys' dorm and she went to her own room. Edna Enge was there, at her study table, peering at a book.

"It's a beautiful day," Sara told her. "You should be out-side."

"I should be, but I feel sort of lonely, and I've learned that I can stop feeling sorry for myself if I study."

Sara dug into her trunk, found the brass-knobbed knife she had once used to protect herself from being rolled on the ground, tucked it into her skirtband out of sight behind the folds of her coat, and said, "Joe and I are going on a picnic."

"Alone, or do you want company?"

"Alone, I'm afraid."

Edna sighed. "Have a good time."

Sara went to the bathroom at the end of the hall, stuck the knife blade behind the door facing, and snapped off its point. Then she put it back inside her skirtband and hurried over to the dining room to arrange for a lunch of sandwiches, boiled eggs, and pickles. At the last moment she bought cookies, deciding they would taste especially good with huckle-berry wine.

When she met Joe near the gym, she saw that he had a quart-sized package under his arm.

They walked together for an hour, away from town toward the creek at the foot of the mountain, coming out at last onto a low, grass-covered ledge where the sun beat warmly through a grove of black birch trees.

"Joe, let's have our picnic here."

She spread her coat on the grass, wondering how soon he would notice the knife. "I brought glasses," she said and took them out of the basket.

"Then let's have a drink. This is going to be a surprise to you." He unwrapped the jar and held it up.

"Joe, that's milk."

"Buttermilk."

"Couldn't you get any wine?"

"I didn't try. Sara, I don't know what you're up to, but if I drank wine, I wouldn't trust myself not to roll you on the ground."

"We drank together at Bennacker's and you didn't try."

"There were always other people with us. Now, listen to me. I won't pretend that I don't think about it. Almost more than anything else. . . . Sara, you've got your knife again." The smile left his face. "I don't like this. You asked me to bring wine, and then you brought that knife to protect yourself."

She drew the knife and showed it to him. "I broke off the point, Joe."

He stared at it. "Why did you do this?"

"So I would not be able to protect myself."

"You could have left the knife at home, if you didn't want to protect yourself."

"Then you wouldn't have known that I no longer want to."

"Protect yourself?"

"Yes."

"Sara—are you telling me that you want to be rolled on the ground?"

"Well, not that exactly. I'm trying to tell you that you can do anything you want to do."

He set the milk jar beside the basket, reached for the knife, examined its broken point for a moment, then stuck it into the ground. He pulled her down onto the coat and kissed her, but not quite the way she thought he might. Holding her close, he said, "Sara, I'm not going to roll you on the ground."

"You're not?"

"I'm going to kiss you a few times and then we're just going to eat our sandwiches."

He got up suddenly and began walking around a huge black birch tree nearby.

"What are you doing?"

"Walking around this tree," he said.

"Why are you doing that?"

"To keep from rolling you on the ground. Sara, firecrackers are going off in my brain. You've always wanted to have a Christian wedding."

"I don't care what kind of wedding I have."

"Ever since you were a little Jesus girl on the prairie at home, you wanted to grow up and have a Christian wedding."

"But I don't care anymore. Will you stop walking around that tree, please?"

"You ought to care," he said. "You may have turned whiter than either of us realize, Sara." He came to her, lay down beside her on the coat again, kissed her hard, and said, "Do you want me obligated to you?" He didn't seem angry, but he urged her to understand the implication he must read in her astonishing action.

"Joe," she said, "I'm not trying to do anything except let you know that I don't want you to have to marry me for sex."

He sprang up and started walking briskly around the tree again. "The graduating boys from all the tribes are afraid of this sort of thing, Sara. Didn't you know that?"

"What sort of thing?"

"Getting latched onto by educated girls before they go home. We're going to get married, but for some reason you want to get me obligated to you even sooner."

Angry, embarrassed, yet somehow amused, she said, "You look foolish going around and around that tree, Joe."

"Let's not quarrel again." He came to her. She was sitting up now, and he sat beside her near the picnic basket. "I felt terrible after that quarrel we had. Did you feel terrible about it?"

"I almost died, Joe."

"Sara . . . you know I want to roll you on the ground, don't you?"

"Yes, that's why—"

"Will you give me a sandwich or something?" He uncapped the milk jar, filled their glasses, and began to laugh. "Sara, you're no Jesus baby."

"I'm your woman, Joe. That's all."

"Listen," he said, "I haven't been going out of my mind for nearly six years just to spoil your Christian wedding now. Goddamn it, Sara, I'm going to be walking around trees all spring!"

11

IF the white man had not finally corralled the Plains Indians, Joe and Sara would have exchanged marriage vows in a different way. Running Standing would have waited his chance to slip into her father's tipi and crawl into Crosses-the-River's buffalo robes. If she had not cried out in opposition, she would have become his wife. She would not have cried out, of course, for he would already have bought her from her father with several horses, and she would have known about this payment far enough in advance to object if she had cared to.

But the white man's ritual prevailed. They were married in June at Carlisle by a Presbyterian minister while standing at the altar on a blanket of daisies their admiring fellow students had provided. To strains of organ music played by Edna Enge, they ran down the steps and across the curb, Joe pulling her along in the opposite direction from the waiting buggy she thought they were to leave in.

"Where are we going?"

"Come on! That buggy is a decoy. I've hired another rig— it's across the street in the next block."

"But why?"

"They're trying to kidnap you."

He rushed her to the next corner and helped her into a rig that waited beneath a great elm tree. He leaped up beside her, grabbed the reins, and slapped the horse into a gallop. As they approached the next intersection, she heard the shouts from their friends—the football and track stars—who pursued on foot.

"They were going to waylay us east of town," Joe said. "The Kick and Tuc's crowd. They're waiting out there now, on horses in that old barn beside the junction."

"In feathers and war paint?" she asked, delighted. She could imagine Kicking Boy riding alongside the buggy and literally plucking her out of the seat. "Where were they going to take me?"

"Out to Bennacker's place. The Bennacker girls, your friends, are conspiring against you, too."

Joe wheeled the rig around a corner, up the street for two blocks, around another corner, and into the outskirts of Carlisle near the railroad switching tracks.

Making sure they were out of sight, he drew to a sudden stop. In the cloud of dust she saw a young white boy and girl standing beside the tracks.

"Here you are, Sammy," Joe called to the boy.

"All right, Joe," the boy said.

"Take off your veil, Sara, and give it to Maggie."

Before she could fathom his plan, he lifted her from the buggy, removed the veil from her head, and placed it on the little white girl. "Let it flow out in the wind so they'll be sure to see it, Maggie," he told the girl and helped her up into Sara's seat. The boy leaped up beside her and took the reins.

"Thanks, Sammy," Joe said. "Now, get going. Circle the depot and head out toward the barracks. But don't get too far ahead of them. I want them to follow you all the way."

"I won't. Good luck to you, Joe. And to you, Mrs. Standing," the boy said. He slapped the reins smartly and moved away.

Joe dragged her from the road and pulled her down behind a blackberry hedgerow, ducking from sight just as their pursuers came into view and sped by, chasing the buggy.

She whispered, "It worked, Joe. Look at them run."

"Nobody steals this Indian's bride."

"Who are those children who took the buggy away?"

"Sammy hangs out around the practice field. I'm his hero."

"You're mine, too. Where are we going? Our suitcases are in the other buggy."

"Mrs. Standing," he said, grasping her shoulders in his big hands, looking down in a half smile that was dead serious, "you must learn, beginning at this very moment, to trust your husband. Or you will not have a happy life."

He turned her toward the switching tracks. There, on a siding, stood a fancy private railroad car, glistening in the sun. *Clarissa* was her name. The letters in golden script that formed the word seemed demure against their varnished background.

"Come on," he said and led her toward it. "Up you go, Sara."

"This is trespassing."

"If anybody objects, we'll call them heathens and hold a prayer meeting." He laughed at his joke. "Come on. Up!"

He boosted her out of the ballast onto the step and then up into the car. She gasped. "Joe—look at all this!" She saw the drawing room first—a resplendence of bowlegged furniture, delicate beneath its plush upholstery and heavily stuffed cushions. Flowing ball-fringed draperies drawn over the windows cast all the elegance into deep shadow. As her eyes adjusted, she realized that love emblems were the principal theme of the car's decor.

He moved around her and she followed. As they passed an

open writing secretary, Joe pulled the switch chain and the light came on. Startled that it worked, he switched it off immediately.

"Joe, let's get out of here."

But he dragged her into the dining room, where a table was set with candelabra and silver service for two.

"I wonder what the menu is," he said. "Look in here." He pushed through the passage into the combination dressing–bath room, a cubicle magically arranged to provide a spacious setting for marble plumbing fixtures, bath tub, and wardrobe.

"I wonder if the water is hot." He turned on a faucet for a moment.

"Joe . . ."

He dragged her through the passage again into the bedroom, which featured, beneath a frieze of flying cupids, a huge canopied bedstead with parted silk curtains—a bed of most heroic size. Watching her, Joe grinned. "This beats a buffalo robe, doesn't it? Or a grassy ledge on North Mountain?" He pushed his fists into the bed's abundance and his expression told her he was ready to have her now.

"Joe, for heaven's sake. Not here."

He picked her off the floor for a moment and then, just as she thought he would throw her onto the bed, he put her down. "Scared?"

"Terrified. This isn't ours."

Wheels crunched the ballast outside. "Let's see who this is," he said, leading her back toward the drawing room. A man in butler's clothes appeared at the entrance carrying two suitcases that Sara recognized as theirs.

"Oh, Mr. Standing, you are already here," the butler said from a face that was obviously surprised but otherwise oval, pallid, and blank. He bowed to Sara. "On behalf of Mr. C. J. Roscoe, welcome aboard *Clarissa,* Mrs. Standing. I am Haskins. We had not expected you until this afternoon." The man rushed to draw open the draperies to let in light. Sara stared first at Joe, then at the butler.

"Will you be wanting lunch, madam?" Haskins asked.

"No, Haskins," Joe told him quickly. "Nothing at all."

"You will find the galley well-stocked. And here's your luggage, sir. Your trunks are in the freight room. They'll be loaded before the train moves out. Have a good trip, madam."

Haskins disappeared. She turned to Joe, who shrugged and

said, "Mr. and Mrs. Standing are going on their honeymoon
to New York City in a private railroad car just like a couple
of swells." He grinned foolishly.

"Explain it, Joe. Tell me what you've done."

He told her nothing, but picked her up and carried her
back through the car, pausing only long enough to close the
draperies Haskins had opened. When he reached the bedroom,
he put her down on the bed and began undressing her.

She sighed. And then she laughed wildly, pulling him to her
on the bed. "Good heavens, these sheets are silk!"

"I hope they are top quality," he said and smothered her
into them.

It was almost dark when thoughts of food finally reached
them. He pulled on underwear and went through the passage
toward the drawing room where the butler had left their bags.
Sara had a traveling dress in the suitcase which she would
wear now, a striking dark-blue dress of good muslin she had
made at Bennacker's. She had planned to wear it home this
year.

"I found the galley," Joe said at the door.

He set her suitcase down and watched her dress. He had
not bothered to bring his own suitcase to the bedroom. "You
won't need that until tomorrow," he told her.

"I have to wear something."

"I'm glad they taught my girl modesty."

"Don't try to make me angry," she said, wondering just
how white she had become. She had always thought that she
would approach the marital situation naturally, but of course
there was nothing natural about a railroad car. That ledge at
the foot of North Mountain would have been preferable to
this.

Joe said, "There's a coal-oil stove in there, and an ice
chest."

"Let's see what's in it. You'd better get dressed, hadn't you?
Your man might think he had a low-caste employer if he saw
you that way."

"Men of stature do not care what servants think. We are a
couple of swells, aren't we?" he added, and she realized that
she was becoming frightened.

They found fancy tins of meat and fish. The labels were in
gourmet language that neither of them quite understood.

She whirled toward him suddenly and said, "You have to

tell me now, Joe, what kind of deal you have made with Mr. Roscoe."

He grabbed her shoulders. "I didn't want to quarrel with you before our wedding. We aren't going home, Sara. There's no help for our people."

"Joe, there is! And they need us. Lives-in-a-Tree, Long Neck. My mother and my brother Billy—"

"Trust me. That's all you need to do."

Unable to speak, she whirled and ran back to the bedroom. He followed, controlling his anger. She threw herself on the bed and he towered over her.

"Joe," she said into the silk sheets, "I can't go to New York. You had no right to make this commitment without telling me about it. I've followed every detail of the Sequoyah State movement. I *want* to go home and be a part of it, and I want you to. You could be the governor someday! We're the hope of our people—but without us, they have no hope."

"Sara, goddamn it, you're my woman and—"

"I won't go," she said, instantly stunned by the hideous knowledge that she had taken an impossible position. To soften it, she added quickly, "Let's both try to stop being stubborn, darling, and try to—"

"Can you say 'darling' in Cheyenne?" He sat down on a bowlegged chair, to begin dressing. "Or in Kiowa? 'Darling' is another one of your white-lingo words. Women sometimes change their minds, Crosses-the-River. You have a chance to change yours, if you do it right away."

"I won't go," she said, trembling. "And please don't call me Crosses-the-River."

Now fully dressed, he turned through the door. She ran after him, along the passage, wildly yelling, even screaming, "Joe! We're married . . . under the laws of the United States."

"We are not even citizens of the United States," he said. "If you don't want the honeymoon I have planned for us, you can consider yourself returned to your father."

He picked up his suitcase at the parlor entrance and stepped down onto the ballast. She pulled one of the draperies aside to see him hurry across the tracks toward the depot, and she always remembered that, as she watched him go, her senses were staggered by the feeling that she had at last been rolled on the ground.

She hurried to the bedroom, closed her own suitcase, returned through the car, and leaped from *Clarissa*'s steps to

follow him. He was nowhere in sight. She ran along the cob-
blestones at the street crossing, where, in a din of whoops
and screams, a rider on a galloping horse plucked her Indian-
style right out of the street.

"I've got her!" cried Kicking Boy, and she was thrust into
a waiting buggy and sped out of town by Joe's friends, who
secreted her for the night at Bennacker's farm—the victim,
finally, of their plot to kidnap the bride of Carlisle's most
popular spring graduate.

Sara put a successful face on her wedding night abduction.
Admitting anguish to no one, she even managed to laugh
about the escapade with all her friends.

"Father has a buggy waiting for you in the barn," whispered
Nora, an excited sixteen-year-old who was the younger of the
Bennacker sisters. "He is on your side. As soon as the boys
leave, he'll drive you."

"Where is Joe waiting?" asked Leona, the older sister, who
was Sara's age and went to high school in Carlisle.

"I don't know where he is," she had to tell them.

"Didn't you make an emergency plan to meet somewhere
in case they got you?"

"We didn't think they would. I'll . . . have to stay here
tonight, I guess."

"Oh, that's awful. I hate boys," said Nora, blissfully.

Sara cried herself dry of tears in her old room upstairs
where she had lived as an outing student. When finally there
was nothing left to drain out onto her pillow, she lay in dry-
eyed wonder until the sounds of breakfast downstairs aroused
the household.

She rose, toughened with new resolution. Mr. Bennacker
drove her to town and she went directly to the depot. *Clarissa*
was no longer on the siding.

The agent told her it had rolled out early the previous evening, hooked onto a Philadelphia-bound passenger train.

"Was it going to New York?" she asked.

"Could be going anywhere." The agent was a wizened but
humorous little man with a sharp chin. "*Clarissa* is a wild-
running lady, miss. Only two weeks ago she was in California,
month before that down in Florida. She could be in Canada
two days from now."

Sara asked hopefully whether the agent knew anything
about the servant, Haskins. The agent nodded sadly. "A very

lonely man, Haskins—comes in and talks once in a while when *Clarissa* passes through."

"Where does he live when he's not traveling?"

"Him? Aboard *Clarissa*. When she is in use by Mr. Roscoe or his guests, he travels the sleeper cars, or stays in hotels wherever he happens to be. They say there is big gambling games aboard that varnish car sometimes. Politicians and high-powered people, moguls and tycoons." The agent peered at her. "Are you one of the Indian school girls?"

"Yes."

"Say . . . you are not the bride that had a quarrel yesterday and ran away, are you? The groom came back an hour later."

"Did you talk to him?"

"He didn't say very much. But I knew he was looking for his bride."

"Didn't you tell him that I was kidnapped by our friends from school?"

"I told him I saw you run across the switch tracks carrying a suitcase, and then the telegraph got busy and that's all I saw."

"Do you know where he went?"

"He was still aboard when *Clarissa* hooked onto that Philadelphia train." The agent watched her closely and said, "I seen him through the window just as the train pulled out. Haskins was serving him supper, sitting all by himself there in the fancy little dining room, and it seemed a shame."

"Did he take our trunks?"

"He took one and left one. Put it aboard while I was busy with the telegraph."

"I'd better send a telegram myself," she said, and prepared a message which she sent to her father in care of the Indian agent at home.

12

Sara's father and brother met her at the Territory depot. They wore long hair, in thick flat braids wrapped with rawhide at the ends. They were dressed identically in black full-crowned hats, bibbed overalls, blue shirts, and moccasins. They nodded and grunted a few monosyllabic phrases in white lingo, but mostly they spoke Cheyenne. Sara slipped easily back into her native language. As they loaded her trunk and suitcase into the wagon, she began to follow their conversation.

Her father was huge, fierce-looking but gentle. Now he was troubled. He kept glancing at her ring and presently her brother noticed it, too.

"Do you have a husband, Crosses-the-River?"

She nodded.

"Did you marry Running Standing?"

"Yes, I wrote you that I was going to."

"Did you have a white marriage with him?"

"Yes."

"Where is he now?"

"In New York City, I think."

"Why is he there?"

Because she did not want to admit that Joe had left her, she said, "I do not know."

"When will he be here?" her father asked.

"I'm not sure when."

"If he married you, he should come and take you off our hands." Her father then looked over her clothes and said, "I will buy you a squaw dress. You can't go around looking like that. People will think you are ashamed of yourself."

"I am not ashamed of anything."

Her brother said, "The school ruined her; I knew it would." He turned away, crossing the street toward a general store.

"Wait here," said her father, following Billy.

She waited beside the wagon. People passing stared, their faces revealing curiosity—and open amusement—that someone dressed in white-woman traveling clothes would be connected with such an Indian-looking rig. Away from the wagon she could have passed for a sun-browned white.

It was the same wagon she had gone away in, the orange and black road wagon that Joe had once admired. Its colors were faded now and its size less imposing than when she was younger. The high spring seat had been removed and two straight chairs put in its place. The bed behind the chairs was piled with bags of corn meal, flour, sugar, and feed grains. The horses stood in lassitude beside the rail, now and then stomping the dust.

Uncomfortable to be attracting the attention of strangers, she left the wagon and crossed toward the store to wait on the boardwalk in front. When they came out, her brother had two parcels in his arms and her father carried a huge section of beef on his shoulders with his head up inside the rib cage. She hurried after them and watched her father dump the beef into the wagon, then wipe blood from his hat and straighten it into its natural crown.

They climbed into the chairs to leave town quickly, as though they were ashamed of her. She scrambled over the tailgate and fell among the flour and sugar bags alongside the beef carcass. Flies and bees attacked the meat in swarms as they moved out over the prairie road. She searched for something with which to cover it but could only find a pile of gunnysacks between the chairs in front. Deciding those were better than nothing, she opened and shook them out before covering the beef.

They stopped to water the horses and eat their lunch alongside a stream that fed into the Washita. She had not quite remembered how the land looked here. It was flat, endlessly flat and red, and seeing it recalled to her mind the surprise with which she had first seen the Cumberland Valley in Pennsylvania where earth was black and river water clear, where mountains rose on every side to bring into close intimacy the rim of the world. Here the horizon was distant and the mountains that marked it low and vague.

While unhitching beneath a pecan tree near the stream, her father noticed the covered beef and snatched the gunnysacks from it. The meat needed the sun to start drying, he said. Flies attacked it again as he led the horses to water.

Her brother sat down in the shade and told her there was food in the large brown bundle they had brought from the last store they visited. Obviously he expected to be waited on. "Why did Running Standing leave you?" he asked.

"I did not say he left me."

"We will find you another husband as soon as you get rid of those clothes. Do you also have on underpants and a bosom harness?" His question implied that he was reasonably sure she did have on those garments, and that such things revolted him.

Silently she took the food parcel to the base of the tree and opened it. There was cheese and bread and a tin of sardines. She looked for something to spread on the ground. There was nothing, of course, except the filthy gunnysacks.

Her brother watched her, as curious as the whites who had passed her in town. His face was less square than her father's because he was younger, but the family resemblance was remarkable. He was more cynical than her father, perhaps, again, because he was younger.

"What are you looking for, Crosses-the-River?"

"Everyone calls me Sara Cross now. I mean, Sara Standing." Angered to find herself under such arrogant scrutiny, she dumped the bag of food onto the ground at his feet. This was apparently what he wanted. He reached for the bread, then picked up the sardine tin and handed it to her for opening.

"We bought you a squaw dress," he said. "It is in the other package."

"Billy, I told you I did not want one."

"Everyone calls me Billy Cheyenne."

"Why do they?"

"Because Many Stones likes it better than Billy Cross. She must not see you in that dress."

"Who is Many Stones?"

"My wife."

"I thought you married Walking Fast from the Caddo."

"I sent her back when I married Many Stones."

"I am surprised that you did not keep them both," she said, but sarcasm was lost on her brother.

"Many Stones is plenty squaw for one man," he said.

"Is she a Cheyenne?"

"Part Cheyenne, part Sioux, part black white-woman, part brown white-woman, part wolf."

"Wolf?" Sara suppressed a laugh and studied Billy Cheyenne, hoping he might have intended humor. Apparently he
hadn't; he only nodded and waited for her to open the sardines.

Her father now sat beside her brother and leaned back
against the tree trunk.

"Many Stones has power," he told her. "You will have to
do as she tells you. She will never let you wear that dress. We
have quit the Jesus Road, Crosses-the-River." Then he warned
her solemnly: "Many Stones' power is dangerous. She will be
kind if you do everything she says. If you do not, she will
poison you."

"Has she ever poisoned anybody?"

"Yes," said Billy Cheyenne. "She used to poison me often,
and then she stopped when I began treating her different."

"How were you treating her that made her want to poison
you?"

"She did not like to cut the wood."

"Do you cut the wood now?"

"All the time."

"Don't you feel ashamed for having to do as she tells you?"

"She turns me into a woman," he admitted, "but only while
I am cutting wood. Most of the time I am a man." His chest
swelled noticeably when he said it.

"What else does she make you do?"

"She makes me take the children out back and live in the
tipi with Ma and Pa and our old aunts while she has her
menses."

"How many children do you have?"

"Two. Girls. We need some boys."

Sara turned to her father. "Do you have a tipi on the back
yard now?"

He nodded. "We built it to live in when we left the Jesus
Road. The year after you went away."

"Why did you leave the Jesus Road?"

"I lost my power. I could never pray anyone to death after
I killed Sky-Walker. The Jesus people only let me have the
power to get rid of him, and then they did not need me no
more."

"Does Reverend Holcombe still have his mission?"

"Pole Bean and Round Face Woman? Yes, but we never
go there anymore."

"What happened to Running Standing's mother?"

"She lost her nose," said Billy Cheyenne. "We don't know what happened to her."

"Do you ever see Long Neck?" she asked, remembering the knife fight Billy had once had with Joe's half brother.

"He married Two Bonnet, a low-class Caddo. They work for whites near Fort Sill. They are dapoms now. I was going to kill him once, but I decided not to."

"Why did you decide not to kill Long Neck?"

"Dapom Kiowas are not worth killing. They say he still raises gamecocks. Someday I am going to get a fine cock and send him a challenge, if he ever comes back up this way to live." Billy turned to his father and said, "Crosses-the-River is wearing underpants and a bosom harness."

Her father's face drew into an expression of supreme disgust. "Take them off. Put on the squaw dress we bought for you."

She glared at them. They both sat beneath the tree, waiting. It was clear that they did not intend to budge. Just as clearly she would have to.

She found a striped parcel and took it to the other side of the wagon to change. The dress, a loose-fitting garment of dull brown cloth, might have been an elongated flour sack with holes cut in the closed end for arms and neck. Winter dresses had cuffless sleeves sewn into the armholes and summer dresses did not. Earlier, the same design would have been fashioned from deerskin; when newly tanned and soft, with fringe at the hemline, laces down the front, and beaded designs, they were beautiful. Drably made by white merchants with gaudy cheap buttons from waist to neck for trade among the Indians, they were hideous.

Since she was changing behind the wagon, out of sight, she did not remove her bloomers and bust form. The men in her family were not going to make her *that* Indian.

The sun was setting when the wagon turned across the river bridge and around the bend where her family's house came into view. It was the house of gray cottonwood boards that she remembered, although now it seemed absurdly small. Canvas-covered, the tipi in the back yard was as large at the base as the house itself. A fire with a pot hanging over it was burning in the yard and a trickle of smoke rose straight up. Nondescript fighting chickens strutted and scratched in the yard and a spotted pig dozed beside the corner of the house.

Her mother was waiting in the yard. Everyone had always continued to call her Lamb Woman instead of Rachel, as she had been entered on the Cheyenne roll because some fanciful-minded Bureau official knew that Rachel meant *ewe* in Hebrew. Sara recognized Lamb Woman instantly and it was wonderful to have someone glad to see her. There was no doubt that her mother was glad.

"Is this Crosses-the-River?"

"Yes, Lamb Woman. It is."

Lamb Woman's eyes seemed less dulled by age than her face, which might have been carefully shaped of dried-out doeskin. She was round and heavy-looking. Obviously the family had plenty to eat. "I see they bought you a squaw dress," she said. "I was hoping you would not wear one. Squaw dresses look very funny on a person wearing braids tied up into a white-woman hairknot and sharp-toe, hard-bottom shoes. Isn't it very painful to wear shoes like that?"

"You get used to it," Sara said.

"Come, let down your braids and I will find you some moccasins. You must be tired. You are very beautiful, Crosses-the-River. You are as beautiful as I remembered you."

The two aunts—they were Sara's great-aunts—both peered from the tipi flap, their old eyes squinting warily. In front of them, like soft miniature reflections in a pool, two infants peered from cradleboards hanging from the poles on either side of the flap.

Sara glanced around quickly for a glimpse of her new sister-in-law.

"Many Stones is inside the house," said Lamb Woman, reading her mind. "She lives mostly in the house."

"And these are her babies," Sara said. "My little nieces."

"Grass Girl and Vegetable Girl," said Lamb Woman. "Same litter, last year."

"How marvelous. They are beautiful, Mother—"

"Do not touch. Many Stones will have to give you permission to touch. She will let you, I think," Lamb Woman added with another glance at Sara's squaw dress. "She was afraid you might bring white-child clothes for them. She does not want them to be white babies."

"Well, I might have, I guess, if I'd known they existed."

"Didn't anybody write to you about them?"

"No. I thought until today that Billy was married to Walking Fast from the Caddo."

"He said he would go to the mission and have Pole Bean write a letter to you, but I guess Many Stones would not let him."

"She seems to have all the authority around here."

"She has power," Lamb Woman said.

"I am not afraid of her," Sara said.

Lamb Woman lowered her voice. "You must be careful. Now that you are home again, I do not want her to kill you."

Killer Cross and Billy Cheyenne emptied the wagon of supplies, setting the bags of meal, flour, and sugar inside the tipi.

"Why don't you put those things in the house?" Sara asked.

"We live in the tipi," her father said.

"But the sugar will get very hard if you leave it on the ground."

Her father and brother ignored her and returned to the wagon for the beef carcass, which they dumped near the fire. The two aunts came out with knives and began shaving off thin slices for drying. As they cut, they wallowed the carcass in dust, leaves, wood chips, chicken manure, and whatever lay on the ground.

"Can't you at least put it on a board or something?" she asked. "It won't be fit to eat." Watching the two old women go about their unsanitary task made her sick.

Her father still ignored her. "Crosses-the-River has lost her husband," he said to Lamb Woman.

"She can't hold a husband," said Billy Cheyenne, "but she wants to tell us what to do. Maybe she tried to tell Running Standing what to do, and that is why he kicked her out."

"We will find her another husband," said Lamb Woman simply.

One of the aunts looked up from the beef carcass. "Running Standing's people are all dapoms now anyway."

"At the school in Pennsylvania," she said, "they taught us about sanitation. We will all be much stronger and healthier if we eat clean food." It was not easy for her to find the necessary Cheyenne words. "Dirt and filth contain little bugs and animals that get inside us when we eat the food."

"What kind of animals?" Billy Cheyenne asked skeptically. "I don't see any animals in the dirt."

"They are tiny—so small you can't see them without a special glass to look through."

"Do you have a special glass to look through?"

"No, but I have seen them in the laboratory at school."

"There may be animals in the food in Pennsylvania, but not here."

"They are everywhere in the world," she said. "Wherever there is filth."

"And they get inside us and make us sick?" Billy Cheyenne pondered the curious revelation. "Many Stones puts them there, I guess. But I will cut wood for her, so we do not have to worry about it."

The old aunts resumed their task, draping the meat slices over the pole from which the pot hung above the fire. At least, Sara thought, the smoke would keep the flies away.

"Why do you have to buy meat?" she asked her father. "Wouldn't it be better to raise some cattle and slaughter your own beef?"

"We don't have to do that. We are rich now. We get grass money all the time for the use of our allotment lands."

"How much do you get?"

"Fifteen dollars every moon if we can find the man. Billy Cheyenne knows where to find him."

"That isn't very much to live on, is it?"

"We have everything we need. We eat whenever we want to." Her father said it with pride, reminding her of the teachers' warning at graduation time that coming home would be the hardest thing she would ever have to do in her life.

"I want to see Many Stones," she said.

"I am Many Stones," said a voice from the back of the house.

Everyone looked up. Sara wondered how long her sister-in-law had been listening. Many Stones was a frail little woman, obviously young, wrapped in a blanket as though she were cold even on such a warm day. Her hair was in tiny narrow braids. Her forehead was banded with a doeskin ribbon. But the most important aspect of her on first sight was the sweet expression on her face. It was a thin face with a straight attractive nose and a sensitive mouth. That such an unprepossessing person could have the entire family tyrannized seemed ludicrous.

"I hope we will be friends," said Sara, searching for a way to begin their relationship.

Many Stones did not answer, but stepped from the doorway into the yard. As she approached, Sara realized that she was lame. Her feet, in clean, delicately-beaded moccasins, were tiny even for such a small woman; one of them made a small circle in the air as though the ankle swiveled automatically with each step.

"I am not going to hurt you, Crosses-the-River," Many Stones said, looking up now, for she was much shorter than Sara.

"I did not think you would, Many Stones."

She inspected Sara for several moments, then went to the tipi flap and took one of the babies from its cradleboard. She sat down on the woodpile, opened her blanket, and withdrew a full breast, which the baby attacked noisily.

"Why do you stare at me?" she said at last. "I told you I would not hurt you."

"I didn't mean to stare at you."

Many Stones only smiled and glanced down at her nursing infant.

Sara's own glance wandered back to the flap where the other baby watched, wide-eyed and patient—waiting its turn.

"Which one is Vegetable Girl?" she asked.

"The one I am holding," said Many Stones. "That one is Grass Girl."

"They are beautiful children, Many Stones. May I hold Grass Girl in my arms for a few minutes?"

"If you will first remove the bosom harness you are wearing underneath your dress. Grass Girl would be frightened if she were cradled against a hard breast."

Now Sara realized that her father and brother were glaring at her for having defied them. She pushed angrily past the swinging cradleboard and through the flap into the tipi. She might have cried in frustration if the smell inside had not staggered her. At least it distracted her for a moment. And it brought memories of her own childhood flooding back. The accumulated odors of unclean living had been a natural part of life to her, with no repugnant association; now, in the home where she expected to live, they were unbearable.

The bedding was all on boards that were propped off the ground with flat stones. She could not even sit on it. As she stood, growing slowly accustomed to the tipi darkness, her father appeared at the flap with her suitcase.

"Here," was all he said, and he went away. Nobody brought her trunk, and she realized that, since it was heavy, she could fetch it herself. Her father had only brought the suitcase to emphasize that she must change.

She returned to the wagon, pulled out her trunk, and dragged it over the ground into the tipi.

Her mother came inside and told her it would be better if she removed the bust form. That, apparently, would solve everything. "I think you are still a good girl, Crosses-the-River. I don't believe the school ruined you, but the whites have taught you some foolish things. Bosom harness will ruin your milk if you ever have babies. Take it off, and Many Stones will like you. Now I will find you a pair of moccasins."

Lamb Woman rummaged through her clothing bags, which hung from tipi poles. Many Stones, still nursing Vegetable Girl, came to the flap. The two aunts appeared at the flap behind her, one of them carrying the butcher knife. They were all going to watch Sara change—to see exactly what sort of gear she might have on underneath and to satisfy themselves that she got rid of it. As soon as she was back in the squaw dress, they all seemed satisfied.

Because there was not time enough to sun the bedding before dark, Sara shuddered at the prospects of approaching night. She could not abide the sight or smell of the food they cooked for supper, and when she pretended to feel unwell in order to retire without eating, everyone feared that Many Stones had already poisoned her.

She dug a blanket out of her own trunk and managed to get through the night. Daybreak found her realizing that if magically, somehow, she could be with Joe—wherever he was—she'd be there faster than her family had put her into a squaw dress.

13

Soon after sunrise, she stood before the fire outside the tipi, trying without looking at it to help her mother fry meat and boil coffee.

"How do you feel this morning, Crosses-the-River?"

"Just fine."

"Then you have not been poisoned."

"I am sure I haven't been."

"I did not think Many Stones would do that to you."

Iron-rimmed wheels clattered on the road. An open-topped hack was approaching from the direction of the river, with a white man and woman bouncing in the front seat.

"Morning, Brother Cross," said the man as her father emerged from the tipi. She recognized the voice. These people were the Reverend and Mrs. Holcombe. Pole Bean and Round Face Woman.

"Morning, Sister Cross," said Mrs. Holcombe sociably. "It's early in the day to be visiting, but we wanted to come over before the sun gets hot."

Sara's parents stared at the missionary couple. The aunts peered from the flap. Billy Cheyenne, followed by Many Stones, came from the door of the house; Many Stones was nursing one of the babies.

"We heard at services last night that Sara was home," said the Reverend. "We've missed you folks at services for quite some time now, Brother Cross." He said it without enthusiasm, for he meant to be careful not to encourage them. He'd had trouble enough with Killer Cross's evangelistic impulses several years ago.

Watching them, Sara wanted to laugh. The Reverend and his wife gazed past her, trying to peer into the tipi. They had not recognized her.

"I am Sara," she said. "I arrived home yesterday. It's been a long time, hasn't it, Reverend?"

They made no attempt to disguise their reaction to the sight of her. "She's already back to the blanket," said Mrs. Holcombe.

"I . . . just put on something to work in," Sara heard herself say.

"We have come for you, dear girl," said the Reverend. "We'd have met your train if you had let us know when you expected to arrive."

"Come for me?"

"We're taking you to live with us." Mrs. Reverend's smile bespoke a sense of certainty about what they were doing.

"To live with you?"

"Susan Antelope has left us. There's a wonderful place for you at the mission now. We were so thrilled when we heard you were home."

"Susan Antelope," the Reverend added, "has gone out West to preach for Jesus among the Hopi and the Navajo. Bless her for that, if she does. Quite frankly, our fear is that she has returned to the blanket. However, we have a marvelous new work planned here, Sara, and you are to be an important part of it."

His face, lean and gray, grew even more solemn as he explained their plan to translate gospel songs into all the Plains languages spoken in the area. "Quite frankly," he admitted, "we've been a bit disappointed lately. So many of these people have a momentary joy in Jesus and then backslide. We've decided that actual participation in the songs might help reach them on a deeper level. The gospel rhythms are always infectious, especially to the childlike mind."

"I'm going to live here," she told him, less outraged that he would speak of *these people* as though they weren't present than amused by his admission that he considered gospel hymns childlike.

"But you must not live here, dear girl."

"Why mustn't I?"

"She's already back to the blanket, John," Mrs. Reverend said again. "I told you that we'd have to get one right off the train."

"If you come with us today, it will be much easier for you," the Reverend said.

"Easier than what?"

"Than later, after you've grown back into your old ways. You can't possibly be happy here"—his glance swept the yard —"not possibly."

"But these are my people," she said. "You don't seem to understand why I went away in the first place."

"Of course I understand." His voice took on the edge of thunder she remembered from times past when she had heard him in the pulpit. "You went away so you could return with sufficient education to lead your people to Jesus, didn't you?"

Now thoroughly angry, she said, "I'm here to try to bring my people better living."

"Exactly, dear girl! And through Jesus—"

"Through Jesus they haven't got very far up to now. If you wanted to teach sanitation and health requirements instead of gospel songs, I might help you."

"But that's the Indian Bureau's job, not mine."

"I wish somebody would tell the Bureau." She bent toward

the fire to turn the meat that simmered in a skillet on a little
mound of coals her mother had pulled aside. Suddenly the
meat smelled good. Squatting before the breakfast fire, she
felt herself an Indian again. The feeling would probably pass
before she got the bedding aired, but for the moment she
could have shouted for joy.

The Reverend, at his wife's insistence, gave up and drove
away.

"Quite frankly," was his parting remark, "we believe you'll
come to see us of your own accord after you've been here a
few days. If you do, and if we haven't already found another
interpreter, we will be glad to have you with us."

Many Stones began to laugh. "You were very strong and
brave with him, Crosses-the-River. You are one of us. I did
not think you would be."

Sara was surprised that Many Stones had understood that
much of what had transpired. "Pole Bean means well," she
said.

"All white people mean well. Only Indians mean bad every
thing they do."

"But we won't get anywhere by hating the whites."

"We won't get anywhere not hating them, either."

"We haven't yet tried not hating them, have we?"

"Our ancestors tried it in the beginning, and lost everything
they had." Many Stones' small frame was now erect. Her chin
was high and her nostrils flared. "That is all," she said and
went back into the house.

"I think I will kill Pole Bean," said Billy Cheyenne.

"Don't try it," said Sara's father. "He has power. I know,
because he let me use it for a while one time."

"We all know," said Billy Cheyenne with surprising arrogance. "We were there when you killed Sky-Walker, and yet
you tell us about it over and over."

"It is the Indian way to tell each other about the brave
things we've done. I wish you would do something brave so
I could be proud of you."

"I will kill Pole Bean. If he has power, that would be a
very brave thing, wouldn't it?"

"Much braver," Killer Cross said to his son, suddenly whis-
pering, "would be to make your wife cut some of the wood."

Billy Cheyenne walked toward the woodpile, picked up the
ax, and chopped wood for half an hour. Then he stuck the
ax blade into the chopping stump and stalked across the yard,

disappearing down the road toward the river without talking to anyone.

"When he is angry," Lamb Woman told Sara, "he sits on the bank for a while and then feels better. I would cut some wood for him, but Many Stones won't let me."

14

S ARA spent the morning cleaning and airing everything in the tipi, organizing the woodpile so she could get to the cooking fire without stumbling over split wood, and sweeping the yard. Billy Cheyenne returned midafternoon, on a small spotted Indian horse that he rode with only a faded blanket and surcingle. He leaped down and drew his father aside for private conversation. Everyone watched. The message soon produced a smile on his father's face.

Killer Cross laughed and kicked the ground. "Crosses-the-River, this is a good day. Your brother has already found you a new husband. He gave Billy Cheyenne this fine horse and he is on his way here now with five more horses for me."

The two old aunts broke into a cheer. Lamb Woman did not cheer, but her face revealed that she waited hopefully for Sara's reaction. Many Stones came from the house carrying one of the babies in its cradleboard, which she hung on the pole at the tipi flap. She looked skeptical.

"Who did you find to marry her?" Many Stones asked.

"Three Toe," said Billy Cheyenne. "His woman ran away last year. I thought of him while I was splitting wood. Three Toe has to cut his own wood now."

"He's an Arapaho, but that's all right. Running Standing was a Kiowa," Many Stones said to Sara, apparently explaining everything.

"He's only part Arapaho," said Sara's father. "This horse runs fast, Billy Cheyenne. I saw you coming. Do the others run fast, too?"

"Very fast. We can win some races on Saturday in Cloud Chief."

For Sara to protest that she already had a husband would have had no more point than to insist that she didn't want another one. Her brother had made a profitable deal, producing not only a sudden abundance of horses but joy, it appeared, for everyone.

Even now, a dust cloud near the river announced that Three Toe and his horses were approaching.

"Go inside, Crosses-the-River," Lamb Woman told her. "Comb your hair and fix your braids, so Three Toe will like you. He must be richer than we knew."

Stupefied, she rushed into the tipi, lowered the flap, and sat down hard on her trunk. Wherever Joe was, and whatever he was doing, he could not possibly be in this much trouble.

She heard the horses thunder into the yard amid wild shouts of greeting.

"Did Billy Cheyenne tell you why I am here?" a gravelly voice asked in a fevered pitch.

"Yes, we know," said Killer Cross. "These are fine-looking horses you have brought me."

"They are the best I had," said Three Toe proudly. "Where is Crosses-the-River?"

"Inside, combing her hair," Lamb Woman assured him. "She wants to look good when you see her."

Sara opened her trunk and dug out a pretty dress she had made at Bennacker's to wear to parties at graduation time. It was a dropped-shoulder dress that swept the ground, made of lavender-tucked linen, with a dramatic V-shaped design across the bust and a narrow waistline tied tightly with a lace and velvet-ribbon belt. She found her straw hat with roses, which she had carefully packed into a corner of the trunk, and she searched out her sun parasol, the edges of which, when opened, were deeply fluted and fringed with lavender lace.

Twirling the parasol, she pushed through the flap and made her entrance into the yard. Three Toe, a big strong handsome-looking Arapaho, naked to the waist and with long thick braids down his chest, gaped at her and almost fell off his horse.

She strutted back and forth before the tipi. And her magic worked. Three Toe regained his balance, if not his composure, tightly checked his bridle reins, and backed his horse away from the fire. And soon, at a jerk of its master's hands, the horse reared and galloped toward the river.

"Crosses-the-River," said her father, "I am disgraced. Now I will lose face with all the Arapaho."

"I have put up with enough of this nonsense," Sara told him, her heart pounding wildly. "I can't live like a filthy peasant, and you may as well understand it now. I am going to stay here, and we are going to clean this place up and make a farm out of it. A fine, abundant farm. We are going to plant watermelons again, and cotton and vegetables. We are going to raise cattle, and grain to feed them."

Whirling as abruptly as Three Toe's horse had whirled, she went inside the tipi and brought out the squaw dress. She rushed to the fire and flung it into the flames. "Billy," she said to her brother, "round up these horses and take them back to Three Toe. Tell him your sister has disgraced you and you are sorry but there is nothing you can do about it. Then come straight back here and go to work. We'll begin laying out our fields today."

"We can't return the horses," Billy said, with rage, fright, and a sense of intrigue combining in his voice. "It would be an insult to take them back. You are his wife. He didn't return you to us. He just rode away."

"I am Joseph Standing's wife," she said. "Some day he will come here after me. In the meantime we are going to make something out of this place. If you won't return the horses, we'll use them to farm with."

"But these are running horses!" cried Killer Cross. To him, working a running horse was even more offensive than dressing women in ruffled clothes.

Wondering how far she could get with a further show of strength, Sara's gaze fell on Many Stones, who stood now in the back doorway of the house, nursing her other child, staring as though she were a wizard in some kind of trance.

Sara decided to stare her down. Many Stones did not try to speak, but at last her eyes dropped and she turned, limping more noticeably than usual, back into the house.

"Now she is going to poison you," said Lamb Woman, and her tone suggested that it might be just as well.

The last Cheyenne-Arapaho treaty with the United States, after providing for a headright allotment of 160 acres per person, opened the rest of the·reservation to white occupation. Sara quickly added up what her family had. Her own allotment, and those of her parents, aunts, brother, and sister-in-law, combined into a land area of 1,120 acres. Approximately a third of it lay in the rich river bottom and the rest on the plains where absentee white cattlemen grazed their herds. Curiously, it was her mother, not her father, who knew where all the boundaries were.

"Can you still ride a horse?" Sara asked.

"One does not forget how to ride a horse," Lamb Woman said. "Back in the glory days I used to capture mustangs occasionally, when the men were away at war for a long time."

"Will you show me where the allotment boundaries are?"

Lamb Woman's reluctance to deviate from her squaw-woman role was overcome by pride in her daughter's independence. "I will ride with you, Crosses-the-River."

Together they bridled two of the ponies Three Toe had brought to pay for his new wife. They had no saddles, but blankets were all they needed. Lamb Woman had never been in a saddle, anyway.

Killer Cross protested that women-ridden horses were forever ruined for racing.

"You and Billy can keep one each," Sara said, "and the others are going to learn to plow."

Her father stared at her and said, "I wonder if you are my daughter."

"I am your daughter, but I am different now. You must remember that you wanted me to go away to school."

"I did not." He folded his arms imperiously. "Pole Bean wanted you to go."

"Why don't you come with us today and look at the land?"

"I have already seen it. The grass money will stop if we begin using the land ourselves."

"By using it ourselves we can earn much more than fifteen dollars a month."

"We don't need any more than that," he said.

She rode away with her mother. Frustrated, her father remained in the yard. The two aunts stood beside him.

Bluestem, buffalo grass, and sedge grew on the prairie beyond the river in a deep carpet that moved constantly beneath the breeze. Except for the river and occasional creeks that fed it, the terrain was flat; its only rise and fall were the land swells surrounding shallow drainage depressions in the endless sea.

They reined up at the edge of a tiny creek that marked the far boundary of their land. "It's magnificent," Sara said, fired with the challenge she had now set for herself. "Mother, can you possibly understand that we have a grand opportunity here? Someday I'll have it all fenced and—"

"What will we do," asked Lamb Woman, who had been thinking her own hard thoughts, "if our grass money stops and then Many Stones kills you?"

"I told you not to worry about that."

"We know she has power."

"When she has been assured that she won't have to do any more heavy labor, she'll be content."

"I don't understand."

"She is a frail person, and also lame," Sara said. "She protects herself from heavy work in the only way she can—by making Billy think she has power."

Lamb Woman's face showed instant alarm. "You do not believe she has power, Crosses-the-River?"

"No, there is no such thing as power."

Lamb Woman's eyes grew large. "Of course there is power. Did you know that secretly Many Stones is an old woman, not young at all as she appears to be?"

"She isn't even as old as I am."

"She is old! She does not look old because she was killed many years ago when Custer raided our people on the Washita."

"Many Stones was killed?"

"Yes, and she was even killed one time before that, when our people lived on the Powder River and fought the Crows, when my mother was a girl. She remembers my mother. She does not age when she is dead, and she always comes back to life. Now do you believe me?"

Sara sighed. "Billy tells me she is also part wolf."

"That is true," said Lamb Woman. "Once she came back to life as a wolf. She got her foot caught in a steel trap and a white man shot her. When she came back to life the next time, she had a crippled foot. I am afraid of her, Crosses-the-River."

"You know, I think I like Many Stones very much. She has a resourceful imagination. Somehow I am going to get her on my side. With her power over everybody, we could get a lot done around here, working as a team."

"Then you do believe she has power."

"All women have a certain power."

"I have no power."

"I think you have. You have never known how to use it."

"A moment ago you said there was no power. Now you say there is. I do not understand you, my strange daughter, but I do not want you to be poisoned."

One morning at daybreak a few weeks later Sara became ill. Believing she had been poisoned, everyone was furious with Many Stones. They were too frightened, however, to say anything aloud.

"She should not have done that to Crosses-the-River," Lamb Woman whispered to Billy Cheyenne.

"I did not want her to," Billy's whisper answered.

Sara lay on her bed in the tipi most of the morning, slowly grasping the significance of her sickness. It confirmed what by now she already suspected—that she was going to have a baby. It also confirmed something else: that she was a very white Indian. She had learned about morning sickness from the white women at Carlisle, but had not thought of it as an Indian affliction because she had never heard of an Indian woman having it.

She was excited. "And Joe," she imagined herself saying at some vague happy time in the future, after he had come for her, "everyone thought Many Stones had used her power on me!" They would laugh together and then marvel that their one time together aboard *Clarissa* had produced their first child. To have conceived her child in such a setting must surely be an omen. She was determined to have it under proper conditions.

"Billy," she asked her brother, "is there a doctor in Cloud Chief?"

"An Arapaho *docti* lives up near the mouth of Winding Creek."

"I mean a white doctor."

Billy shook his head. "Charlie at the store could tell you."

"Hitch up the wagon for me, please. I must go to town today."

"You may die on the way if Many Stones has poisoned you."

"I doubt if I will."

As she prepared to leave, Many Stones, carrying a child under each arm, came into the yard and stared at her. "Where are you going?"

"To Cloud Chief. Would you like to come with me? I wish you would."

Many Stones hesitated, obviously tempted. "Why are you going?"

"To find a doctor."

Many Stones considered what to say next, for she wished to leave open any possible belief that Sara had been the victim of her power. "You are sick," she said.

"I think I am going to have a baby."

Many Stones hefted her own two babies into a higher position under her arms. "Why do you want to see a doctor?"

"Because I want to have my child under proper medical conditions." Clearly, Many Stones did not understand. Sara added, "I am also going to stop at Charlie's store and buy material to make some baby clothes."

"Then you want to have a white-child baby. Why do you?"

"My child will be happier if it is raised in the white way. Lamb Woman will take care of your babies for a while. Come with me."

For a moment she thought Many Stones was deciding to go. She tried again: "Perhaps we could look at some dresses ourselves while we are there. You would be simply beautiful in white-woman dresses. Charlie may have some that we could look at."

Many Stones' mouth curled fiercely downward. "We have no money."

"I have some money that I saved while I was at Carlisle. I would like to buy you a dress for a present."

Many Stones teetered on the edge of what must have seemed to her a perilous decision. Then she regained her balance and whirled in anger back into the house.

Sara drove to Cloud Chief alone.

The town had changed incredibly. An occasional Indian could be seen on the streets, but there were no watermelon stands at the edge of town, no chicken fights near the watering trough, no displays of bright beads in the stores to attract the attention of Indians. Cloud Chief was thoroughly white. A stranger set down here would not possibly guess that he was deep in the Oklahoma Territory that ten years earlier had been inhabited only by whatever Indians had survived the U.S. Cavalry.

She found a sign hanging over an entrance on the wooden sidewalk:

DOCTOR'S OFFICE

Wills Freeland, Physician

Teeth Pulled

A fat man with a gold chain across his belly leaned against the doorjamb. "If you're aiming to see Doc, he ain't here."

"Do you know when he will be?"

The man drew out his watch and peered at it. "About half an hour, if he comes when he said he would. He ain't the promptest man in the world, but everybody says he's a pretty good doc for somebody that fools around being artistic in his spare time. Comes from back East."

"I guess I'll go to Charlie's and return later."

"He won't be long with me," said the fat man. "Just a tooth-pulling. They say Doc Freeland gets them out of there fast, for a man with delicate hands."

She went up the street to the general store where her family had always traded. It had changed little.

"My goodness, Crosses-the-River," Charlie said when she identified herself. "Of course I remember you. So grown-up!"

She had never liked Charlie because she knew he cheated her people whenever he could; but she did not thoroughly despise him because his conscience would not let him cheat them very much at any one time. She bought a few yards of white muslin, some embroidery thread, and some ribbon and lace, and then looked over the store dresses he had in stock.

"These are too small for you, Crosses-the-River. Over here is your size."

"I want a small one, for someone else."

She selected a bright gingham dress with tucks at the waist and ruffles at the throat and sleeves. Exacting Charlie's promise that she could exchange it for another if it did not fit properly, she bought the dress.

Back at the doctor's office, the fat man was still waiting. "Here he comes now, miss."

A shiny black one-horse buggy approached with its calash

up against the sun. The driver was a tall, hatless young man
with flaming red hair and side-whiskers. Even though the day
was warm, he wore a properly fitting dark single-button sack
coat and gray plaid trousers. You would expect to see someone dressed like that in Harrisburg, she thought, but not out
here.

"Eastern clothes," the fat man remarked. "He's supposed
to be a very educated young doc. They say he likes Indians—"
The man looked at her more closely. "Are you Indian, young
lady?"

"I am."

"With those clothes on you could be took for white."

The doctor pulled up to the hitchrail and climbed down
with his pill bag. "Good afternoon, folks," he said, escorting
them inside.

"I'm first, Doc," the fat man said. "It won't take but a
minute. I just need this tooth pulled." He opened his mouth
and pointed inside.

"We'll have a look in the examination room." The doctor
turned to Sara. "Maybe you'd like to read something while
you wait." He indicated a small bookcase beside a chair.

"Thank you," she said. He looked her over with such
deliberation that he seemed to embarrass himself.

"There aren't many Indians who dress as you do," he
explained, and she was pleased that he had not taken her for
white because of her clothes. "Have you been away to school?"

"Carlisle."

"I know the Cumberland Valley country of Pennsylvania.
Please be comfortable while I take care of this patient. A
tooth?" he asked the fat man and led him through the door
into the other room.

Sara found herself less interested in the bookcase at her
side than in the walls of the office where a dozen Indian
portraits hung. They were marvelous paintings, one of them of
a Cheyenne subchief she remembered. She was getting up to
look at it more closely when a scream from inside pierced the
air. She could hear the doctor's voice say, "There . . . that was
quick, wasn't it?" And the fat man's voice answered, "Everyone said you was quick, Doc. . . ."

The Indian portraits gave her the greatest sense of ease
she had felt since returning from school. For a moment, at
least, she seemed not in a hostile environment. Since there

was no other patient after the fat man left, the doctor sat down in a chair opposite her in his tiny reception room and talked in a friendly, almost sociable way.

"I will be glad to attend the birth of your child," he assured her, "but you must alert me in time to get there."

"Have you attended the birth of any Kiowa or Cheyenne babies yet?"

"No, I haven't."

"My child," she said with an incredible surge of feeling, "may be the first of his race to be brought into the world by a doctor."

"By a civilian doctor, possibly," he said, and she knew that he had grasped the symbolic magnitude she felt. "Army doctors have probably delivered Indian babies. Meanwhile, drink lots of milk, or the child will deplete you of calcium. I'll give you some medicine to take for the nausea." He went inside and returned with a bottle of green fluid and a pad and pencil. "May I have your name for my records, please?"

"Crosses-the-River—" She stopped and laughed. "I have heard nothing but my Indian name lately. On the Cheyenne rolls I am Sara Cross. My husband is Joseph Standing, a Kiowa."

He listened to her thoughtfully, then lifted his pencil. "Mrs. Sara Standing," he said as he wrote.

"Those are fascinating paintings you have collected, Doctor," she told him to cover her self-consciousness.

"Do they seem accurate representations of the subjects?"

"The Cheyenne subchief is a perfect likeness. He is the only one I know. The Arapaho woman over there is dressed authentically, but I don't recognize any of the other tribal costumes."

"That's because they are Eastern. The old man in the corner is a Penobscot from New England. These two are Mohawks and the small one is a Tuscarora woman."

"The only Eastern Indians I have known were those at Carlisle. There weren't many."

"Tell me about your family," he said, and to her astonishment she heard herself launch eagerly into the story of her return home to an undeclared war between herself and Many Stones.

"I bought a dress for her today. I only hope she can be persuaded to wear it."

"She may be an Indian version of the suffragette, you know.

More than anything, she is rebelling against the oppression of
being a woman."

"Heaven knows I don't want to kill that impulse in her,"
Sara said, rising. "I have stayed too long."

"The pleasure has been mine, Crosses-the-River." She felt
crestfallen that he had used her Indian name, but it was
refreshing to have talked to an educated person again.

"How much do I owe you for this visit, Doctor?"

He did not hesitate to answer. "That will be one dollar. But
you can wait until—"

"I have enough money," she told him and dug a dollar from
her handbag, which he accepted, making a notation on the pad
beside her name.

15

SHE drove to the edge of town, where a new-looking farmhouse stood on the spot on which her family had once
operated their brush arbor watermelon stand. The great
cottonwood tree from which Joe had watched his brother and
hers in a knife fight was the principal ornament inside a well-
fenced front yard. In the lot, beside an imposing barn, were
several milk cows.

She stopped her team at the gate. A young girl of ten or
eleven peered from a curtained window beside the open front
door.

"Hello," Sara called to the child.

The girl came to the doorway and stood silently with one
foot on top of the other.

Sara tried again. "Is your mother home?"

The girl walked from the porch toward the gate, where she
paused to look at her visitor more closely. She still remained
silent.

"I would like to see your mother for a moment if she is
here," Sara said.

The girl's small mouth opened slowly. "Are you a Indian?"

"Yes. My name is . . . Crosses-the-River. What's yours?"

"Maude."

"Is your mother here, Maude? Or your father?"

"They're both dead."

Sara gasped, "Dead?"

"Indians killed them." The child then burst into a shriek of laughter. "No, they ain't dead! I just said that." She ran to the side of the house and shouted: "Ma! They's a Indian woman out here dressed like she ain't Indian."

"Who's out there?"

Sara watched a tall skinny woman appear in sunbonnet and apron with a garden hoe in her hand. "Who is it?"

"Hello. My name is Sara Standing, ma'am. I live just down the—"

"That ain't her name, Ma," cried the girl. "It's Over-the-River."

"My Indian name is Crosses-the-River."

The girl's mother was now close enough to stare as her daughter had. "What do you want?"

"I noticed your nice place when I passed by on the way to town. My family used to camp here, when I was a young girl. I wondered whether—"

"We're homesteading this place fair and square," the woman said. "It ain't yours. The government gives you people land of your own."

"Yes," said Sara quickly, "we live below here about a mile. I need a milk cow, and I was wondering whether—"

"You can't get no cow from us. You Cheyennes always come around trying to get a pig or some *wo-haw* or something. Now, I ain't got any cows to spare."

The woman was frightened, and Sara, in exasperation, said, "I'm not begging, lady."

"You ain't?" The woman's eyes narrowed, but the touch of hysteria had left her voice. "You speak real good for an Indian."

"I have been away to school at Carlisle."

"Where's that?"

"In Pennsylvania."

"Pennsylvania State?"

"Yes. I just returned home a few weeks ago."

"I ain't been to school much myself," the woman said.

"You ain't been any," the girl taunted.

"Shut up, Maude."

"I been more than you have," the child said and ducked when her mother's backhand flew toward her.

"You want to buy a cow, did you say?"

"If I have enough money, I would like to. How much would you want for a fresh milk cow? It wouldn't have to be a terribly good one."

"How much you got?"

"Very little, to tell the truth."

"If I don't know how much you got, how could I tell if it's enough?"

"I suppose you couldn't," Sara said, controlling her anger. "Well, good day." She picked up her reins and slapped the team.

"I bet she ain't got a cent," the girl cried as Sara's wagon moved ahead.

"Wait a minute, there," the woman called. Sara's impulse was to continue without looking back, but the larger purpose of providing herself with milk commanded her action. She swallowed her anger and drew up.

"Git down a while," the woman said. "I'm Jennybelle Wilson. We might as well be neighborly. I ain't afraid of eddicated Indians."

"Don't let her git down from there, Ma!" cried Maude. "Her folks killed Grandpa, remember?"

"Shut up, Maude. I reckon Grandpa killed some of her folks, too."

The girl backed halfway across the yard as Sara looped her reins over the brake handle and climbed from the wagon.

"Your rig looks funny with them two chairs instead of a front seat," Jennybelle Wilson said.

"Yes, I agree that it does."

"What happened to the seat, anyway?"

"My father sold it. To buy the chairs, I imagine."

Jennybelle looked puzzled for a moment and then burst into laughter with Sara. "I ain't ever been visited by an Indian woman yet. Come set on the porch."

"You ain't been visited by anybody," Maude cried from her safe position in the yard.

"You better shut up, Maude. I am telling you."

"Then you better watch out," Maude insisted. "Crosses-the-River is going to look the place over good and tonight her folks will come and scalp us all."

"That done it, Maude," Jennybelle said. " 'Scuse me just

a minute, please. I got to whup that young un again. Ever since she caught on she's got more schooling than I have got, she acts smart-aleck."

"Ma—don't you dare whup me in front of company—" the girl began and then turned to run.

Before pursuing, the mother laid down her hoe and removed her apron and bonnet. The apron, Sara assumed, would hamper her pace. Maude had a good start, but it was soon apparent that Jennybelle knew how to catch her. Fists doubled up close to her chest, in the manner of the distance runners at Carlisle, the woman set out in a casual jog to run her daughter down. They circled the garden, the lot and barn, and the cottonwood tree, and made two turns around Sara's wagon before the gap closed significantly. It was plain that Maude knew that in the end she had to lose.

"You got more wind than I got!" she called over her shoulder. "It ain't fair!"

Jennybelle sprinted suddenly, caught the girl's flying hair in her fist, and pulled her to a stop.

"You got more schooling but I got more wind," she said. In a deft motion suggesting that she had done it often, she whirled Maude around, bent her over a knee, pulled her dress up and her bloomers down, and spanked her bare bottom with a bare right hand.

The girl took it without screaming but sniffed as she walked out of sight at last.

"She's always saying Indians going to get us, just to plague me. Sending them to school seems to ruin them sometimes and it hadn't ought to," Jennybelle Wilson said, returning to the porch. "She's got plenty of wind to get away from me, but she don't know how to use it yet, thank God. Are you folks Jesus Indians, Crosses-the-River?"

"Yes," Sara said, amazed. "Backslid a bit, maybe."

"Everybody in this part of the country is a bit backslid, and it's no wonder, considering the caliber of preaching nowadays. Tell me . . . why do you need a cow? For milk, or to eat?"

"For milk. I'm going to have a baby."

"Been to the new doctor in town?"

"Yes, I have, as a matter of fact."

The woman shook her head. "Not many Indians go to doctors but they ought to. Doctors are a good thing if you don't pay too much attention to them. They don't puke folks for fevers no more, and that's pure foolishness. Some of them have got a little too much schooling. We have a fresh heifer you can borrow if you'll take the calf, too."

"Borrow?"

"We aim to butcher the calf when it's old enough, so we'll want it back. But you take care of it and you can have a side. You got any feed for the cow? Any grain at all?"

"No," Sara admitted. "Just grass."

"We better talk to Harley, then. That's Mr. Wilson. Maude ain't his daughter. My first husband, Harold, he was Harley's cousin, so Maude's name is Wilson and all. Harley likes her real good. I never could seem to have any children of Harley's own. He's chopping cotton this afternoon. I and Maude ought to be helping him, but Harley don't like to see women in the fields. He ain't near as backslid as some of the men around here."

"Do you want some cake, Crosses-the-River?" Maude asked from the doorway inside the house. "I made some flour cake yesterday."

"A whupping does her a lot of good, sometimes," Jennybelle said. "Why don't you have a piece of cake? Bring it out here, Maude, and a pitcher of sweet milk to go with it. We'll set on the porch and have it, if Crosses-the-River don't mind a few flies. Then run tell your pa they's somebody here to see him." She turned back to Sara. "You'll like Maude's cake."

"Thank you very much," Sara said, overwhelmed.

"Lots of flies bother me," Jennybelle said, "but I don't mind a few."

Maude brought the cake but her mother would not let her sit down on the porch to eat with them.

"You're always afraid I'll listen to grown-up talk," Maude complained. "I don't listen."

"You listen. Now, run down to the fields after your pa."

"Aw—"

"Scat!" cried Jennybelle, stomping her foot. The girl leaped from the porch and ran out of sight past the barn.

"I was scared to death of Indians before we come out here," Jennybelle said. "All the stuff you hear about them."

"Where did you come from?"

"Southern Illinois. We've always been farmers. There ain't

no Indians at all up there anymore. I never seen one in my life until we come here. That's a pretty dress, Crosses-the-River. Must of cost you a penny."

"I made it, while I was in school."

"Lands, you did? I sew, but not that good. Where's your husband at?" Before Sara could find words for the sudden question, Jennybelle Wilson added, "I ain't trying to be shrewd or nothing, but it seems like he'd be out looking for a milk cow."

"My husband is in New York City. He'll be here later."

"New York City . . . sounds important. He must be eddi-cated, too."

"Yes. He is a Kiowa."

"Eddication is all right if you don't get like Maude and think you got a right to plague people."

Maude returned from the cotton field, running in long easy strides with which Sara believed she could easily outdistance her mother if she didn't panic and sprint.

"Pa says can it wait till dark? He's got a lot of cotton to chop after the rain the other day."

"Did you tell him I sent for him?" asked Jennybelle.

"No'm, I said they was a stranger to see him."

"Maude, I am going to—"

"That's all right," Sara insisted. "I'll be glad to come back later. I'm sure Mr. Wilson has a lot of work to do. We only live about a mile from here."

"I'll get the heifer and the calf for you, then—and you come back tonight. Now, don't forget. Mr. Wilson will talk to you about some feed grain."

"The cake was delicious, Maude," Sara said.

"Ma didn't teach me how, Crosses-the-River. She can't cook worth a hoot. I just have a natural gift for it, I guess." All the while, Maude kept a safe distance from her mother's backhand.

With the cow tied to the tailgate of her wagon and the calf following, Sara drove home.

The place seemed utterly deserted when she got there, but a closer look revealed the two babies hanging from the tipi entrance poles. She knew that Many Stones was a devoted mother and would not be far away.

By now Sara grudgingly accepted the fact that her father and Billy Cheyenne spent most of their time in the shade of one side of the house or the other. A pecan tree protected the east side in the morning and three tall cottonwoods spread over the entire west yard and the tipi. The two men, sitting there on a pecan log, talking and whittling, or just watching in distress as she directed the women in her campaign to clean and organize the place, had become a familiar sight. The yard seemed naked without them.

There was no movement at all, not even in the house. The back door was open and she could see through to the front. She listened and heard nothing. From the cradleboards, the babies stared at her with huge solemn eyes. The flap between them was down, which was odd. She had a feeling that it had just been closed as she approached, and pushed through it quickly.

There knelt Many Stones, deeply embarrassed, caught in the act of trying on one of Sara's dresses, which she had taken from the trunk. Spread out on the trunk lid were Sara's vanity mirror, hairbrush, and an assortment of ribbons and beads.

Half-rising, Many Stones remained essentially in a crouch, as though ready to fight, eyes flashing. The dress, much too large for her, swept the ground comically. Except for the cornered-animal look, Many Stones might have been a child playing grown-up.

"I bought you a dress of your own, Many Stones," Sara said, handing her the package.

Many Stones hesitated before accepting it. "I told you I did not want a white-woman dress."

"It has marvelous ruffles on the neck and sleeves. You will be very pretty in it. If it doesn't fit exactly right, we can exchange it for another."

Sara watched her sister-in-law struggle with the conflict between her instinct to resist and her desire to accept. There was resolution in Many Stones, and resourcefulness. And also vanity.

"I am not part wolf," she said.

"I know you are not."

"How did you know?"

"Nobody is part wolf."

"Are you going to tell them that I am not part wolf?"

"I have already told them but nobody believes me."

Considering that information for a moment, Many Stones straightened out of the crouch, more relaxed.

"You have pretty things, Crosses-the-River. I have been hoping you would show them to me, but you did not. You don't like me."

"I like you very much, Many Stones."

"Why didn't you show me any of these things?"

"I didn't believe you were interested in them."

"Are you going to tell Billy Cheyenne that I tried on your dress?"

"Of course not. Here, let's try yours and see how it fits." Sara reached for her arm and Many Stones backed away, striking her hand.

"Go outside and I will change," she said.

"Why?"

Many Stones' nostrils flared and she said, "I have on your bosom harness. I don't want you to see me."

Sara did as she was told. The wide-eyed babies watched her pass between them and stand with her back to the flap until Many Stones appeared.

"Now," she said. "This is how I look."

Sara turned and saw her, and she was beautiful. The dress fitted perfectly. "I want to be like you, Crosses-the-River."

"You can be. And we can make more dresses. I know how to sew white-woman things. I can teach you exactly as I learned in the school."

"I would like to have many white-woman dresses!"

"You will have."

"I will help you start the farm, Crosses-the-River. Billy Cheyenne will do everything I tell him to."

"I know he will. If you will help me, we can have a wonderful life here. We can have everything we want, if we work for it the right way."

"I am not an old woman, either," said Many Stones. "I was not killed when Yellow Hair massacred our people at the big river bend. I was not even born then. I am young!"

"I know that, Many Stones."

"How did you know?"

"People do not come back to life."

"Don't tell Billy Cheyenne. I won't be able to get him to do anything if he knows I have no power."

"You have power."

"I am not an old woman, though."

"Where is everybody this afternoon?" Sara asked.

A glint of amusement struck Many Stones' eyes. "Three Toe came again and they decided to have a horse race."

"Why did he come? I hope he didn't change his mind about me."

"He didn't." Now Many Stones burst into a giggle. "You frighten him. He said he found a better horse at home than one of those he brought to your father. He said it would be cheating to keep it when he had told your father he brought his best ones."

"Did my father accept it?"

"He could not insult Three Toe. They are racing now from the Winding Creek bridge to Rainy Mountain and back, to find out which horse is best."

"Where are Lamb Woman and my two aunts?"

"They are watching the race from the prairie above the river bend."

"When my father and Billy Cheyenne get back, I have some work for them to do. Will you make them do it for me?"

"I will," said Many Stones. "What is it?"

Sara told her about the visit with Jennybelle Wilson and showed her the cow and calf. "Mr. Wilson is busy chopping weeds from his cotton fields. He has more work than he can do. I want Billy Cheyenne and my father to go help him."

"This will not be easy," said Many Stones, "but they will not wish to be poisoned." She smiled. "If we learn from Mr. Wilson, we can have our own cotton fields, can't we?"

"That's the idea," Sara said, thanking whatever gods there were for Many Stones and her incredible power. "We can have a vegetable garden, even this summer. And somehow I am going to get some cattle started on our pasture land. And a barn for milk cows. And some laying chickens. Many Stones, do you realize that all we have here are old fighting chickens?"

16

MANY Stones put Billy Cheyenne and his father to work on the Wilson farm that afternoon, and within two weeks they not only had Harley Wilson's cotton fields weeded but, with his help, a garden of their own laid out and spaded, a brush arbor shelter for the cow and calf, and a lot fenced in with new rails they split from logs they cut along the river.

Harley Wilson was a strong, knowledgeable, quiet-spoken man with huge tough hands and a gentle wind-browned face. One thrust of his big foot could send a spade haft-deep into the ground. Billy Cheyenne and Killer Cross tried digging with moccasins on their feet, but the spade cut through the soft bottoms and lacerated them.

"They need work shoes," said Harley Wilson one morning. "Doesn't the government issue shoes to you people?"

"The government did," Sara said, "but they were all for the same foot. My father sold them, don't ask me how."

Mr. Wilson returned from Cloud Chief the next day with new brogans from Charlie's store.

"This is to pay for helping me chop cotton."

"We don't like white-man shoes," Billy Cheyenne protested, "but," he added, seeing Many Stones' eye hard upon him, "we will wear them."

Sara had enough money left from Carlisle to buy garden seeds and six pullets. To her father's dismay, she cooped up the fighting chickens and killed them one at a time for the table. Jennybelle Wilson showed her how to make a roost in one end of the arbor and, with Maude, helped her plant the garden.

"Pa is going to lend you a plow," said Maude, who was caught up in the excitement. "He says Indian ponies can learn to plow as quick as Indians can and maybe quicker."

"Maude, shut that big mouth of yours, or I'll shut it for you," Jennybelle said.

Harley Wilson made a deal with them for feed grain. In return for their helping pick his cotton in the fall, he would provide them with grain now and with cotton seed for planting next spring. With diligent use of his plow, they could have their cotton land broken by then.

Exhausted but exhilarated, Sara sat on the chopping block late one afternoon listening to the clatter of approaching wheels. Looking up, she recognized the black buggy belonging to Dr. Wills Freeland. Hatless, he sat before the dash, straight-backed in his sack coat, his red hair and side-whiskers glistening in the low sun.

"Hello, Crosses-the-River. I was passing by. Do you mind if I stop for a while?"

"I don't," she said. "Would you like some coffee?"

"I would," he said. She liked his direct manner.

She filled the coffeepot, hung it over the fire, and threw on chips. While the fire blazed she went into the tipi and brought a cup, sugar, and cream from a cupboard she had made by stacking together three wooden packing boxes Jennybelle Wilson had brought her from town.

"We use creek water," she said. "I hope you don't mind."

"If it doesn't hurt you, it won't hurt me."

"I get it at a place where an underground spring pours into the creek."

"How far is it?"

"Not far." She motioned toward the river. "Winding Creek flows into the Washita just below here. The spring is half a mile above the mouth of the creek."

"Do you carry the water yourself?"

"Yes. I go every morning. It is a nice walk, and everyone else is doing the heavier work."

"How do you feel?"

"Fine."

When the water boiled, she pulled a bed of coals aside, put the pot on it, and poured in coffee to simmer.

Wills Freeland sat on a log, watching, and once when she glanced at him, she was startled to recognize a certain speculation in his expression.

"Crosses-the-River," he said, "I am rather a direct person."

"I have noticed, Doctor."

"My friends don't call me Doctor. They call me Wills." She said nothing, and he added, very directly, "You are beautiful, Crosses-the-River."

She lifted the coffeepot and poured into his cup. "The cream is fresh this morning. It will keep for a day, even in hot weather."

He smiled hugely. "Now let's talk about the weather. We could use some rain, couldn't we?"

"Yes," she said, trembling, "we could."

He watched her silently for a moment, then said, "Where is your family?"

"My mother and aunts are inside the tipi staring at us from the flap. My brother and sister-in-law are inside the house, staring at us from behind the door. My father is standing behind you."

Which was true. Killer Cross, wearing moccasins to rest his tired feet, had walked up quietly. Towering over Wills Freeland, he looked down, Sara thought, with an expression so enormously blank it was comical.

Wills turned, rose quickly, and offered his hand. "I am Dr. Freeland from Cloud Chief, Mr. Cross."

Sara's father gave his hand a solid up-and-down pump. "Rain makes the weeds grow," he said in his best white lingo. "We don't need no more rain just now, Doc."

"It makes the cotton grow, too. And the garden."

"Sunshine makes all that stuff grow," Killer Cross said. His voice was rimmed with mystification, but his face showed nothing. "Crosses-the-River already got two husbands, Doc," he remarked simply and disappeared into the tipi.

"Two?" Wills Freeland said to her.

Killer Cross stuck his head back around the flap and held up two fingers. "Two. One kicked her out. Other one ran off when she acted white." The flap then closed summarily.

Wills said, lowering his voice, "I would like to visit you again, Crosses-the-River."

"If I need a doctor, I will send for you," she told him, feeling a certain sadness; for she would never send for him now. Unless another doctor could be located in the community, her child would not be born under the conditions she had dreamed of.

Aware of her discomfort, he drained his coffee cup, stared into it for a moment, poured out the grounds, and got up to go.

"At Carlisle," he asked, "did you happen to study any literature at all? Any poetry?"

"A few poems," she said.

"There is a poem, I can't remember it exactly, about the eternal mystery of the way of a ship at sea, a serpent upon a rock, and a man with a maid."

"I do not understand," she said, although she vaguely did.

"I am going home now to look up that poem, Crosses-the-River. There may be a lesson in it for me." Then, with a gesture of hopelessness, he said, "I am sorry if I have embarrassed you in front of your people."

"My people do not embarrass easily."

"They don't, but I think you may." He climbed into his buggy. "It's astonishing, the way a person can create an impression the exact opposite of his intention."

She did not answer and he drove away.

Her family poured into the yard from both directions, so excited they forgot to revert to their own language. "White man no good for third husband, Crosses-the-River!" cried Lamb Woman.

"White docti bad, bad," said Billy Cheyenne.

"He not even a Jesus docti!" her father said.

Both the aunts, in unison, said, "Na, na, na!" and shook their fingers at her in scorn.

Only Many Stones did not chastise her. She said nothing until she could speak privately.

"He will come again, Crosses-the-River."

"Maybe he won't."

"You do not have two husbands. You have none. He has a very man-look when he sees you. Let him come.' Many Stones' eyes flashed mischievously and she added, "If Billy Cheyenne and his father do not like it, I will poison them for you."

Sara burst into laughter.

"Many Stones, I love you. But I do not wish to see the white docti anymore."

She saw him shortly after daybreak the next morning. Carrying two water pails up the path along Winding Creek, she came out into a grassy clearing beside a flat ledgestone where the spring bubbled up, and there he was. He stood before an artist's easel with palette and brush, so intent on the canvas before him that he did not hear her approach. He was wearing Levis and a blue work shirt with rolled-up sleeves. Smears of paint from his brushes were on the sides of his Levis.

She stood debating whether to ease away and disappear back down the path. But he sensed her presence and turned.

"I found it," he told her. She thought he meant the spring in the creek until he said, " 'There be three things which are too wonderful for me; yea four which I know not: the way of an eagle in the air; the way of a serpent upon a rock; the way of a ship in the midst of the sea; and the way of a man with a maid.' The Proverbs of Solomon."

Again she said, "I do not understand." But again she vaguely did.

"Solomon also spoke of disaster, Crosses-the-River. He said, 'Under three things the earth trembles: a slave when he becomes a king; a fool when he is filled with food; and an unloved woman when she gets a husband.' "

"I must fill my water pails now."

"You can see that I am caught between two incredible forces," he went on. "Imagine my plight. Because your husband has abandoned you, the earth must tremble beneath me —a man floundering before a woman who interests him greatly."

"A serpent upon a rock, perhaps," she said. She could not despise him. He was much too formidable a person to pity, as she had pitied Three Toe: at once too gentle to hate and too compelling to ignore.

"I have a husband," she said.

"I know that, of course."

Embarrassed, she asked, "Did you paint the pictures that hang in your office?"

"Yes."

"That had not occurred to me." She tried to remember what she had said to him about them. "I do not understand you," she said, and this time she meant it.

"Would you like to hear a brief story of my life? It would make me utterly transparent. If you will sit on the rock, facing the light, for a little while and let me work on the details of the face, I will tell you more about myself than you could possibly wish to hear. When you've heard enough, all you have to do is raise your hand."

She glanced more closely at the easel. The painting in progress was a portrait of her, sitting on the ledge above the spring. It was only sketched in, but already recognizable; and it depicted her in Cheyenne clothing: a fringed doeskin dress with intricate embroidery of porcupine quills; beaver-skin hairbraid ties; a necklace that might have been chinaberry seeds.

"You did this from memory," she said. "It's amazing."

"I could finish it from memory if I had to. But it will turn out much better if you pose for me."

"For how long?"

"That's quite impossible to say. No longer than you would like, certainly."

She studied the canvas for several moments, then put down her pails and sat on the stone as nearly as possible in the position he had placed her in the picture.

"Is that all right?"

"Perfect."

"You put Cheyenne clothing on me."

"I prefer it that way."

"It is not an honest portrait. You have never seen me in a doeskin dress and moccasins, or with my hair in braids."

"Do you think it is dishonest of me to imagine you that way?"

"Is an untrue picture not dishonest? I am certainly not that person."

"Are you sure, Crosses-the-River?"

"I am not even Crosses-the-River."

"You told me that was your name."

"I told you my name was Sara Cross." She laughed. "I am sorry—does that ruin your picture, if I laugh?"

"Not if the laugh is honest," he said, and she wondered whether he was mocking her. "You were born Crosses-the-River, weren't you?"

"Why do you insist that I must stay the way I was born?"

"I don't mean it that way. I happen to think Crosses-the-River is a beautiful name. Anybody could be named Sara Cross, but only you could be Crosses-the-River."

The irony of his attitude struck her. He was probably more interested in Indians than any white person she had ever known except the teachers at Carlisle, yet he did not want them to do the one thing they must do in order to survive in this world—which was to change.

"We're talking about me," she said, "but our agreement was that we'd talk about you."

Painting in swift little movements of his brush from palette to canvas, he asked, "For a starting place, is there anything specific you'd like to know?"

"There are two things about you," she said in parody of
his quote from Proverbs, "that I know not: the way of a
docti when he paints; and the way of a white man who only
paints Indians."

"Every person has a hero. When I was very young, my
hero was an artist named George Catlin. Do you know who
he was?"

"I know he painted pictures of many Indians back in the
glory days."

"He lived among the tribes of the West for several years,
painting the great chiefs and warriors and their women and
medicine men. His work remains as a remarkable account of
more than forty tribes, made before the white man took over
the West. His was the most romantic life I had ever heard of,
and I used to dream of doing the same thing."

"They taught us at school," she said, "that George Catlin
was a documentary artist. He painted my people exactly as
he found them, not as he wished them to be."

"Whether you know it or not, Sara," said Wills Freeland
slowly, "you have just hit me a very hard blow."

"I hope so," she said with more than passing satisfaction,
no small part of which derived from the fact that at last he
had called her Sara. She noticed that her heart pounded in
comically thundering accompaniment to the sense of victory
she felt over a young white man who intrigued her more than
she desired to be intrigued by a man . . . especially a white
man . . . especially a docti.

Several meetings by the spring were required for Wills
Freeland to complete his portrait of her. It was obvious by
the end of the second sitting that he intended to work slowly.

He was from Pennsylvania, the only son of a physician who
had raised him to follow his father's profession. But his talent
for drawing and painting had surfaced early. He defied his
father's wish that he be educated in medicine and was cut off
from the family coffers. To establish a studio, he found em-
ployment in a factory. That had seemed romantic in the beginning. He fell in love with and married the factory owner's
daughter. A sense of true love, he told her, was less romance
than liberation—and a special sound came into his voice,
filling in more than his words possibly could the depth of his
feelings. The girl was a frail but rebellious creature. Calling
her a creature was to Sara vastly exciting; a savage was one

thing—a *creature* quite another. The girl was disowned by her people when she married the struggling artist, and soon afterward Wills was fired from his job.

"Her name was Adrienne. She died of pneumonia during the second month of our life together, even before I found another job. Because we had so little money, she did not receive medical attention until it was too late. I returned to my father, who then put me through the Eclectic Medical College in Cincinnati."

While still a student, he had been connected with a field research team that ministered to a small group of Shawnee Indians who had remained in Ohio when most of their people accepted reservation life in the Indian Territory. Because he thought their faces were marvelous, he had not been able to resist painting them. The present pattern of his life—of treating people physically as a profession and painting them for joy—evolved naturally, although he had not left for the West until after his father died.

"Where do you live, Wills?"

"On the other side of Cloud Chief. I'm a homesteader, like your friends the Wilsons."

"You—a farmer?"

"Not a very good one, perhaps, but my intentions are good. A single man doesn't have as much incentive."

She let that point go and said, "Do you have a house?"

"Yes, but again, not a very good one."

"Did you build it?"

"With the help of two Arapahos."

"Is it a large house?" She could not imagine a man as formidable as Wills Freeland living in anything small.

"It has three rooms. Sometime I would like for you to visit it."

"Do you have more pictures there?"

"Many more. Most of them are dishonest, according to your standards."

"I had thought," she said, "that you might change my clothing in this picture after our discussion the other day."

"Never. This is a portrait of Crosses-the-River. I'll do Sara Cross later, if you'll let me."

"I do not understand," she said, "why you wish to paint the picture of a Cheyenne woman who wears white clothing and lives in a tipi behind her father's house, and who is soon going to become the mother of another man's child."

"That is not precisely the woman I wish to paint. I am interested in a very beautiful woman who is leading her family through a thousand years of evolution almost overnight. You are doing something incredible, and you haven't even asked the Indian agent for help."

"I do not want help. The white man could not defeat my people even with superior weapons until he put us on reservation handouts by killing off our food supply. The agent came to see me the other day. He wanted to give us seeds, but I prefer to get them myself. As long as we depend on him, we are in prison."

"I would like to paint the girl who knows that."

"Why didn't you, instead of painting someone who does not exist and never did?"

"It is important to maintain some sense of the past, don't you think? Some of the traditions of one's culture?"

"Then why don't you paint yourself in powdered hair, silk stockings, knee breeches, and big-buckled shoes? That is the way your ancestors looked."

She rose from the ledge and took her pails to the spring. Without even glancing at her portrait on his easel, she started toward the path and came face to face with her father, who stood quietly, wearing the blank expression he usually wore in the presence of whites.

"How long have you been watching?" she asked in Cheyenne.

"Every morning lately I come. You are very white-woman now, Crosses-the-River. You have learned to tell lies to me all the time." He said it not in anger but as a matter of curious fact. He walked to the easel and peered at her portrait. "You make picture of me, too, Doc?" he asked in white lingo.

"I would like to," Wills Freeland said.

"Then I will come after the water for a while and sit on the stone every morning in place of Crosses-the-River."

"I think," said Wills, "that we should paint your picture standing up. Very tall and straight—an hereditary chief."

"Stand-up picture?" Distaste flooded his face, for he much preferred sitting down. "What kind of chief, Doc?"

"He means," said Sara in Cheyenne, "that chiefs do not sit down in pictures. Women sit down."

Her father maintained his white lingo. "Woman ought to stand up beside sit-down man. I seen white pictures that way already. Woman has hand on back of man's chair."

"Then let me paint a portrait of you and Lamb Woman," Wills Freeland said, seizing the idea. "I will come to your tipi and make it."

"Good, good," said Killer Cross. "You come every morning, and while you make picture, Crosses-the-River can bring water pail here."

During the closing weeks of summer, Wills Freeland painted everyone in her family—not as they were, she noted, but depicted in proper, almost elegant white attire. There was now, however, an aggressive purpose in his method. She discovered it when he eliminated the hair braids from her father's and Billy's portraits. Both men were so intrigued at the sight of themselves thus rendered that they cut each other's hair.

"Only the most backward Indian wears hair braids now, Doc," her father said, using his white lingo proudly. "You feel like you got any clothes on, Billy Cheyenne?"

Her brother shook his head. "Haircut makes you feel like you ain't got any head."

They hung their pictures in the house. Killer Cross liked them so much that he moved Lamb Woman and himself back inside with his son's family, leaving Sara to live with the two old aunts in the tipi.

She brooded about Joe in New York City. As she grew bigger with his child, she frequently found herself at the verge of tears. She brooded over the fact that each time thoughts of Joe led her into the abyss of despair, in fantasy she found Wills Freeland there and talked with him as she had not dared to talk with him at the Winding Creek spring.

But he left you. He abandoned you. *He'll return, Wills, I know he will.* The earth trembles when an unloved woman gets a husband. *Solomon is right—the earth does.* After your baby is born, if he does not come back—? *Oh, Wills, please don't say anything. . . .*

Nor in her fantasy did she correct his calling her Crosses-the-River, understanding that her own very private feelings caused him to do it. She wondered why she preferred her Indian name in secret, and she decided to give her child a resoundingly Indian name: Running Stone, after Joe, if a boy; Crosses-the-Prairie, after herself, if a girl.

17

As her father had predicted, the white cattlemen objected when the lowlands along the river were broken that fall for planting. Two of them, a Mr. Green and a Mr. Baylis, rode into the fields and confronted Killer Cross, Billy Cheyenne, and Harley Wilson, who were busy taking turns with the plow. Harley Wilson laughed about it later, saying they had taken him for Indian, too.

The men argued that they had an agreement to use this grass near the river and they didn't want it plowed under. Killer Cross said they might have an agreement but he had a willful daughter who had managed to get control of his daughter-in-law.

"What's that got to do with it?" asked Green.

"Many Stones has power," Killer Cross said. "We got to plow up this land or she will poison us. I had power once, but the Jesus people took it away from me."

Green and Baylis shook their heads, as they often did when confronted with the endless voodoo of the Indian country. "We'll have to stop paying you," Baylis threatened.

"Go see my daughter," said Killer Cross. "She speaks white lingo."

They rode into the yard, where Sara stood at the tipi flap, waiting. She had been watching the confrontation out in the field, and had guessed what it was about.

The tall one with a mustache was Green and the chunky one was Baylis. "Gentlemen," she told them, summoning her best vocabulary, "we have decided to use our lands for our own purposes. I had been planning to contact you soon, to request the removal of your herds entirely. Now you will kindly arrange to vacate our range as soon as possible."

The cattlemen were slack-jawed at her articulation. "Your father said you spoke white lingo," said Green. "Are you folks Jesus Indians?"

"I think I must be," she told them enigmatically.

"We have a grass agreement with your people," said Baylis.

"I have spoken to my lawyer about it," she said in casual rejoinder. This was not true, of course; she had discussed the problem with Wills, who had told her that any attorney would advise that an agreement in the absence of a legal instrument approved by the Indian Bureau was merely a month-to-month arrangement. She was amazed at how easy it had become for her to lie. "He assures me that you have no recourse."

The men gaped. "Who is your lawyer, miss?" asked Baylis.

"Why do you want to know?"

"We would like to talk to him."

"You may talk to me."

"We don't want to talk to you," said Green.

"If you don't wish to remove your herds immediately, you may continue to graze them for a while on our land above the river. About seven hundred acres—land we do not plan to use for cotton planting."

"But we couldn't pay as much as we have been paying—"

"I do not want money," she said.

Their faces brightened. Living eternally in the white man's breast, she knew, was the hope of getting something for nothing.

"You may use our grassland for one more year, in return for which I want a bull calf and twelve heifers from next spring's crop."

"What?" cried Baylis. "That's too much. We'll give you three young steers."

Sara said, "Do you believe that Jesus is the son of God?"

"Yes, of course," said Green impatiently. "But—"

"You must not forget that He is watching all the time, gentlemen, and always knows what is in your hearts."

A stricken look, suggesting exasperation with her if not a fear of God, came over Baylis's face. "You can have a bull calf and twelve heifers next summer."

"Which I will select myself," she said. "Meanwhile, you must instruct your line riders to keep your herds away from my cotton fields. We plan to plant early in the spring."

"I don't know whether cattle eat cotton shoots or not," said Green as they rode away, his voice registering melancholy regarding the cowman's plight.

She rode a pony over to Wills' house that afternoon as soon as the sun was low. The blessed cool breeze, which always blew away the worst of a summer day, now bore a penetrating chill. Although he had invited her a number of times, she had never been to his house before. The prospect of acquiring a nucleus cattle herd of her own was so exciting she had to tell him. Her own family had been unmoved. The only flicker of interest was her father's initial belief that although the grass money would stop, they would have plenty of meat to eat now. When she told him he could not butcher any of the calves, he only walked away, stomping the ground clumsily with the heavy brogans he would never be comfortable in.

"I told you to stay off horses until your baby comes," said Wills.

"Don't worry," she told him. "Lamb Woman got down off a horse to have me in the Winding Creek arroyo. She showed me exactly where the other day."

Sara slid from the blanket to the ground and looked around the place. Wills' house was adobe over a dugout cellar, well-sealed with good clay and roofed Spanish-style with sloping long straight poles and mill-made shakes that must have really cost something. Inside, she found books everywhere, on shelves and tables, in piles on the floor. An easel much larger than the portable one he often carried around in his buggy stood near the front door.

"You're not very tidy," she said.

"I need a woman here. Badly."

"You need a housekeeper, anyway."

Wills had the best furniture she had seen in the West—a real settee with matching chair and two carved tables with fancy-globed spirit lamps on them. A huge polished Franklin stove in one corner warmed the place nicely, and she was grateful for the warmth.

He stood near the door listening as she related the encounter with Baylis and Green. Shades of early twilight settled in the contours of his face.

"You are a miracle," he said. "You do have power."

"Soon I will have a bull calf and twelve heifers. In time, I will have a large cattle herd, and that will be power."

"Basic lesson in economics," Wills said. "Have you eaten supper?"

"No."

"You could eat with me if you'd like some smoked ham. I'm going to drive you home when you are ready. I don't want you riding that horse."

"I'd like to have smoked ham. May I cook it for you?"

"If you want to."

"Cooking on a stove will be interesting for a change."

She went into the kitchen, a well-equipped room no better organized than the rest of the house, and searched for something she could add to the dinner.

"Have you ever tasted vinegar pie, Wills?" she asked when he brought the ham up from his cellar.

"I never even heard of vinegar pie."

"A Cherokee girl taught me to make it at Carlisle. You have the ingredients here. Fortunately, not many are required —which is the vinegar pie's greatest asset. I'll make one if you will put a fire in the cook oven."

She rolled out two thick crusts, using a round fruit jar for a roller. The filling was a simple mixture of flour, butter, sugar, vinegar, and water. While the pie baked, they cooked and ate smoked ham, store bread, and greens from his garden. Vinegar piquance filled the darkening room. Wills brought another lamp from his parlor.

"You say this is Cherokee pie?"

"That's what Mary Half Bird told me. Shall we set it out to cool?"

Wills lifted it from the oven with a huge potholder and set it on a split-log bench he used for a cook table. "It's the right shade of brown," she said. "While it cools, will you show me your paintings? You said there were many more."

The third room of his house, opposite the kitchen, was his studio. An easel, even larger and more professional-looking than the one by the front door, stood beside a wide north window that was made of four glazed sashes installed into a permanent rectangle; on the easel, half-finished, was a portrait of a Kiowa woman with a rag tied around the middle portion of her face.

"She is noseless," Wills said. "Her name is Lives-in-a-Tree. She's a medicine witch who lives on Owl Creek."

The detail in the portrait was incredible. Wills had been intrigued by the texture of the skin, he said, and by the pattern of creases around the eyes and over the brows. Sara gaped, suddenly unnerved by the sight of Joe's mother staring at her from the easel—stern and accusing. She might have been saying to her daughter-in-law: *Do not lose your nose.*

"When were you on Owl Creek?"

"Last month," he said. "I had heard of Lives-in-a-Tree

when I was down there before. We are in the same business,
so to speak, and last month I went to see her. Some of the old
Indian remedies have a certain medical soundness and it always fascinates me to find them. Nobody had told me that
she was noseless. Does this picture seem honest to you?"

"It does." Sara moved around the easel and the eyes of the
portrait followed her exactly. If she had been a little more
primitive, she might have fled in fright.

"Lives-in-a-Tree has a special medicine," Wills told her.
"The land she was allotted has an oily spring bubbling deep
in a sandstone crevice. She lives on a ledge above it in a hut,
and she treats white people for rheumatism and dropsy. The
white homesteaders on the Kiowa reservation call it Indian
Oil. Several of them go regularly for treatments."

"Does it cure them?"

"No. I can't cure them, either, so there's no harm done."

"Does she treat Indians with it?"

"I don't think so. She uses an old medicine of dried owl
skin, pounded into a powder, for her Indian patients. I think
she knows the medicine oil is a hoax, but I may be wrong
about that. It's really only a hunch."

Sara said with a touch of anger, "Then you suspect that
she is deliberately fraudulent with whites but not with Indians."

"Maybe I am wrong."

"You are. Does she live alone?"

"Apparently. They say she has had many husbands, even
since she lost her nose. But in the end, she frightens them
away with her chants. She preaches bitterly against the Jesus
Road and sometimes goes into a trance."

"Do you have any more Kiowa pictures?"

"A few, and some pencil sketches."

He showed them to her, and one prominent observation
struck her hard. None of them seemed accurate except possibly the portrait of Lives-in-a-Tree. He had painted her as
she must surely look today, with remarkable fidelity to contemporary clothing. All the others he had romanticized or
rendered comical in one way or another, by exaggerating the
Indians' confused attempts to accommodate themselves to the
white civilization, as he had in the paintings of her own parents, or by placing them back fifty or even a hundred years
in depicting them in adornment no longer worn by anyone.

"You don't like them," he said.

She didn't want to answer. Wills was gentle, intelligent, strong-minded, and sensitive; but his work revealed something in his attitude that she could not possibly discuss calmly.

"You are my only important critic, Sara. You must have something to say."

Her pulse pounded. "I suspect that the only one you painted accurately was the mutilated woman."

"It seemed a shame to alter her."

"I would think that to an artist it would seem a shame to alter anybody." She turned from his studio. "The pie must be cool by now."

He followed her in silence.

She took a knife and cut the pie with more of a slashing gesture than she intended. She put out wedges on delicate saucers he took from his cupboard. They ate the pie, which she thought had turned out well. It was obvious, however, that he didn't like it. Which would have been all right, if he had not lied about it.

"It's delicious," he said, but later, while preparing to take her home, he wondered aloud whether some eggs might have given the filling a lighter texture.

"It would not be vinegar pie that way," she said.

Leading her horse behind his buggy, she reached home without revealing to Wills Freeland that Lives-in-a-Tree was her husband's mother.

In Sara's mind, the noseless face staring from Wills' canvas seemed to watch her wherever she went for days. She decided in November, after the cotton was picked and the fall plowing finished, that she must go to Owl Creek. She confided in Many Stones, who said, "Do you believe Lives-in-a-Tree knows where Running Standing is?"

"She may have heard somehow. That's why I am going."

Many Stones, always practical, tried to prepare her for disappointment. "Since he said to consider yourself returned to your father, she probably won't tell you where he is even if she knows."

"I must see her."

"If she hates the Jesus Road so much, she may not like you. Everyone thinks you are a Jesus Indian."

"I'll wear a squaw dress."

"You burned up the only one you had."

"You haven't burned all yours. I'll take two of yours apart

and make a larger one. You'll never wear them again, will you?"

"Never," said Many Stones, digging the old dresses out of a box at the end of her bed. "Let's cut them up."

Sara and Many Stones had made several dresses for themselves and for Many Stones' daughters. By midafternoon they had a squaw dress ready.

"It is terrible-looking," Many Stones said as she stepped back to survey their labor. "You will not look like a Jesus Indian in that. I will braid your hair for you and Lamb Woman has a pair of very old moccasins you can wear."

Her trip to the Owl Creek village was delayed the next morning by an unexpected visit from the Holcombes.

"It's Pole Bean and Round Face Woman," said Killer Cross, who had brought a pony, bridled and blanketed, from the brush arbor stable.

Mrs. Holcombe sat regally on the buggy seat. The Reverend started to climb down, then changed his mind as she spoke to him.

"Just look at her," Mrs. Reverend said. "Home less than six months, and look at her."

Sara stood before the tipi flap in her braids, squaw dress, and outsized moccasins.

"Good morning, Reverend," she said. "You are here early again."

"Just passing by," he told her tentatively. "We thought perhaps—"

"It's no use, John, no use at all," his wife insisted. "Every member of this family is dressed better than she is. Look at that one over there"—indicating Many Stones—"so neat and pretty. She's left the blanket of her own accord, and this one who's been to school and should know better . . ."

The Reverend nodded sadly. "We hope everything is going well for you folks, Brother Cross." He glanced at the brogans. "They tell me in town you're putting in several acres of cotton."

"Yep," said Sara's father. "How you like my plow shoes, Reverend? We're damn good farmers now."

Mrs. Holcombe coughed and Sara said, "Father, you should not use that word in front of ladies."

Nettled, Killer Cross coolly remarked, "Crosses-the-River is ashamed of her own damn folks."

"Let's be going," said Mrs. Holcombe to her husband, and

Sara turned to hide a smile. Round Face Woman was not as indignant as she would have you believe; she simply didn't want to risk any more sociable exchanges between her husband and Brother Cross, lest the inevitable invitation to attend services might be accepted. She'd had enough of Killer Cross in action on the Jesus Road.

"Well, good day, then," the Reverend said and drove away.

Billy Cheyenne watched them leave and remarked that they still had no one to take Susan Antelope's place. "That's why he come here," he said to Sara. "While you're down there, give that noseless woman a message for Long Neck, in case he ever comes to visit her. Tell him I am going to get me a gamecock the first chance I have, and I will challenge him to pit one of his cocks against it."

She wondered whether he meant the message literally or was sending a veiled challenge for Long Neck to fight him in person. Probably both. "We don't need any cockfighting," she said, conscious of her bigness as she climbed upon the pony's back. To do this easily, she thought, a pregnant woman should ride every day.

"Wait," said her mother in Cheyenne. "You can't go on that pony to Owl Creek."

"Why not?"

"He's one of those that Three Toe brought. He might not know his way home. You must ride one of the old horses today. Then if you start to lose your baby on the trip, you can lie down on the blanket and turn the horse loose. He'll return by himself and we can come looking for you."

"I won't lose my baby."

"You don't know what you will do, Crosses-the-River. You are not very Indian anymore, but we need you here now. If you die, we won't know what to do next." Lamb Woman was stern about it. "Go and bring one of the old horses," she said to Billy.

Sara's brother nodded and went to the stable. Sara dismounted, and while she waited, her mother grabbed a chicken from the yard, wrung off its head, and said, "You must take a gift with you." When the chicken stopped flopping, she brought a butcher knife from the house, opened the chicken, flung the insides away, and held it out to drip.

Billy Cheyenne returned from the arbor with a swaybacked horse. "This one ain't much good. It wouldn't be no loss if you left him there and walked home."

"She no walk home," said Lamb Woman in white lingo.

"Why she got to go there?" asked Billy. "To try to find Running Standing again? She don't need no dapom Kiowa. Three Toe would take her now, dressed that way."

"No he would not," Lamb Woman shrieked. Billy's eyes and his father's bulged with surprise. Lamb Woman had never before raised her voice to a male member of her family. Billy Cheyenne and his father both made threatening gestures toward her. One of them might have struck her, Sara thought, except for the quick movement of Billy's wife.

Many Stones, her lame foot swinging in its strangely delicate orbit, stepped directly in front of them. Hands on hips, she thrust out her pretty chin and looked up at her angry husband.

"Don't be a damn fool, Billy Cheyenne," was all she needed to say.

Billy backed away but his father argued. "It ain't right for you to protect her, Many Stones. Lamb Woman should not talk like that to us."

Many Stones remained silent, but stood her ground and stared him down. Finally, abandoning himself to confusion, he stomped the ground with his now fairly broken-in brogans. Lamb Woman wiped her hands, rolled the chicken into a flour sack, and tied it to the horse blanket.

Sara rode toward the Kiowa prairie, her senses acute with the picture she must surely make, disguised to fool her noseless mother-in-law into talking to her—a traitor to her people.

18

BECAUSE the Kiowa-Comanche reservation was not opened to white homesteading until 1901, ten years after the Cheyenne-Arapaho reservation was opened, Running Standing's village, the most backward of them all, remained very much as it was when Sara last saw it. His people had land of their own—160 acres each, as had the Cheyennes and Arapahos; but having no idea what to do with it, they remained huddled along the stream, the canvas of their tipis sagging, the stench of their village reaching for a mile in every direction. Other Kiowa villages, where missionaries had brought agricultural methods along with Jesus Road ferment, were mostly abandoned now, in 1905—the people living in good tipis or small wooden houses on their own lands, their futures clutched in their own trembling hands.

On reaching the edge of the village, Sara saw Little Moccasin and Medicine Water, sitting together on the trunk of a fallen tree. She did not know their names but remembered them vaguely as old friends of Rabbit Hand. Their hair was in braids and they wore issue clothes and moccasins. Both stared as she rode up.

"I am looking for Lives-in-a-Tree," she said, summoning the best Kiowa she could from what she had learned from Joe.

"Are you sick?" asked Little Moccasin.

"Yes. I need a medicine."

"Are you Cheyenne?"

"Yes."

"She does not treat Cheyennes or Arapahos."

"I have heard that she even treats white people."

"If they have money." The eyes of Little Moccasin and Medicine Water suggested that it might be unsafe to reveal that she had money. They were, after all, dapoms.

She rode past them, past the curious quiet faces of other Kiowas who peered from their flaps or paused around their fires to watch. At the upper end of the tipi circle, off to itself, she recognized the Grandmother Keeper's tipi. Approaching it, she slid from the blanket as an old man came from behind the flap. He was Weasel Ear, Joe's ancient uncle, still quite alive although dramatically feeble. For a moment she thought he might have become the high priest of the village, but realized when he spoke that he had not.

"I am the Keeper's principal assistant," he said. "Do you bring an offering?"

"Yes. A fresh-killed chicken."

"I will give it to him."

The Keeper appeared at the flap. "Weasel Ear is not my helper," he said, and she saw immediately that he was blind.

"I bring you an offering," she told him. "A fresh-killed chicken."

"Thank you, my dear young woman. You have a kind

voice." He held out an eager hand for the chicken. "Your words tell me that you are not Kiowa."

"I am Cheyenne. I wish to see Lives-in-a-Tree." She unfolded the flour sack and placed the chicken in his hand.

"Are you sick?" he asked.

"Yes, I am."

"You will find Lives-in-a-Tree near the rocks above the lower bend of Owl Creek. A path leads down the creek from here."

"How far is it?"

"One mile, maybe."

"Is she the same woman who was once the wife of Rabbit Hand?'

The old Keeper hesitated before answering. He hefted the chicken, touching its cavity with his fingers and tasting them. "Yes," he said at last. "Rabbit Hand cut off her nose and kicked her out. Her own people would not take her back, so she returned here. I let her live behind my tipi until the land allotment, and then she dug a hut on her own land. She is not a good woman, but she has strong medicine."

"Do you know where Rabbit Hand is now?"

"After they let him out of prison, he stayed at Fort Sill. I am told he still lives on the farms there."

"And his sons? Long Neck and Running Standing?"

Again the Keeper hesitated. Sara feared she had asked too many questions.

"Do you have more offerings for me, dear young woman?"

"No," she said. "I have nothing else."

"I do not know where they are," the Keeper said. "Running Standing ran away a long time ago. Long Neck married Two Bonnet, a Jesus Caddo. I do not know where they live.'

"I have a blanket on my horse," she said. "I would like to give it to you, to make your bed softer."

He waited at the flap while she removed the horse blanket. Still clutching the chicken in one hand, he accepted her blanket with the other.

"Long Standing and Two Bonnet may also live near Fort Sill," he said. "They may work for a white cow rancher there."

"And Running Standing? Have you seen him lately?"

The old man shook his head. "He never came back."

She was crushed, for she believed the old man was telling

the truth. He might hijack her for information, but would tell the truth if he told her anything at all.

"Not even once?" she asked.

"You do not sound sick to me, young woman. You sound inquisitive."

"I am very sick. I must go now and ask Lives-in-a-Tree for a medicine."

"If you have nothing more for an offering, she will not make a medicine for you."

"I will ask her anyway," Sara said. For she did have something to give Lives-in-a-Tree. She had the purple beads she had given back to Joe after his mother had lost her nose. He had brought them to Carlisle and had given them to her the following Christmas. His mother, for whom they had been originally intended, would get them now.

She turned to her horse and hefted herself onto it. The trail down Owl Creek was worn smooth from considerable traffic. Hot November sun beat down through the barren treetops. She reached the bend and followed the trail northward through an eroded gully away from the creek. On the Kiowa prairie, where the land appeared endlessly flat, one could suddenly come upon drainage arroyos like this, slashed deep into the red subsurface. No stream flowed here, although the trough of the gully quickly rushed and swirled during flash rains.

Lives-in-a-Tree's hut was a roofed-over dugout in the side of the ledges at a point where a natural crevice in the sandstone had widened the arroyo. Eroded layers of rust red, purple, beige, and eggshell white made a pillared wall below the hut. The trail led down and across the trough, then upward in easy ascent to the side of the hut, apparently ending there.

As she began the ascent, Sara saw Lives-in-a-Tree emerge from the hut, a white rag around the middle of her face, exactly as Wills had painted it, and a rifle in her hand.

"Leave your horse below and come up on foot," she called out in Kiowa. "Whoever you are, do not speak white lingo here." There was strength in her voice.

Sara did as told, noticing the stamped-out area at the bottom of the erosion where many horses had waited while their riders visited above.

Lives-in-a-Tree did not aim the gun, or even hold it at the

ready. It was an old lever-action carbine with a scarred stock and a rusty barrel—the gun once used by Sky-Walker to shoot the heart out of Killer Cross's effigy. Medicine Water had given it to Wolf's Tongue, who had given it to her.

"Are you Lives-in-a-Tree?" Sara asked in Kiowa when she reached the top of the incline.

The woman's eyes bored into her from above the bandage. "You know I am. There is no other noseless woman around here. Why do you come to see me?"

"I come for a medicine." Sara had rehearsed her lie and the performance that would accompany it. While walking up, she had twisted the fingers of her left hand into an awkward and useless position. Now she held them out. "Rheumatism. They say your medicine oil cures rheumatism."

If Lives-in-a-Tree so much as glanced at the hand, Sara could not detect it; she seemed not to have taken her eyes off Sara's face. "You come with lies on your tongue. That hand is not sick. You hold it that way to deceive me."

Stunned, Sara tried to insist—raising the hand higher as though to prove her affliction. "It is very painful."

The woman's eyes narrowed above the bandage. "You speak Kiowa words the way Cheyennes speak them."

Sara decided suddenly to end her pretense. "I am Crosses-the-River," she said.

Lives-in-a-Tree's eyes widened. "I have heard that my son married you on the Jesus Road."

"That is true."

Lives-in-a-Tree considered for a moment and then said volubly: "Come on inside. You may want to sit down. I see you are going to have a baby. I must be its grandmother. I have a good chair inside. You will be comfortable in it, I think. Do not be afraid of me. I have been hoping you might come to see me, but I did not think you would, because I have no nose."

Lives-in-a-Tree held open a canvas flap that hung across the doorway to her hut and Sara went inside, marveling that her fingers did not want to relax from their awkward position. They had rebelled against her lie and were now determined to turn her words into the truth.

Lives-in-a-Tree had done a miraculous job of building her hut. Having first dug clay from between two ledges, deepening the natural depression there, she had dragged and laid up sandstones to form an abutment against further erosion on the lower side. Then she had arranged more stones on the ledges themselves, to raise their height; and across these rows she had placed boards, pitched downward for drainage, and covered them with sod. Grass grew on the sloping roof exactly as on the adjacent prairie. Approaching the gully from the north, one could walk right onto her roof without knowing it—unless it was very cold and she had a fire going inside, in which event smoke would be coming out of the ground through a small smoke pipe stuck into a hole in the sod.

The room was larger than most tipis, and the clay floor was hard and dry. The chair proved to be a ladder-back rocker of good design, if badly in need of varnish. Lives-in-a-Tree had accepted it as payment for medicines from a white settler who came for treatment regularly. Her hut had in fact been well equipped from the medicine offerings.

"My spring has made me a rich woman," she said. "Wolf's Tongue wants to come live with me. That is why I keep my gun in hand, so he can't slip up and throw me to the ground. He is sorry he gave me the gun. He kicked me out after I lost my nose, and I will not have him now. Would you like some coffee and a smoke, Crosses-the-River?"

"I would like some coffee."

"A good smoke makes coffee taste better. Look, I have sixteen tobacco pipes." Lives-in-a-Tree opened a tin box and showed Sara her pipes. They were long-stemmed and short, cob bowls, clay bowls, and some very good briars. "Smoking keeps the teeth nice and yellow," she said. "I hate white teeth." She smiled and her teeth verified her predilection.

"I don't smoke," Sara said, but added quickly as her mother-in-law's smile disappeared in a sense of rebuff: "But I would like a smoke with you today. With our coffee."

The smile returned to Lives-in-a-Tree's face. She placed the box of pipes in Sara's lap. "You sit here and rock your baby. While I build a fire, you can select the pipe you like best."

She picked up her carbine, lifted one corner of the entrance flap, and peered out. Then she hung the flap on a nail at the top of its opposite corner, leaving it open. Sara could see her outside at her firepit, kindling a coffee fire; and she could hear Lives-in-a-Tree softly singing a Kiowa song.

Lives-in-a-Tree had not seen Joe since he went away as a boy. She believed that shame had prevented his coming to see her, and to an incredible extent she seemed to have understood and forgiven.

"He probably knows I am rich now," she added reflectively as they sat smoking in her dugout. "Otherwise he would come and see about me."

Sara had stopped rocking because the tobacco smoke had made her queasy. "Does Rabbit Hand know about the medicine oil?"

Lives-in-a-Tree nodded. "I went to see him myself after the allotments. I staked out his land acres alongside mine. After I discovered the medicine oil, I thought he might come here to live with me again, because we would be rich." She shook her head sadly. "I still hope he will sometime."

"Would you want him after what he did to you?'

The woman nodded. "When he is older, he will need looking after, and I could do it."

"Where does Falling Water live now?"

"She is dead and gone to hell. She was traveling on the Jesus Road when she died, so she must be burning right now." Sara had stopped smoking and her mother-in-law noticed it. "Here, you need another light." Lives-in-a-Tree took a match from a bowl on her shelf. "This is good tobacco, no?'

Sara held the match unstruck for several moments, wondering if she could avoid lighting the pipe again. "Yes, it is good."

"After I last made hominy, I strained the corn hulls from the lye water and dried them in the sun. They add a nice flavor to the tobacco, especially when you put in some dried sumac leaves." She watched until Sara struck the match and lit up again.

"Have you no idea where Running Standing is? Not even a guess?"

Lives-in-a-Tree shook her head. "None." She smiled. "I am very glad you do not wear white-woman clothes. It makes my heart sing to see you so pretty.'

"Sometimes I wear white-woman clothes," Sara admitted.

Lives-in-a-Tree looked at her over the white rag exactly as she had from Wills Freeland's canvas. "When you go to see the picture-man docti?"

"How did you know that I go to see Dr. Freeland?"

"He told me about a Cheyenne girl named Crosses-the-River. I did not tell him I knew you. He spoke of you with a certain sound." Lives-in-a-Tree's eyes focused squarely on

Sara's nose. "Take advice from an old woman. Keep wearing your squaw dress and do not go see that docti any more. I will give you a few bottles of medicine oil to take when you feel sick."

Lives-in-a-Tree got up, reached for her carbine, peered around her flap, and went outside. Sara followed, glad at last to leave the smelly pipe behind on the table. Lives-in-a-Tree walked down the incline into the arroyo and up the trough to a point near the bottom of the sandstone outcropping directly below one end of her hut. A small well with a stone ring and a wooden cover was cleverly camouflaged behind a cluster of tumbleweeds that seemed to have blown there idly.

"I have to watch, or people may steal my medicine oil," she said. "Wolf's Tongue already knows where it is."

"And he steals it from you?"

"Yes. I took a shot at him once, although I did not try to hit him."

"Don't kill him, for heaven's sake."

"I won't. If I decide Rabbit Hand is never coming back, I may want to take Wolf's Tongue again. Otherwise, I would already have killed him."

She lifted the wooden lid and there on a stone shelf beneath the rim of the well Sara could see many bottles of greenish brown fluid. Two feet below, not bubbling exactly, but roiling with perceptible movement, was a pool of water upon which the green oil floated. Sara stared down, deeply touched that Lives-in-a-Tree, though jealously guarding the well, had so willingly revealed its location to her.

"I make everybody bring me bottles," Lives-in-a-Tree explained. "I won't give them any medicine oil if they don't. I used to be out of bottles all the time."

"What does it cure?"

"Everything."

"How did you happen to find it?"

"I first made my house down here, because I wanted to hide in the gully and never let anybody see me. I dug out this place and began dragging in stones. A hard rainstorm came one night and you never saw a gully so full of wash in your life. I climbed to the rocks up there'—she pointed toward the abutment of her hut above them—"and when the day got bright and the water ran out of the gully, I saw the green color in the clay where I had been digging."

"How did you discover that it had curing power?"

"I tasted it and suddenly I felt better. I had not even known I felt bad until then. I knew right away that I had medicine oil." Lives-in-a-Tree took several bottles from the shelf, handed them to Sara, closed the lid, glanced around, and covered the lid with tumbleweeds. "You don t look too good, Crosses-the-River. Maybe you ought to take some medicine oil now."

"No, I am fine." Sara still felt the effects of smoking the pipe, but she wanted to leave with a good face lest her mother-in-law force some of the oil down her.

Fortunately, at that moment other visitors approached on the trail below, distracting Lives-in-a-Tree.

"Somebody comes. They must not see me here at my spring. You go to meet them, Crosses-the-River. When they ask for me, tell them I am up in my hut. Bring them up slowly and I will be there."

"How will you get there without being seen?"

"I can climb the ledge," she said.

Sara hurried down the trail to where her own horse waited. The riders were three white men dressed similiarly in khakis and field boots—not western men but by no means strangers to the prairie. To intercept them, she stood beside her pony in the center of the trail at the bottom of the incline as they approached.

"We came to see Lives-in-a-Tree," said the lead rider. "Understand white lingo?"

Although the voice seemed instantly familiar, the full impact of staring into the smiling, easygoing face of Buck Failey did not hit her for several moments. But caution struck her the instant his voice seemed familiar and she waited before answering to let him satisfy his interest in looking her over. His blue eyes peered from beneath the brim of an expensive sweat-stained hat. What he saw was merely a squaw woman of indeterminate age and indifferent character: and there his curiosity ended.

She said in barely comprehensible white lingo: "Me under-stand-em little bit," and waited to see if he would recognize her voice. If he did, she would try to laugh it off. But he didn't.

"You guard Lives-in-a-Tree now?" he asked. "No let any-body up trail? Understand me?"

"You come for medicine oil cure?" she said, feeling certain that Buck Failey was not Joe's friend and never had been.

He glanced back at his two companions. All three of them grinned, and Sara thought they were evil. "Yes, we come for medicine oil cure. I see you have some bottles in your hand. That is medicine oil, no?"

She nodded uncomprehendingly and said nothing.

Again Buck Failey turned to his companions and said, as though she were not within earshot, "This woman is probably going out to peddle it for the witch. She doesn't understand very much white lingo."

"Use signs on her, Buck. Ask her if we can have a look at one of those bottles."

Buck Failey answered the man, whom he called Frank, saying that the squaw woman was fairly young and that the young ones seldom understood signs. To Sara he said, "You sell-em bottle of medicine oil? Understand? Comprendo?"

She uncapped a bottle and held it up. "You smell?" she said. "Maybe-so you buy? Cure foot ache and arm ache?'

Failey took it and held it to his nose for a moment before passing it to his companions. "Now, Frank, you'll see what I've been talking about. This is crude petroleum if I've ever smelled it."

The man named Frank both smelled and tasted it. He nodded. "If we could only be sure where she gets it." He handed the bottle for inspection to the third man. "Take a whiff, Jack."

This one also put a fingertip to the bottle, then to his mouth. He let out a low whistle. "Be careful what you say. I've heard these people often pretend not to understand in order to get information."

Failey reached for the bottle. "If you know Indians, Jack, they can't fool you. She only understands that we're talking about the medicine oil." Again he asked Sara patiently, "Where this come from? You understand me? Where does Lives-in-a-Tree get this medicine oil?'

"Where?" Sara said.

"Yes. The medicine oil. Where does it come from? Out of ground?"

"You buy ground-water medicine oil?" Sara asked.

Failey explained triumphantly to his colleagues that this stuff was coming out of the ground here somewhere, right on the noseless witch's allotment, probably in this very gully. "She thinks she is rich," he added, "because she can make forty or fifty dollars a month selling it as medicine oil."

"Do people actually believe it cures anything?" asked Frank.

"It's mildly laxative, I understand, so they feel that something has happened to them." All three men laughed.

Hoping to hear more, Sara motioned for the men to dismount and follow her up the incline. Lives-in-a-Tree met them, carbine in hand, at the top.

"These men are dishonest," Sara said in Kiowa.

"I know," Lives-in-a-Tree answered. "They want to steal my medicine oil spring. One of them has been here many times. Do not say anything. They may understand everything we say. It is a trick of the white man to pretend he does not understand. He gets information that way."

Sara nodded and backed to the doorway, where she stood aside while the three visitors attempted to coax from Lives-in-a-Tree the location of her spring. But Lives-in-a-Tree merely placed three bottles of her medicine on the table and held up three fingers. "Three bucks," she said in her best white lingo and with her most stupidly ebullient smile.

They paid and Failey asked for three more bottles. Lives-in-a-Tree shook her head. That was enough to sell them at one time.

"We'll need more than this to run a good test," said Frank.

"At a dollar a bottle," said Jack, "she is doing relatively better than we could ever hope to."

The men smiled covertly at their joke and soon departed down the red clay incline toward their horses.

Sara stood on the ledge outside the hut and heard one of them say, as they rode away, "So that's Joe Standing's mother. No wonder he won't talk about his background. I tried again the other day, but he wouldn't tell me a thing."

"I told you he wouldn't," said Buck Failey, "and so did Doc Freeland. Don't press him about it, or he'll clam right up about everything."

As they disappeared, she felt violently ill. She sat on the ground and held her heaving stomach. Lives-in-a-Tree reached her quickly. "You need some medicine oil, Crosses-the-River. Here, swallow this."

Sara protested, but Lives-in-a-Tree unscrewed the cap from a bottle and held it to her mouth. Before she could fend it off, she tasted it and retched.

"You are now better," said her mother-in-law.

"Yes, I am fine," Sara gasped.

"It is very good medicine."

"I must go now. I brought you a present." She unbuttoned her dress at the throat and removed the purple beads, placing them over Lives-in-a-Tree's head. "Running Standing bought them for you many years ago but gave them to me instead. I'd like for you to have them."

Lives-in-a-Tree fingered the beads, marveling at their beauty. "Thank you, Crosses-the-River. I always wanted some beads like these."

Central to Sara's tangle of feelings as she rode bent forward on the barebacked pony was the revelation that Wilis Freeland had not told her all he knew. She left the prairie trail, fearful of becoming ill again, and went home on the main road, annoyed with herself for being so exhausted. She wondered if she was becoming white-woman fragile and decided on impulse to remain in the squaw dress.

"Hello," said Many Stones demurely at the flap. Ostensibly Many Stones had come to hear about the trip to Owl Creek. But the real reason for her immediate appearance was obvious: She was wearing a new shirtwaist of black and white check cotton with a black sateen collar, the piped edge of which continued down either side of the opening to outline a smart vest front. Laced into a whalebone corset, she was scarcely bigger around in the middle than a miniature hourglass. She was also barefooted . . . and smiling.

"Many Stones! How beautiful."

"Do you like it, Crosses-the-River? Jennybelle and Maude came over and helped me."

"We must get you a pair of shoes."

"I don't need no shoes, but I wanted you to see how this new outfit looked without moccasins. Arent you going to take off that ugly old thing?"

"I think I'll wear it for a while. I may have been too white lately."

Many Stones' eyes widened as they always did when she threatened to poison the men in the family. "I see something in your face. What happened?"

Sara told her about the three men who had come to Lives-in-a-Tree's arroyo for samples of medicine oil. "They are crooks," she said.

"But you are not afraid of them. It is something else. Why don't you talk to Doc about this?"

"No," she snapped, not yet willing to reveal that she had learned something new and repulsive about him, too.

"Are you afraid of Doc?" Many Stones asked.

Sara refused to answer. She lay back on her bed, brushed her hair up from her ears, and massaged her temples.

"He was here this afternoon," Many Stones said. "He got mad when I told him you had ridden alone to Owl Creek. He went across the grass to look for you."

Sara sat up suddenly. "I did not come back that way. I came on the road."

"I hear Doc outside now," said Many Stones. "I will go and meet him so you can change out of that dress."

"I will see him in this dress," Sara said. "And Many Stones, please do not interrupt us. I have a lot to talk to Doc about."

Many Stones paused at the flap. "Then I will borrow your shoes," she said.

Surprised, Sara dragged them from underneath her bed. "They'll be too large for you."

"At least I won't be barefoot," said Many Stones, sitting to put them on and hardly able to bend the whalebone in which she was wrapped. Sara watched, marveling at Many Stones' revealed vanity and hoping that her sister-in-law's fever to be a white woman was not becoming too hot too soon.

Many Stones went out and spoke with Wills.

"Crosses-the-River is inside. Changing her clothes."

"Is she all right?" Wills asked.

"She is tired."

"How pretty you look, Many Stones."

"You paint my picture again, Doc?"

"I'd like to."

"In new clothes? Not in doeskin dress and braids?"

"Yes, in your new clothes."

"Start now?" said Many Stones. Wills did not answer and Many Stones explained for him in a perky voice: "You see Crosses-the-River first, Doc. I don't blame you. She is good-looking and she has no husband."

Sara sat on her bed, unmoving. Wills had once painted Many Stones as her Cheyenne grandmother might have looked and now he would paint her, as he had painted Sara's father and Lamb Woman, outrageously overdressed in white adornment. The shoes in the picture, she knew, would be even more outsized than they actually were. Perhaps she would take back the shoes and give him a portrait he'd really enjoy: Many Stones with an hourglass figure, in a piped shirtwaist and fitted skirt, barefooted.

Many Stones returned to the flap. "Come on—oh, Crosses-the-River, you don't want Doc to see you that way."

"I don't care how he sees me."

"May I come in?" Wills asked behind Many Stones, who stood protectively in the tipi entrance. "Hello, Sara," he said.

"Hello, Wills."

"I went to meet you on the grass trail."

"I came by the road."

"You look exhausted."

"I look like a squaw woman, which I am."

The angle at which he stood in the entrance left his shock of red hair backlighted by the sky and his face in shadow. "What happened, Sara?"

She realized that her reaction to him was a kind of fear. "I will tell you nothing until you answer a few questions for me, Wills."

"Anything you wish to ask," he said.

"Do you know the exact location of Lives-in-a-Tree's medicine oil spring?"

"Yes. The old blind Grandmother Keeper told me several weeks ago. I have never actually seen it, but I know it is in the ravine below her hut, covered with tumbleweeds."

"I wonder how he knows?"

"Everyone in the village knows. They steal it from her all the time. Little Moccasin, Medicine Water, and Wolf's Tongue frequently go out selling it together."

"But she guards it all the time."

Wills laughed. "Wolf's Tongue lets her chase him, some-times even shoot at him, to distract her while Little Moccasin and Medicine Water steal from the spring."

"And you think it is all very comical, don't you?"

The smile didn't leave his face as she thought it would. It stayed warmly there as he moved inside, letting more light in through the entrance to the tipi.

"Sara, I think that everything, in a sense, is comical. Even you and me. Observe," he told her with a sweep of his arm, "a redheaded artist from Pennsylvania masquerading as a doctor in the wild Southwest, desperately in love with an Indian woman who is soon to have another man's child. Isn't that a comical picture? I just can't believe it is tragic."

"Masquerading?" she said, her resolve to hate him softened.

"At heart I'm a painter. I don't quite have the courage to practice it. No doubt that is why all my pictures are bad. No courage. And yet I don't know how I'd paint any differently. If I painted Many Stones in her new clothes, would I make it clear that she is wearing someone else's shoes? Or is that sort of thing important?"

"How did you know she was?"

"They are much too large for her, and one of them has a scuff on the toe that I happened to notice when you came to visit me and cooked a vinegar pie." He moved a step closer, still smiling at her, and went on with a rush: "Suppose I painted you right now, in that ugly dress that you made to masquerade as a squaw woman. Would it be an honest picture unless I somehow depicted you, Sara Standing, hiding inside the squaw woman who rode up the arroyo on a barebacked pony?"

"Do you know where Joe is?"

He hesitated, but only for a moment, and said, "Yes, but I'm not going to tell you."

"Why won't you?"

"He abandoned you . . . and I am in love with you."

She ignored that and glared at him. "Do you know a man who works for Roscoe Petroleum named Buck Failey?"

"Yes. I met him once. I only know that he is a friend of your husband's."

"Please go away from here and don't come back."

Now he stood for a moment in silence. The smile left his face in a hurry. He had not expected her to say that.

"And stay away from me," she said.

He turned stiffly at the flap and went toward his buggy. Soon she heard the clatter of his wheels on the road.

19

Throughout the winter she worried about Buck Failey's presence in the Territory. But she resisted every attempt Many Stones made to convince her that she should stop sometime in Cloud Chief and see Wills again. Her refusal was a puzzle even to her father. Although he had believed he wanted the white docti to stay away from his daughter, he confessed that he was troubled. "He is a pretty good guy," Killer said. "Crosses-the-River is mean to him."

"Running Standing kicked her out," said Billy Cheyenne, "and Three Toe does not want her. She ought to have a husband, and Doc ain't got no wife. I hope her baby is a boy. We need some boys around here."

"Maybe she does not love Doc," said Many Stones. "Maybe she loves her husband."

"Which one?"

"Running Standing. She does not consider Three Toe her husband."

"She can't love nobody she ain't got," Lamb Woman said with finality.

Sara sometimes heard them but paid only scant attention. She felt certain that Joe would return to her someday, and for now—beyond the approaching delivery of her child—the progress she was making on the farm was uppermost in her mind. With Many Stones' help she made several children's dresses, which Charlie bought from her to stock his store. The whites in Cloud Chief loved the Indian designs she stitched onto the collars and aprons. With the money thus obtained, she bought lumber for good chicken coops, wire for the garden fence, paint for the cottonwood house, and a churn and butter mold.

"If the baby is a boy child," said Killer Cross in December, "we will have a celebration."

"Suppose it is a girl child?" Sara said.

"Then we don't want it," her father replied. "Me and Billy

Cheyenne have too much work to do. Even if it is half Kiowa, we need a boy. We don't want no girls."

Not that the family disliked Many Stones' twin daughters. They were all right, the family thought, but a lot of bother when one stopped to realize that they wouldn't be worth anything to anybody until they were old enough to have babies of their own and might then possibly produce some boys.

Winter chores were completed by January and everyone waited for the new arrival . . . and for spring.

As the time grew near, Billy Cheyenne suggested to his father that they have a chicken fight for the celebration if his sister's baby proved to be a boy. "I think she will have a boy," he said. He could not explain why he thought so, but his father liked the idea of a chicken fight.

"The trouble is," Killer said, "we ain't got no gamecocks."

"Let's trade a few hens for one. I know an old Tonkawa up on Winding Creek that likes to eat eggs. The whites call him Old Tonk. He has a fine red long-heeled cock that could surprise a lot of chicken fighters around Cloud Chief, whites and Indians both. We could pit him and win a lot of money." Billy thought about it and added, "If that damn dapom Kiowa, Long Neck, ever comes back to Owl Creek, we would have a well-trained cock to challenge him with."

Killer nodded. "That ain't a bad idea, Billy."

That night they crept into Crosses-the-River's new chicken coops and took two hens each.

"We ought to make it look like a fox got them," Billy said. "We don't want Many Stones to poison us for stealing, and she would do it for Crosses-the-River, you know she would."

But Killer was not afraid. "Many Stones don't care what we do as long as you keep the wood cut. But we might as well throw a few feathers around."

The hens squawked raucously when the feathers were yanked. Killer and Billy Cheyenne ran toward Winding Creek as fast as they could, telling each other that they would scatter more feathers for evidence on the way back.

Old Tonk was glad to trade his cock for four laying hens. Billy carried the rooster home under his arm. Only then did they realize they had no place to keep him out of sight.

"Do you know who would keep him for us?" Billy said. "Maude Wilson would."

"Do you think Maude would?"

"She's scared of Indians. If she don't want to, I'll tell her that we are going to kidnap her. She'll do it."

"That's a good idea, Billy Cheyenne. If her papa gets mad, we will cut him in as part owner."

"Let's don't cut him in unless we have to," Billy said. "I'll go see her in the morning. You hide on the river tonight and keep this fighter out of sight."

"All right," Killer said. He went down to the sandspit at the water's edge, holding the rooster in his arms, and felt sorry for himself. The night was cold. It seemed that his son might have stayed out here with the chicken. Anyone could go over tomorrow and frighten Maude, if she needed frightening.

As he thought about it, Killer could not maintain his enthusiasm for the celebration he and Billy were planning. He brooded that even if the new child proved to be a boy, it wouldn't be old enough to do much work for at least ten years, and that was a long time to wait for help. His muscles had barely recovered from the soreness of winter work, and now spring planting stared him in the face.

Clutching the chicken and shivering in the night air, he walked from the sandspit up through the low ground that he had so laboriously plowed during the fall. At the point where his land jutted into a bend in the river, he came upon the depression where he had dug his grave a few years ago when he thought the Kiowa owl prophet was going to pray him to death. The sides of the grave had eroded, but its perimeter was visible in the moonlight. He lay down in it for a while, stroking the rooster, thinking that it would only take a few minutes to dig it out again. Planting cotton would take all spring.

The next morning Billy Cheyenne found Maude near the rail fence behind her father's barn trying to kill a cat with a stone.

"Why do you want to kill him?" Billy asked.

"He ain't any good," Maude said.

She picked up the stone, which was the size of a small cantaloupe, and stood away from him, backed against the fence, wary-faced and skinny. The cat lay in the end of a furrow, badly battered and no longer trying to escape. Billy couldn't honestly say that he liked Maude, but he didn't especially dislike her, either. She was too talky, of course, but

being a white female, she couldn't help it. She was afraid of
Indians, which was nice—and, Billy thought, to her credit.

"Want me to kill him for you, Maude?"

"I can do it," she said.

"Go ahead, let me see you."

"Stand over there and I will."

"Are you scared of me?"

"Not with this stone in my hand."

Billy backed away several paces. "Is this far enough?"

For an answer, Maude eyed the cat, aimed the stone, raised
it deliberately over her head, and heaved it with all her might.
It struck the cat's head and bounced off. She pounced on it
and backed instantly to the fence, her self-protection intact
once more.

Billy Cheyenne bent over the cat. "You got him, Maude.
You want me to bury him for you?"

"I can bury him," she said.

"I'd help you if you wanted me to."

"Why do you want to help me do things all of a sudden?"

"Because I like you."

"I'm too young to like."

"You ain't too young."

Maude raised the stone. "You better watch out what you
say to me. If I tell Many Stones you said I was not too young,
she would poison you."

Which, Billy thought, was undoubtedly true. He backed
away, perplexed to realize that he had come to frighten Maude
and she had frightened him instead.

"Do you know how to give that cat an Indian burial?" he
asked.

"Any old burial is good enough for that cat."

"He's an Indian cat, so he ought to have the right kind of
burial."

"How do you know he is Indian?"

"On account of his eyes. They are about like mine, aren't
they?"

She leaned over the cat, which lay open-eyed in the furrow.
Then she stared at Billy. "He's Indian, all right. How do you
bury him?"

"Standing up."

"On his hind legs?"

"Yes, facing the morning sun."

"I don't believe you, but I will go get a shovel."

Billy waited beside the dead cat, and when she returned, he carefully dug a cylindrical hole deep enough to leave room for a furrow above the grave. He lowered the cat, hind feet first, turned it to face the east, set its forepaws in a praying position, and filled the hole with dirt.

"That's stupid," Maude said.

"Lots of Indians been buried that way."

"It's stupid, anyway. I ought to know, I been to school a lot and you ain't been any."

"You want to make some money?" Billy said, understanding now that only a very direct approach could possibly succeed with Maude.

"Make some money?" she said. "You better watch out what you say to me. I am a young girl."

"On a cockfight?"

"I ain't got nothing to bet on a chicken. Whose chicken?"

"Ours," Billy said confidentially.

"Who is ours?"

"Yours and mine and Killer's."

"Have *we* got a chicken?"

"Yes, all three of us has."

"Me, too?" Maude said.

"Yes. Me and Killer have got a long-heeled chicken that nobody knows about in Cloud Chief. We need somebody to take him a few days while we trim him for the pit. If you keep him here for us and don't tell Crosses-the-River or anybody, he can be part yours. And if you don't," he said carefully, "you may get kidnapped and run off with some dark night."

Maude only blinked. "One third mine?"

Billy nodded.

"I been to school," she warned. "I can do fractions. You would not be able to cheat me."

"We wouldn't try to."

"I will do it. What is our chicken's name?"

"He hasn't got one yet. You want to name him?"

"How about Long Heel?"

Billy nodded and left. Symbolic touches appealed to him, and good ideas from a girl were a miracle.

He hurried to the river and found his father sitting on a log with the rooster.

"Maude will do it," he said. "But I had to give her one-third interest."

"Couldn't you frighten her?"

"She had a big stone in her hand, and I couldn't scare her at all. Come on, let's take him over there. We are going to call him Long Heel."

"You take him," Killer said. "I have been up all night." He handed Billy Cheyenne the rooster and stalked up the bank, stiff and cold and feeling alone. When he reached home, Maude was there. She had run all the way to tell Crosses-the-River about the chicken—and to tell Many Stones that Billy Cheyenne had said she wasn't too young. Crosses-the-River had asked too young for what; and Maude had answered bitterly: "You ought to know about buck Indians! '

The anger that met Killer Cross at his own threshold was more than he could face. Crosses-the-River had already deduced that he had traded away four of her laying hens. He wished he were in the grave by the river with a peaceful mound of dirt over him and a cool wind blowing.

"Where is the rooster?" Crosses-the-River asked.

"I ain't saying," Killer told her and went back outside to sit for a while on the fallen pecan tree. He felt even sorrier for his son than for himself. If Many Stones' face reflected her intentions, then poor Billy Cheyenne was certain to be poisoned.

Billy didn't return for a long time, and he came without the chicken. His angry wife met him in the yard.

"What did you tell Maude she ain't too young for?" Many Stones asked. Killer Cross studied his son closely, and he almost wept to see that Billy, to, would have liked to be in a quiet grave somewhere. But he was proud of his son. Billy refused to answer anything.

Nor could Crosses-the-River get a word out of him. Later, sitting beside his father on the log, he confided: "I took old Long Heel over to Three Toe. He's our partner now. We'll go there to trim the bird."

"Crosses-the-River will never let us pit that chicken," Killer said.

Billy Cheyenne shrugged. "She will probably have a girl child, anyway. She has a very girl-look on her face lately."

Sara had her baby on the fifteenth day of March, late in the afternoon. Lamb Woman midwifed the birth and began a lighthearted song the moment she saw that it was a boy. A mockingbird in one of the cottonwood trees sang with her and nearby on the fallen log Killer Cross and his son whittled. They were supposed to be in the fields planting, but when they came home at noon for dinner and found Sara in labor, they stayed to find out what she would have.

"Do you hear Lamb Woman?" Killer asked. "That means it's a boy."

"We could have the celebration over at Three Toe's place. Chickens don't care where they fight."

Killer shook his head. He was bone weary from spring plowing and heart weary from life in general. "I think I will go clean out my grave," he said. "The sides of it are all caved in."

He went for a shovel, put it over his shoulder, and trudged across the cotton field to the river bend. There he dug contentedly for a while, sharpening the sides of his grave into neat perpendicular walls. The digging was easy and pleasant; the river bottom dirt was rich and soft and sweet.

"If you had ever been anything more than a dog soldier," said his son, who had come along to watch, "you could be buried standing up."

"I want to lie down when I die," Killer said.

"Do you think you will die soon?"

Killer nodded. "As soon as I finish cleaning out my grave, I will go home and tell Crosses-the-River we are going to have a chicken fight to celebrate her son. If she won't let us have it, I will begin my death chant."

"You don't start a death chant until you have been wounded in battle."

"I have been wounded," Killer Cross said.

20

MANY Stones insisted for several days that Sara move into the house before her labor began. But Sara was adamant; she wanted to be in the tipi where the atmosphere of the old aunts would keep her as Indian as possible. On delivery

day, however, Lamb Woman instructed the aunts to take their
bedding to the floor inside the house and leave the tipi for
Sara alone.

It was an easy delivery, so easy in fact that Sara marveled
at all the fuss made over childbirth among the whites. It
gave her confidence to know that she had not become as white
as she had feared.

With her child warm and noisy at her breast she sat propped
up on her bed and asked her father how far they had got with
the planting today. He admitted that they had done nothing
since noon because they wanted to find out whether she had
a boy.

"Now we are going to celebrate," he told her.

"Not with a cockfight," she said.

"I do not understand you anymore, Crosses-the-River. You
waste money painting the house and you ruin our good racing
horses and you won't let us have any fun. If Many Stones
would not poison us, we would not do anything you tell us
to. I am sorry you went away to school and I am sorry you
came back. It ruined you, and now you are trying to ruin us."

She smiled at him, feeling strong. "In a few years, when
the farm is prosperous and the cattle range well-stocked,
you'll be glad we did all this."

"A few years is too long to wait," he said and went straight-
away to one of the cottonwood trees outside, where he started
his death dance—chanting mournfully.

Harley Wilson crossed over from his own fields to Killer's
late in the afternoon to inquire about the state of Sara's
pregnancy. Both Jennybelle and Maude were rooting for a
boy, and they'd had no news for several days. Neither Harley
nor his wife knew that Maude had told Sara and Many Stones
about the secret rooster.

When Harley found no sign of Killer and Billy Cheyenne,
he hurried on to the Crosses, certain in his mind that this
was the big day. He got there in time to hear the baby's first
cry, and was still there, sitting outside on the pecan log with
Billy, when Killer stalked out to the cottonwood tree and
began his chant.

"What is he doing?" Harley asked Billy.

"It's his death dance."

"What does that mean?"

"He is going to dance around that tree until he dies."

"Why is he going to do that?"

"He has been wounded. If he chants until death comes, he dies with honor. But if he just lies down to die, there is no way to know whether he faced the end with courage."

"How was he wounded?" Harley asked.

"I don't know," Billy Cheyenne admitted. "I didn't see it happen. He told me."

Harley watched for a while. Killer Cross danced around the great bowl of the tree, limping on first one foot and then the other. His chant rose to shrill peaks of sound and then lowered into resonant and mournful wails.

Many Stones came into the yard, hands on hips, shouting for him to stop. First in Cheyenne and then in white lingo she threatened to poison him unless he stopped. Killer kept dancing.

"Has she really got power?" Harley asked Billy Cheyenne, the top of his mind amused at the antics of his Indian friends while at a deeper level quite absorbed with respect for the supernatural.

"She has power, but if he is going to die, he does not care if she poisons him." Billy had to laugh at Many Stones' sudden impotence.

Harley Wilson eyed his friend closely. All winter he had pondered Billy's sad plight, for he liked Billy and wished Many Stones did not dominate him so. He had no idea that without her power the Cross cotton fields would not have been broken and planted. He asked, "Where was your father wounded?"

"I told you I was not there when it happened."

Harley went home to inform Jennybelle and Maude that Crosses-the-River had a boy. They all drove back to see him the next morning. Killer still circled the cottonwood tree, his step noticeably slower. Maude was so fascinated, when told it was his death dance, that she forgot to go into the tipi to see the baby. She studied Killer's face each time he came around the tree, shuddering to realize that she was looking at death—living, breathing, dancing, singing death.

She sat on the pecan log, chin in her palms, all morning. Toward noon her parents were ready to go. They called, but Maude failed to hear them. And just as Jennybelle Wilson went to fetch her, ready to blister her bottom for disobedience, Killer Cross swung into the southernmost quadrant of his wailing circle and met Jennybelle face to face. She, like

Maude, stared into the eyes of death; and like Maude, mesmerized, she sat down on the log to watch.

By now several people had gathered in a great circle in the
yard: an Arapaho family; three Caddo children; a sprinkling
of white strangers. Two of the whites grinned meaningfully
at each other from time to time and tried to catch Harley
Wilson's eye to exchange grins with him, but, out of respect
for his Indian friends, he wouldn't let them. Other passersby
had gone on to town and talked along Main Street about Killer
Cross's death dance. By midafternoon, people began flocking
in from every direction. Even Three Toe came and stood off
to himself, watching.

Inside the tipi Sara said to Many Stones, "Can't you stop
him?"

"He no longer cares if I poison him. My power is helpless."

"Can't you force Billy Cheyenne to stop him?"

Many Stones shook her head. "He, too, is about ready to
rebel against my power. If we decide to let them have the
cockfight, Crosses-the-River, everything will be all right."

A chorused gasp and then a hush came from the crowd
outside. "Go see what happened, Many Stones."

Sara waited in a wandering melancholy until Many Stones
reported that Killer had stumbled and fallen, but had got
promptly to his feet again and now continued around the
tree. "He looks half-dead," she said. "Crosses-the-River, Doc
is here again."

Sara glanced toward the flap as Wills' face appeared. He
asked if he could come in.

She didn't answer. Pill bag in hand, he came in anyway.
Many Stones discreetly disappeared.

"Congratulations on your son," he said, putting down his
bag. "I don't suppose a doctor has seen him."

Unable to resist, she handed him her son. "His name is
Running Stone."

Wills listened to the infant with a stethoscope. "He's wonderful. I hoped you'd send for me."

"White women need doctors. We don't."

"How long has your father been chanting?"

"Since this time yesterday."

"He could die of a heart seizure with that much exertion."

"There is nothing I can do about it."

"You could let them have their chicken fight."

"Wills, please go, will you?" she cried, taking back her child.

He made no move to leave but said, "You have brought your family a long way in a hurry, but you should let up a little. You are about to kill your father."

"Perhaps," she said, "you'd like to sketch a big chicken fight celebration for a painting of the savage in his natural habitat."

He watched her intently. "Agree to let them have the cock-fight and I will tell you where your husband is."

"Will you also stay away from me?"

"If I didn't intend to, I wouldn't tell you where Joe is." Then he sat on the trunk beside her bed and told her.

Joe had returned from the East and was living over in the Indian Territory, deeply involved in the political move for the admission of a new Indian state. And above all he was reading law under the guidance of a white attorney connected with the Roscoe Petroleum Company. He had decided as soon as he left Carlisle in C. J. Roscoe's private railroad car that he wanted more than to be a professional ballplayer. He wanted to go into politics. Roscoe had given him the opportunity to come out here and begin plans to become a lawyer.

"Mr. Roscoe," she said, "wants Joe's land and his mother's land. That's why."

Wills smiled and said, "The Owl Creek land is of no value. It would never have been given to Indians in the first place if it had been of value. You must know that."

"How long have you known where Joe is?"

"Quite a while."

"Why didn't you tell me?"

"He abandoned you."

"Do you know whether he is aware of the fact that he is a father?"

"I doubt if he knows, but I'm not certain."

"When did you last see him?"

A sardonic smile touched his face. "If I'm not ever to see you again, I'd rather not answer that question."

"Please go now, Wills."

He was silent for several moments. Finally he got up and stood at the flap waiting for her to relent.

"As you leave," she said, "send Many Stones in, please."

He nodded stiffly and disappeared.

Many Stones came inside and said, "Doc looks sick."

"Go back out and let them have the chicken fight."

"You don't care anymore?"

"I have decided to let them have it."

Many Stones rushed out with the good news, and presently everyone cheered. Killer Cross abruptly ended his dance, and Billy Cheyenne, with Three Toe at his side, announced to Indians and whites alike that he had a rooster he'd pit against all comers. Betting began even before the chicken was produced for inspection.

Sara watched from the flap. Many Stones said, "Billy Cheyenne and his father will have some fun now. Doc said Running Standing is going to be something, but I do not understand what."

"He hopes to become a lawyer. That means he will be able to manage things in the white-man courts."

"How far is the Indian Territory from here?"

"It's about two hundred miles to where Joe is."

"Will you go there to look for him?"

"As soon as Running Stone is old enough to travel."

"How will you get there?"

"On the train. Billy Cheyenne will take me to the depot."

"Why don't we live in the Indian Territory instead of here?"

"We are Plains Indians. We are not considered civilized yet."

"I would like to see a train," said Many Stones. "Can I go with you to the depot? I could hold your baby partway."

Sara nodded and Many Stones suddenly said, "If Running Standing kicks you out again, you can come back here and marry Doc. He would take you, even in a squaw dress."

"Joe will not kick me out."

"How do you know?"

"He will love his son."

"Will you give Running Stone a white name?"

"His father will," Sara said.

21

BY the end of April she felt strong enough to look for Joe but she kept putting it off. Plowing and planting consumed her and she drove her family hard. Many Stones had told them she intended to leave soon and they watched her expectantly.

"Why ain't you gone yet?" her father asked one day in May, using white lingo to impress her. He was weary from long days in the fields and not particularly friendly to anybody.

"I'm afraid you'll stop working the minute I leave."

"We can't quit. Many Stones will poison us."

"I will go when Running Stone is old enough to travel."

Killer Cross turned abruptly at the tipi flap. He called for Lamb Woman and instructed her to tell Crosses-the-River that Cheyenne women always traveled with their babies as soon as they were born.

Lamb Woman nodded but said nothing.

"She does not want me to go," Sara said to her father. "Why do you want me to?"

"We need your husband, even if he is a dapom Kiowa. Go and find him. If he won't have you back, come home and marry Doc."

"Doc is a good man," Lamb Woman said. "For a white man."

"He offered me his horse and buggy," said Killer Cross, "if you would marry him."

"And Doc ain't Indian," Lamb Woman reminded her. "White men don't usually offer nothing for a wife."

"I will go," Sara promised, "before the week is out."

Still she did not go, but let each day slip into the next, believing that tomorrow she would make specific plans.

Many Stones told her toward the end of the week that she was afraid to go. "I have been watching you. Fear guides everything you do."

"That isn't true." Sara drew her bag from beneath her bed

to prove it. "I will go tomorrow. Please tell Billy Cheyenne to have the team ready at daybreak."

Many Stones nodded and turned away. Her lame ankle swung in its delicate arc. She went toward the barn where Billy Cheyenne and his father were trimming their fighting cocks.

Sara made a cooking fire in the yard at daybreak the next morning. Lamb Woman came to the back door. "Are you really going today?"

"Yes. Wake up Billy Cheyenne and Many Stones, too. She wants to go with us to the depot."

"She is up," said Lamb Woman.

"I am over here." Many Stones spoke from the pecan log where she had been sitting in silence, nursing one of her babies.

Lamb Woman went back inside and Sara asked, "How long have you been there?"

"I came outside before you began the fire. I have been watching you. I wanted to try my power once more. It works on the men but it does not work on you."

"Were you trying to poison me?"

"Yes. I am glad I couldn't. Power may be a bad thing."

"You must keep your power and make the men work in the fields."

"That's what Doc told me, too."

"Wills? Have you seen him?"

"Last night I went to see him. I wanted him to ask you not to go away."

"I don't like this," Sara said.

"He will be here in a few minutes to take you to the depot. You have power over Doc. I talked to him a long time. He told me you put a spell on him the first time you came to his office. You say there is no such thing as power, but you have been using power on Doc all this time."

"You had quite a visit with Dr. Freeland, didn't you?"

"Did you know that he'd cut wood for you?"

"Did he say that?"

"Yes. Here he comes now. I'm going with you to see the train, and then coming back with Billy Cheyenne in Doc's buggy. I will hold Running Stone for you part of the way."

"Wills' buggy isn't big enough for all of us—"

"He has a new one. A two-horse one, with two seats."

The new rig was a shiny black Texas-made drummer's surrey drawn by a handsome team of grays. Wills waved as he drew up and jumped from the seat.

"Good morning."

"I asked you to stay away from me."

He tied the reins to the dash and came toward her. "The coffee smells good. You wouldn't deny a cup to a sojourner, would you? Sara, I have something to say to you. It is well-rehearsed, and brief. Will you listen?"

"No."

"She will, Doc," said Killer Cross, stepping suddenly from the tipi. Sara's two aunts were at the flap behind him, their faces barely visible.

"How did you get in there?" Sara asked her father.

"I seen Doc coming and I slipped inside. Sometimes you forget that we are Indians. Now, you listen to Doc. He wants to marry you and I think you ought to let him even though he is a white man."

"So you can have this new buggy and team, I suppose."

"Not this one," Wills corrected. "This is a hired rig, Killer. I offered you my own rig, and I meant it."

"And I will take it if she marries you, which she ought to do."

Lamb Woman and Many Stones went inside for Billy Cheyenne and returned presently with him, dressed for the trip. Killer told them, "Doc wants to make a speech. Everybody shut up and listen."

All eyes turned to Wills, who said, "It isn't a speech exactly, and it is only for Crosses-the-River to hear."

"Has she still got a spell on you, Doc?" Killer asked.

Wills grinned. "Have you heard about that?"

"Many Stones told us. Is it the truth?"

"Yes, she has a spell on me."

"Then don't marry her if you can help it." The look on Killer's face was not exactly disgust, Sara thought, but disgust was in it. He stalked toward the pecan log, sat down, and began whittling absently. "Go ahead and tell her whatever you want to, Doc," he added. "We ain't going to listen."

Sara's glance caught Wills' and she suppressed an urge to smile. "Well?" she said. "I don't mind my family hearing whatever you say."

"I suppose I shouldn't mind either, but an ear-straining audience is calculated to take the edge off a man's ardor."

"A man's what, Doc?" asked Killer from the log.

"Ignore him, please," Sara said, "and continue. He won't understand anything unless you talk down for his benefit."

Wills thought about it for a moment. There was a look on his face that she hadn't seen before. "The devil with it—I have no speech to make. You mustn't wear that dress. Your husband is coming out to the Comanche pasture with a group of important Eastern Indians to see the President of the United States. I am going to take you there and help you find him."

"The President is out here?"

"Yes. Wear your best clothes. You'll want to be Sara Standing, not Crosses-the-River. Your husband is on a statehood committee that is urging Mr. Roosevelt to support the admission of Sequoyah State."

Killer asked, "Is the big white chief the one they call Teddy?"

"Yes," said Wills. "President Teddy Roosevelt."

"They say he is a good friend of Chief Quanah. Maybe Quanah could get him to do something for us."

Sara poured coffee for everyone and left them to drink it while she rushed into the tipi and began digging for her best clothes.

"Wear the gray one," said Many Stones, "and take your high-collar silk dress with the lace sleeves."

"A silk dress might look ridiculous out in the grass."

Killer Cross appeared at the flap and said, "If you find Running Standing, tell him we don't want no Indian state. If we get one, them damn Cherokees and Creeks will run it. They are all Jesus Indians."

"Oh," Sara cried, "please leave me alone. I have to get ready."

As she packed her things, her father stared, not liking what he saw but holding his tongue.

They departed in half an hour. Wills told her that Joe and the other Indian committee members would reach the Comanche country on a passenger train from the east. A cattle train from the north, usually carrying a passenger car, also crossed the Kiowa-Comanche reservation, passing a few miles above Rainy Mountain at a junction near Elk Creek, which was their destination now. It was twenty miles away but the road was hard red clay, and they could expect to make good time if they rested and watered the team at intervals.

"Will we find Joe today?" she asked.

"Tonight or tomorrow, I think. If we can get on this train. The President is supposed to be in San Antonio. He is coming north to Frederick, in Quanah's country."

"Why would the President of the United States come out here to see a Comanche chief?"

"He is going wolf hunting with Quanah and a man named Abernathy who catches wolves alive with his bare hands. Teddy wants to see it."

"How do you know about all this?"

"I have seen Joe's name on a list. I am on another committee, which is why I have seen the list."

"And your committee is opposed to statehood?"

"Opposed to the Indian state. We favor the admission of both Indian and Oklahoma Territories as a single state. To be called Oklahoma."

"You'll have it so the whites can dominate it, won't you?" was all she said.

They made good time and arrived at the Elk Creek junction by midday. The sky was hot and the land was hot and shimmers rose from the ballast in the railroad bed. They waited beside the tracks and were disappointed when the cattle train arrived, for there was no passenger car on it. Wills spoke to the flagman at the caboose while the engine was taking on water.

"Do you mind if we ride in one of those empty cattle cars down to Frederick?"

The flagman considered the request and said, "It's again' the rules."

Wills stepped forward suddenly and peered into the flagman's eyes. "I'm a doctor. Have you had an examination lately? I think you have a noticeable contraction of the muscular partition in both irises."

The bell sounded. The flagman quickly said, "Would you and the lady like to ride the caboose, Doc? There's a bench inside. It's better than the cattle car."

"We wouldn't mind. Maybe I could give you something for that partition contraction."

The flagman assisted Sara up while Wills hurried to the surrey for the baby and their bags. He said good-bye to Many Stones and Billy Cheyenne and leaped to the rear step as the train began to move.

"Now let's have a look at you," he said, peering into the

flagman's eyes again. "Lucky this isn't aggravated. I'm going to give you a pill. You should stay in a darkened room for a few hours if possible."

"I could stay in one of the cattle cars and keep the doors shut, Doc. Frederick is the next water stop and I won't need to come out until then."

"Good." Wills rummaged inside his bag, withdrew a bottle of pills, and gave one to the flagman. "It's very sweet. Chew it slowly and keep your eyes closed as much as you can."

"Thanks, Doc," said the flagman, disappearing with his pill. Wills dragged a bench out of the caboose onto the rear platform. They sat on it and watched down the track.

"What kind of pill was that?"

"Sugar."

"Contraction of the muscular partition. Of both irises, at that."

"Light causes it. Back there in the darkened cattle car, those partitions will expand. This is a nice way to travel, here in the breeze, isn't it?"

"I am sure we could not have a better ride into Comanche land."

"Would you like to hear my speech now? I couldn't say it in front of your family."

"No, Wills. Please."

"Since we have been thrown together this way, it would seem to me that utter silence would be both unnatural and unfriendly. Politics bores me, if you must know the truth, and philosophy, while fascinating, would lead us inevitably to the spell I am under. What else can we possibly talk about?"

"We can simply watch the prairie go by." Her gaze swept the grassy horizon where on either side of the disappearing railroad track clusters of cattle stood on the hot land in mesquite thickets near small water holes. "Or you could tell me what you know about my husband," she said.

At last he told her, and he answered every question she asked. A few months ago, before her visit to Lives-in-a-Tree, Wills had made a trip into the Indian Territory with a statehood committee from Oklahoma Territory. Indian Territory was sure to be admitted to the Union soon. The question was: Would it be strictly an Indian state called Sequoyah? Or would it include Oklahoma Territory and be a white state called Oklahoma? To Wills' surprise one day he had found himself talking to Joe Standing, a member of the Sequoyah committee. Until then he had not known that Joe had given up football to return West and take up the study of law. Everyone over in the Indian Territory seemed to believe that he had a great political future.

"Did he know you were from Cloud Chief?" she asked.

"Yes. I told him I had met the Cross family. I said their daughter was building a farm on the allotments. I said she was a beautiful woman, doing a perfectly remarkable job."

"What else, Wills?"

"I asked if he had known her at Carlisle. He replied only that everybody knew everybody at Carlisle. That made me angry and I didn't talk to him anymore."

"Didn't you tell him I was going to have a baby?"

"No. He didn't even admit that he was your husband."

They were silent. As the train rolled ever deeper into Comanche land, the prairie seemed to rush past the cattle caboose into the hot receding distance.

22

WHILE Sara and Joe were at Carlisle, the Comanche-Kiowa country had been opened to white settlement with a land lottery, which had produced towns and villages overnight. Pretzel vendors arrived on the prairie along with beer and whiskey wagons; jewelry stalls appeared alongside Chinese laundries; grocery stores that sold just about everything except razors popped up everywhere: Few white men shaved here in the beginning.

Now, four years later, some of the yeasty aspect of the frontier towns—Frederick, Oklahoma Territory, among them —had settled into a milder quality of life. Churches had begun to thrive, wooden houses had displaced the tent communities, and society had taken a gentler turn, men often tipping their hats to ladies on the street . . . and ladies carrying parasols against the sun as well as the rain.

A crowd had gathered at the depot as word of the President's impending visit had preceded him. All three wagon-yards in town were full. Wills and Sara said good-bye to the flagman, who admitted that his eyes felt much better after a stay in the darkened cattle car.

"You keep this pill," Wills said, giving him another bit of sugar, "and take it in a week. Then I am sure everything will be all right."

"Thanks, Doc," the flagman said.

Sara carried her basketed baby and Wills carried their bags. They hurried across the cinder siding and through the depot. A drayman, with his rig hitched to the center post outside, bowed at their approach. "I'll take ye wherever yer please t'go for four bits," he said, "but they ain't much choice because the hotel is full and Mrs. Finley's—that's the boarding-house—is full. They's no place left to stay in town, and no place out of town, either, closer than about two miles, at Mrs. Ormandy's on the north road. She still has some rooms."

"Four bits is a lot," Wills said.

"For two miles it ain't." The drayman frowned, looked Sara over impudently, and said, "Yer a full-blood Cheyenne or I miss my bet. At first I thought you might be part Arapaho. Them white duds fools a fellow."

"We will need two rooms," Wills told him. "Do you suppose Mrs. Ormandy could give us two?"

"Then you ain't husband and wife?"

"No, the lady is Mrs. Joseph Standing. I am Dr. Freeland from Cloud Chief in the Cheyenne country—"

"I know where Cloud Chief is." Again he surveyed Sara, but less critically. "Is your husband that educated Kiowa they call Running Standing that used to play football up at Carlisle, Pennsylvania?"

"Yes, do you know him?"

"I seen him this morning at the hotel."

"Then take us there, please."

"Whatever you say, but the price is still four bits."

At the hotel Sara inquired about Joe. The clerk was a lean rail of a man in sleeve garters and tiny gold-rimmed spectacles. He nodded and said yes, he'd heard of the man. Joseph Standing was registered . . . but no, none of the Indians from the Sequoyah State crowd was here at the moment. They had put their suitcases upstairs and then left the hotel.

"Have you any vacancies? I am Mrs. Standing. My husband did not know I would be here. I wonder whether it would be possible for you to shift some of the guests around so that I might be able to—?"

"I got no way to know you are his wife."

"Well," said Sara. "I guess you haven't, at that."

She turned and went outside. Wills instructed the drayman to take them to a livery stable. The drayman shrugged, pulled out into the street and said, "This will be another four bits, Doc. Did you find out where your husband is, ma'am? Not that it's any of my business."

"No, I didn't, and four bits is too much."

"Then two bits to the livery stable, since you are already a customer. Like I say, it's none of my business—but all six of them Indians went over and rented horses and they are out on the pasture looking for Chief Quanah right now."

"I thought Quanah lived near Fort Sill, below the mountains," Wills said.

"He does, but once or twice a year he loads up his family and camps out on the pasture for a few weeks. It takes three or four wagons to haul all of them. Quanah's still got several wives, you know. The womenfolks hereabouts don't like him, but Quanah's a good Indian."

The drayman did not know where Quanah's present camp was, exactly, but it was somewhere north of Frederick, he imagined, and west of Manitou.

"Could you tell us how to find it if we rode out there?" Wills asked.

The drayman was emphatic. "They's a heap of grass west of Manitou."

At the livery stable Sara stood aside while Wills rented a lightweight double-shafted buckboard drawn by a high-rumped old roan gelding whose ability to draw it seemed doubtful. "He's the only harness horse I've got at the moment," said the liveryman. Wills nodded and led it out of the stable.

The single seat was wide enough to accommodate Running Stone's basket between them, and they drove out to Mrs. Ormandy's place on the north road.

"Good afternoon," Wills said to the woman who stood in the front yard near a gate that separated two wild-rose hedgerows.

"I'm Liz Ormandy," said the woman, squinting. "Looking for rooms? They say everything in Frederick is full. Teddy

Roosevelt is all right, but I don't know why he wants to go wolf hunting with that old buck they call Quanah."

Mrs. Ormandy had almond eyes, a swarthy complexion, straight black hair—part Indian, Sara thought, probably Caddo—and no apparent menfolk. "We'll need two rooms, Mrs. Ormandy," she said.

"For how long?"

Wills said, "Two or three days."

"Git down and come in. Will chicken do for vittles? Fried tonight and stewed tomorrow?"

"Yes, chicken will be fine. I'll be glad to pay you in advance, Mrs. Ormandy."

"No need to, I ain't a hotel." The woman swooped to grab a chicken that had trapped itself between her and the porch. She wrung its neck and left it flopping on the ground. "If I lived closer to town, I'd start a regular rooming house. You'll like my dumplings. Lucky for you that I've got rooms. Six Indians rode by a few minutes ago, and when I seen them coming I said to myself, 'Liz Ormandy, you are just about to rent every room you've got.' An' when they didn't even stop I said, 'Liz, old girl, your rooms is still empty.' " She smiled through missing front teeth.

"How long ago did those Indians pass here, Mrs. Ormandy?" Wills asked.

"Them six? Half an hour."

"Have you any saddle horses that we could hire?"

"One, maybe."

"Have you an extra saddle that I could use on this old fellow?"

"I have four good saddles, but you ain't going anywhere very fast on that old piece of flesh." The woman glanced up at Sara. "Are you aiming to follow them Indians?"

"One of them is my husband. He doesn't know I am here." Sara indicated the baby in his basket beside her. "My husband has never seen his son."

Mrs. Ormandy's expression suggested, as one woman to another: caution. She said, "You aiming to take the baby with you onto the prairie?"

"Yes."

"I've got a cradleboard in the barn. Git down, honey. Come with me. I'll let you have two horses," she said to Wills. "One is my own saddle pony, but I won't need him right away. I'll ride this old swayback of yours to town if I need to. Let me get a fire going and I'll cook this chicken for you to take."

"We'd rather hurry," Sara said. "Could we take it and cook it ourselves later this afternoon?"

"Why not?" said Mrs. Ormandy. "Hurry now. I ll make you up a chuck bag. Did you ever use a cradleboard with that child?"

"No, but I'm sure I can."

"I know you ain't Comanche or Kiowa, honey, but save my soul if I can figure out mainly what you are."

"Cheyenne."

"Part Caddo, too?"

"No, full-blood."

"You look part Caddo. I'm partial to Caddo, don't ask me why." She turned toward the house. Sara followed, carrying her basketed son, smiling at Liz Ormandy's remark.

"Do you know Chief Quanah?" Wills asked.

"Him?" Liz shrugged. "Jacob, that's my late husband, he knew him. I know him, too. Quanah has too many wives."

"Would you have any idea how we might find him?"

The woman nodded. "When Quanah is out this way, he generally camps on the shelf below the south curve of the big west bend at Red Canyon. Go north on this road here about five miles and then straight into the sun until you hit the canyon. Then follow it north a ways and you will find Quanah's outfit up on the rim. He ought to keep one wife and give the others up. It sets a bad example for the other bucks around here." She glared at Sara. "But you know about buck Indians, I guess, being a full blood."

The big Comanche pasture was a thousand square miles of rolling grass swells whose surface bobbed in the constant breeze. The only breaks in the monotony of bluestem, wild oats, buffalo grass, and sedge were the wooded lines along the tiny creeks that formed the upper Red River. The canyon had no stream at its bottom; its rim was a flat treeless shelf in the grass. One came upon it suddenly.

Sara drew up, facing the sun. "Comanches and Kiowas," she said, "used to kill buffalo by chasing them over these bluffs."

Wills drew up beside her. "I've never seen them before." He pointed toward the north. "That must be Quanah's camp up there."

The sun was on his face. Suddenly she said, "If you were

an Indian, I would probably be willing to go away with you right now. If you wanted me. You have been wonderful and I have behaved badly at times—"

"I wouldn't take you until you had seen him, Sara."

"May I ask one more favor? Will you ride into Quanah's camp and inquire whether Joe is there? If he is, ask somebody to tell him there is a woman out here in the grass looking for him, and then leave without letting him know who brought me?"

"Of course." He wheeled his horse around and left without saying good-bye.

She watched him ride toward the Indian camp. Her baby became restless in the cradleboard. She dismounted, hobbled her horse, then swung the baby from her back and put him down in the grass. She dug dry swaddles from the saddle pack Liz Ormandy had given her, washed the baby with water used sparingly from the canteen, and laid him naked in the sun to air. All the while she kept an eye on the distant camp and at last she saw Wills leave toward the east. The sun was bright in his hair.

She had to wait a long time for Joe to come. While waiting, she created a careful picture for him to see. In a sandy crevice at the canyon's rim she built a fire for roasting the chicken. Liz Ormandy had supplied not only forked sticks for a spit but a few pine knots to cook with. By now the heat had subsided and the prairie wind swept across her. She drew a blanket from her pack, draped it over her shoulders, and huddled before the fire, nursing her baby.

Joe did not ride out from Chief Quanah's camp. He walked slowly across the grass and she saw him coming. His long arms swung easily, and she was gratified to see the high attitude of his head. The sun was in his face as he approached. He paused for a moment to peer at her.

"When they told me a woman was looking for me," he said, "I thought it might be you."

She said nothing, marveling at her urge to be a squaw— obedient, respectful, patient. Perhaps it was not even ridiculous.

"Is that my child?" he asked.

She nodded.

He stepped closer, took it whimpering from her breast, and unwrapped the swaddles to see whether it was a boy or a girl.

Only then did he smile—the Joe Standing victory smile that came over him in moments of great achievement.

The baby, separated from his milk and summarily unwrapped in the grass, began crying. And she watched, amazed, as Joe picked him up, held him high in the air, and said in a booming voice, "Hey, now, you stop that. Indians don't cry!"

And the crying ceased as though the child had understood.

"What's his name?"

"Running Stone, after you."

"He needs a white name, too. We can't avoid it."

"I thought you might give him one."

Joe held his son aloft once more and said, "Your white name is Jeremy, boy. After the most powerful white man I know—Mr. C. Jeremy Roscoe. You were conceived in his private railroad car, and if you'd been a girl your name would have to be Clarissa."

And there, Sara thought, was an incredible truth that she must live with. Her little son had been named by his white-hating father after a powerful white man who, she felt sure, was out to swindle him. It was a contradiction so obvious that it almost explained itself. For Joe's hatred was not of the whites; it would always be of himself for not being one. But who could tell him this? A squaw-woman?

The baby stared solemnly down at his father for several moments before being thrust back, still naked, to her breast inside the blanket. The gesture told her something fundamental about her husband and son. They were males together, would always be males together—and her duty was simply to do whatever she could for them. At that precise moment, of course, the most she could do was feed the baby. Then, with her free hand stirring the coals and turning the chicken on the spit, she knew that she could also feed her husband. She looked at him and saw him watching the fire hungrily.

Tears stung her eyes and she was unsure whether she resented her son for being his son, too, or was incredibly glad to be here and able to do these basic things for them.

The baby fell asleep and was returned to its cradleboard. They ate the chicken. She waited for Joe to show his feelings and was relieved at last when he said, "I came back to *Clarissa* that day we quarreled, but you had left."

She prayed that she could talk to him without making him

angry. "I tried to follow you, Joe. Outside near the tracks Kicking Boy grabbed me and took me out to Bennacker's. When I finally got back to town, *Clarissa* was gone. The depot agent told me you were on it when it pulled out of Carlisle."

He cracked a chicken bone with his teeth, sucked on the marrow, and stared at her. "Do you want to live with me now?"

"I would not be here if I didn't."

"Who was the man that came into Quanah's camp and told one of the boys that a woman was out here looking for me?"

She braced herself and said, "It was a doctor from Cloud Chief."

He fished a sliver of bone from his mouth, threw it into the embers, and asked impassively: "Would that be Dr. Freeland?"

"Yes."

"I met him over in the Indian Territory. Why did he leave without speaking to me?"

"I asked him to."

"Is there anything important between you and him?"

"No."

"I hope that is true."

"It is . . . at least from my point of view."

Joe cracked another chicken bone, sucked the marrow, and said, "You remember what happened to my mother, don't you? If I take you back, Crosses-the-River, I will be as jealous as Rabbit Hand ever was."

She nodded silently, marveling at the intensity with which he laid out the rules. At last she said, "I'll be flattered to have a jealous husband. What do you want me to do? Shall I return to Cloud Chief and wait for you, or do you want me to stay with you now?"

He thought for a moment and asked in a flat voice: "Where is that doctor staying?"

"At Liz Ormandy's farm north of town. You passed by there on your way here. Running Stone and I have a room there, too."

"Did you know that your doctor is opposed to Sequoyah State?"

"He told me he was."

"What do you think about it?"

"I want whatever you want, Joe."

"That does not exactly sound like you, Sara. The girl I left in Carlisle always knew what she wanted, and she always said so."

"I am not exactly the girl you left in Carlisle."

"Wait for me here. I must go and talk to Quanah. I'll be back soon."

He left her for half an hour and she waited with her sleeping baby. He returned riding the horse he had rented from the livery in Frederick. "This old fellow can carry all three of us to town from Ormandy's," he said. "Let's go." He leaped from the saddle and unpicketed her pony while she fastened the cradleboard to her back.

"The baby has gone to sleep," he said. "I think he has muscles. I want to have more sons."

"I hope you will," she told him, stepping up into the saddle.

Joe laughed and she welcomed the sound of his laughter. "He looks out of his pack as though he's been riding this way for years."

"In a sense he has been. For generations. He'll be the last in his line to ride this way, I imagine."

"Sara, I want you with me tonight."

"I want to be with you."

"I must go to the hotel first, but I will leave quietly, after my Sequoyah State friends have gone to bed, and come to you."

"Where will I be?"

"We'll make a camp of our own. Out on the grass somewhere."

"I'd like that," she told him, wondering why she seemed to view his behavior as Indian and her own as white.

PART THREE

Running Standing

23

Joe rode with her back to Liz Ormandy's farmhouse. If he was making a fool of himself, he would simply do it—and worry about it later.

Wills Freeland was not there. Liz Ormandy said to Sara, "When the doctor told me he would not be back, I figured right then you had found your man."

"We're leaving, too," Joe said. "I'll pay you for Mrs. Standing's room and for the supplies you let her have. You have been very kind to her and the baby."

"Lands!" Liz exclaimed. "It don't seem right to accept money for rooms that ain't even going to be slept in. If you want to pay for it, Mr. Standing, then you-all ought to keep that cradleboard. I sure ain't never going to use it again."

Later, as they rode toward Frederick, Running Stone peered toward the rear from the cradleboard on Sara's back while she sat on the pad and held onto Joe in the saddle. The basket with its cargo of baby things hung from the saddle horn.

Joe hired a wagon and bought a bundle of supplies including a can of kerosene, a few sticks of cooking wood, slab pork, eggs, bread, sardines, and cheese. He borrowed a lantern from the liveryman and drove Sara and the baby out of town on the road south, veering into a gully barely visible in the settling darkness.

"We can make a fine camp here," she said.

"I'll come back as soon as possible. Light the lantern so I can find you."

"Please hurry, Joe."

The other members of his committee had arrived at the hotel ahead of him. All of them except Black Bird Davis had gone to bed. Black Bird, a Cherokee National Councilman who had argued vigorously for young Standing—a Plains Indian, at that—to be placed on the Sequoyah Committee, waited for him on the hotel veranda. Joe was his protégé and he was worried.

"Was that woman your Cheyenne wife?"

"Yes, Black Bird," Joe admitted. "I made a camp for her south of town."

"And you will go to her later tonight?" Black Bird was a strong, heavy-jawed man with big ears and a brush mustache. Taciturn by nature, he spoke with authority when he chose to speak at all. He studied his young friend and framed his words carefully. "I am going to be blunt with you, Joe."

"Haven't you always been?"

"Many of our people believe that you are much too white to be of any help in the cause of Sequoyah State. If you take that woman back, it will suggest a woman weakness. I wouldn't be your friend if I didn't tell you this."

"Thanks for telling me."

"There's no doubt in my mind that if you go to her tonight, you'll keep her. And I will lose face for having put you on the committee in the first place."

"I talked to Quanah today," Joe said. "Privately. There is going to be no Indian state, in Quanah's opinion. And he knows what he is talking about." Joe found it curious to realize that holding his ground with Black Bird Davis was suddenly easy.

The huge Cherokee was aghast. "You dared to discuss this with Quanah in the absence of the committee?"

"He didn't mind. He'll tell the entire committee what he told me. He thinks it's humorous for us to use the President's hunting trip as an opportunity to apply political pressure, but he doesn't mind."

"You had no right to speak to him, Joe. We were trying to demonstrate our friendship to Quanah before asking for his help."

"If it is bad to find out the truth, then I have done a bad

thing. Quanah knows that the President is against Sequoyah State, and will oppose it in Washington. If you'll listen to me now, Black Bird, and forget the attempt to use Quanah, you'll save the committee a lot of embarrassment. Because Quanah is prepared to turn you down."

Black Bird Davis rose in the darkness. "I think I made a fool of myself when I nominated you to our committee." He stalked from the veranda and disappeared into the hotel.

Somehow, from the moment he found Sara waiting for him in the grass near Quanah's camp, Joe had been able to hold his agony in check. For by all odds, Black Bird was right: He would lose face with a lot of people if he took Sara back. Well, he thought, I've done it; I'll find out later how I feel about it.

Still sitting in the darkness of the frontier veranda, he remembered the glittering lobby of the hotel in New York City where he had spent his honeymoon alone. Buck and Cora Failey had been incredibly resourceful in helping him over the embarrassment. He would never forget the searing moment when he was forced to tell them that Sara had left him before the train pulled out of Carlisle.

"Buck, don't you believe it," Coral Failey had said. "I am sure there's an Indian custom of brides remaining out of sight for a certain time—something that we don't know about because we are ignorant. Why don't you give Joe the hotel reservation and let them go alone if they want to?"

"Why . . . sure. That's a good idea, Cora," Buck had stammered, relying as did most white men on the adroitness of their women. "Forgive us if we've done anything stupid, Joe. Here's the letter confirming the reservation of the bridal suite in your name. Now remember, Mr. Roscoe does not intend for you to pay for a single thing while you are here. I'll be in touch with you around noon tomorrow. Will that be all right, Joe?"

"Yes," he had said because going along with their improvisation was less painful than any further explanation of Sara's absence.

"You can get a hack outside on the street. Room service there is good. Just buzz the bell and a boy will come right up to take your order for anything you and Sara want to eat or drink. Well, we'll see you later. Come on, Cora, let's leave these two alone, for heaven's sake." And they left, no doubt as glad to get away as he was to be alone.

They not only briefed Mr. Roscoe well, they did it quickly. A letter arrived the next morning by messenger, handwritten by Mr. Roscoe himself on engraved stationery.

> Dear Joseph:
>
> I hope you and Mrs. Standing have found everything in good order at the hotel and that your trip here on *Clarissa* was pleasant. I always find traveling aboard her a tranquil experience. Naturally Mrs. Roscoe and I are eager to meet you both, but that can wait—until your next trip to New York, if necessary. Buck Failey has explained to me that we have inadvertently trodden upon one of your marriage traditions, namely, the custom against public appearances of the bride, and I wish to apologize for our ignorance. Do convey our apology to Mrs. Standing.
>
> I do not know whether you wish to see me in person at this time or not, but if you do, you need only present yourself at my office any morning or afternoon this week. I have some ideas in mind that far transcend our thoughts of a football team under the company banner. Mrs. Roscoe and I, and the Faileys of course, all look forward to the pleasure of seeing Sara whenever it is proper for us to do so.
>
> > Yours sincerely,
> > C. Jeremy Roscoe

Joe both admired and resented the man's cleverness. Standing at the window of the bridal bedroom in his underwear, fingering the engraving on the stationery, he finally burst into laughter. You had to hand it to them: These whites were a smooth tribe.

He'd go see Roscoe right away. Not today—he would be expected to stay pretty close to his bride-in-hiding for a while. But he'd go to Roscoe's office soon and learn what it was that transcended thoughts of football in the rich white man's fertile mind.

He waited, alone in the hotel, and heard from no one. He was amused to realize that even Buck Failey would stay away until he himself made a move to contact his friends. He told himself that of course nobody really believed she was there;

and he also told himself that they might believe it, they just might.

When Joe summoned the courage to visit Roscoe's office, he found it comprised the entire top floor of an eleven-story building in the heart of the city. Its reception room was not large, but the walnut-paneled resplendence of the great man's private office made up for any initial lack of impressiveness.

"I hope, Mr. Roscoe," Joe said, determined to appear in command of himself, "that you and Mrs. Roscoe will understand if my wife and I postpone accepting your personal hospitality until the next time we're in New York City."

As he spoke, Roscoe's head swung away, facing the window, providing a profile for Joe to observe—a long, lean face with prominent nose and chin and a lot of shaggy hair down over the collar at the back of the neck. Then, in a manner as studied as the profile maneuver, the head swung back and the face was full upon Joe, not long and lean but frighteningly square . . . as wide at the cheekbones as an angry Sioux.

"Joseph," said C. Jeremy Roscoe in a hard bass voice, "if you are the man I hope you are, there is no need for us to lie to each other about anything. If you are not that man, then I am wasting my time and I will soon know it." He paused, blinked slowly, and said, "I know that your wife did not come with you from Carlisle. That is absolutely none of my affair. You may be surprised to learn that the Faileys actually believe she is in hiding at the hotel. Cora Failey, an essentially stupid woman, is oddly endowed with cunning instincts. To mitigate the initial embarrassment of your arrival alone, she thought up the idea that your wife was beholden to some Indian custom. When she told me about it, I assured her that she had accidentally hit upon the truth. I told her I knew that the Cheyenne, Arapaho, and certain Apache and Hopi bands did indeed practice such a custom. I don't suppose they do, of course, but Cora swallowed my superior knowledge, as will most anyone if you make him think he has been instinctively shrewd or wise. I am saying more about this than is necessary, Joseph. Let us simply drop that subject and continue with our business."

Joe straightened his spine, squared his shoulders, and with great effort somehow made himself taller before C. Jeremy Roscoe's eyes. Otherwise he would have shrunk into extinction. As the silence continued, he understood that Roscoe now waited for him to speak and therefore reveal something more of himself.

"I don't know anything about you, Mr. Roscoe," he finally said. "I don't see how we can have any business until I do." He paused and added, "Do you?" He almost said "Sir," but checked the craven impulse. From somewhere the idea streaked through his confusion that it was time to let Roscoe do a little revealing and that it would be wise to withhold his own inclination to show excessive gratitude. For in essence, when you came down to it, Roscoe could be no more than one more greedy white man.

But Joe soon altered his appraisal. C. Jeremy Roscoe put his arm around Joe, led him through the door onto a terrace overlooking New York's Fifth Avenue, pointed to the parade of passing traffic below, and asked how Joe would like to have a motorcar of his own. A Reo runabout, a Winton, or even a new rear-engine Cadillac. If his plans worked out, Joe could have as many automobiles as he wanted.

"Mr. Roscoe, football players do not have motorcars, as far as I know."

"It is my plan for you to become a lawyer, Joseph."

"A lawyer, sir?" This time the "sir" slipped out involuntarily.

"Exactly. I intend to train you briefly here to acquaint you with the general structure of our company and then send you out to Muskogee, Indian Territory, to work for us and read law under the guidance of our attorney there. By the time of Statehood, which will be soon, you can be admitted to the bar. There is a great future for you. In politics, in business— or in both."

Joe backed away. He did not like for Roscoe's arm to stay around him so long. "I still don't know anything about you, Mr. Roscoe," he heard himself say, and he liked hearing it, for he was surprised that he had been able to say anything in the least coherent.

Roscoe considered the remark and then laughed jovially, implying that there was no reason anyone should know very much about him. "Know thyself, Joseph," he said, "and fear no man."

"Why have you picked me to become a lawyer for you?"

"That question makes sense. I picked you because I need the help of an Indian. To be worth a great deal to me, he must be intelligent, popular, and acquainted with the white civilization. You fit the bill better than anyone Carlisle has turned out in the past five years. I have been looking for someone that long."

"I can only say, sir, that it is difficult for me to understand how an Indian lawyer could be of such great value to you."

"That's another good question. If you intend it as a question. The answer is that a great deal of wealth lies in the ground in your country. Petroleum mineral wealth—waiting to be drilled and exploited. I can get it out of the ground, but I must have clear mineral titles to the land. Your people do not trust mine, and with good reason. But a new era is before us. I need your help, and in return for it, I will help you make a lot of money."

Joe did not quite know when Roscoe's arm went back around his shoulder, but it was there when he was ushered out the door an hour later with instructions to return to his hotel and think about it. "I would suggest," Roscoe added, "that you keep a pad and pencil by your bedside and write down any other questions that occur to you. Come back as soon as you're ready to talk to me again. And don't forget that I will know a little more about you by how long it takes you to return. I learn about people by judging their actions. That is how you must learn about people, too."

The more Joe thought about the last remark, the more confused he became. Did it mean that haste would signify immaturity? Or that leisurely digestion of the idea would indicate Indian lassitude?

During the night he wrote down questions on hotel stationery, filling several pages. The next day he tore them up. There was only one question in the bottom of his mind and he asked it the next morning when he returned to Roscoe's office.

"You have come early, Joseph, and I am glad. It's a tired but true maxim that he who hesitates is lost. Alas, those who associate with me must suffer my use of maxims to emphasize my points. That they are old and worn only proves their verity. Have you any further questions since yesterday?"

"Basically, one question, Mr. Roscoe. What's in all this for me? *Exactly,* I mean."

"I hoped you would ask that question bluntly when it occurred to you, and I confess that I had supposed it would take several days for you to understand that you should ask it. I'm beginning to like you as much as Buck Failey said I would. First, I intend to help you become a lawyer." Roscoe's eyes were intent upon him. "Then if all has gone well, I intend to make available to you a partial ownership in the Roscoe Petroleum Company."

"A partnership, sir?" Joe asked, astounded.

Roscoe smiled tolerantly. "There are no partnership shares in a corporate entity, Joseph. Ownership derives from shares of capital stock. The acquisition of a considerable stockholding in Roscoe Petroleum would be made available to you, but I would not want you to make any such decision until you had qualified yourself in the law and were then able to understand all the ramifications of associating with me in business."

"Mr. Roscoe, you must admit that it sounds as though you would like to use me eventually to work for you against my own people."

"Does it also sound as though I would let you make a great deal of money for doing it?"

"Yes, on the surface, at least."

A certain glint in the gray eyes deepened. Roscoe asked in a surprisingly mild voice, "Would you be willing to work against your people if the price were right, Joseph?"

"No."

"Even if there were millions in it? The ideas I have in mind involve possibly millions of dollars."

"No."

Roscoe grinned; perhaps, Joe thought, he even sighed. "Thank heaven. I hope you mean that, and I believe you do." The hand came around his shoulder and again he was led toward the terrace outside the office. "I want you to work *for* your people, not against them. Always. Together we are going to make a lot of Indian families rich beyond their wildest dreams. It has been said that money is the mother of evil. If that is so, then it must follow that money is also the mother of good. For wealth is only a means to an end, and the quality of the end it seeks is determined by the quality of the people seeking it. If we are evil, our work will be evil; if we are not evil, our work will not be."

They stood together on Roscoe's terrace. One out of every ten vehicles on the street below was motorized. Joe's mind reeled as Roscoe described the endless prospects of a young educated Indian in the worlds of petroleum exploration, Wall Street finance, and frontier politics.

"As you can see," Roscoe said at last, "it is good that you ask the crass question. There is a lot in it for you."

"Yes, Mr. Roscoe," he said. "Apparently there is."

Sitting on the darkened veranda of the hotel deep in Oklahoma Territory, Joe leaned against the banister of the wooden front steps and closed his eyes . . . remembering the maze of traffic on New York's Fifth Avenue below Roscoe's terrace . . . and remembering Buck Failey, his best friend in the world of whites, but a friend, nevertheless, whom he had not yet been able to trust.

"Joe," Buck had said recently when Joe bumped into him on the street in Muskogee, "you were afraid of C.J. in the beginning, weren't you?"

"It amuses me, Buck," Joe had taunted, mimicking Roscoe, "to wonder whether you would ever have the guts to call him C.J. to his face."

Joe had always enjoyed nettling Failey when he could— because he had never been truly comfortable in Failey's presence. He knew that Failey kept him under constant surveillance on Mr. Roscoe's behalf, but that did not bother him. The thing that rankled was Failey's idea that without him Joe's connection with Roscoe would deteriorate in a hurry.

"Nobody calls him C.J. to his face," Buck replied. "You shouldn't let him intimidate you, Joe. You're going to own a lot of Roscoe Petroleum stock one of these days, especially if you learn how to play your hand. Did you know that you have a weapon over C.J. that he doesn't know about?"

"Weapon?"

"A tremendous power, actually. Hasn't he ever explained to you about leverage? 'Give me a lever long enough and a place to stand, and I can move the earth.' " Joe had laughed at Failey's imitation of Roscoe's delivery of one of his favorite truisms.

And Failey had leaned toward him with lowered voice: "He thinks you're stupid, Joe, and that's your weapon. It could be your undoing . . . or it could be the key to your undoing of him. He's going to offer you a lot of stock in Roscoe Petroleum in return for mineral leases on your lands at Owl Creek. If you could get enough stock, either in your own name or in the name of other people friendly to you, you could take charge of the company affairs and let people call you C.J. behind your back." Leaving Joe to think it over,

Buck slapped him on the shoulder and departed down the street.

Although the remark had made an impression, Joe had not for a moment believed that Mr. Roscoe thought him stupid. But the idea that he might some day begin trading land interests for an ever-growing ownership in the petroleum company intrigued him beyond any previous consideration of his life. He now often found himself, wherever he was, deeply absorbed with thoughts of the power that would surely accompany the control of a dynamic business organization. Sara hoped to improve her people's lot with Jesus Road manners, but a more direct way of helping them might be available. If Indians in sufficient numbers put their mineral rights into Roscoe Petroleum and eventually commanded the company—the American Indian Oil Company, for instance!— who needed Sequoyah State? If all the tribes put land into it, the company could become more powerful than the state could ever be. This was the white trick the Indians ought to learn: that business could control government—and all you needed, really, was some Jesus Road hollering to cover it all up.

Black Bird Davis appeared in the darkened doorway again and came outside. "I could not go to bed without making one more try to persuade you to stay away from that Cheyenne girl. I am glad you haven't gone yet. It pleases me to believe that I have at least given you some doubts."

"I'm going to her, Black Bird."

"Then you show a weakness that will destroy your value to the Sequoyah Committee."

"Since you are the chairman," Joe said, "I offer my resignation now."

Once more the Cherokee councilman nodded curtly and stomped up the stairs in a quiet rage.

Sara waited for him in the grass south of town. The moon was rising when he got there with blankets, a skillet and pot, two canteens and a glass jug of water.

"You haven't even built a fire," he said.

"I thought I'd wait for you before using up the kindling."

She hung the lantern on the running gear of the wagon and made a pallet on the grass beneath the tailgate. She changed the baby while Joe built the fire, and finally she nursed the infant as she cooked. Joe sat opposite her and watched every move.

She thought he might rise and come to her, but he didn't. He said instead, "Tell me about Cloud Chief and your farm."

She told him eagerly and he asked many questions, some of them surprisingly shrewd. He wanted to know whether Many Stones' babies had been entered on the rolls for allotments and how many Cheyenne and Arapaho families nearby were friendly to her. She did not care what he asked; as long as he seemed interested, she told him everything, including the attempt of her father and brother to marry her off to Three Toe. And she described her quarrel with them over cock-fighting.

He laughed at her for caring. "Whatever we do, the white man will not change his basic point of view about us. The best thing is to ignore the whites and go our own way. Do you think we could live together and ignore them, Crosses-the-River?"

"Yes, I do."

"Would you like to stay on the farm at Cloud Chief?"

"Joe, I only want to be with you. Wherever you are."

"Sequoyah State is dead. Both the territories are going to be combined into a single white state called Oklahoma. Mr. Roscoe has told me there is evidence of oil on our land. Sara, I have a big, wild dream."

And he told her about it. The white way of life was a simple but well-made pattern—when you finally got to see through it—wherein rich and powerful people controlled the government by putting their own people into the law-making bodies. On every level. "And they use the Jesus Road as a smoke screen to hide it all from the common people. Haven't you ever wondered why rich men give so much money to the churches? We don't need an Indian state, Sara. We need Indian *business*. Business powerful enough to control politics. That's what the white way of life is all about. That's civilization."

"Joe . . ."

"Listen to me." He was excited. "Lives-in-a-Tree's medicine oil is crude petroleum. Roscoe believes that mass production of motorcars is just around the corner, and he is gambling his fortune on it. Because he thinks we are simple savages, we could surprise him. Sara, I'm going to take that petroleum

company away from him and put it into the hands of our own
people and maybe even rule the politics of Oklahoma with it.
Just think. The Plains Indian Petroleum Company!"

"But Joe, how could you possibly do such a thing?"

"There's a way. If we take a leaf from the white man's
book. His real book, and not the one with gold edges that he
reads in church."

Slowly she said, "I'm proud of you, but I'm frightened."

He rose and came around to her. He took the stick she had
been using for a poker and pushed the skillet of frying meat
to the edge of the coals. He pulled her up from the grass and
said, "Crosses-the-River, there are some things a man is more
interested in than either money or food."

"I have heard," she replied, "that such a matter depends
upon his bank account and how recently the man has eaten."

Joe drew her down onto the blanket beneath the wagon and
made love to her. They lay quietly at last between the wheels,
and the odor of sweet grass reached their nostrils along with
the scents of woodsmoke and cooked meat.

Still they did not eat. They talked instead of his plan for
organizing enough Indian allotment land to take over the big
petroleum company. At the edge of her growing terror, Sara
was proud. Joe could not possibly succeed with such an ex-
travagant dream. But to tell him so, she feared, would drive
him away from her, and she did not believe he would ever
return if he left her again.

Take over a petroleum company from a powerful white
man? She wept silently beside him. But silently.

24

Joe's campaign began soon after he quit his job with Roscoe
Petroleum and returned with Sara to Cloud Chief. He
quickly discovered that influencing Killer Cross and Billy
Cheyenne would be easier than influencing Lamb Woman
and Many Stones. It appeared to be a contest of the men
against the women.

"Running Standing," said Killer Cross in white lingo early that summer, "I am damn glad you took Crosses-the-River back and came here to live with us."

"Me too," said Billy Cheyenne. "Somebody ought to do something about her, and maybe you can do it."

They were standing at the edge of a field of young cotton near the river. The bolls had already formed, spreading the message across the bottomland that abundance was here, awaiting a rich harvest.

Killer Cross kicked a stiff brogan at a clod of dirt and said, "These damn shoes hurt my feet."

"Mine too," said Billy Cheyenne, also kicking the dirt, "but we can't work in moccasins. That hurts even worse. We don't need these fields."

"But you need money," Joe said.

"We can get all the money we need from renting out the grass, but Crosses-the-River won't let us."

"We also win money on chicken fights," Killer said. "We have got the best fighting cocks around Cloud Chief, but Crosses-the-River does not like for us to fight them."

Joe kicked a clod with his own brogan and said, "Men should not let women run their lives."

"That is right," said Killer Cross pensively. "That's why we are glad you're here."

"Crosses-the-River tells me," Joe said, "that Many Stones has power."

"She has," said Billy Cheyenne, relieved to know that the truth was already out, for explaining things like that to an outsider was embarrassing. "We must do whatever Crosses-the-River tells us to, or Many Stones will poison us."

Joe bent toward them in the furrow and said, "Maybe Many Stones is faking. Maybe she has no power. Had that ever occurred to you?"

"We thought of it," Billy said, "but we can't take a chance because she is also part wolf."

That seemed to settle the issue in Billy's mind, and Joe decided not to press the subject of Many Stones' power too hard too soon. "There is a way," he said gently, "to get a lot of money from this land without planting any cotton."

He explained to them the phenomenon of crude petroleum deposits, the possibility of exchanging them for shares of a large oil company, and the power that went with such ownership.

Billy Cheyenne was eager to cooperate with Joe, but his father was dubious. "Maybe we ought not to trust a white-man oil company, Running Standing. White men got most of our land already."

"We must get enough of our people into that company to take it away from the whites. Then we could change the name of it to Indian Oil Company, or something like that."

"Indian oil is damn good oil," said Billy Cheyenne, and they stood at the end of the row and talked about all the things they could do if they suddenly had a lot of money and the leisure to spend it.

That evening Joe marveled at the speed with which family discussion brought the entire subject to Sara. When he had moved into the tipi in the back yard with her, he had made a bed of ropes and bought a feather-filled tick from Jennybelle Wilson. They were saving feathers for another tick, which they hoped to complete before cold weather. Undressing by lantern light, Sara said, "Many Stones tells me that Billy Cheyenne and my father would like to let you make them rich."

"I'll make us all rich if Many Stones doesn't stupidly spoil our chance. She's willful, Sara. She prances around in white dresses that accent her bosom and her tiny waist, but pretends she's part wolf and has a dangerous power."

"She is very beautiful and sweet," Sara said, "and she's a good mother."

"Being a good mother is not especially to her credit. Women should be good mothers as a matter of course." Joe sensed that beneath her obedient expression Sara was laughing, and it made him angry. "What do you know about this power of hers?"

"Only that they think she has it."

"Will you tell her to stop it?"

"She needs her power over Billy. Without it to protect her, he'd be a brute."

Joe sat heavily on the featherbed to remove his shoes. "Then will you try to convince her that she should encourage them to cooperate with me?"

"Give her time to get acquainted with you, Joe. There's no reason for her to trust a stranger."

"She trusts you. Will you try to convince her?"

Sara nodded, wondering if she really would, in view of her belief that Joe's plan could not possibly succeed.

Her son stirred in his basket, which sat on two short pieces of log beside the tipi flap. She went to the baby and held him to her breast. Joe listened to the noisy nursing sounds and his feeling of frustration rose rapidly. When she came to bed at last, he took her with a storming intensity. She felt herself obliterated beneath him in the featherbed. For he seemed to sense that she could not bring herself fully to cooperate with his dream.

As calmness returned to the tipi, she clung to him and said, "Darling, I'm glad you're home. Tomorrow I wish you'd make the baby a bed. He's outgrown his basket. Unless . . . you want him to continue sleeping with us."

"I'll make a bed for him," Joe said.

The next day he gathered a few pieces of whipsawn lumber, some rope, and two feather pillows. He placed them in the yard near a stump that he intended using for a workbench. Billy Cheyenne and Killer Cross protested at having to go to the fields without him. "Why ain't you going to chop cotton weeds today?" Billy asked.

"I'm making a bed for the baby."

Many Stones, who had been listening while working at the breakfast fire, put down her poker and came toward them. Her lame ankle swung into its peculiar arc. Joe had noticed that when she was determined about something, the ankle always swung with a certain deliberation. He was reminded of a cat flicking its tail.

"Go to the fields," she said to Billy. "Running Standing will come as soon as the bed is made." She turned to Joe and said evenly: "Won't you?" It was not really a question. He marveled at her apparent belief in her power. He hated her, but feared her, too—for she could undo all his plans.

"Yes," he said, but the word was involuntary. He did not know why he said yes. He glared at her and she glared back, not fiercely, but with intimations of her power showing catlike in her female face.

While nailing the frame together, he watched her come and go, shepherding her two little daughters who were playing in the woodchips around the fallen pecan log—the whittling log, as Crosses-the-River referred to it. From time to time he noticed Many Stones glancing at him, as aware of him, certainly, as he was of her. He made up his mind to confront her with the part-wolf hoax, to chastise and shame her, the first time he had her alone.

His chance came before noon. Lamb Woman went to the

henhouse and Sara disappeared with water pails toward the Winding Creek spring.

"I want to talk to you," he said.

"I know you do," said Many Stones.

"How do you know?"

"I have power and I know these things."

"You are not part wolf. Let's get this straight, between you and me, once and for all. You have no power and you're not part anything except possibly part cat."

Her glance darted at him. "I may be part wildcat."

He grabbed her arm and twisted it until she sat on the whittling log. "Now, I'm telling you that I know you have your husband fooled—"

She leaped from the log, clawed him on both arms with her fingernails, kicked him in the groin with her sharp-toed shoe, and butted him in the pit of the stomach with her head. So sudden was her attack that he stumbled, completely off-balance, and fell into the woodchips. When he scrambled to his feet, he found her sitting on the log again, with a hunting knife in her hand.

"I will cut you, Joe." Her voice bore tones of sweet, sweet reason.

It occurred to him that Many Stones was an incredibly good-looking woman, and he despised her all the more for that; it occurred to him also that with the slightest provocation she would cut him.

"I think we could be friends," he said.

"I do not think we could."

"If you'd stop pretending that you have power."

"I do have power."

"You have woman power, but not wolf power. There is no such thing as wolf power."

"If you would stop pretending that you are not a white man," she said, "you would have some power among our people."

He stared at her, conscious of the knife, and he decided to take it away from her. With a sudden movement, he grabbed for her wrist. She darted beneath his hand and swiped at him with the knife, cutting him severely on the forearm as she stepped gingerly out of reach and turned to face him, glaring.

He looked down at his bloody sleeve and then at her. She said, "I am surprised your blood is red."

He pulled up the sleeve. "I want to know," he said, holding out his arm to let the blood drip, "why you hate me enough to cut me like this."

"You are no longer one of our people. Carlisle made you a white man, only pretending to be Indian."

"Many Stones, your head is full of hoot owls and rattle-snakes. Why do you believe I am white, pretending to be Indian?"

"You want to swindle us. That is how I know you are white."

"Swindle you? I am going to make all of us rich."

"You want to use our land to make yourself rich. You do not care about us."

"Don't you understand that if I make myself rich, you will be rich too?"

"You have the very look of a white man when you talk about it. And the smell of a white man is on you. I feel sorry for Crosses-the-River. She has to sleep with you and smell you every night in her featherbed."

Many Stones turned away, still watching him as she went to her baby girls. She kept the knife in her hand until she was out of his reach and only then put it back inside her belt.

He went to the washstand on the east side of the house, poured water into the basin, and removed his shirt. The arm would not stop bleeding and finally he twisted a rope around it below the elbow.

Many Stones asked if he would like her to bandage the cut. "Doc taught me how. I have some clean white rags under my bed."

"I'll make my own bandage," he said.

He went inside and fished a bundle of rags from beneath her bed. When he returned to the yard, she was sitting on the pecan log with her blouse off, nursing both her little girls at once. The knife was sticking in the log beside her. She said, "You got a pretty deep cut, didn't you?"

"Don't tell me you're sorry."

"I am not."

"I've decided to let you bandage my arm."

"Now you will have to wait until my babies have nursed."

"Couldn't disturb them, could we?"

"You are such a very white man. I don't like you, but I don't hate you, either."

"Maybe your power doesn't work on me because I am so white."

"I did not say it will not work on you."

"I'm sure you'd have used it before now, if it would work on me."

Her face was serene. "I have all the power I need."

After she had burped her babies and returned them to play in the wood chips, she put on her blouse and bandaged his arm in a good, tight, neatly formed crisscrossed pattern.

"Doc showed many Cheyennes and Caddos how to do this. We went to the agency several times, and he came to teach us. Crosses-the-River should have married him instead of you."

"She was already married to me when she met Doc."

"You told her to consider herself returned to her father. She could still marry Doc if she wanted to."

Many Stones slowly moved away from him, retrieved her knife, and tucked it inside her belt.

"Thank you for the bandage. Somehow I am going to convince you that I can make all of us rich if you will help me."

"Make yourself rich first," she said, "and let us see how you do it."

Frustrated and angry, he decided to join Killer and Billy in the cotton fields before Sara returned from Winding Creek. He put on a clean work shirt, intending to keep the sleeve down over the bandage.

But the sun was hot and Killer Cross said, "What's wrong with you, why ain't you got your sleeves rolled up?"

"Something is wrong with his arm," said Billy Cheyenne. "He ain't using but one arm to chop weeds with."

Joe shrugged and rolled up his sleeves. "I cut myself."

Their essential indifference to his wound fairly described their feeling for him. "When Many Stones poisons you," he asked, "how do you know you have been poisoned?"

"She tells us," Billy said.

"Have you ever refused to do what she wants you to—just to see what would happen?"

Killer became angry. "You are trying to get rid of Billy Cheyenne!" And Joe realized that whatever he said seemed to solidify them against him. He found himself wondering whether Many Stones might actually have some kind of power.

25

DURING the next few weeks Sara watched Joe's maneuverings. Buck Failey came twice and took him on long horseback rides, during which they no doubt endlessly probed their plan to get rich. Her dislike of Failey grew with each visit.

She watched her husband spend the rest of his time trying to work himself into the confidence of her father and brother. He offered to help them trim their fighting cocks, and he was making some headway, she thought, when an Arapaho friend of Billy's stopped by one day to visit in the yard.

The Arapaho's name was Big Oak, but, as Many Stones pointed out later, he looked more like a stunted willow tree. "I have just come from the Kiowa country," he said, "and someone you know has recently returned there from Fort Sill."

"Long Neck!" cried Billy Cheyenne, who had never ceased smarting from the knife fight he had once had with Joe's half brother.

"Yes," said Big Oak knowledgeably. "And he has taken Running Standing's white name. Everyone now calls him Long Standing."

"Long Standing," said Billy in disgust. "That dapom is turning white! Does he still have any chickens?"

Big Oak nodded. "He brought many gamecocks with him."

"I have a chicken that I would pit against the best he's got."

"I'm going back down there soon," said Big Oak, "and I will tell him."

A few days later Big Oak appeared once more in the yard. Billy Cheyenne, who was sharpening a pair of steel gaffs, straightened his back and expanded his chest. "Did you see that damn dapom?"

"Yes, I did. He wants to come to Cloud Chief on the Fourth of July and pit his five best cocks against the five best you can get together."

"No dapom in this world has got five good cocks," Billy snorted.

"He has joined with Little Moccasin and Medicine Water. They have five. I saw them." Big Oak lowered his voice. "Old Tonk has two sons of Blackbreast ready to pit. I happen to have a very good cock myself, and my brother has one. Together, with Old Tonk, you and me and my brother could pit five against those Kiowas if we wanted to."

"We will do it," said Billy, "and Running Standing's half brother is going to have a lot of dead chickens to eat on the Fourth of July."

"The trouble," said Big Oak with a sigh, "is that he has no wagon to bring them in."

"Tell Long Neck," said Killer Cross, lifting his shoulders imperiously, "that I will send my road wagon after him and his cocks. But I won't send him home after it's all over. He won't have no birds left, anyway."

Joe's hope of becoming more deeply involved with Billy and Killer through their chickens thus came to an end. They no longer thought of him as Crosses-the-River's husband; in their minds he was Long Neck's half brother, a member of the enemy.

The Fourth of July fell on a Monday, and the day before, as Billy Cheyenne's fever rose, he told Joe bluntly to stay away from his cages. "We can't be sure you would not dope our cocks," he said.

Many Stones put a sudden end to their male bristling. "You had better go to the fields and chop weeds for a while and let yourself cool off, Billy Cheyenne."

"This is Sunday," Billy protested.

"You ain't on the Jesus Road."

The threat to use her power was ominous. Billy Cheyenne turned from the yard and went to the barn to seclude himself with his chickens.

Killer Cross muttered that ever since Running Standing had come here to live, Billy seemed to have no peace. "And I ain't got much either," he added pitifully as he went to help Billy Cheyenne.

Sara felt sorry for both of them and made up her mind to talk to Joe about the pressure he had them under. She waited until they were alone that night in the tipi, but all she achieved was a burst of rage so intense that the impending cockfight was forgotten.

"It is time," he said, "for the men in this ridiculous family to stop letting the women run their lives. Your father and brother have been stripped of their manhood by that crippled bitch."

"You must admit that she has some kind of power, Joe, or she could have no effect on them. Will you let up on them a little? Please?"

"Let up?" he shouted. "We have a chance to make a fortune and all they can think about is cockfighting. You have influence with Many Stones. If you would help me, I could get control of all this land. But suddenly, when I need you most, you act like a white woman."

"Oh!" she cried. "I am so tired of hearing everyone around here yell white man this and white woman that! We were doing well until you came."

"Do you want me to leave?"

"I want *us* to leave, Joe. And have our own lives somewhere, together."

"How long do you think your farm would last without you here to push everybody around?"

"Many Stones can keep it going."

"I wonder if I'm beginning to understand you at last, Crosses-the-River. Now that you've set up everything so that your brother and father can never be men again, you're willing to go away and leave them. Do you think you'd have a better chance to take my manhood from me if we left here? Do you want to work on me in private so I won't have the example of Killer and Billy around to show me what will happen if I'm not alert to the modern Cheyenne woman? If I leave here," he added to bombard her with a final threat, "I'll go alone."

"If you want to leave me, Joe, please go as soon as possible," she said softly.

He could not answer for a while. She was glad that finally she had met him head on, even though her heart pounded wildly.

She changed into her nightgown and lay on the bed. After a few moments her baby began crying. He cried more than most Indian babies, and this worried her. Many Stones' babies never cried.

She got up and took her son from the new bed and nursed him. Joe sat, still fully clothed, and watched.

"Do you like that baby?" he asked in a different voice.

"Of course I do."

"Don't you think I like him, too?"

"You have never said so, but you made a new bed for him."

"I like him very much and I want to make him rich. That is the way of civilization. Men work to make their families rich. I could be one of the first successful Indians in the white world, and my son could go to an Eastern academy instead of a government school and he could have the best of anything he wants. I could give it to him, if you would help me with Many Stones."

Lying very still, she said, "I will help you with my own land, but not with my family's lands. I don't trust Buck Failey, Joe."

"It isn't a matter of trust. Buck works for Roscoe on salary. He doesn't own a single share of stock in the company. I am going to give him five percent for working this out for us. He knows the corporation lawyers, and he is white."

"You need him for a front," she said, "and Mr. Roscoe needs you for a front."

"You say that as though you feel there is something wrong about everything I'm trying to do."

"You can have my land," she said quickly. "And our son's."

"But you won't help me with the others?"

"I just couldn't, Joe."

"Because you think I will lose it all to Roscoe?"

"Yes, I think that in the end you will."

He slapped her twice, once with his palm as his hand shot out and once with his knuckles as he brought it back.

She lay hard in her featherbed, her face stinging. She had no urge to cry. She felt weirdly sorry for Joe. Each day she had realized more and more the extent to which he'd been twisted by the world of whites. Running Standing, grandson of Spotted Foot, believed himself to be faced with the choice between playing pawn to a greedy white man and, worse, playing the greedy white man himself.

She closed her eyes and wondered what he would do now if he were Spotted Foot. Would he strut around the tipi and yank her up from the bed and hit her again? And maybe lop off one of her ears to make it forever clear that he had been forced to discipline her for disobedience?

She opened her eyes and saw that he was dressing again. "Are you leaving?"

He didn't answer. She remembered the day in the railroad car. Trying to talk to him would be futile. She could have no influence on what he would do when he was angry.

"You are my husband, Joe."

"Then you must do what I tell you."

Again she was silent. He glared down at her, flung open the tipi flap, and disappeared. She heard the whinny of a horse from the direction of the barn, and soon she heard hoofbeats as he rode away, fast, in the direction of Cloud Chief.

26

RAIN came down hard as Joe rode into town and the clay beneath his horse's hoofs became dangerously slippery. He reined the animal to a slower pace and slogged on; hail pelted him as he reached Cloud Chief. Shielding his face with both arms, he made for the hotel on the south side of Main Street.

It was called the Iron Hotel because its sides and roof were constructed of sheets of galvanized iron. Joe tied his reins to the hitchrail and hurried inside.

"That's coming down out there," he said, dripping in the doorway.

"Man, just listen," the clerk said.

Joe flung water from his hat. He had to raise his voice to be heard. "I'm looking for Mr. Failey. Mr. Buck Failey, from Pennsylvania."

The clerk thought about it. Joe was not sure he had heard above the noise of the hail. "I got a Mr. Failey from Muskogee, Indian Territory, that comes once in a while."

"That's the man."

"He ain't been here lately."

"He'll be here again by tomorrow. I'll take a room and wait for him."

"You're Joe Standing, ain't you?"

"Yes, that's who I am."

The clerk entered his name in the book. "Room number three, through the hall there. Key's in the door."

"I'll take my horse to the stable and be back."

"Here early for the rooster fights tomorrow, are you? Your folks' cocks against your wife's folks' cocks?' The clerk's face was spuriously solemn, barely obscuring the special grin he and every other white man had for the spectacle of Indians doing the things they enjoyed.

Joe said nothing. He went outside and stood on the porch underneath the iron overhang. Even in the dim light of the lantern in the hotel window he could see hail bounce everywhere. Presently it stopped with a suddenness that was loud. He climbed into the wet saddle and slogged down the street a block to the wagonyard, woke up the night man, got a stall for his horse, brushed it down, and watered and fed it.

The night man stood nearby, watching.

"I know who you are, I think," he said finally.

"In case you are wrong, I'll set you straight. I am Joe Standing, recently from Carlisle, Pennsylvania."

"Then I was right. You played football and everything, didn't you?"

"Yeah, I did. And now I'm in town cockfighting. My folks' cocks against my wife's folks' cocks. Isn't that right?"

" 'Pears like it," the night man said, walking away. Joe could not see whether he was grinning or not, but if he was, it was doubtless a bit twisted.

He returned through the mud to the hotel. He stomped on the porch and scraped his boots. The clerk met him at the door and said, "My name is Hobart Jenkins. No hard feelings about what I said about the cockfights, I hope."

"None at all. How are you, Hobart?"

"Just fine." Joe went past him toward the hall door. "Do you want me to hang your clothes up back there in the kitchen where they'll dry out?"

"Yes, I'd appreciate it."

"You played football against Harvard College and Yale and them places, didn't you, Joe?"

"Yes, that's right."

"Leave them outside your door in the hall. I've got to pick up another fellow's in number five directly."

While Joe slept, his clothes dried. The storm passed, and he awakened early in the morning at Hobart Jenkins' knock on his door. "Your clothes are ready, Mr. Standing."

He got up and cracked open the door.

"Delma Sue Raven Rock ironed them for you. She's an Arapaho girl that works in the kitchen. A granddaughter of Chief Little Raven, but she's civilized like you. I mean," said Hobart quickly, "that most of you-all's people is getting civilized these days." Then, embarrassed, he handed Joe the clothes. "I didn't mean nothing by that, Joe. It's just that—her in-laws is pitting some of the chickens with your in-laws today. And yet you and her has both went away to get educated. It seemed funny there for a minute, but I guess it ain't." Hobart handed Joe the clothes and pushed on down the hall to deliver number five's.

Joe dressed and went to breakfast in the little dining room that separated the lobby from the kitchen on the east side of the hotel. The waitress was a young dark-eyed Indian woman who wore a sack-style blue calico dress that came just to her knees, where it met beaded buckskin leggings that encased her legs down to her moccasins. Her hair, parted straight in the middle, hung in brightly-tied braids down in front of her shoulders.

Because she did not seem stricken with shyness, he knew that she had been to school somewhere. "Are you Delma Sue Raven Rock?" he asked. Her attitude had already told him that she knew who he was.

"Yes, I am. I went to Haskell while you and Sara were at Carlisle. We heard all about you. We wished you had been playing on the Haskell teams."

"Thanks for pressing my clothes, Delma Sue."

"You are welcome, Mr. Standing."

"You could call me Joe if you wanted to."

"Thank you, Joe." Her smile broadened. She was exceedingly attractive and younger than he had thought at first.

"Why are you wearing Indian clothes?" he asked. "You're a good-looking girl."

She glanced down at her leggings, but she was not self-conscious. Her easy manner astonished him. "It is a curious thing that here in my own country I am a colorful freak. Times change fast, don't they? The hotel wants me to wear these things. Travelers like to go home and tell about a full-

blood Indian in beaded leggings that waited on their table."
They laughed and she asked, "Did you like your eggs, Joe?"
"Yes, I did."

"Your wife is beautiful. When I have a chance I always
watch her. The way she walks and everything. And I listen
to her. I run over to Charlie's store sometimes and stand
around when she is in there. Are you in town for the chicken
fights?"

Joe grinned at her. "I understand that your in-laws have
joined forces with my in-laws to put five cocks against my
half brother's crowd from Owl Creek. Big Oak must be your
brother-in-law."

"He is. Are you going to bet on your half brother's cocks?"

"I hadn't thought much about it. Are you betting?"

"Of course not, and neither are you, Joe Standing. We can't
bet on cocks anymore." She laughed and said, "What I think,
Joe—sometimes—is that those of us that went away and got
educated have to miss a lot of the fun of being Indians. We
can't be natural anymore and join our folks' fun, and the
whites won't let us into whatever kind of fun they are having.
Had you noticed that?"

She was both merry and sad. He studied her for a moment
and asked, "How many brothers and sisters are in your
family?" If she thought the question at all strange, she did
nothing to indicate it.

"Three older brothers, and one older sister, who is Big
Oak's wife, and one younger sister."

"And you're the only one that's been educated?"

"My brothers went to reservation school."

"Do your people trust you?"

"Oh, they trust me. They just don't have any fun with me."

Joe's mind spun ahead. "How many people are in your
whole family? Sisters-in-law, brothers, babies, everybody?"

Now Delma Sue seemed puzzled. "About two dozen or so,"
she said at last.

"Two dozen allotments, all told?"

"About that. Why did you ask me?"

"Do you know what, Delma Sue? I haven't the faintest idea
why I asked you. Maybe I was just wondering how many
people there were to keep you out of their fun at home."

A little peal of laughter burst from her and she shook her
head. "Sometimes I think our education has addled us, but it

will be good for the next generation, I suppose. I have seen your son, Joe. He is beautiful."

"I don't know whether Sara is coming to town, but if she does, would you go to the fights with us?"

Delma Sue was surprised. "Do you think she would go? Everybody knows she almost killed her father last spring trying to stop him from cocking."

Delma Sue Raven Rock now laughed again, strangely, and this time the pink tip of her tongue covered her upper teeth and smothered the laugh before it was full born. She said, "My family would never believe it if they saw me there."

"Well," said Joe, "we can't stop cockfights just because we went away to school and learned how barbaric they are."

"We don't have to watch them, though," she said and turned toward the kitchen before she laughed again.

Buck Failey arrived an hour after Joe had finished eating. It was a tedious hour during which Joe added up the number of Kiowa, Comanche, Cheyenne, Arapaho, Caddo, and Wichita headrights he might eventually hope to command if he handled all his friends right. He would have to establish himself as the legal spokesman for those headrights, of course; Failey would know how to accomplish that. And before this day was over, Joe intended to count Delma Sue Raven Rock's family in the total. He intended to become very friendly with her brothers and brothers-in-law during the cockfights in the wagonyard.

Failey reached town with a drummer who peddled, among other things, fireworks that he said had been made in China. They came in a hard-topped jump-seat wagon drawn by a pair of aging roans.

"He was headed out this way from the depot," Buck said. "Cloud Chief isn't the easiest place in the world to get to. I kept thinking those fireworks would start going off in all this morning heat."

It was hot, all right. It must have been approaching a hundred degrees. "Well," Joe said, "you're here now, and listen, Buck, we're having the biggest chicken fight of the summer. You've got to learn how to take things easy when you're in Cloud Chief, Oklahoma Territory. It doesn't matter how you got here."

Buck Failey said, "You're in a better mood than when I last saw you. Making progress with Sara's family, are you?"

"No, but I have a substitute family in mind. Come on inside and I'll tell you."

He resisted an impulse to carry Failey's bag and led the way into his room. He didn't speak until the door was closed and then he kept his voice low. He might have a wrong estimate of the situation, he admitted, but he believed the Arapaho family could be persuaded because of the girl's attraction to him.

"Their land is above the bluffs on the river bend. They might open the way to a lot of Arapaho land."

"C.J. will be interested," said Failey. "I have recommended that he buy up the mineral rights to anything he can possibly get on these reservations."

"I'll need a power of attorney, won't I?"

"That's no problem. I brought forms this time. You'll need three witnesses. The lawyers want white witnesses, and I can be one of them. Charlie over at the store would be good, if we can get him. There's also an Indian Bureau man coming out here soon who's a friend of an old pal of mine back home. He'll cooperate with us. The agent here won't like it, but we'll have the powers of attorney before he knows it. What's this Charlie fellow's name?"

"Delma Sue Raven Rock will know."

They went to the kitchen and Joe called her aside. "His name is Charlie Goodsen," she said. "Joe, if your wife comes to town, I will go to the cockfights with you, if you want me to."

"Good. We will come after you, if she does."

Delma Sue laughed, suddenly very self-conscious, and said, "But you know perfectly well, Joe Standing, that educated Indians don't bet on chickens."

Out of a sense of sportsmanship, Billy Cheyenne's friend Big Oak provided a camping space on Arapaho land for fifty-seven Kiowas who came across the grass from Owl Creek. The caravan was half a mile long. Harley Wilson was agreed on by everyone as the man to drive Killer Cross's wagon. Even though he was white, you could trust him because everybody knew that the whites in town looked down on him for living in a community of Indians.

Charlie Goodsen, having purchased everything the drummer had for sale, set up a fireworks stand at the wagonyard entrance, and firecrackers began going off sporadically around town twenty minutes later. Hobart Jenkins, the hotel night clerk, didn't mind having his sleep interrupted because he had to get up anyway and help his uncle Ellick Jenkins, the wagonyard proprietor, construct the cockpit. They used boards that had been purchased to repair a row of stables. The pit was octagonally shaped and twenty feet across, its sides draped with gunnysacks.

"You're on something of a spot here today," Buck Failey said to Joe. Failey, true to his race, was letting himself be expansively amused at the spectacle of nonwhites having fun. "You'll need to get lease papers signed by people on both sides of this chicken war, and feeling is running pretty high."

"My people fight hard, make peace hard, and then play hard," Joe answered as enigmatically as he could.

A commotion at the street entrance announced the arrival of the Kiowa chickens. The crates were lashed together on Killer Cross's wagon. Harley Wilson sat in the driving chair, Long Neck in the other giving instructions, Little Moccasin and Medicine Water on the tailgate. Long Neck shouted that he didn't want anyone near his birds, then leaped from the wagon.

Joe was surprised by his half brother's appearance. Naked to the waist, with impressive hair braids, issue pants and shoes, and a knife at his belt, Long Neck was a well-fed version of the way Joe remembered their father.

"Are you Long Neck from Owl Creek?" Ellick Jenkins asked.

"I am Long Standing from Owl Creek," Long corrected.

"Pull her over there, Long. You can set your cages in the back entrance to the yard."

"My birds stay on the wagon," Long told him, "and they will be guarded every minute. I don't trust nobody in Cheyenne country."

Billy Cheyenne's voice was heard from the back of the crowd as he made his way forward. "They won't be no doped cocks here unless some dapoms I know sneak around and dope them!"

Long Neck turned, raised his shoulders high, and said, "Who is that talking back there?"

"That is me talking." Billy Cheyenne came into the open near the wagon. "I see you let your hair grow out again, and you ain't even wearing a shirt to town. Just like old Rabbit Hand used to come to town before they put him in jail for what he done to his wife's nose. You are here in a borrowed wagon, and besides that your wife is a Caddo."

"If you have got a good knife, Billy Cheyenne, you had better put it into your belt because you may need it any minute now."

Billy unbuttoned his issue shirt, revealing his knife. He folded his arms across his chest and said, "You would not be afraid to bet a horse on each cock today, winner of the odd to take all, would you? I don't guess you have got five horses."

"I will bet five horses on the odd with you. I will win in three fights and then bet ten on the next. But first I would have to see your horses. I ain't going to put up good horses against any old hides you Cheyennes might have staked out somewhere."

"I will bring five horses to the stable, Long Neck, and I want to see yours, too."

"My name is Long Standing now, and I guess you had better call me that."

Billy's shoulders rose yet higher. "I don't know why you took your brother's name. It ain't yours."

Long Neck jumped from the wagon, ducked into a crouch, and drew his knife. The crowd backed away. Billy Cheyenne removed his shirt, deliberately threw it aside, and drew his own knife.

"I'd better stop this, Buck," Joe said and hurried into what now amounted to an arena. As he stepped in front of his half brother, Killer Cross stepped in front of Billy.

Joe said, "We had better settle our differences with them in the pit, hadn't we, Long?"

Long Neck remained in his crouch for a moment and stared. "Running Standing, you growed a lot."

"Everybody calls me Joe now."

"Whose cocks are you betting on, Joe?"

"Yours, of course." A flicker of a smile touched his half brother's troubled face. "I'll help you pit them if you want me to."

Long considered for a moment. "I could use some help."

Joe grinned. "You and me together, Long. Come over here and talk to me for a while."

They moved the wagon into the back of the yard and stood aside from the crowd. Long kept looking Joe up and down, marveling, and finally he said again, "You sure growed."

"I am glad to be home, and I'm glad you are home, too."

"You made Standing a good name."

"When did you decide to use it?"

"They put us on the allotment roll and we had to have a name or they would give us one. They did that to all the Indians that didn't already have a name."

"What about Rabbit Hand?"

"He is Rabbit Standing now. Do you know what he done? He come back to Lives-in-a-Tree, so she can doctor him with her medicine oil."

"What is her name now?"

"Tree Standing."

"I hear you married a Caddo girl named Two Bonnet."

"She is Two Standing now and we have two sons. We all live together in Tree Standing's hut. She ain't got a nose but we don't care."

"I am going to see her soon."

"She is here with us, but she don't want you to see her because of her nose."

"But she doesn't mind if you see her?"

"I ain't her real son."

"Is Rabbit Standing at the camp with her?"

"Yes, over on the gyp bluffs. You gave all of us a name, Joe. Rabbit Standing is very proud."

Joe had thus established a harmony with his half brother that weeks of effort had failed to establish with his brother-in-law. "Have you got five horses?"

"Medicine Water and Little Moccasin have gone to our camp after them. They are real dapoms, but don't tell Billy Cheyenne. If you come back to Owl Creek, I ain't going to have anything to do with dapoms no more. It ain't good for our name."

"I have a plan," Joe said carefully, "that will make us all rich—if you will help me."

"I will help you all I can. You are a smart boy, Joe. You married a Jesus Cheyenne, but you can bring her to Owl Creek with you because I married a Caddo myself. We are all mixed up now. Here come the horses."

Dust rose in the road leading to town from the west. Several Kiowas, including Medicine Water and Little Moccasin, led the horses toward a small corral behind the stables. Long Standing ran to let down the gate. Then he climbed onto a barebacked pony and said, "Don't let nobody near our cages, Joe. I am going to count Billy's horses."

While he was gone, Joe stood near the tier of chicken crates. Little Moccasin and Medicine Water stood nearby to back him in case there was trouble. Everyone else kept a respectful distance. When Long returned he asked: "Where's your chickens at, Billy? I ain't going to quarrel with you anymore until after your cocks is all dead and I have got your horses and all your money. Then I aim to quarrel with you."

"My chickens will be here any minute, Long Neck, and when you are ready to quarrel with me, I will be ready."

The tension was broken when somebody set off a package of firecrackers near the cockpit. Chickens squawked and flapped against the cages and everyone jumped and then began to laugh.

27

HARLEY Wilson was chosen to referee the fights. Ellick took him aside and warned that these angry bucks were tempestuous when aroused. But Harley declared that he was not afraid of Indians; he was proud, if you wanted to know, that both sides trusted him.

At Joe's elbow, Buck Failey said in a lowered voice, "You did a good job on your brother. You can bet on his birds, and I can bet on Billy's. We'll be friends of both sides and protect each other at the same time."

Appreciating the element of immediacy in the white man's cunning, Joe laughed to cover his true feelings and thought to himself that someday he would figure out a way to tie a proper can to Buck Failey's tail. Meanwhile, he would cooperate with Buck and tie one to C. J. Roscoe's. Doing in one white man at a time wouldn't rid the earth of them, but doing in selected white men for selected reasons would be a satisfaction.

Ellick Jenkins, standing on a box in the middle of the pit, shouted: "Now, folks, I see a lot of you has brought birds today. After these fights is through, the pit will be open until dark for any hack fights that anybody wants to have. Remember now, the rule will be nobody in the pit except the referee and the handlers. All right, handlers . . . go to your birds. Harley will call the first match in twenty minutes."

Joe said to his brother, "I'm going over to offer a side bet to Billy Cheyenne."

Long Standing's high-cheeked face broke into a sensuous appreciation of such a show of faith. "Joe," he whispered, "bet all you've got, if you can get it covered. Billy's cocks is all doped." He glanced about, decided they should be alone, and took Joe around behind the stables. He explained that Big Oak had once been in prison at Fort Sill for shooting a cavalry officer. He had escaped from a work gang and Long had helped him hide out on Saddle Mountain. "Me and him set this whole thing up, Joe. That's why he come to Cloud Chief and challenged Billy for me."

"Won't Billy know his cocks are doped?"

"He can't do nothing if they're already in the pit."

"What does Big Oak get for selling his side out?"

"Two horses. Me and Medicine Water and Little Moccasin is getting the other three."

They returned to the wagonyard and Joe went past the cockpit to Billy's cages. Billy watched him approach and said with contempt: "I always knew you was nothing but a dapom."

Joe kept a straight face. "A man backs up his brother, doesn't he?"

"Do you want to bet on his chickens?"

Joe took five dollars from his pocket. "Who'll cover this on the first fight?"

The Cheyenne-Arapaho crowd probably didn't have five dollars among them. Buck Failey, standing now behind Billy, said, "If you want to lose your money, I might as well take it as anybody."

"You wouldn't want to make it five dollars a bird on the odd, would you, Buck?"

"Sure, if you'd like to."

"It's a bet. Now I'm going over to the hotel to see somebody for a moment before the first pitting."

Several Kiowas had followed to watch Joe bet. When he left, they offered bets of their own. Four bits and nickels and dimes. Cheyennes and Arapahos covered. The drummer got a three-dollar bet with Hobart Jenkins.

At the hotel Joe found his wife talking to Delma Sue Raven Rock in the dining room.

"I saw her go into Charlie's," Delma Sue explained, "and introduced myself. Since I already met you this morning, I almost feel I know you-all by now."

"How do you feel, Joe?" Sara asked.

She was a miracle of poise. The gentleness of her face betrayed no indication that he had slapped her last night. A white woman would have cared, he thought, and he wondered what marriage to a white woman would be like. If you hit one, would she forgive you immediately and expect to be hit again? An overwhelming idea about Sara reached him. No matter what he did to her, she expected to remain his squaw. That could put him in a sort of prison.

"Did you come to town for the chicken fights?" he asked. "Delma Sue will watch them if you will."

"We'll be there later. After Many Stones gets here."

"Where is my son? Isn't Many Stones keeping him?"

"Lamb Woman is minding the babies today."

"Did you walk to town?"

"Dr. Freeland came along and gave me a ride. Many Stones is walking."

"Well," said Joe coldly, "I am going back to the wagon-yard."

As he approached the street entrance to the yard, he noticed a group of whites staring toward the road that led from the east. They were watching the approach of an Indian entourage, amused, in their white way, by what they saw. Joe turned to look. Many Stones came carrying his son in a cradleboard on her back. Lamb Woman followed, leading a milk cow—across whose withers were slung two cradleboards containing Many Stones' wide-eyed twins. Behind them came Maude and Jennybelle Wilson, each carrying a bundle and a pail.

"Look at that," whispered a white woman.

Joe ducked out of sight into the yard and reached the cockpit as Harley Wilson announced the first fight.

"I want honest cocking in this pit and I don't want no trouble," Harley shouted. "Billy Cheyenne, are you ready to bill?"

"Yes," said Billy, stroking his rooster's head.

"Is that a Mug?" Harley asked.

"Purebred Mug." The chicken thrust his head from beneath Billy's hand and peered insolently about.

Harley turned to Long. "That's Roundhead, ain't he?"

Long nodded, holding out his black rooster whose eyes, like the Mug's, surveyed his scene with knowing arrogance. "He's part Roundhead and part something better, and he is ready."

"All right. Now, step up here, boys."

Long and Billy came to the center of the pit and thrust their cocks at each other. The beaks clicked. Hackles rose, wings came out, and the crowd murmured. Harley instructed them to bill again, for added agitation, and said, "Ready, now."

Billy and Long backed to opposite sides of the bunker. Each held his chicken out on the ground. "Pit!" Harley shouted.

The birds were released. Their wings came out and up. Bred only for the moment of death or victory over another male, they surged toward each other. When they were six feet apart, they took to the air and their beaks flew open. Somebody set off a firecracker that shook the wagonyard.

"God a'mighty," cried one of the Kiowas in white lingo as the birds fell in a gyrating ball of chicken wings.

"If that Mug can get loose," someone said, "he'll spar."

He got loose. As though shot from a gun, the Mug spun away, turning as he hit the ground. The Roundhead was on him instantly, and, to the crowd's disbelief, the Mug stayed on the ground.

Joe noticed his half brother's grin. The Mug sat dazed and made no move to defend himself.

"Handle!" Harley cried.

Long and Billy rushed for their birds. Billy Cheyenne held up the Mug and said, "Some son of a bitch has doped my cock."

Three Toe, Big Oak, and Old Tonk came forward quickly. Harley Wilson yelled, "Nobody in the pit except the pitters!" But he was ignored.

Big Oak sucked blood from the Mug's face. "Has he been doped?" Billy Cheyenne asked.

"Might have been," Big Oak said. "He's blind, Billy."

Little Moccasin and Medicine Water came over the barrier and stood at Long's side. "You aiming to accuse all of us?" Medicine Water asked Billy.

Harley Wilson stepped to the center and said, "Now, you boys listen. They's money been bet, and I will call a foul if everybody but the pitters don't get out of here, right now."

They knew he meant it and backed away. Grinning, Long took his place with the Roundhead as Billy Cheyenne crouched with the blind Mug.

"Pit!" Harley cried.

The Mug stayed where he was, turning instinctively toward the onrushing sound. As the Roundhead took to the air, expecting to be met head on, one wing bobbed crazily. He veered away and fell to the ground, kicking.

"That goddamn cock's been doped, too," shouted Harley Wilson. "This is the crookedest fight I ever got myself into. All bets is off!"

Long and Billy drew their knives and faced each other. But Joe quickly put his arm around his brother and pulled him toward the back entrance. "Let's go where nobody can hear us."

Buck Failey, taking his cue from Joe, led Billy Cheyenne to the other side of the pit.

Long and Joe reached the tier of cages at the rear opening and Joe said, "Keep your voice down, and tell me. How did Big Oak dope the Mug?"

"With ground-up peyote in their corn feed."

"Do you have any idea how your Roundhead got doped?"

"Little Moccasin did it, I guess."

Long explained that Little Moccasin's wife had left him several months ago and was now living with Three Toe over near Cloud Chief. She was a very pretty part-blood Kiowa, a dapom of course, or she would never have married Little Moccasin. Everybody at Owl Creek had heard the story of Three Toe giving Killer Cross all those horses for Crosses-the-River, only to back out when she proved to have all-white ways. Three Toe had hated to lose those horses almost as much as Little Moccasin hated to lose his wife. Long now believed that maybe Three Toe took Little Moccasin's wife away from him just to set up something like this.

"I know one thing," Long said, firming up his suspicion. "Little Moccasin has made at least five or six trips to Three Toe's cabin trying to get his wife to come back to him."

"What would that have to do with doping your cock?"

"If Billy's cocks beat mine, Three Toe would have some

horses again, and I imagine Little Moccasin would get back his wife."

Suddenly, warning shouts came from inside the yard. Joe and Long turned to see Billy Cheyenne facing them, fifteen paces away, with a burning Roman candle in each hand.

Both the candles went off, sending balls of fire that landed near Long's feet.

Long cursed and scurried away. Anticipating Long's movement, Billy corrected his aim. Two more balls of fire surged forward, one of them hitting Long broadside in the back.

Little Moccasin now appeared in the rear entrance, firing candles at Billy. And from farther inside, Old Tonk and Killer Cross fired at Little Moccasin. Presently half the Indians in the yard were shooting candles at each other. Somebody anchored a skyrocket in the cockpit and lit it. The rocket ricocheted off Three Toe and landed beside one of the chicken crates, setting fire to a bale of hay. Another rocket ignited the straw in one of the stables.

"The bucket line!" cried Ellick Jenkins. "Hobart, get to the pump! Stop shooting them goddamn fireworks around here!"

Joe rushed to join the brigade. Harley Wilson and Hobart Jenkins did the pumping. Buckets full of water were sent down the line, but the stable fire was out of hand in a hurry. Five stalls and a barn burned up despite the best fire-fighting efforts of the volunteers.

At last Joe stood in the street at the front entrance, realizing that Sara was beside him and that his arm was around her. It was late afternoon and their faces were scorched.

"This is terrible, Joe."

"There should never have been a chicken fight."

"I killed their chickens two or three times, and then I gave up trying to stop it."

Long said, "Hello, Crosses-the-River. You growed a lot, too, since I last seen you."

"Hello, Long Neck."

"My name is Long Standing now."

"I suppose it is," she said.

"Joe, if you want to come with me, you can see your mother and Rabbit Standing. She is ashamed of her face, but maybe she can put a coat over her head or something. I guess we'll all go on back to Owl Creek tonight, since we didn't have the cockfights. My roosters is all burned up, anyway."

Long found Little Moccasin and Medicine Water in a cluster of Kiowas near the horse trough. Joe heard him say, "Little Moccasin, me and Medicine Water need to have a talk with you."

"Do you think our cocks was doped?" Little Moccasin asked.

"It happens that I seen you throw two of them, crates and all, into that burning barn. Now, let's go to camp, and on the way maybe you can tell us what ought to happen to somebody that would dope his friends' cocks."

"Do you mean me?" Little Moccasin asked.

Not bothering to answer, Long spun him around and shoved him toward the road. Little Moccasin began running. He didn't even glance over his shoulder to see if he was being followed. Nor did he run toward the gyp bluffs. He cut across the prairie, directly toward home.

Sara stood beside Joe, watching. "What will they do when they catch him?"

"They may cut off more than his nose."

"Did he really dope their cocks?"

"I guess so. He was trying to get his wife back from Three Toe."

"Why would he want her back if she left him for another man?"

"They say he likes her. That's the kind of Indian we are growing these days."

"Little Moccasin is not growing. He is from the old way of life. Nowadays, people like you and I are growing an entirely different kind of Indian."

"We just don't know what kind yet, do we?"

She was silent for a moment, looking at him. And then she asked, "Joe, can't you do something to keep Long from hurting that man?"

"I'll try, don't worry about it. I am going to see my father and mother now. Would you like to go with me? You could leave the baby with Many Stones."

He turned toward the road. Sara followed, walking fast. Joe caught up with his half brother and asked what he would do to Little Moccasin.

"Scare him a little, I guess."

"Don't hurt him."

Long became indignant. "I won't. We had it coming to us.

We had their cocks doped, too. What they did is fair, and Little Moccasin was only trying to get his wife back."

Joe laughed loudly and said to Sara, "There you are, Crosses-the-River. In the end, us Indians are always fair."

The Kiowas on the gyp bluff broke camp even before it was completely organized. Their disappointment over the aborted cockfight was not especially keen; Owl Creek Kiowas had come to accept unfulfillment as a natural condition.

Reaching the bluff, Long ran ahead to warn Joe's mother that her famous son and his very-white Cheyenne wife were approaching.

"He must not see my face," said Lives-in-a-Tree.

"He knows you have no nose."

"I will keep my back to him," she said. "I will face the sunset and talk to him for a while."

Rabbit Hand, now fiercely sensitive to her feelings even though she was a woman, said, "Tell him that I will face the sunset with her."

"Why don't you want him to see your face?" asked Long, accustomed to puzzlement and therefore not especially surprised by anything.

"Shame is on her face and on mine, too," said Rabbit Hand. "A man does not wish to reveal shame to his son."

"I am your son, and yet you show me your face all the time."

"I did not cut off your mother's nose."

Long returned to meet Joe and Sara on the road and proudly escorted them into camp, nodding to everyone. Lives-in-a-Tree and Rabbit Hand were waiting. They sat beside each other on a stone beyond their firepit, facing the sun-streaked west. Nearby, Two Standing stood with her own small sons close at her side.

"Lives-in-a-Tree," said Joe, staring at the knot of cloth at the back of his mother's head, "it is me. Running Standing. Crosses-the-River is with me."

"I know," she answered. "You must call me Tree Standing now. All of us took your name."

"And I am Rabbit Standing," Joe's father said, sitting perfectly still beside his wife. "We have decided not to let you see our faces."

"It will be difficult to talk," said Joe, "if we can't face each other."

"We can talk," Tree Standing replied in a determined voice. Joe marveled at her curious strength—strength derived, no doubt, from the ascendancy her husband's cruelty had finally given her.

"I have come home to make us all rich." Joe glanced at Sara, whose expression did not change. "I know many powerful white people, and I know a way to make us comfortable for the rest of our lives."

"We are already rich," his mother said. "We have found medicine oil on our land. Sometimes we can get a dollar a bottle for it."

"It cures everything," Rabbit Standing said, "but I am too old to go around selling it. We need your help."

"I will help you. Leave everything to me, and I will help you." Sara's eyes were on him; her face was serene and her expression told him that she would be as loyal to him as Lives-in-a-Tree was to Rabbit Hand. It also told him that she would not try to influence her own people.

"We did not want you to see our faces," his mother said, "but if you decide to come home and help us, we will let you see them. Our shame will pain us less if you come home again."

"I will come home. And Sara Standing will come with me. Now, stop hiding yourselves."

Slowly they turned around. Above the bandage, his mother's large dark eyes swam with tears, but she did not let them roll. The beautiful young woman he remembered was miraculously still there—peering shyly from behind the badge of shame and smiling, even, through the stockade of leathery wrinkles.

Beside her, Rabbit Hand's mouth sagged partly open. He blinked against his own tears and said in broken Kiowa, "This is how white we have become." Even his own language was now confused, perhaps, Joe thought, from so many years in prison where he seldom heard Kiowa spoken. "Back in the glory days," he said, "a man would leap off this bluff before he would cry."

"We must forget the past," Joe said, despising himself for the excess of his feeling.

"Did they tell you," his mother asked, "that your small sister died?"

"Yes, they told me. And that our two old aunts died, also."

"And now so has Weasel Ear," Rabbit Standing said.

"Everybody is dead except us, and we are dying, but we can't die like we could in the glory days."

"We are so glad to have you home," said Tree Standing to her son, "that we don't even care about the glory days no more."

28

THE wretched part of moving with Sara to Owl Creek, Joe found, was the way she watched in silence whatever he did. He could not say whether she went willingly or unwillingly. She packed up their son, all their things, said quick good-byes, and followed. Her father drove them over in his wagon.

There were several unused tipis in the village because so many people had died or had gone away since the government began issuing canvas. With Long's help, Joe cut poles and established a tipi on the edge of the gully below his mother's hut. He ditched around the tipi and channeled the gully away from their clay floor. When the ditching was complete, Long offered to bring Two Standing and their sons to live down here, making room for Joe and Sara and Running Stone up in the hut. But Sara preferred privacy.

"She likes you, doesn't she, Joe?" Long asked. "Me and Two Standing both noticed it. Who is this coming up the ravine on a horse?"

It was Buck Failey, with his big bland smile of self-assurance, and a bundle of papers.

"Where can we talk, Joe?"

"In here. Long, why don't you go up to the hut and help Tree Standing bottle some medicine oil?"

Long did not mind being dismissed. There was importance attached to his new relationship with his half brother, and he would do whatever Joe wanted him to.

"Come on inside, Buck."

Failey reported that he had got Billy's mark on a lease this morning—witnessed by a Bureau official. Furthermore, he had got Billy's children's leases, with Billy as guardian, and also Killer's, Lamb Woman's, Many Stones', Three Toe's, Old Tonk's, and all the Wilsons', including the lease of that awful little girl Maude that somebody bigger than her Mama ought to spank once in a while.

Joe whistled. "How did you ever convince them?"

"I didn't. Sara convinced Many Stones before she came here with you. Many Stones asked me not to tell you."

"Why did you tell me, then?"

"Because," said Sara's voice from the darkness of a back corner of the tipi, "he does not believe that Indians are people." She rose from the rope bed where she had been lying. "And he knows there is no honor among animals. I'm sorry I overheard. I was resting for a few minutes when you came inside. I didn't intend to eavesdrop."

"You convinced her?" Joe asked.

"I only told her that I was going to sign for myself. She admires you, Joe, even though she once cut your arm."

"Did she tell you about that?"

"The day it happened."

Sara pushed beyond them and past the flap. Joe and Buck Failey followed her outside. In the light, they saw that she was in an old squaw dress, and Failey gaped.

"You're the woman I talked to when I came here for medicine oil samples."

"Me understand-em white lingo pretty good sometimes, no?" she said and went up the clay path toward the hut.

Joe laughed. Failey did not consider it an especially funny joke, but he remained in good humor. "As soon as you can get these people here lined up," he said, "I'll bring the witnesses and we will sign everybody at once."

"They're ready now."

"Then we'll do it tomorrow. Let's sit down and add up how many acres we'll have. I'm going to see the lawyer tonight at the hotel. Joe, you haven't even got a table in here."

"No, I haven't got a table," Joe said, again laughing: at what, he did not exactly know, unless there was something humorous about an Indian planning to overthrow the ownership of a petroleum corporation when he didn't even have a table to sit at while adding up his holdings.

During the next few weeks Joe's view of Buck Failey's capacity for spurious sincerity reached new heights. Every facet of Failey's plan was explained to Joe as they proceeded toward their goal, and Joe's contempt for the man grew along with his admiration for Buck's essential cunning.

Roscoe would soon arrive in Oklahoma Territory with sufficient capital to buy outright as many mineral leases as were necessary to make a lot of money if the exploratory drilling proved successful. But Roscoe was greedy, Failey pointed out, and would want to spread his cash far. He would trade stock ownership in his company for mineral rights wherever possible. And that would be his undoing.

"Won't he know how much control he is giving us?" Joe asked. "He can't be stupid or he wouldn't be rich."

"Greed often makes rich people careless," Buck replied in a manner reminiscent of Roscoe's own theatrical delivery of a truism. He pointed out, with some logic, Joe thought, that Roscoe wouldn't know one batch of Indians from another. They were putting the leases covering Joe's family's land and Sara's under his power of attorney. He would have to bargain directly with Roscoe on them. And they were setting up several lease-buying companies to control most of the other allotments Buck had acquired. Joe would control them in the background, of course, but lease-dog friends of Buck's would be dummy owners for the purpose of bargaining with Roscoe. Additionally, Buck had a few individuals waiting for Roscoe to approach personally.

"Won't he be suspicious?"

"When minerals are discovered, speculators swarm in like flies. Sometimes, even, when you think not a soul knows about it. Roscoe would be suspicious if there were no outside speculators to deal with."

"If there is real petroleum here, Buck, I want to take that bastard over. I want to be the first Indian to whip a powerful white man at his own game. It will be a kind of warfare my fighting forebears couldn't even imagine, but somehow they'll know."

"Spotted Foot will know?" Buck said. "Wherever he is in the Happy Hunting Ground, he'll know?" Failey could have been an Indian himself for all his face told you, but Joe suspected that he was secretly laughing. "Roscoe has been luckier than anybody has a right to be," he went on. "All rich men have been. To bring him down, you'll have to be luckier than he is."

"I feel lucky. If there's no oil here, I'll end up owning a

substantial piece of his company anyway. He'll need to get along with me, don't you think?"

Buck spread out his hands. "What else could he do?"

Clarissa came hooked onto a Texas-bound cattle train one day in early August and stayed several weeks. Roscoe brought with him a geologist and a lawyer, a male secretary, a notary, Buck Failey, and his man Haskins to take care of their needs. A surrey and team and three saddle horses appeared out of nowhere the day he arrived. The driver, a tall man with a very Western accent, established a temporary stable near the water tank and then drove Haskins into Cloud Chief for supplies. Word spread of the sight to be seen.

Clarissa, her golden script glistening, was the greatest curiosity since the giant windmill the railroad company constructed to pump water up into the Elk Creek tank. Many Indians had come then, from every direction, to watch the goings-on. They came again now, solemn-faced, vastly more contemptuous than any white man knew or cared—and they returned to their tipis and huts to talk about what they had seen. Roscoe, they had learned, wanted a lot of medicine oil and would pay a considerable amount of money for it. He was even going to try digging it out of the ground himself.

Buck Failey soon appeared at Joe's tipi flap. "I thought he'd never send me, Joe. He's been expecting you to come to him. I'm glad you waited him out. I know C.J. pretty well, and you've riled him up."

"Is that good or bad?"

"Good, I think."

"This is one Indian that won't look like all the others when I get through with him."

Buck grinned. "Stick to your guns. Make him come to you."

Joe had to wait another week, and then Roscoe came—in riding pants, field boots, an expensive shirt, and a big hat. He came alone. Joe and Sara watched him approach in the gully.

"So this is C. J. Roscoe," she said. "He looks sad about something."

"He knows there's some money in the world that isn't his yet. That makes a man like Roscoe very sad."

"I'll wait and meet him, and then go up to the hut. He probably won't talk about anything important until I'm gone."

She was wrong about that. Roscoe, still in the saddle,

swept off his hat, said a gracious good-morning, and surmised that the lady must be Mrs. Standing, whom he had looked forward to meeting for a long time. He did not even pause to be told that his guess was correct. Looking her over as though divining her quality, he provided his profile for them to study —the same deceptively lean face, prominent nose, and shaggy hair that Joe remembered.

"I am glad to find you together, for I have business to discuss that concerns you both. The essential nature of it you are familiar with, of course. After we have completed our business, which will take a few days, I imagine, I hope you will come aboard *Clarissa* for dinner one evening."

His remark sounded more in the nature of an amenity than an actual invitation.

Amazed that this man could have provided not only the setting for her son's conception but his name as well, Sara said, "Could I give you some tea or coffee, Mr. Roscoe?"

"Nothing, thank you, my dear Sara. Joseph, let me proceed quickly to the point of my visit. As you know, a stitch in time saves nine. Many of your people have leased me their mineral rights for exploratory purposes. Since you have not, I assume you have prudent reasons for making me come to you. If so, it only proves the soundness of my earlier judgments about you, and I am highly pleased. I would give a great deal to have you back in my organization."

"Well . . ." said Joe, but that was all Roscoe wanted to hear at the moment.

"I suppose that you will by now have realized that my remarks to you in New York City about the growing importance of petroleum were not idle. I am prepared to offer you a generous royalty on everything developed on your lands and your families' lands"—he glanced at Sara—"in return for the drilling and production rights to whatever oil I can find."

Joe nodded. "I have the power of attorney for my entire family, Mr. Roscoe, and for my wife's family, also."

"That is wise. I much prefer to deal with them through you. As I once told you, I would not like to run the risk of seeming to take advantage of people whose values and interests are so different from my own. Have all your papers been witnessed, Joseph? If not, I would like to assist you in putting them into proper order."

"They have been witnessed, Mr. Roscoe. By an agent of the Bureau."

"Good, good. If that is so, then I need to talk only to you."
He glanced at Sara, silently dismissing her.

She was glad to go. "If you will excuse me now, Mr. Roscoe, I will leave you together."

Still astraddle his horse, and looking ridiculous, Joe thought, he bowed.

As she went up the clay path toward Tree Standing's hut, she heard Roscoe ask to see Tree Standing's medicine oil spring. Joe's answer was a blunt refusal, but that was all she could hear. She stayed in the doorway and watched below. Roscoe did not dismount, but he talked animatedly with Joe for half an hour. Tree Standing said in Kiowa: "Why don't you sit down and have a pipe with me, Crosses-the-River?"

"I will sit, but I do not care for a pipe."

Two Standing sat on the floor and smoked one of her mother-in-law's pipes and nursed her tinier son. Rabbit Standing sat in another corner on a slab of log. Presently he got up, went to the door, peered down the incline for a while, and then returned to his seat. "Why doesn't that man get off his horse?"

"He wants my medicine oil but he won't get it," Tree Standing said, as though that explained why he stayed on his horse.

"White men get whatever they want," Rabbit Standing warned.

"This one won't. Running Standing promised me."

Sara prayed that Joe would be able to keep his promise.

Roscoe finally left, with a grand bow, and Joe came toward the hut. She ran to meet him. He put his arm around her and together they went up the incline. "I'm going to take stock shares in his company instead of cash for the leases. Buck is right, Sara. He's a greedy man."

In the hut he explained to everybody that soon some very strange machinery would be brought to the prairie, but the medicine oil spring in the gully beneath the hut would not be touched.

Sara noticed that every time Joe looked at his mother she turned away. She could never be comfortable facing her son without a nose. For Lives-in-a-Tree was awed by Joe. She not only loved and respected him; she feared him, and would probably not object in the end, Sara thought, if he should lose her spring. For a Kiowa woman—especially a noseless one—

had no right to expect anything of a Kiowa man she loved
and feared . . . even if the man were her son.

Excitement over the oil well overshadowed everything else
on the prairie. Roscoe's invitation to dinner aboard *Clarissa*
did not come, and one day in early October the car disappeared. Buck Failey returned between Thanksgiving and
Christmas to report that detailed plans for drilling were
rapidly shaping up. It was only a matter of time until the
action would begin.

Twenty-one wagonloads of pipes, machinery, derrick lumber, and wood for firing the boilers arrived during February.
A crew of workmen, a chuck wagon, and a cook arrived early
in March. Roscoe's drilling engineer, Sara noticed, was the
man called Frank—Frank Holloman—whom she had first
seen the day Buck Failey came for medicine oil samples. He
chose a drilling site directly toward Owl Creek from Tree
Standing's medicine oil spring, at a point where the prairie
had barely flattened out above the bank of the stream.

Indians lined up every day across the creek to watch. All
of them had financial interest in the unfathomable proceed-
ings. Roscoe had acquired mineral leases from everyone in the
village except the blind Grandmother Keeper, who could not
be persuaded to make his mark for a white man, and Little
Moccasin, who hadn't been seen since they caught him doping
cocks on the Fourth of July.

"If I knew where to find Little Moccasin," Long said, "I
would tell him to come home and sign up so he could get
rich with the rest of us."

"He got his wife back and they ran off together," Medicine
Water said. "Old Tonk told me."

"Was you in Cloud Chief?" Long asked.

"Yes, just the other day."

"Did you see Billy Cheyenne over there? Because I am
looking for him."

"He is looking for you, too. At least that is what I heard
in the new wagonyard."

"One of these days I am going to kill him."

"You aren't going to kill anybody," Joe told him. "I have
been listening to you, and I think you ought to forget all
about Billy Cheyenne."

"Billy ought to forget about me," Long replied with a grunt.

He straightened himself to his full height, his manner suggesting that a man could grow weary of looking up to his younger brother. The oil well had produced tensions in everyone.

The boiler was steaming now and the hoist in the derrick's crown had lifted the pipe into position. The members of the drilling crew began shouting to each other in new voices, their animation conveying something to the Indians on the bank. It was the beginning of the spudding-in operation, as the driller called it: the first moment of actual drilling.

Hissing steam with its magical pressure turned the small wheel on the engine shaft. The long belt turned the big wheel near the wellhead. The walking beam, attached by a swiveling pitmans rod to the big wheel and stretched across a fulcrum called the Samson post, raised and lowered the cable bearing the heavy bit. The bit was soon into rock, slowly pounding its way into the hole.

Earth tremors raced along the bank. Aghast, the older Indians swept back into their tipis. When the tremors continued, many of them sought solace from the Grandmother Keeper who, as frightened as anyone but loath to admit that he no longer had much faith in the powers of the Grandmother, prayed more or less constantly—whether offerings were left at his flap or not. He didn't pray for the discovery of oil—he had no conception of that phenomenon—but for deliverance of his people from whatever it was that could shake the earth.

Whatever it was yielded nothing in Owl Creek that summer. The old Keeper's prayer seemed to have been answered when the drilling ceased.

"We're shutting down temporarily," Frank Holloman said. "Mr. Roscoe is on his way here."

"How does it look?" Joe asked.

"We're deeper than Spindletop now, without the slightest show. I'd have bet my last dollar against a dry hole here."

A week later, C. J. Roscoe shook his fist and said, "I *am* going to bet my last dollar!"

He had brought two new geologists with him—a Texan intimately acquainted with South Texas oil from the first discovery at Spindletop six years earlier, and an old-timer who had been through it all at Oil Creek, Pennsylvania.

"There is no reason to believe, Mr. Roscoe," said the

Texan, "that the formations here are similar to those on the coast."

"Nor is there any reason to believe that noseless witch's medicine spring comes out of nowhere," was Roscoe's exasperated retort. "It doesn't take a goddamn geologist to see that oil is in the goddamn ground around here some goddamn place, does it?"

Joe was too concerned with the failure of the well to appreciate the spectacle of Roscoe with less than complete control of himself.

"I want to examine that medicine oil spring," the Pennsylvanian said. "We found a hundred seepings along Oil Creek in the early days. Some as far up as New York State."

"Come on," said Joe, and he led them up the ravine below Tree Standing's hut.

As they neared the spring, a shot rang out and lead ricocheted off the sandstone side of the gully. Carbine in hand, Tree Standing stood on the shelf above them. She shouted in understandable white lingo: "Get away from there! Nobody is allowed near my medicine oil!"

"Go inside and put that gun away," Joe shouted back.

The old woman raised the gun to her shoulder. "I will shoot anybody that lifts my lid!"

"Then shoot." Joe stepped up to the spring trap, pushed aside the tumbleweed camouflage, and removed the wooden lid. A bullet splintered through the lid as he held it up.

He whirled quickly. His mother still held the carbine on him. Before he could say anything, she put another shot through the lid near his hand.

"I'm coming after you, old woman!" he shouted. And he scrambled up the incline on all fours while she got off two wild shots at Roscoe and the geologists. He reached her on the ledge outside her hut and took the gun away from her.

"That was my last bullet," she said, her eyes fiery above her bandage.

"They aren't going to hurt your spring. The man from Pennsylvania only wants to look at it."

"I am going to buy myself a better gun," she said.

"Now, you come inside and calm down."

He led her into the hut. The entire family sat in the darkened room, on chairs and benches and on the floor. They had been watching, of course. Rabbit Standing said, "We don't like what you are doing."

"All of you stay in here and behave yourselves," he told them. "I'm going back down there with Mr. Roscoe, and I don't want any more foolishness."

Sara said, "You promised your mother not to tamper with the spring."

"Looking at it is not tampering with it. These men are scientists and they need information. Now I want all of you to stop acting like a bunch of Indians."

He grinned at Sara and hurried down the incline.

The two geologists stood over the oily spring and talked about buried salt domes and structural traps and pore spaces. They argued about sandstone, shale, and rimrock faults, and finally returned to the drilling site to examine again the cutting samples the driller had collected from the bailer.

"Note," argued the Pennsylvanian, "that the seepage is on the other side of the ravine. If that gully is a structural fault, then we could expect the pore spaces on the other side of it to be draining into the underground spring. My guess is that the pool is shallow. This hole is not only in the wrong place, it is much too deep."

"All this voodoo talk of geology!" Roscoe said. "I don't understand why we haven't been drilling right into the mouth of that spring. We can see oil there. A bird in the hand has always been worth two in the bush."

"Can't drill into the spring, Mr. Roscoe," Joe reminded him. "It's in the contract. My mother would not have signed otherwise."

"In business, contracts are made to be changed."

"Mr. Roscoe," said the Texan, "I, too, believe this hole is on the wrong side of the fault. But I don't think the oil is leaking out of a shallow pool. It is coming up from pressure —tremendous pressure—enough in all probability to blow a flimsy derrick off the ground. I saw what happened in Spindletop. But I go along with my colleague from Pennsylvania on the location. I believe our pool is on the other side of the fault."

"How deep?" Roscoe asked with a glazed look.

"Very deep. Maybe two thousand feet. You'll need a steel derrick, anchored in concrete, and I would recommend a rotary rig. Cable strings are all right for shallow wells, but I can't advise you to begin another hole unless you are prepared to go deep."

Roscoe glared at him. "To be penny wise and pound foolish

is not my penchant, sir." He walked away and communed with himself for several moments. Then, without turning his body, he looked back over his shoulder. "I will have to raise more money. Select a site across the ravine, if you can agree on one. I must go to New York City. Failey will return with instructions within a month. Meanwhile, begin excavating for a concrete base. Holloman, can you run a rotary outfit?"

"Yes, sir."

"I'll check up on you. If I find that you've had successful rotary experience, you can drill a new well here. If you're not telling me the truth, I'll hire another driller. No offense intended. I have no reason to disbelieve you."

Frank Holloman smiled hugely. "I'll begin setting up, Mr. Roscoe. Meanwhile, it wouldn't cost much to go a little deeper here."

"He who chases two rabbits catches neither, Holloman." Roscoe strode summarily toward his horse. He mounted and galloped toward Elk Creek where his private railroad car waited on the siding near the water tank.

29

FAILEY arrived in exactly a month to report that Roscoe had raised the money for a rotary well.

"He said he'd bet his last dollar, and he's doing it. He mortgaged everything to an investment house and even sold *Clarissa*. A rotary string is on its way up from Texas by freight train—an outfit that'll dig three thousand feet if necessary. He means business."

"Wow," Joe said. "You know, Buck, I'm beginning to admire him again."

"C.J. is a son of a bitch," said Buck Failey, "but somehow we have to respect him for it, don't we?"

The day the new rig arrived, Joe and Long went to Elk Creek to watch the unloading. Sara and Two Standing left

their children in .the hut with Tree Standing and spent the
morning along Owl Creek gathering plums. Sara had learned
by now that Long's wife was permanently primitive. Unlike
Many Stones, who had shown imagination and a fiery spirit
from the beginning, Two Standing, forever dissembling, spoke
only when spoken to, and softly. She was a slim and willowy
woman. Her eyes were deep in a dark countenance and they
moved slowly, as did her entire body, never darting. She
seemed not to resent her husband's constant reminder that a
nonfighting tribe of mixed-bloods had produced her. She
moved about day after day in contented silence—nursing her
babies, cutting wood, cooking, and keeping order in her
mother-in-law's house.

On this morning, they emerged from the creek bend below
the Kiowa village and heard a clatter of buggy wheels. Wills
Freeland drew up and waited for them to reach the road.

"Wills," Sara cried, "you shaved off your whiskers."

He removed his hat. His unruly hair was shaggy on the
back of his head and his bare face glistened. "Makes me look
younger, doesn't it? Sara, I have some information you'll want
to know about. Can I see you alone?"

"You can say whatever you wish in front of Two Standing.
She won't understand very much."

Wills told her that the agent had been out from Anadarko
making inquiry about the details of all the Indian leases now
in the possession of Roscoe Petroleum Company. There was
talk that a group of congressmen and several representatives
of the Indian Bureau were coming in a few days to investigate
the need for greater protection of Indian rights in business
deals.

"I have heard," she said, "that there is a plan afoot to
assign us guardians."

"It might be a good idea."

"Especially for politically connected white lawyers. They
could make a lot of money by *protecting* us into doing whatever they want us to."

He paused for a moment, saw that she was hostile to this
point of view, and then told her something else. C. J. Roscoe
had pledged all the assets of his company as collateral for
extensive loans. If the new well was a failure, Roscoe Petroleum would be bankrupt.

"I would be very happy to see him bankrupt," she said.
"We could then forget about oil and go back to developing

our farms. All we'd lose would be rights to nonexistent minerals and dreams of wealth and white-man glory."

"The company that loaned him money is called Interstate Investments Trust Company. Mr. Roscoe is one of its principal stockholders. Does that mean anything to you?"

She stood silently trying to grasp it. Wills was telling her something she needed to listen to. There was no doubt about it. She felt stupid.

He said, "I have been over to Elk Creek. Joe refused to talk to me. You must tell him that Roscoe has used one of his own companies to loan money to Roscoe Petroleum. I am sure Joe doesn't know that."

"Does Buck Failey know it?" Meaning was coming through to her now.

"Failey is also a stockholder in Interstate Investments. He is working for Roscoe, not Joe." Wills returned his hat to his head. "Tell Joe I investigated because they tried to buy my mineral rights, too. I went to Philadelphia and looked up some old friends of my father's. One of them is a lawyer who knows people in New York City. I went there, too. And I found out about Interstate Investments. Roscoe is a ruthless man. I hope you can persuade Joe to come and see me very soon. If the new well is dry, Roscoe Petroleum will go bankrupt and Interstate Investments will have everything. If oil is found later, in other locations, Roscoe will have it all."

Wills then nodded, tipped his hat, flicked the reins sharply, and drove away. Sara stood beside the road wondering whether Joe would hit her for lying when she told him.

Supper with his family up at the hut was always an ordeal, but Sara never objected openly because Joe loved being their hero. Tonight, as Long listened, smiling and filling in an irrelevant detail or two, Joe told about the machinery that had been unloaded onto wagons at Elk Creek that day, and he reminded them that he had kept his promise. There would be no drilling into the medicine oil spring.

Finally he teased his mother about having missed him with the old carbine. He offered to buy her a new one and teach her to shoot straight. The noseless woman puffed on her pipe and laughed. Sara noticed that she did not turn her face away from him as they talked. Her attempt to kill him had got something out of her system, and she was relaxed.

Sara wrapped Running Stone in his blanket, the preliminary

motion for going to her own tipi. To her surprise, Joe reached
for the baby.

"Let me carry him."

It was an expansive gesture. She knew that Joe felt good.
In the tipi she fumbled for a match and lighted the lamp.
Running Stone was asleep in Joe's arms. She put him to bed
and, with her back to Joe as she undressed, she told him about
Wills Freeland's morning visit.

He did not hit her. He laughed instead—good humor
seemed to command him completely—and reached for her,
drawing her alongside him on the bed, and made love to her
with a bursting energy. Finally he said, "Crosses-the-River,
don't listen to that doctor. He's trying to provoke me into
doing something rash. Maybe into killing somebody. He'd
like to see me in prison, or shot by the marshal. Then he
could have you."

Joe lay quietly for a while, and she lay beside him, wondering if he could possibly believe what he had just said. And
wondering, too, if he could possibly be right.

"Sara, did you know that the white sons of bitches all look
at you in a certain way, wherever we are? There isn't a one
of them that doesn't get a lust when he looks at you. It's
true of Many Stones, too. Did you know that some of you
Indian women look pretty good to those buggers?"

He seemed to wait for an answer and she said, "You called
me both Sara and Crosses-the-River."

"Sometimes I think of you as Indian and sometimes as
white. Do you ever forget that you're not white?"

"No, never."

"Sometimes I do. When I'm around Buck Failey. I have
to give him credit for that." He rolled over in bed and laughed
again. "Imagine that doctor trying to get at you by making
me kill a white man."

Joe then talked expansively about his observations of the
white man's sex life. The whites were afraid of their women,
he said. Even the tough ones who pushed women around were
afraid that getting into bed with a woman was something that
could be taken away from them. "Did you know that they go
and pay money sometimes for sex?"

"Yes, they told us about it at Carlisle. In the girls' health
class."

He was silent for a while and then he rolled to her and
made love again with a new intensity, and she wondered

whether, at the moment, she was Sara or Crosses-the-River
and decided that she was Sara, his white woman, who could
take sex away from him, and that he was afraid.

30

NEITHER of them thought to blow out the lamp. October
breezes pushing underneath the canvas moved upward
inside the tipi. He lay beside her in the flickering silence,
wondering if he had got her pregnant again and whether she
cared, hoping she cared and that he had, and yet hoping he
had not. What was the point of one more Indian?

Why, for that matter, had she not become pregnant again
before now? Had that doctor given her something? Did Wills
Freeland know more about his wife than he knew?

He tried to concentrate on the doctor, to take him apart
and analyze him bit by bit. He wanted to despise—and to
enjoy despising in carefully reasoned detail—every aspect of
Freeland that could be isolated. It was easy, and cleansing,
to hate Wills Freeland, for the simple reason that Sara loved
the man. The white part of her loved him; the Indian part
of her could never love a white man, of course, and that, Joe
knew, was her pain.

She had taken the Jesus Road instinctively as a child. Once
on it, did a Jesus Road victim travel through hell all his
life on the way to heaven? And was it conversely true that
Indians, free from the tortures of white acquisitiveness, spent
their lives traveling through heaven on the way to hell? The
thought was satisfying, but it was a white thought and he
decided that he did not like it.

Slowly, from wherever truth comes, he knew that he was
fooling himself, that only the top of his mind was thinking
about the doctor from Cloud Chief. Every deep part of him
was raging at Buck Failey. For he was certain that Freeland
was right, that Sara had told him the truth, and that Buck was
double-crossing him.

It was not Freeland he needed to talk to, it was Roscoe's

boy, Failey. He needed to get Failey alone for a few minutes —very alone—and beat the truth out of him if he had to.

Joe eased out of bed, standing still for a moment to be certain that Sara remained asleep. He picked up his clothes from his footlocker, blew out the lamp, and pushed quietly through the flap. The moon was rising. He sat on a log and put on his clothes. He turned toward the tipi, to give himself a final chance to change his mind about whatever he was on the verge of doing to Buck Failey. Then he found himself headed down the trail toward the gully where Long kept the ponies. He saddled one and then seemed not to want to ride to Cloud Chief. He wanted to run. As he had run years ago with produce his mothers had raised for trading at Charlie Goodsen's store. As he had run the day he first saw Crosses-the-River at her father's watermelon stand near the bend of the Washita. He left the saddled pony in the corral and headed for the grass, elbows against his sides, fists clenched and raised, strides long and easy, anticipating distance. She had been so pretty that day, in a yellow buckskin dress and chinaberry beads. He wondered where the purple beads were now.

He reached Cloud Chief without altering his pace, satisfied to know that he still had wind. At the edge of town he began walking, quietly, past the wagonyard and livery. A horse whinnied, but there was no other noise until he neared the Iron Hotel. A watchdog barked in the store next door. Soon the storekeeper appeared at the front—and so did Hobart Jenkins, the hotel night clerk.

"What is it?" Hobart called, crossing the porch.

"I don't see anything," said the other man, carrying a shotgun.

Joe slipped to the hotel door, let himself quietly through, and tiptoed up the stairs without being seen. The dog downstairs still barked.

Failey usually stayed in number six. Joe knocked quickly, and then again, hoping to get an answer before the commotion below was quieted.

"Buck, are you in there?"

He heard a grunt and the squeak of bedsprings as Buck got up, heard fumbling for matches and the lighting of the lamp, heard Buck's footsteps . . . and then the door opened.

Buck stood there in his nightshirt, squinting. "What is it, Joe?"

Joe went inside and closed the door, deciding to get a nightshirt of his own, and then despising himself for the impulse to imitate a white man. Hobart Jenkins' voice came up the stairs.

"Who's that up there? Anybody?"

Joe motioned for silence. Hobart's footsteps came into the hall, then slowly went down again. He would soon be asleep at his desk once more.

Buck said, "Are you in trouble, Joe?"

"I just killed Roscoe."

"*Killed* him?" Buck was wide awake now. "Where?"

Joe thought fast, absorbing with surprise the lie he had just told. All the way across the prairie he had tried to plan an attack on Failey, a strategy, but cunning was not in him. He could only improvise.

"Out by the medicine oil spring. He slipped back there with his geologists to get more samples."

"And you killed him for that?"

"No, for something else. That was the first chance I had. Buck, he's been framing us. You told me that he mortgaged all the leases to Interstate Investments."

"That's right. He raised every cent he could for the rotary outfit."

"I discovered that he also owns Interstate Investments."

Even in the lamplight, Buck's face went pale. Something sucked in his face, leaving his skin not only pale but crinkled, as though in the instant of that remark he had aged ten years.

"Are you sure, Joe? How did you discover that?"

"I've had somebody investigating him. In New York City."

Buck made a noiseless whistle. "Jesus Christ, Joe. You've got to do something. Get away from here. Can you hide some place?"

"I'm going to turn myself in. I wanted to tell you first."

"They'd swing you, Joe. Killing a prominent man like that —who saw you do it? Those two geologists?"

"They don't know why I did it. I have a good excuse. I heard a prowler at the spring. Yelled but he wouldn't stop. Fired a shot and got him. Right at the base of the neck, by God." Joe watched Buck closely. The man was thinking fast —the way big, blond, crooked white men always thought fast.

"Joe, listen to me. A white court, white jury . . . everything would be against you."

"You'd testify that he was a friend of mine, wouldn't you, Buck? Terrible accident. Too bad and everything, but that's all there is to it. With you in my corner—good friend of both of us, the grand jury probably wouldn't even indict me."

"You know I'd do anything at all." Now he was talking fast, letting his mind run far ahead. "Joe . . . I'm afraid of it. The way you gobbled up control of all your friends' and relatives' mineral rights. They'd make it look as though you wanted to do Roscoe in. You were planning to ruin him eventually. It would all come out."

"Whatever I've done has been for all my people. And nobody knows about it except you and me."

"Joe, did the geologists keep going, or—?"

"They came back after him. Five minutes after I shot. They had a lantern. Must have had a buggy nearby. I hid near the creek and watched them. That Pennsylvania fellow said the bullet hit the bottom of old C.J.'s neck. Broke his spine, I guess. You know how the Pennsylvanian talks, with that Dutch accent."

"Where could we go, right now? The two of us, until we have had time to figure this out. You can turn yourself in tomorrow as easily as tonight."

"Maybe it would look better, more honest, like an accident, if I turned myself in right now."

"Joe," Failey began again, and this time Joe whirled on him.

"You want me to swing, don't you? If I run, they'll gun me down, or bring me back and then I'll swing for sure. You know that, Buck. Why are you trying to get me to run?"

"Really, Joe, I—"

"Listen, you white son of a bitch. I found out something else about Interstate Investments." He waited, watching Buck, but Failey had become cautious. "I discovered that you are part owner of that big finance company. Part owner along with Roscoe. You've been double dealing me ever since the first time I laid eyes on you at Carlisle. You've been setting me up and I am going to beat the liver and lights out of you, right now, right here in this room. You better listen to me. I'll give you ten seconds to start telling everything you've been doing behind my back, and if I think you have told me the truth, the whole truth, I'll only bust your face. But if I think you have held back anything, I'll break your

white Jesus Road neck and leave you here as dead as I shot
C. J. Roscoe tonight."

"Joe, I swear to God you're wrong."

Joe swung as hard as he could. The blow felt as though it
began somehow in his heels, ran up and out his arm like
lightning, and exploded in the general vicinity of Failey's
nose. The man went back as though flung by a cyclone. And
the base of his neck, ironically the very anatomical spot Joe
claimed he'd shot Roscoe in, smashed into a pointed brass
finial on the footpiece of the bedstead and was impaled there
momentarily before the limp largeness of his body pulled it,
gushing blood, to the hotel floor, with no more than a gentle
thump.

Joe looked down, hoped the man was dead, knew he'd
better leave as quickly as possible, unlocked the window,
eased it up—and then had an idea. He turned back to the
bureau and opened all the drawers, tumbling all of Failey's
clothes into disarray. To further the appearance of a hurriedly
ransacked room, he upended the suitcase and emptied the
briefcase onto the floor. Then he crawled outside the window,
swung for a moment on the sill, and dropped to the ground,
remembering how he used to land at the end of a pole vault
at school. But there was no spaded pit with sand and straw
in it here. The impact of the hard clay stunned him for
several moments. But he'd been quiet about it; at least, the
watchdog around front remained silent.

He rubbed circulation back into his ankles and knees, got
up slowly, tried them, found that they worked, moved through
the moon shadows to the street, hurried out of town and ran
across the grass all the way home.

At the tipi he stopped, sat on the log where he had dressed,
got his breath and cooled off, removed his clothes and shoes
again, crept to the flap, listened to Sara's breathing, laid his
clothes and shoes on the footlocker, eased himself into bed
beside her, closed his eyes—and saw Buck Failey impaled on
the brass finial and didn't care.

When daylight came Sara waked first. She watched him
until he opened his eyes. She searched his eyes for daylight
signs of fear and decided that she might have been wrong
last night . . . that Joe might not be afraid of anything.

And then she got up and discovered his clothes on the
footlocker, still damp and smelling of perspiration. He took

them from her, mumbled uneasily about the heavy dew these past few mornings, and spread them outside on the log.

"Where were you, Joe?" she asked. He pretended not to hear. She looked at him again for any sign of fear, and this time she saw it. Not a cowering fear that spreads through the shadows of a relationship, but fear that reveals itself in the form of impotent bluster, as the puff adder strikes because it has no other defense against its enemies.

"You were somewhere," she said. "Your clothes did not get this wet from dew."

"Where is my breakfast, Crosses-the-River?"

She stopped questioning him and built a fire outside the tipi at her cooking tripod. He ate voraciously, scarcely glancing at her as she changed and fed the baby.

Long came down the incline from the hut and paused to pass a few words. He noticed the clothes spread out and asked about them. Joe ignored his questions and said, "Are you going to watch the oil well today?"

"Later. Now I'm going to Cloud Chief to buy some tobacco."

"I haven't been to Cloud Chief lately."

"Come with me. If I should happen to see Billy Cheyenne, I might try to kill him unless someone is there to stop me."

"We don't want any killing around here," Joe said.

When they reached the corral, Long discovered that one of his ponies was already saddled. "But he ain't been rode, Joe."

"All kinds of people wandering around these days, I guess," Joe said, and Long shrugged, satisfied at least for the moment.

31

WHILE Long and Joe were riding across the grass to Cloud Chief, Wills Freeland drove out on the Owl Creek road to tell them what Hobart Jenkins had discovered when he went to investigate why Buck Failey had not come down to breakfast as usual that morning. Wills had been called to the hotel immediately and it was his medical opinion that Failey had been killed around midnight.

"Where is Joe?" he asked so suddenly that Sara thought he was trying to take her by surprise.

"He went with Long to Cloud Chief, half an hour ago."

"I didn't meet them on the road."

"They often ride across the grass."

"Sara, I hope he was here all night."

"He was," she said.

Joe's clothes were still spread out on the log. Wills glanced at them but said nothing.

"Do they have any idea who killed Mr. Failey?" Sara asked.

"I must confess that you don't seem surprised to hear that he is dead."

Terrified that whatever she said might be the wrong thing, she admitted that she had never liked the man, wouldn't pretend that she had, but was truly sorry when anybody died. And she added compulsively, "Joe was with me. All night. Right here in bed . . . and I will swear to it."

Wills nodded and turned to his buggy. "Tell him to come to me, Sara, if he is in any trouble."

Cloud Chief was swimming in its first sensational mystery. Heretofore the killings had all been done in the open—in the street or the saloon or the wagonyard.

"We heard something around midnight," Hobart Jenkins told the marshal. "Me and Barton Light. That's the man with the store next door. Well, Barton, he keeps a watchdog in there, and the dog barked a right smart around midnight and once I thought I heard somebody on the stairs, but I never seen a soul. That dadgum killer must of been lurking around right then, and that's what that son-of-a-gun old dog must of heard."

Joe and Long stood in front of the hotel, listening to the group gathered around the marshal. Apparently there was not a single clue.

Noticing Joe, Hobart Jenkins said, "There's Joe Standing right over there, marshal." Apparently everybody had already told the marshal that Joe was Failey's best friend in the vicinity of Cloud Chief.

T. Rowley Duggan, the marshal, was known familiarly throughout the western end of the Territory as T. Rowley— some people didn't even know his last name was Duggan. He was a wiry man with a square gray mustache, dark heavy eyebrows, and shaggy hair. He wore a vest with a badge on it winter and summer. During winter, regardless of the cold, he kept his coat open enough to display the badge. He'd killed several bad men. People respected him.

"Howdy, Joe. I have heard a lot about you. I am Marshal T. Rowley Duggan. We ain't met before, I don't guess."

"Pleased to meet you, Marshal," Joe said as the knot of men automatically opened up a passageway for him to approach the hotel porch.

"Looks like a good friend of yours has been killed."

Joe stared steadily at the marshal and said, "I just heard about it. I don't suppose there is any mistake about it, is there?"

"No, he's dead. Doc Freeland examined the body."

"I mean about the identity."

"I already identified him," said Hobart Jenkins. "It's Buck Failey, all right. I heard this noise and—"

"Might be a good idea to have another identification," the marshal said. "Come over to the funeral parlor with me, Joe, and let's make sure."

The marshal seemed honestly to believe there was merit in having a known personal friend of the deceased view the body before it was buried. Gravediggers were already at work in the cemetery and the undertaker, who was also the local hardware merchant and laid out bodies in the corner of his storage room in the rear of the store, was already making a pine box. The hammer could be heard from where they were standing.

"If you think it's necessary, Marshal," Joe said. "I'm pretty shaken by this. I can't imagine that anybody had anything against Buck."

"Did he have any quarrels lately that you knew about? I was hoping maybe you could give me some names to look into."

"I can give you the names, Marshal," said Hobart Jenkins, "of everybody that ever came to see Mr. Failey at the hotel."

"You do that," said the marshal. "While Joe and me are viewing the body, you make up a list and write it down on a piece of paper, Hobart. Think hard, now, and put down every name you can." Everybody except Hobart was amused at the marshal's manner of pushing him aside. Hobart's mind was already at work on the list.

Joe and the marshal fell into step together and the crowd

followed across the street toward the hardware store. Joe noticed at one moment that they were walking in perfect cadence with the hammering and he deliberately broke the step.

"The two mainest things about murder," said the marshal, "is that in the first place, you don't get very many of them that ain't solved before you reach the scene. And in the second place, a man's wife or his partner or his best friend ain't always the least likely suspects, even though folks generally think so. Enemies don't tend to kill one another, did you know that?"

"I guess I hadn't thought much about things like that, Marshal."

"Well, there's no reason you should. In my line of work, of course, we think about things like that all the time. When a bunch of law marshals gets together, that's just about the only sort of thing we talk about. Most people don't realize that there ain't much passion in being enemies. Passion comes between lovers and friends. Something goes terribly wrong between them, and you have got what I call negative passion. And that's what opens up the instinct to kill. Everybody on earth has the instinct, but something has got to open it up. It's just my own opinion, of course—but it's based on considerable experience—that negative passion is what opens it up ninety to a hundred percent of the time. Who else was this Mr. Failey's good friends around here, Joe? Besides you?"

"Well . . . I'll have to think about that."

"You are probably still a little bit stunned. I'll give you time to think, and then I want you to make up a list, too. Put everybody on it that you would say was a good friend of the deceased and you will have my word, as a lawman with a reputation he is jealous of, that every last person on the list had better have a good alibi for where he was about midnight last night."

The crowd muttered and nodded. T. Rowley was not letting them down. One good thing about him was that he did not try to work in secret. He went about his business right out in the open where everyone could see.

Otto Finlater, the undertaker-hardware dealer, a heavy, hard-eating man who had recently come to Oklahoma Territory from Tennessee, said: "I've examined your corpse, Marshal, and mind you I ain't no doctor. Any postmortem that I can give you is just one man's opinion, but I believe the blow in his face killed him, even though Doc says the place on the back of his head is what done it."

"You are entitled to your opinion, Otto," said the marshal noncommittally.

"Because that face is sure bashed in. Let me tell you that man could've been hit with a singletree."

"Otto, you're acquainted with Joe Standing here, aren't you?"

"Howdy, Joe. I've knowed who you was ever since you came here to live with your wife. You done real good up there in Pennsylvania, boy. You have been a credit to your race, and don't let nobody tell you different."

Joe said, "Howdy, Otto."

"You and Failey was good friends, wasn't you?" Otto Finlater did not ask the question with any hint of suspicion. His bulbous face bore a constant sincerity, whether selling nails, conducting a funeral, or passing the plate at church. Neither subtlety nor the capacity for insinuation was in him.

"Yes, we were friends, and I've come to identify him. I won't deny that I'm hoping there has been a mistake in identity. I didn't even know that Buck was back in Cloud Chief, and usually I know."

"There's no mistake, if you allow that one side of his face don't look very much like him anymore. When I was a boy I seen another white corpse with a face just like it one time, back in Tennessee—my daddy was an undertaker before me —and that one was hit with a singletree, which is why I thought of it in connection with this case, Marshal."

Otto drew back a canvas and exposed Failey's body, lying on some heavy boards that were stretched across sawhorses. Joe approached the body, stared down at the crumpled structure of bone and jellied flesh beneath its black-and-blue, formerly white, skin covering—glad, still glad, he'd done it.

"It's Buck," he said.

"Now, Marshal," said Otto Finlater, "you notice the massive coloration on the left side of the face from the nose across to the ear. You can always see more in a white corpse. A black man or an Indian don't color up like that when the flesh is bruised."

"Nice observing," said the marshal with a straight face. "We know now that the victim was a white man. I must get along, Otto. If you think of any more interesting aspects to

this case, I want you to make a list to show me when I have
a little more time."

"Sure, Marshal, be glad to."

T. Rowley Duggan swung toward the door, motioning for
Joe to follow him. The crowd of onlookers, all the way inside,
parted again to make a passageway.

"I believe," said a tall skinny man to a short fat man among
the spectators, "that T. Rowley is already on to something.
Did you notice him keeping a straight face?"

"I sure did," the short fat man replied. "If he's as good as
they say, he's on to something."

Three Indians huddled nearby—an Arapaho, a Delaware,
and a Tonkawa. They looked at each other and said nothing.

"Now, folks," said the marshal when he reached the center
of the street, "I have got some talking to do that needs to
be private. I want you-all to go wherever you would be if I
wasn't here on a murder case. I appreciate all of you-all's
interest and help, and if anybody has any suggestions, I wish
you'd write them down on a piece of paper for me to look into
as soon as I can."

Nobody moved for a moment. Then a few started backing
away, others followed, and presently Joe was alone with the
marshal in the middle of the street.

"Them's good folks," T. Rowley said. "All of Oklahoma is
full of good folks nowadays. They's good Indians here now,
too . . . folks like yours, Joe, and your wife's. I can remember
when there wasn't a Kiowa or a Cheyenne in the world that
it was safe to be around. I believe you're a Kiowa married
to a Cheyenne, ain't you?"

"Do you have any ideas yet, Marshal? About my friend?"

"Yes, by golly, Joe, I believe I have got my first idea, but
it ain't clear. Sometimes they clear up and sometimes they
don't. You was his friend, so I would like to ask if you have
got any suggestions where I should start looking? Or maybe
you are still too stunned to think about it."

"I feel pretty bad, I'll admit."

"Then let's have a quiet ride out to your place together
and not even talk about it. We'll leave our minds open for
ideas. The mistake sometimes, on a law matter, is not leaving
the mind open enough for anything to get into it."

Stunned to find himself so suddenly under scrutiny, Joe
entirely forgot that he had come to town with Long. He
found himself instead riding over the grass with T. Rowley

Duggan, a federal marshal legendary in his own lifetime for always getting his man.

The pattern of T. Rowley's investigation took shape on that first visit to Owl Creek. Always sociable, pleased to meet everybody wherever he went, forever confiding his technique and philosophy as he probed, he gave the surface impression that the last person he might suspect was Failey's good friend, Joe Standing. Yet, at the most disarming moments, he would return to his basic belief that murder tended to be the province of lovers and friends. And, above all, he kept coming back to Owl Creek.

"Take a bank or a train robbery," he said one day while Joe was showing him around the drilling site of Standing No. 2, "and somebody gets killed. It's murder, of course, but it's the direct-fear type. Your robber-killer fears getting caught in the act, or he tries to strike fear into those that might get testy and resist his heist. That sort of direct-fear killing is a by-product of the other action, and the lawman thinks about it differently."

He waited for a response, his gray eyes narrowing into little searchlights beneath the bushy brows.

"That stands to reason," Joe said, determined to hold a rein on his rising anger. "I don't suppose there was any evidence that Failey was robbed, was there?"

T. Rowley's square little mustache twitched. "Yes, there was. I have sealed off that room, and I go in there every once in a while to see if I have overlooked anything important. Lots of people was in and out before I arrived on the scene, but Hobart tells me he was careful from the first moment he saw the body on the floor, because all the bureau drawers was ransacked. Hobart ain't as stupid as he looks. He cautioned everyone not to move a thing until the law got there."

Joe felt a cascade of relief until the marshal went on: "But it never did look like an honest direct-fear robbery-killing to me. Things was throwed all over, not just moved around like a robber would do it. Somebody was trying to make it look like a robbery, but he didn't stop to put himself into a robber's frame of mind. I say 'he' although, as a lawman, I know that a woman might have done it. Negative passion comes naturally to women."

"I doubt if any woman could swing a singletree that hard."

"It wasn't done with no singletree. The undertaker has not

got his mind open. He heard about a singletree killing one time and it closed his mind forever. Have you ever noticed that undertakers tend to have closed minds?"

"No, I haven't."

"It's the sort of thing that a lawman would notice more than a layman would."

"I doubt if anybody would carry a singletree up into a hotel room, anyway."

T. Rowley agreed. "What I think is that messing up the bureau drawers and the papers was a case of direct-fear action *after* a negative-passion murder. Do you suppose your good wife could give us a cup of coffee? It's a right chilly day."

Joe realized that he would probably have to kill T. Rowley. He would not do it, of course, until he made absolutely certain the marshal was closing in on him. T. Rowley was an interesting man. Killing him would be too bad; but he was white, so it wouldn't be a shame.

"She'd give us some coffee, I imagine, Mr. Rowley."

"The surname is Duggan." T. Rowley grinned with every feature of his face except those hateful eyes. And he went on genially: "But I ain't offended that you forgot. You are most likely still a little bit stunned. Your friend has only been dead four days. A person in my business has to take into consideration that suspects are generally apt to be a bit stunned for a while. You know of course that you are automatically a suspect, being a friend of the deceased. No personal offense intended, mind."

Joe nodded and began searching for a plan. If they were alone right now, and not in the presence of the drilling crew, how would he do it? This marshal was clever and no doubt resourceful. Joe measured the man tactically and found himself facing a poised officer whose feet were planted firmly apart, whose coat was open, whose badge was shining, and whose pistol grip seemed to reach from the left side of his belt buckle toward his dangling but poised right hand. The man's entire posture said that he employed the cross-draw technique of gun fighting and there was no doubt about it: T. Rowley Duggan was already prepared for attack.

"Maybe my good wife will also give us some sweet cake," Joe said.

He waved good-bye to the drilling crew and led the way toward the eroded gully above the creek. At several points he paused, trying to get the marshal around in front of him, but

T. Rowley Duggan always stayed behind, adroitly maneuvering Joe back into the lead.

As they approached the tipi at the foot of the clay incline, Sara stood before the flap nursing her baby. Seeing Joe and the marshal, she slipped discreetly inside to finish her task. It was the white in her, Joe thought, to fuss with modesty.

"This is T. Rowley out here with me," he called. "We want some coffee."

"I saw you coming, Joe. I'll be out in a minute."

Joe raked back the ashes and built a cooking fire. The marshal's mustache twitched. He watched in silence and Joe's troubled mind leaped to the conclusion that T. Rowley was amused at the spectacle of an Indian doing women's work.

Angered—perhaps to his own peril, he realized—Joe straightened up and stood before the marshal, towering over him. "There's a look on your face," he said. "I believe you are laughing at me."

T. Rowley automatically assumed the stance that readied him for action. "Nobody is laughing, Joe, except in your imagination. As a lawman, however, imaginary things always interest me."

"Is that so? I would assume that a law officer would not be interested in anything but facts."

The marshal said genially, "Looking into killings takes a lot of imagination. Your public imagines things—you're on the stage, you know, and the public is your audience. And of course your suspects imagine all sorts of things."

Sara came outside the flap. "Do you consider my husband a suspect, Marshal?"

T. Rowley Duggan spread his hands. "No offense intended, but every known friend of the deceased has got to be a suspect until the crime is solved."

"My husband was with me that night, right here in bed, all night."

"My problem, Mrs. Standing, is that you are his wife and any suspect's wife is apt to give him an alibi. Now—purely as a part of routine, mind—I would like your help in finding another element to his alibi. Somebody else that knew he was here. Did you folks have any visitors that night?"

"No, and there is nothing unusual in a husband and wife being alone at home with their child."

Sara's anger was white-hot but her control of it was perfect. Proud of her, Joe said, "Put the coffeepot on now, will you? The marshal wants to get going. He has many more suspects to look into, haven't you, Marshal?"

T. Rowley ignored him and said, "You mentioned imaginary things—do you know what I have been imagining? An Indian—not real, but made up just to fit this killing. Want to hear about him?"

"Not particularly," Sara said, "unless you have a reason to believe it was an Indian and not a white man."

"I am purely convinced that an Indian done it, so I made up one that fits into what I know in order to study him."

Sara could not resist a note of sarcasm. "It's the sort of things Indians do, isn't it, Mr. Rowley?"

"The surname is Duggan." Keeping his right hand poised near the butt of his left-side pistol, T. Rowley lifted his left hand and removed his hat in a courtly manner. "Ma'am, don't jump to no conclusions about my conclusions, please. Now, I don't want to rile you, but you had better listen to me. If the Indians that live around the scene of a killing are pretty sure that a white man done it, they always tell everything they know and often a whole lot more. If they are pretty sure that an Indian done it, they won't say nothing. I speak a little bit of Kiowa, Cheyenne, and Arapaho, even a smatter of Comanche, and I'm as good on signs as you'll find these days. But I can't get a word out of any Indian about this case. That means they know—or they are pretty sure—that an Indian done it." T. Rowley returned his hat to his head. "Would you like for me to describe what I know about him?"

"We'd just as soon you'd leave here, Marshal," Joe said quickly, knowing in his heart that if T. Rowley Duggan once turned his back, there'd be a killing on the prairie more intentional than the one in the Iron Hotel.

"The man I am looking for," the marshal went on, his voice as gentle as his eyes were hard, "knows that I am closing in on him. Being a negative-passion killer, he is in what us lawmen call his post-crime panic period. That means he is apt to indulge in one fear act after another, on account of what he already done and is about to be caught for. His first fear act was to tumble up that room. I imagine that when I find him, he is going to claim he didn't know that room was tumbled up. By the way, Joe . . . up to now, you are the only man I have talked to that claims he didn't know Failey's room was tumbled, and I am looking for somebody else that don't know it."

"I didn't say that."

"You asked me if there was any evidence of robbery at the scene. Ain't that the same as saying you didn't know it?"

Joe stood silently, his gaze dropping to the marshal's poised right hand, then lifting to meet the man's eyes head on.

"You had better go, Marshal."

"No, I had not better do no such of a thing, Joe, because I am here as your friend today, besides being here as a marshal of the law court, and I still ain't had my coffee that I came for. I wish you would give it to me, Mrs. Standing, and let me tell you about how I sometimes go visiting my suspects as a friend instead of as a lawman, especially if I like them. Don't forget that a lawman is also part plain ordinary man that has feelings and likes coffee and bleeds if you cut him." T. Rowley smiled, this time even with his eyes.

Struggling not to tremble, Sara set a pot of coffee water to boiling on the fire. As she worked, the marshal talked on about the imaginary Indian he was looking for. Unless he missed his guess, Failey's death was an accident resulting from a fist fight. Accidental homicide after a quarrel was a vastly lesser crime than robbery and murder. Doc Freeland would testify that the brass finial on the bedstead had been the direct cause of death, and no judge or jury would ever believe anybody threw the bed at the deceased. T. Rowley himself would testify that the tumbled room had all the earmarks of a fear act and did not appear to be the result of robbery.

He moved to the other side of the fire so they could both see him and said, "If I can talk my Indian into turning himself in, they would give him two or three years—maybe no more than a suspended sentence, if he was a good Indian with a good reputation. On the other hand, if he don't come out of his panic period pretty soon, he is liable to commit any number of fear acts that could get him in a lot worse trouble, and I hope he don't. Some lawmen wouldn't care, because the more crime, the better their business is, but them lawmen ain't worthy of their badges. I am passing the word in the hope my man will volunteer to face the lesser charge. Because if he goes on a rampage, some of them other type of lawmen is bound to be brought into this case with me and they like to shoot down their criminal sometimes, especially if he is Indian."

Sara dumped coffee into the pot and set it back on the coals to simmer. Afraid to speak, she went inside, returned with cups, and poured before the coffee was completely brewed. "We haven't got any cream today, Mr. Rowley."

"Duggan," the marshal said. "I generally like cream with breakfast coffee, but later in the day, especially if it's chilly out, I take it black." He blew steam from the rim of his cup—which he held in his left hand—and sipped.

"Marshal," said Joe, "my wife and I will be glad to pass your word along. Maybe your man will hear it and come in. Where would he find you if he decided to?"

"At the Iron Hotel. If I was out at the moment—and I would be, because I am hot on this man's trail, gathering evidence—he could wait there in the lobby until I got back. I would appreciate you good folks helping me. You are very respected Indians. Being graduates of Carlisle—and just about everybody has heard of Joe Standing in football and track—you folks are truly a credit to your race. I can tell you that all the white folks in the country believe you are good Indians, and that would include the federal court judge that I work for."

Wishing desperately that he would leave before agitating Joe further, Sara emptied her cup onto the ground and said, "This is terrible coffee, Marshal. I must apologize. Please don't think you have to drink it if you don't want to."

"It's very good coffee, ma'am, but I had better get going after my man. In my line of work, you need to stop once in a while and let ideas come into the mind. But if you sit around too long, your man sometimes gets a big start and ideas won't hardly do you no good even if they come."

T. Rowley set his cup on the log, turned away toward his horse, and after four steps turned back suddenly—his right hand still casually poised. He smiled, tipped his hat with his left hand, said: "It is purely a lawman's habit that I have got into, always suddenly looking to see if anything is going on behind me. No offense intended," got on his horse, looked back again, and rode away fast.

32

ALTHOUGH Joe admitted nothing to his wife and family, everybody discussed what he should do, always carefully referring to him as the man the marshal was after.

"He will stay hid out and T. Rowley won't ever catch him," Long repeated over and over, his smile huge and satisfying, his respect for Joe at its peak. "Because that's one smart Indian he's looking for, ain't he, Joe?"

Sara urged him, when they were alone, to take the marshal's advice and turn himself in. Tree Standing, black eyes blazing above her bandage, suggested that if she had a new rifle, no lawman in the world could get near her hut alive. Rabbit Standing, nursing his memory of prison years, counseled against anybody admitting anything to anybody, ever. Two Standing remained silent but her peace-loving instincts were all toward cooperating with the law, an attitude her husband could only attribute to her Caddo blood.

"When I saw that saddled-up pony," Long remarked to Joe, "I knowed something had happened that night." He was proud to believe that his illustrious half brother had killed a prominent white man.

Joe seemed, Sara thought, to ignore all of them. When alone with her, he talked only to himself.

"An Indian hasn't got a chance in the white courts," he said aloud at the tipi flap, pacing before the cooking fire. "They don't think anything about giving an Indian ten years for nothing. Look at Rabbit Hand. All those years in prison and he didn't even break the law. He had a right to cut off her nose. If he'd been rich, the whites would have left him alone. A rich Indian could turn himself in and get out of it, but a poor one would go to jail."

Sara watched him, and they both listened to the grinding sounds of the rotary rig at work up on the other side of the cleft.

They could not actually see the rig from either Lives-in-a-Tree's hut or their own tipi base at the foot of the incline, but their need for riches had brought the clanking sounds closer each day. And the clanking, as the drill bit reached toward its destination, inevitably brought C. Jeremy Roscoe to the prairie.

Roscoe came with his two geologists one morning in November. An Owl Creek Kiowa saw him and told Long, who was whittling with Medicine Water near the Grandmother Keeper's tipi.

"The big white man with the big boots and two more white men with big boots have come again to the big medicine hole."

Long knew immediately who it was and ran to tell Joe. "They say two men are with him." And Joe hurried to the rig, where Roscoe's greeting took the form of mutual condolence for the loss of their good friend.

"Joseph," he began, holding onto Joe's hand, "I give you my word, I shall see that justice is done. The cruel murder of Buck Failey will be avenged. Somehow I am going to have that killer tracked down if it takes every last dollar I've got. Which may not be much," he added, mixing his grammar uncharacteristically and landing two emotional blows on Joe at once. "According to my drilling engineer," he went on, removing his hat with a certain reverence, "we are on the verge of bankruptcy. We are in a sorry situation, my boy." His lips trembled.

Joe stood, aghast and tired, watching Roscoe, listening to the incredible words . . . searching for meaning. Roscoe on the prairie beside a saddle horse seemed, despite his theatrical bluster, much less formidable than he had seemed while commanding a railroad car or pompously parading in the paneled office in New York City. Here, in knee-high grass beneath an endless sky that white men had not yet come to understand they did not and would never own, he was no more than a greedy clown—a clown, withal, whose contempt oozed through the surface concerns of the moment and spread into every crevice of his stocky face. Joe looked at his hair, long, wavy, gray, shaggy at the neck, curling at the ears, and imagined it suspended high on a stick in a dance around some Kiowa fire of the past . . . a scalp lock with which a brave warrior could proudly count coup.

"You are smiling, Joseph. Does it entertain you to be told that our company faces bankruptcy?"

"I was thinking of something very funny, C.J., but I didn't quite realize that I was smiling."

It was the first time he had ever addressed the man by his initials, and Roscoe stiffened perceptibly. "Perhaps you'd like to share the joke with me."

"My elders used to tell stories, when I was a boy, about the old glory days when they danced around fires waving scalp locks. They counted coup against each other and had a good time."

"Counted what, Joseph?"

"They told one another of their exploits, the way your friends sit around sometimes and talk about their killings on the stock market. They showed each other their evidence when they could. The scalp of a white soldier or, better yet, a blond woman, proved one's bravery and daring. You have probably never heard of my grandfather, Spotted Foot. For years he went into battle with a white woman's scalp lock attached to his shield."

C. J. Roscoe's lips became both heavier and darker. He put his hat back on and said in a quavering voice, "I have come here to investigate the death of a friend. Now I am told by Mr. Holloman that I may soon be presiding over the demise of my company. You will understand, I'm sure, if I seem puzzled to find a major stockholder amusing himself with antic thoughts about the customs of his ancestors."

Joe understood that Roscoe had read beyond his words and was frightened. To test it, he took a casual step forward. Roscoe instantly backed three steps away. Joe grinned, hating the man as he had never hated anyone, including the late Buck Failey.

"What about our company, C.J.?"

"It is proper for you to think of Roscoe Petroleum as *our* company, Joseph. A corporate business belongs to its stockholders, and certainly not to its management. I am aware of the extent of your stock interest, naturally, and have been profoundly impressed by the investment courage you have shown. Against the urgings of many of your people, you have—"

"*What* about our company, C.J.?"

"We are on the verge of bankruptcy, my boy. It is as simple and as terrible as that. Holloman can find no hopeful sign of oil in the drill cuttings. It appears that we have gambled and lost."

Roscoe waited for the impact of his pronouncement to sink in, and then assumed a gentle and paternal voice. "Joseph . . . in business these things happen. This is not the first time I've gambled and lost, but it is probably the first time you have. I've always managed to come back, and I'll come back again. When I do, there'll be a place for you in my organization if you want it. Right now the Oklahoma and Indian Territories are being combined into a new state. There's a great opportunity—"

"For an educated Indian who'd like to be your lackey for the rest of his life."

Instinctively, Roscoe backed away and shouted for his geologists, who were at the derrick with Frank Holloman. They came on the run—the Pennsylvanian and the Texan— and described, at Roscoe's request, the discouraging picture.

They were nearly as deep as they could go. Three thousand feet. There was no salt dome here, the Texan insisted; neither the cuttings from the hole nor the general terrain resembled anything he had seen on the Texas-Louisiana coast. Joe tried to remember what this man had said before the second drilling location had been selected and could not.

The Pennsylvanian agreed that their hole was dry but adamantly insisted that the seepings on Oil Creek in his native state had resembled this one here in the Kiowa land. They had made an unlucky guess as to where to drill.

Which was now academic, Roscoe added, inching himself, Joe noticed, ever closer to his two geologists, remaining as wary in his own way as had T. Rowley Duggan.

Joe said, "If these gentlemen don't mind, C.J., I would like to talk to you alone."

"They're privileged employees, Joseph. You're perfectly free to discuss anything pertaining to company business in their presence."

"I want to talk to you alone."

"That would serve no useful purpose."

"Are you afraid of me, C.J.?"

"Fatuity doesn't become you, Joseph."

"I don't know what that means."

"I respect a man who doesn't try to bluff his way through moments of ignorance. It means that I consider it ridiculous of you to ask if I'm afraid. Of course I'm not afraid." Roscoe then deliberately plunged further into the subject and asked with surprising bravado: "Why on earth would you think I might be?"

"I happen to know that you own a major interest in the investment company that put up the drilling money for this well. I imagine your lawyers have everything prepared for you to squeeze me and my people out. If I were in your shoes, I would not want to be alone with a man that knew I was cheating him out of his mineral rights."

"It pleases me," the white man said with unbelievable arrogance, "to discover at each new juncture in our association that you are every bit the man I thought you were in the beginning. I like the forthright manner with which you have approached this difficult aspect of our gamble."

Roscoe paused and Joe glanced at the men around him. Both geologists stood with their coats open, pistol butts showing. Joe could not remember guns during their previous visits here.

The truth of his predicament seized Joe in its jaws, shook him mightily, and swallowed. These men were as one against him, had always been . . . and would always be. And behind them were the courts and the Congress—white judges, white lawmen—united in the proposition that white men had inalienable rights to acquire by cunning or force whatever they coveted.

Roscoe said, "Joseph, I won't pretend that this is an unpleasant moment for me. I always find satisfaction in winning a contest. You've been a competitor of a different sort. From your athletic days, you know what it means to win. Don't deceive yourself, my boy . . . I'm not a pirate who preys on innocents. If you think of yourself as an innocent victim, self-pity will destroy you."

"Go on, Roscoe."

"I admire the resourcefulness with which you made plans to wrest my company from me. I know exactly how many shares of stock you command. If you'd managed to defeat me, I'd have shaken your hand and offered genuine congratulations. If you're the man I believe you to be, you will in exactly the same spirit offer congratulations to me. How about it?"

Incredibly, Roscoe extended his hand and took a step forward. For reasons he could not begin to understand—and could never have explained to Spotted Foot—Joe found himself, dazed, extending his own hand. And they shook, sealing yet another unfathomable agreement between an Indian and a white man.

"I'd have gambled that you'd take it this way," said Roscoe with a new note of gravity. "I'm seldom wrong about people. I don't mean to brag, but I seem to have inherited the capacity to judge people with considerable accuracy. It is intuition rather than reason."

"Then I am to understand, Mr. Roscoe"—Joe deeply offended himself by calling the man *mister* and could not comprehend why he had done it—"that your investment company will take over the assets of your petroleum company and all the stock shares of Roscoe Petroleum will be worthless?"

Roscoe's nod was solemn. "But you're more fortunate than you can understand at the moment. You'll find, if our association continues as I hope it will, that I don't carry grudges. We can have a rewarding future together. Come to the hotel this evening and I'll tell you about it."

"Why not tell me now?"

"It would be better if you had a few hours to absorb the shock of learning that our drilling venture has been unsuccessful. I expect to be in Cloud Chief for several days. Come tomorrow if you don't feel like coming tonight. I'll describe the place awaiting you in Interstate Investments." He paused and his eyes, not unlike pistol barrels, took steady aim at Joe. "I also want to hear any ideas you may have about the tragic death of our friend. I promise you, Joseph, that the man who killed Buck Failey is going to pay the supreme penalty unless he is shrewd . . . very shrewd indeed."

Joe spent the rest of the afternoon alone on the bank of Owl Creek below the village. He sat on the sandstone ledge where he had once ached to roll Crosses-the-River on the ground.

He thought of Pole Bean, Round Face Woman, and Carrot Nose who had lured him ever closer to the mission school. He remembered the night Chief Killer had prayed Sky-Walker to death, thus putting more Kiowas on the Jesus Road than Pole Bean had imagined possible.

He stared down at the water, following a leaf in the current. The leaf moved lazily across pools and swiftly through little eddies, obeying whatever pressure the stream held. It occurred to him that he had not been exactly like the leaf. He had resisted at times, and not always feebly. He had plotted against one grasping white man and had killed another. The killing had been accidental, but the white dominion now held that the man he'd plotted against in business would swallow him up and use him . . . or have him hunted down as a killer. For there was no doubt in Joe's mind that Roscoe, like everybody else, knew him to be T. Rowley's Indian.

At dusk he went to Long's corral, saddled a pony, and rode to the hotel in Cloud Chief. Roscoe, with his entourage, was still in the dining room. Delma Sue Raven Rock met Joe at the door.

"Mr. Roscoe said you might come this evening. He is waiting for you, and T. Rowley is at the table with him. I hope the Indian T. Rowley is looking for does not give himself up."

Joe smiled hugely at her. "Delma Sue, if T. Rowley's man is smart, they'll never catch him."

"I hope and pray that he is smart," she said.

Joe wondered, as he approached Roscoe's table, whether after all these years he could turn himself back into an Indian. And what the reaction of these white men would be if they suddenly found themselves talking to some old Kiowa whose hatred of them was pure because he desired nothing of them except their early demise.

"I'm pleased that you could join us," said Roscoe genially. "I understand that you've already met Marshal Duggan. You know everybody else, of course." Everybody else consisted of his secretary, his driller, and his two geologists. "Will you have something to eat, Joseph? This nice young Arapaho girl could work a miracle in the kitchen if we asked her to, I'm sure."

"Some coffee would be enough," Joe said.

"How about some whiskey?" asked one of the geologists. "It's against the rules for Indians, but we could give Joe some, couldn't we, Mr. Roscoe?"

Roscoe's manner maintained its highest geniality. "I've known Joseph rather well for quite some time and I am certain he never takes spirits. Nor do I, as you know. You gentlemen are welcome to imbibe, of course." With which he ordered a bottle of whiskey to the table.

Then, to Joe's astonishment, Roscoe openly outlined the future of Joseph Standing as he saw it. He made no attempt to hide the fact that he had squeezed the Indians out of their mineral rights. He put a different face on it, however. He described the contest for control that Joe had waged, remarked respectfully on Joe's adroit maneuvering, complimented himself for having spotted these attributes in Joe long before their contest here began, and described the urgent need in business for men of Joe's initiative and intellect.

"There's an old saying that beauty is as beauty does," he added, "that is equally true of courage and leadership. I was able to defeat this young man only because of my greater financial resources. The reason I want him in my organization again is the way he took it. He understood that business is business and offered me his hand. Some day he'll be the Western representative of Interstate Investments, or perhaps even a vice-president."

"I'll drink to that," said the Texan and lifted his glass with the driller and the Pennsylvanian. No one else was drinking.

Roscoe talked expansively for a while, entertaining his guests with stories of his many successes, topping his own arrogance at last by explaining the role he intended to play in a forthcoming congressional investigation of the Indian problem as related to petroleum exploration. Two very good friends of his—congressmen from the East, fine sensible men —were on their way here to make a study and recommend that the government provide a guardian system of some kind to protect Indian rights.

"If Joseph's people had had such protection, he wouldn't have been able to take their lease rights and squander them in an attempt to corner control of my company. This is not to demean you, Joseph, but the fact does remain that many people have suffered losses they'd have been spared if a system of adequate guardianship had been in effect. After you've been trained in law and business, you'll be in a position to do a great deal for your people. Until then, it is obvious that their respect for your limited education places their interests in peril. For you are, as we know and appreciate, a very aggressive young man."

"I'd like to suggest, Mr. Roscoe," said the geologist from Pennsylvania, "that Joe might want to leave with me tomorrow for the East. I'm going by way of the Texas oil coast. We'd have several days together and I could explain to him many aspects of mineral exploration. By the time we reached New York, he'd have a much better background with which to apprentice in the law. I can already see that Joe is cut out for the law, so I won't try to persuade him into a professional career in geology."

"I hope you won't do that," said C. J. Roscoe, "because I've wanted Joseph to become one of my lawyers for a long time."

"Then it's settled?" the Pennsylvanian asked. "We'll leave together tomorrow? You can send for your wife and family after you are established, Joe." He smiled knowingly and added, "I'm familiar with Mr. Roscoe's policy on that sort of thing. He never likes to separate a man from his family any longer than absolutely necessary."

All eyes at the table swung down hard on Joe. Before he could even begin to react, Roscoe said, "There is one small complication to be overcome. As it happens, Joseph is technically a suspect in the death of our good friend. Perhaps the marshal would permit him to leave the jurisdiction, however, if I personally vouched for his return in case he is needed here. Would that be possible, Mr. Duggan?"

"I think it would be all right," T. Rowley Duggan said, and Joe's eyes searched the man and drew out of him the truth. He'd been paid off, or somehow intimidated, and was no longer the man of strength Joe had come to respect and even fear. "Yes," the marshal said, not looking at Joe, "he can leave my jurisdiction. As long as he's working for you, Mr. Roscoe, I'll know where he is."

Roscoe nodded and smiled, remarking casually that Joseph would want to talk this over with his wife. Sara was a fine girl. She'd want to cooperate in every way. Roscoe was sure she would.

33

I N his tipi bed that night, Joe lay beside Sara and pondered her silence. Because she was not asleep, she had to be thinking about something. He wondered whether Rabbit Hand had ever worried about what his wives were thinking . . . or Satanta or Big Bow or Spotted Foot? With several wives in your tipi the tendency to concentrate on one woman and be controlled by your desire to look good to her would be less acute. Perhaps the white man's monogamy, enmeshing him in his woman's desires, robbed him of manhood and thereby made him mean. Why else would his life be devoted to making a profit on others? Why else would acquisition, regardless of honor, be his lifetime symbol of success?

"Joe," she said, startling him, "you are very still, and yet your heart is pounding faster than usual."

"How do you know?"

"When I lie close to you, I can always feel your heart beat. Tell me what you're struggling with."

Angered, and wishing to pain her into silence, he said, "I was just thinking that monogamy has ruined me."

"Do you feel ruined?"

"You've made me white. If I had several women, you could never have done that."

"Many tribes were monogamous but they didn't turn white because of it. The changing world is turning all of us white."

"My ancestors weren't monogamous and neither were yours. We're living together unnaturally."

"Do you wish you had other women?"

"I wish I wanted to."

"I'm terribly glad you don't."

"Naturally. You've always been a white Indian."

"Are you sorry you married me, Joe?"

"No, I'm only sorry that we're the way we are. I've become so white I hate myself."

"Why do you?"

"I have used my people. Trying to make a profit."

"You were trying to make a profit for everyone."

"They trusted my wisdom, and now they have lost their petroleum rights to a scheming white man. Sara, I killed Buck Failey."

"No," she said quickly, "the man T. Rowley is looking for did it, and T. Rowley will never find him."

"I've been planning to kill T. Rowley, too. Did you know that?"

"Yes, and so does he. I've prayed that you won't. You'll be hunted down and shot if you kill a U.S. marshal."

"Sara, don't talk to me for a while. Everything you think and say and do is white. I would rather be dead with honor than alive and greedy."

Whatever she was about to say next, she thought better of it and remained silent.

Neither of them slept. He listened to the pulse beat in his ear against his pillow and marveled that it had become appreciably slower. No Indian would ever settle his pulses by talking to his squaw.

At last he abandoned any hope of sleep. He got up, lit a lamp, and reached for his clothes.

"Joe, where are you going?"

"To the creek. Lying beside a woman, a man can't think. He can only scheme. I have some things to think about and I want to be alone."

Outside, the air was cold. He wished for the great coat of buffalo hide that he remembered old Sky-Walker used to wear. And for the knee-length beaver-skin leggings with the fur warm against his legs.

He walked down the gully, took the path to the creek, sat again on the sandstone ledge, and found that sitting there in agony did not help him at all. "What can ever help me?" he said aloud, and immediately, as though in cosmic answer to his cry, a screech owl wailed nearby. The Indian in him shivered, awestricken. The white part of him laughed at the Indian part, and the Indian part lifted its shoulders, threw out its chest, folded its arms, and stared in stony defiance.

He stood aside and looked at the two people he was—and pondered the spectacle of a boy, ambitious to become his village's owl prophet, growing instead into a white man's puppet. For he knew—the screech owl told him, certainly— that he would have to do C. J. Roscoe's bidding or die. The government people, the Indian Bureau men and the congressmen, would gather with the business men and the cattlemen and agree on a system of guardianship that would forever deepen the Indian's despair.

The owl screeched again and he walked toward it, mesmerized to think of himself as part owl, capable of flight, a winged man-creature cannily endowed with wisdom. The owl moved upstream. Slowly, silently, he followed, glimpsing the owl occasionally in the moon-brightened tops of leafless trees.

Daybreak found him at the edge of the tipi village. Two Kiowa women were at the creek, one standing on the bank, the other naked in the cold flowing water. The woman on the bank was a medicine woman; the other was cleansing herself of childbirth stains, making her body fit to return to her husband's tipi.

A new umbilical cord, he knew, would now be hanging outside the Keeper's tipi, to indicate, if it remained intact and dried into a sinewy string, that the new baby would lead an honorable life, or to foreshadow, if it disintegrated, fatal weaknesses.

He said nothing as he passed, but felt the women's scorn. His eyes had looked upon an unclean state, telling the women that his own umbilical had no doubt fallen apart before he had even begun to grow.

He went up the bank and through the village to the Keeper's tipi where the umbilical, black with drying blood, hung from a string attached to a forked stick in the ground. He summoned his best Kiowa and said at the flap, "I am Running Standing. I have come to see you."

The old Keeper peered out as though he could see and asked, "Have you brought an offering, Running Standing?"

Joe gave him whatever coins he had in his pocket and they were eagerly received.

"Come inside and talk to me, my son. Maybe you will build up my fire. I am so old now that I feel the cold long before winter begins."

There were fire logs and cedar knots and remnants of kindling in a pile near the tipi entrance. Soon Joe had a fire going in the ring of stones at the center of the tipi floor. The old Keeper stood before it, spreading his hands, and said, "Do not leave until the fire has died down into a bed of embers, for I am now completely blind. When you ran away with the Cheyenne girl I could still see a little. Why have you come to me, my son?"

"Because I have ceased to be an Indian and I do not like myself."

"And you want me to tell you how to become an Indian again?"

"Yes, if you can."

"You are not the first one who forgot who he was." The Keeper squatted down beside his firestones. "Sit here, my son. Your question may not be difficult. First, tell me why you feel that you have ceased to be an Indian."

Joe sat beside the Keeper and the flickering warmth spread deep into their faces. "I struck a man who had betrayed me. He was accidentally killed."

"Surely that does not trouble you." The Keeper seemed genuinely surprised. "If the man betrayed you, he deserved to die. Our Topadoga council would have directed you to kill him. When you struck this man, did you intend to kill him?"

"No. His death was an accident. He hit his head on a piece of iron when he fell."

"If you had not lost your sense of Indian honor, you would have struck such a man intending to kill."

"We live under the white laws now. They say their courts take the place of our Topadoga council."

"They lie, of course," the Keeper said gently. "The whites use their courts only to protect themselves. There is no safety in their presence unless you understand that they are the exact opposite of everything they say. You must never tell them the truth and you must never fear them. To fear a white man is more cowardly than to fear a hungry panther. The panther can only kill you and tear your flesh. But the white man robs you of honor and shames you for who you are."

Joe was silent for several moments. The Keeper gave him some time for reflection and then asked, "Have I answered the questions that trouble you, my son?"

"I mean no disrespect," Joe told him, "but I have known these things about the white man since I was a child."

"And you are still troubled?" The Keeper was truly puzzled.

"Yes. I understand what a white man is but I do not know what an Indian is. I have never known what an Indian is."

"Perhaps you were born too late, my son. The very first clothes upon your back were probably white-man clothes issued to our village after they took away our hunting lands. You should have been dried with soft doeskin and wrapped in rabbit fur. A baby must have the power of animals rubbed into him or he never develops the instincts necessary for survival. That is why the Indian in you died. You probably have poor eyesight and a limited sense of smell, also."

"I seem to see and smell all right."

"Can you smell a deer upwind? Or count the tail feathers of an eagle in flight?"

"No."

"Your ancestors could."

"Can you?" Joe asked.

"You forget that I am blind now. When I was younger I could. You will begin to feel better, my son, if you take off your white clothes and wear animal skins for a few days. And you should speak no white lingo for at least one whole moon. If you find that you are feeling better, then you will know that you have taken good medicine. Perhaps you will continue wearing the skins and speaking your own tongue. It might also be helpful, for a while, not even to *listen* to white lingo. Your hearing sense may become sharpened by the sounds of your own people."

34

WHILE sitting before the old Grandmother Keeper's tipi fire, Joe had sought wisdom from the Kiowa past that would finally point a way to death with honor. Perhaps that was what triggered his decision. He visited his mother's hut to begin assembling a warrior's wardrobe.

"I am going into the woods for a while," he said.

"Why are you speaking Kiowa?" his half brother asked.

"I have been to see the Grandmother Keeper and I have spoken only Kiowa since I left his tipi."

Long was puzzled. "Why did you see that old Keeper?"

"Running Standing is tired of being a white man," said Tree Standing with a nod of satisfaction. She puffed on her pipe, blew smoke from beneath her bandage, and rocked with purpose.

Joe dug into his bag and found his grandfather's whitewoman scalp lock. He had kept it with him during the years at Carlisle, as a sort of talisman, but had not unrolled it in years. He unrolled it now, remembering how he had rubbed warm tallow into it when he was a boy. Inside the scalp lock he found his old knife, its blade well-protected by the tallow. He tested the blade with his thumb.

"You can use my oilstone," said Rabbit Standing.

Joe removed his coat and shirt, skinned out of the upper half of his underwear, letting it dangle, and buckled the scalp lock onto his belt. He stood naked to the waist before his mother's fire, whetting his knife on his father's stone. The sound of the blade could barely be heard above the fire-crackle.

"I have a breechclout you can wear if you want to," said Long, fascinated. He dug into the cowhide case beneath his bed and found it. Joe removed his pants and kicked his underwear aside. Watching, Tree Standing clapped her hands excitedly and rocked.

The clout was a wide piece of soft doeskin, six feet long, which passed between his legs and up beneath his belt; fringed at the ends, it dangled down from his belt, both fore and aft, as far as his knees.

Two Standing said in Caddo, "I do not believe this."

Long Standing said, "Speak Kiowa or shut up."

Sara said, "Why are you doing this, Joe?"

Joe said, "I need leggings and a buffalo coat. I am going into the woods for a while."

"I will go with you," said Long. "I have another clout—"

"I must go alone. I am going to look for owls," Joe said, placing a pall of mysticism over his action.

Rabbit Standing said, "I think you are going to kill a white man and I wish you great success."

"It is my intention to kill a white man," said Joe, referring to the white-man part of himself but pleasing his old father nonetheless.

With Long's help, he found among the villagers buckskin leggings that buckled onto the belt, buffalo boots with lots of hair still intact, and Sky-Walker's old buffalo coat. The coat had been given as an offering to the Keeper, but Joe was able to trade his shoes for it.

He went into the woods beyond the creek that afternoon, hearing, even as he left the trail, the hoofbeats of horses bringing Roscoe's geologist and T. Rowley Duggan to escort him to the train. He had no idea how Crosses-the-River would explain his absence. He had told her nothing of their plan to get him out of sight before the investigation of Indian rights by the men from Washington.

After two days and nights in the woods with nothing to eat but a few overripe persimmons, Joe began wondering why he had not brought food along. The answer, he knew, was simple. He had assumed that he could live as an Indian and fend for himself in a natural way. Hunger, however, soon drove other considerations from his mind. He sat on a stone in a spongy hollow at the foot of the mountain, knife in hand, waiting for some animal or bird that he could possibly kill to show itself.

At last he heard a noise . . . the breaking of twigs. He had no idea what it was. He'd had no training for living in the woods. He crouched, waiting. Soon it came closer, and there was Long: in clout, leggings, boots, and a hairy coat. "Hello, Joe," he said in white lingo. "I have been watching you for an hour. You'll starve if you stay here."

"I'm hungry. I must kill an animal."

"I'll help you."

"Why did you come here?"

"I went to see the Keeper. He told me your eyes and ears had went bad and that you could not smell anything. I thought you might need me in the woods. Joe, you ain't any good as a Kiowa. You ought to stay white."

"I'm hungry. Let's kill something."

"Let's kill a white man and eat him." Long grinned but Joe thought he meant it.

"We aren't cannibals."

"We could see what he tastes like and then throw him away."

"I want to kill a rabbit or a deer. Or a quail or a dove or a turkey."

"They ain't any deer or turkeys left, and they ain't many rabbits, either."

"Let's try."

Together they searched the woods but they had neither the stealth to flush game from its hiding nor the cunning to remain still enough for game to come out of its own volition.

"There's no animals in these woods," Joe said.

"I told you," said Long. "Above the village, at the edge of the grass, they's a few stray cattle. We could kill a calf and have some fresh liver."

"Come on."

They hurried around the village to the border of the woods where a remnant of cattle from a white man's lease-grass herd had strayed. They picked out the animal they wanted, a nice fat strong-looking castrated bull calf.

Joe said, "I'll kill him," and ran the animal down with an ease that surprised his brother. He grabbed its neck, plunged his knife into its jugular, twisted its head, and held on until the bawling ceased. Slowly the animal crumbled. When it fell, he was on top of it, slicing its belly open, reaching into the steaming cavity, searching among the incredibly hot entrails for the liver. He brought it out at last, severed it from the tissue it clung to, found the gall, squeezed it over the liver, sliced off a piece, and began to eat.

Now covered with blood, he almost retched at the taste.

"I can't eat this," he said and spat it out.

"I can," said Long, who promptly took the liver and knife, sliced a piece for himself, and ate with relish. "You just ain't a Kiowa no more, Joe."

Disgust replaced hunger. Joe watched his brother eat slice after slice. "All this blood is beginning to dry on my body," he said. "It feels terrible. I'm going to the creek and wash, and then I'm going to go to my camp and cook some calf meat over a fire."

"I saw your camp. In the pecan grove where a hackberry tree has fallen. You made a bed of leaves beside the tree trunk and slept under Sky-Walker's buffalo coat."

Joe was surprised. "When did you see it?"

"I watched you quite a while. You ain't mad at me, are you?"

"No."

"The Keeper told me you wanted to be a Kiowa again. You can't do it, Joe. There ain't anything wrong with being a white Indian. Everybody expects it of you. Even the old-timers know you had to turn white at Carlisle. Everybody has turned white that ever went to Carlisle or to Haskell—or even to a mission school."

Long paused, and then urged his case even harder: "Everybody knows you didn't go to Carlisle on purpose. Crosses-the-River lured you there. Nobody holds it against you. There ain't any need under the sun for you to be a Kiowa again, because everything is gone now. Even old Kiowas ain't real Kiowas no more. I wish I'd of gone to Carlisle so I could be like you. I can't ever be like you because I've got too damn much Indian in me."

Joe was deeply moved by his brother's argument for him; he was also embarrassed by the display of so much sentiment.

"Long Neck," he said, "I had better go to the creek and wash." They were speaking white lingo now, having switched over without realizing it.

"Don't wash the leggings or the clout," said Long. "Let the blood dry and shake it out."

They cut hunks of meat from the calf carcass, then went to the creek together. Joe stripped and waded into the cold water. He washed quickly and came out shivering.

Long said, "You just ain't much of a Kiowa, but I like you. I'll help you kill T. Rowley if you'll help me kill Billy Cheyenne."

"You're not going to kill Billy Cheyenne. He's Crosses-the-River's brother."

"But she lured you to Carlisle and made you unhappy."

"I'm not unhappy."

Now they hurried through the woods toward the pecan grove where Joe had left his coat. "If you're not unhappy," said Long, "then why did you ask the Keeper how to be a Kiowa?"

"I'm trying to find out how a man dies with honor."

"You ain't going to die, are you?"

"I think so."

"Who's going to kill you?"

"I don't know."

"If anybody tries to kill you, they'll have to kill me first."

It occurred to Joe that perhaps Long could tell him something about Kiowa honor that the Keeper had failed to explain. He asked, "What is honor, Long? Do you know?"

"I ain't got none, I know that . . . but we don't need it no more. I'll be honest with you, Joe. I ain't nothing but a dapom now. I sunk pretty low when I married a Caddo girl."

"You said you'd die trying to protect me."

"But that ain't honor. You're my brother."

"Billy Cheyenne is Sara's brother."

"But he ain't got no brother. He has only got a sister and his father has only got one wife and they ain't nothing but corn-growing Jesus Cheyennes anyway. But I won't kill him if you don't want me to."

Joe stopped shivering only after he had been inside the buffalo coat for half an hour. They made a cooking tripod beside the hackberry log and tried to build a fire. They fashioned a firebow with a lace from one of the leggings but they couldn't get the spindle hot enough.

"What kind of wood did our people use for fire spindles, Long?"

"I always thought it was just any piece of wood."

"We're not even getting smoke."

They tried every kind of wood they could find. For tinder

they tried dry moss, crumbled dead leaves, and bark, both shredded and pounded into pulp. Nothing produced a fire. "Long," said Joe, "did you see the two men who came after me the day I left?"

"Yes. T. Rowley was one of them."

"Do you know what Crosses-the-River said to them?"

"No."

"Do you think I'm hiding from them?"

"I think you came here because you do not want to kill T. Rowley. But you're going to starve unless you learn to eat raw meat, and you're going to have to kill him anyway."

"Go home and bring matches. Tell Crosses-the-River that I must know exactly what those men said to her."

"I'll bring us some food, too, Joe." Long disappeared quickly toward Owl Creek.

While he was gone, Joe tried again to start a fire. He considered another attempt to eat raw meat but the smell of it, when he put his knife to a chunk, disgusted him. He lay down to wait in his bed of leaves beside the log. Warm in Sky-Walker's coat, he dozed for a while, and when he woke the woods were alive. He watched a weasel stalk a rabbit, saw a hawk swoop down on a field mouse. Darkness slowly came, but Long did not.

An owl screeched nearby. "I don't believe you're talking to me," he said, astonished that he would speak aloud to a bird.

The moon was bright through the barren treetops. He looked at it for a while, and listened to the swelling night-sound of the woods, and once more fell asleep.

Long awakened him at daybreak.

"You ain't much of a Kiowa, Joe, and I ain't either." Still wearing his clout, Long carried a bundle and a bucket.

Joe sat up. "What time is it?"

"Just good daybreak. I couldn't get away from T. Rowley until dark last night. And when I reached the woods, I couldn't find you. I had to wait for daylight before I knew where I was."

"Did you talk to T. Rowley?"

"He figured I knew where you was hiding. He followed me everywhere, so I waited until after dark and slid down the ledge and crept out past Tree Standing's medicine oil spring."

"Did you talk to Crosses-the-River?"

"T. Rowley was always there. I couldn't speak to her alone."

"What did T. Rowley say about your clout and leggings?"

"I changed at the creek before I went home. And changed back again after I got away from him. My clothes are inside a log. I also hid a Winchester rifle in the log. I borrowed it from Medicine Water. Here's some food, Joe."

The bundle contained corn bread, roasted meat, and ground coffee in a jar. "We can make us some coffee in this bucket."

"I hope you didn't forget to bring matches."

"I brought them. Joe, you ought to listen to me. We've got to kill him. I could lure him into the woods and—"

Brush broke nearby. They looked around, heard the metallic click of a lever, and saw, larger than life, with a rifle in his hands, T. Rowley Duggan. His feet were apart, his coat was open, his face was incredibly empty of expression, and his gun muzzle was all-seeing. It was Medicine Water's Winchester.

"I took it out of the log where you left your clothes. I followed you, Long Neck." T. Rowley's little gray square mustache twitched. "You boys ain't about to go on the warpath, are you? Because it's too late in this world for Indians to get away with that sort of thing." He looked Joe up and down, amused by the Indian garb but not smirking. "I've tried to warn you. The panic-period fear act is what mostly gets people into trouble."

"I thought you were talking about criminals when you said that, Marshal," Joe told him steadily.

"You ain't thinking, boy." T. Rowley's deep eyes swung over to Long. "You couldn't lure me into ambush in one hundred and sixty-seven years of steady trying. Because I always keep one eye looking over my shoulder. It's a trick that only a good lawman learns. If you was to try to kill me, you'd end up one of the deadest Kiowas of all time."

The marshal then let the hammer off the Winchester, unloaded it, put the shells into his vest pocket, tossed the gun into the leaves at Long's feet, stood with his right hand near the butt of his left pistol, and said to Joe: "I'm taking you to town, boy."

"You're calling me 'boy' all of a sudden, Marshal. You're not the same man you were before C. J. Roscoe bought you off. Or found out something about your past. Or told you he would find out something and you know he could if he tried."

"You're under arrest for killing the late Buck Failey," T.

Rowley said. "I gave you a chance to leave my jurisdiction under the custody of Mr. Roscoe's geologist, pending the completion of my investigation. Since you decided to hide out, I reckon the jury will have something to go on when I put you up in court."

Long turned suddenly and walked a few quick steps away— at a right angle.

"You had better stop, Long," the marshal said. "You are under arrest, too, for aiding a fugitive."

Long turned back toward the marshal. "You don't realize it yet, T. Rowley, but we have got you now."

A flicker of amusement crossed T. Rowley's face. "You ain't got nobody. I'm taking you to town with your brother. Let me warn you before anybody gets hurt that I have killed more than one dozen outlaws since I started marshaling, and I was a scout in the mountains before that. Because of where-all I've been and all the things I've done during my busy life, I've got more Indian ways in me than you boys has got, both combined."

Long said, "You're just a part-white man that is also part dog. We've got you and we're going to kill you."

Amused or not, T. Rowley's body, anticipating action, bent slightly forward. "You'd better put your hands up now, Long."

Long slowly raised his hands. Joe marveled at his brother's poise. He feared that Long was on the verge of getting himself killed, but some echo from his Kiowa past told him not to interfere with whatever his brother was doing. There was honor here, whether Long believed himself to have honor or not, and Joe watched.

Long said, with his hands now high above his head, "You can't shoot us both at once, T. Rowley. We're going to come for you at the same time, and while you're shooting one of us, the other one will kill you. Did you know that I've been wanting to find out what a white man tastes like even though I ain't a Tonkawa?"

"If you ain't a Tonkawa, for talking like that, you're a goddamn fool. I can draw and shoot with either hand. My reputation is far and wide."

"Me and Joe is the two fastest Kiowas that ever lived and we ain't afraid of no white-man gun. Come on, Joe, let's go at him."

Completely captivated by his half brother's dazzling courage, Joe heard himself say, "Let's go!"

They sprang toward the marshal. T. Rowley's right hand cross-reached for his left-side pistol. As it came out of his belt, a rifle blast shook the woods. His right hand flew into the air and his pistol sailed over the hackberry log beyond the buffalo coat.

"I got him!" cried Tree Standing in Kiowa as Long and Joe swarmed over the wounded marshal and subdued him. She came into the open, cocking her old carbine again. "Get out of my way, boys. I will finish him."

"No," Joe shouted, shielding the marshal from his mother's aim with his own body.

"Joe, get back and let her kill him," Long cried, stepping aside to give Tree Standing a clear shot.

Joe pulled the other gun from T. Rowley's belt, then sprang toward his mother. He wrenched the carbine from her hands and unloaded it onto the ground. She stood, eyes blazing beneath her bandage, speechless.

Joe looked down at the marshal who held up his bleeding right hand and said, "By God, I'm ruined."

"You ain't ruined," Long Standing said, "but you ain't got no honor. You'd better start looking over your shoulder once in a while, T. Rowley."

Long had left his knife near the cooking tripod where he'd been whittling shavings for tinder. He now picked it up and walked toward the marshal with an expression of supreme relish on his face. T. Rowley's face was a portrait in horror. He had been around Plains Indians in the old days and knew how quickly he'd be dispatched if Long reached him.

Once more Joe intervened. He lunged at his brother, blocking him, football-style, out of the way. "Long, we're not going to kill this man."

Tree Standing, from the hackberry log, said in white lingo: "Yes we are." She had picked up the marshal's pistol that had been shot from his hand. She aimed it at Joe and said in Kiowa: "Don't move, son. Kill the marshal, Long."

Joe saw the pistol tremble in her hand. Whether because she was nervous or too old to hold it steady, he didn't know— but the chances were good that if she actually fired at him, she would miss. Ignoring her, he grabbed Long's wrist, wrenched away the knife, and once more put himself between his mother and T. Rowley Duggan.

Tree Standing's mouth gaped. Her chin quivered. She lowered the pistol to her side and accepted defeat.

T. Rowley looked up at Joe. "During the last two minutes you have saved my life two times. My right hand is shot all to hell. Please get me to a doctor quick, or else let her shoot me, if you would be so kind. I ain't ever going to be any good unless I get my right hand fixed."

"You can shoot with your left hand, can't you, Marshal?"

"I ain't going to continue marshaling."

"Why not?"

"You folks could all be prosecuted for one thing or another —homicide, assaulting an officer with a deadly weapon, aiding a fugitive from justice. But you saved my life, Joe, and I could never put you up for prosecution even if you should let me go and I got good use of my right hand back, which I am afraid I will not, although Doc Freeland might be able to do something for me if I could get to him right away. So I will have to give up marshaling." With his left hand he removed his badge and put it into his vest pocket, symbolically retiring himself from the law . . . an act, Joe thought, with honor buried in it somewhere, even though the man had no doubt been bought off by C. J. Roscoe.

Long said, "A white man's liver with his own gall squeezed on it might be too bitter to eat. I am going to try yours with goat gall if my brother decides to let me kill you."

T. Rowley replied stoutly, "You boys look ridiculous in them breechclouts."

Long said, "Joe followed a Jesus Cheyenne all the way to Carlisle, Pennsylvania, and got turned white up there, or you would be dead right now."

"You are the talkingest Kiowa I ever seen, did you know that?"

"You ain't got no Indian ways, T. Rowley, or you'd never let a noseless old woman track you down in the woods."

35

THEY took T. Rowley to Tree Standing's hut. Joe sent Long to saddle a pony and ride fast for Doc Freeland. Sara insisted that he put on clothes first. "You'll panic everybody you meet on the Cloud Chief road if you go like that."

As Long dressed he said, "I left me and Joe's other clothes in a hollow log."

"I will go after them," said Tree Standing in Kiowa, pleased to let her family know that she understood as much white lingo as she wanted to.

"You don't know which hollow log I left them in."

"I know. I followed you right down my ledge last night." She and Long went away together.

Sara took a rag from a nail where Tree Standing kept her nose coverings and made a tourniquet for T. Rowley's hand. He sat on the floor in the darkest corner and brooded. Rabbit Standing sat cross-legged nearby and studied him. T. Rowley finally complained. "He is just about to drive me insane. He ain't took his eyes off me once."

"What are you looking at, Rabbit Hand?" Sara asked.

"The white man," her father-in-law answered and would say no more.

Two Standing, whose habit was automatically to tend Sara's little son as well as her own babies when Sara was busy, seemed fascinated with T. Rowley's mutilated hand. At last he asked, "Would you like to have a good look at this thing?" He held up the hand.

She put the baby down and bent to examine the hand. After a while she shuddered, turned away, picked up Sara's son, and began nursing him from her own breast.

Wills Freeland arrived in his buggy, with Long following on his pony, before noon. He examined T. Rowley, gave him morphine, amputated the forefinger, and repaired the palm as well as he could right there in Tree Standing's hut, steriliz-ing his instruments in water boiled at the cooking tripod

outside. Joe held the man's arm steady and Sara mopped
blood as Wills directed.

Tree Standing, who had returned with the cache of clothes
before Wills arrived, held her carbine in her hands and
watched the operation for a while. Then she hung the gun
on the wall and summoned Long's wife outside.

"Two Bonnet," she asked in her own language, "do you
trust that white docti in there?"

"No, I do not. He makes pictures that look just like us. He
has a weird power. I am afraid of him."

Tree Standing nodded. "He also cuts the flesh and heals it.
Do you think he could make a nose that looks like a nose?"

"We could ask Crosses-the-River. She understands more
than we do about everything."

"I may ask her one of these days," Tree Standing said,
certain, of course, that she never would. She did not wish to
encourage Crosses-the-River's friendship with the red-haired
docti. It was a dangerous friendship. You had only to look
at their eyes when they spoke to each other to know that. The
docti's eyes told you the instant truth. Crosses-the-River's
eyes told the truth also, but somewhat less instantly. . . .

Inside, Wills Freeland finished the operation, bandaged the
hand, and made a sling. "I think you'll have considerable use
of it again," he told the former marshal. "I'll show you some
exercises to strengthen it after it heals. There was nothing I
could do to save that forefinger, but in time you should be
able to control the rest of your fingers."

T. Rowley listened and blinked his morphine-glazed eyes
and mumbled, "I ain't marshaling no more, anyway."

"You still got a trigger finger on your other hand," Long
pointed out, hoping the man would go on marshaling. Some
day he would kill T. Rowley and it would be a vastly greater
satisfaction to kill a marshal than a plain white man.

The self-retired marshal spent three days in the hut of
the woman who had ended his career. After the first day he
became talkative again but said little to her. He watched her,
however; even while addressing himself garrulously to others,
his eyes followed her around.

During the recuperation, Joe dared not leave T. Rowley
alone with his mother and brother, for they might yet kill the
man if they had a chance. He stayed in the hut or made sure
that Sara stayed there when he was away. Sara had a great

deal of control over his family's actions. Any Indian who had been to Carlisle or to Haskell had enormous prestige despite everyone's reluctance to admit it.

Joe added a fringed buckskin shirt to his leggings and clout and trimmed his hair into a pattern of straight bangs combed over his forehead. He would let his hair grow long, he thought, and braid it—if he lived. Frequently he went into the woods for a while to contemplate himself.

Wills Freeland came each day to visit his patient. On the third day he told them that a new marshal had been assigned to the Buck Failey case.

"Is the new marshal a skinny man with eyes like a lizard?" T. Rowley asked.

"I didn't see him close up," Wills said.

"Does he wear cavalry boots and a badge on his hat?"

"Yes. They say in town that he wears his badge up there to give outlaws something to shoot at."

Contempt swam across T. Rowley's face. "That ain't why. A lawman knows that just about everybody shoots high because they are expecting their gun to kick and ain't been trained against the flinch. I would not tell this if I was going to continue marshaling. His name is Dutchy Gilmore and he is mean. You folks got to hide me somewhere or let me go. If you would be so kind."

"Has Dutchy Gilmore got something on you?" Joe asked.

T. Rowley nodded. "I done a very foolish fear act after a negative-passion thing one time back on the Ohio River. That is how I first came to understand the criminal mind. I studied myself."

"Then you're an outlaw," Sara said.

"A former outlaw, ma'am. Lots of your lawmen is . . . just as many of your very best preachers is former drunkards. They know about hell and sin. I was a good marshal because I had a firsthand study of how the criminal mind is apt to work when you push him hard."

"Did C. J. Roscoe find out what Dutchy Gilmore knows about you?" Joe asked.

T. Rowley sighed dolefully and explained that if he hadn't found out, he would soon. "Dutchy come with a gleam in his lizardy eyes and told me that Mr. Roscoe was paying him to look into me with a fine-tooth comb and the only way I could keep him quiet was to let you leave my jurisdiction. Roscoe don't want you around when them Washington fellows get here. He has the goods on you, Joe. Somebody knows you done it to the late Buck Failey, but honest to goodness, if you can believe a white man, I don't know who it is."

"Then why does Roscoe want me to leave? He could simply let them prosecute me for murder."

T. Rowley blinked and said, in tones of wisdom, "He wants to use you, after this is over, for the rest of your life. To help him slick more Indian folks out of their oil rights, just like he slicked you. Now, I could get something on Dutchy Gilmore if I had time. Which I ain't got, I guess."

"Where would you have to look?"

"I'd hide first in a dugout that I know on Saddle Mountain and concentrate on Dutchy for a while. I could figure out where to look, if I put my lawman's mind and my criminal instincts both to work on it."

"Don't trust him," Tree Standing said in Kiowa.

"Ma'am," T. Rowley told her, "I am able to understand your lingo. You are a good shot with that carbine, but I ain't mad at you. I done a fear act when Dutchy Gilmore threatened me and that is what cost me my trigger finger."

"Do you have a family anywhere?" Sara asked.

"I used to have a wife, back in Ohio, but I lost her in all the commotion over that negative-passion thing I mentioned."

Long, who had been sitting on a box near the fireplace, rose suddenly, paced the floor, and said to Joe: "We can't let him go. He'd turn us all in. Let me hide him in Medicine Water's tipi."

"Will you promise not to kill him?"

"I'll promise, but you've got to tell me why so that I can understand it. Remember, I ain't been to Carlisle or anywhere. But I could kill him and nobody would ever know about it, not even the new marshal with the badge on his hat."

"This is important, Long. I'm in the way of a powerful white man's greed. I have a feeling that I may be about to die and I'm trying to decide how to die with honor. I'm going to tell the truth about some things that might help our people if I can decide the right way to do it. They may put me on trial, and then I may need T. Rowley's testimony."

Sara and Wills watched Joe intently. Tree Standing saw them glance at each other and did not like what she saw. "Running Standing," she said in Kiowa, "if you are going to die, I want you to die with honor and so does Rabbit Hand and so do all your dead ancestors. I do not understand honor anymore. I went to the Grandmother Keeper after Long Neck went there. The Keeper told me that honor might be dead. If it is not dead, I wish you would find it. And when you are through with T. Rowley, I wish you would give him to Long Neck and me."

"I will turn him over to you," Joe promised, "if I decide he ought to be killed."

"Then come on," Long said and placed his knife inside his belt.

"Doc, is your patient able to go?" Joe asked.

"Yes," said Wills. "I'll visit him again at Medicine Water's tipi in a day or two. He's doing all right."

Joe's mother and half brother prepared to escort their captive into the village. Joe decided to go with them on his way to the woods. "I have some more hard thinking to do and I don't believe there is very much time," he said.

"I wish you'd do some of your thinking here," Sara said, "and let me in on it."

"I've told you, Crosses-the-River, that a man can't think around his woman."

"That is purely the truth, ma'am, if you'll pardon me," T. Rowley assured her. "That's how I got into that negative-passion situation out in Ohio."

Joe turned to Wills Freeland. "You're leaving now, aren't you, Doc?"

"I'd appreciate a cup of coffee before I go . . . if Sara would give it to me."

"What are you going to tell the new marshal if he comes while you're here?"

"It's none of his business why I'm here."

"Sara doesn't have time to give you coffee."

"Very well," said Wills, closing his pill bag. He went stiffly down the incline toward his buggy and drove away.

Sara held her temper. "Joe, Wills is our friend."

"He's your friend. I have no white friends."

"You're becoming too fanatic about this."

"I'm becoming a Kiowa Indian, Crosses-the-River."

He put on his buffalo coat and went with his mother and half brother to escort T. Rowley Duggan into the Owl Creek village for safekeeping until he could be useful.

Marshal Dutchy Gilmore didn't come that day, but late in the afternoon Sara's entire family came. She was helping Two

Standing with supper at the cooking fire outside the hut because Joe had announced, when he returned from the woods, that he would not stay alone with her in the tipi any longer. He wanted to be with his family. After supper he intended to bring their bedding up to the hut. Six adults and three children would make the hut crowded, but Tree Standing was delighted with the idea. They would all feel close to each other, and loyal.

Creaking wheels on the clay path below the incline caught Sara's attention. She looked down to see her father's old road wagon, drawn by a team of good mules, loaded with her entire family.

"That's Killer Cross's wagon," said Rabbit Standing, peering down.

"And that's Billy Cheyenne up there driving," said Long, reaching for his knife. "Billy is a goddamn fool for coming into Kiowa country."

Joe took Long's arm. "Give me the knife."

"I'm going to need it."

"I'll take it away from you."

Long pulled himself free and went into a crouch. "You may not be able to."

"I'm prepared to die, and you know it," Joe told him steadily. "I'm going to take that knife." He moved toward his half brother, grabbed the wrist of Long's knife hand, spun him around, and pushed the hand against the doorjamb until the knife fell. Then he picked it up. He noticed with satisfaction while wresting the knife free that Long had not tried to slash him.

Billy Cheyenne climbed from the driver's chair and shouted: "Long Neck, are you up there?"

"I'm up here, Billy Cheyenne."

"I came to give you my knife."

Long was astonished. "Why are you giving me your knife?"

"They say in Cloud Chief that you and Running Standing has went Indian to hide out from the law. I came to make peace. Me and Killer Cross is ready to go Indian and help you."

"Then come on up and have some coffee with us," said Long. "Two Bonnet, you had better put on another big pot of coffee now. My wife is a Caddo, Billy, but she makes good coffee."

"I don't know what mine is no more," Billy replied, leading the family up the incline.

He came holding his knife handle forward. When he was ten feet from the hut, he tossed it onto the ground at Long's feet. "There," he said with the friendliest smile Sara had seen on his face since she returned from Carlisle.

Long picked up the knife, examined it with pleasure, and said, "Why don't you folks stay for supper?"

"We brought side meat and a chicken with us," said Billy.

Lamb Woman, wide-looking in her inevitable brown squaw dress and moccasins, followed Killer, who wore overalls and new brogans. And behind them came Many Stones, proving beyond a doubt her husband's statement that he did not know what she was any more. She wore a picture hat with a velvet crown, a brim of gathered satin, and two ostrich fan feathers, one upright and the other swept around the crown. And a dressy coat of Astrakhan cloth with a handsome collar of rich seal plush. And high-laced kidskin shoes with patent leather tips and cuban heels—one shoe swinging in its delicate arc with each movement of her lame foot. And she carried her two babies proudly, one in each arm.

"The men is going Indian," she said to Sara, "and I am going white like you."

Thoroughly delighted, but also apprehensive, Sara glanced for Joe's reaction. She need not have worried. The men were already inside the hut, talking about going Indian, and above all paying no attention to women. "Many Stones," she said, "you look beautiful. Did you make the coat and hat?"

Many Stones nodded. "Nowadays, Charlie gets good goods. The patterns came all the way from Saint Louis."

"Your white lingo has improved, too."

"I listen to it whenever I can. I had to sew a lot of things for Charlie to get these goods. I made a dress for you. It's in the wagon."

Many Stones came onto the clay landing at the top of the incline. Sara introduced her to Long's wife who, with her own two babies in her arms, stood stiffly in a squaw dress and was speechless. Instinctively, and not to be left out, Sara picked up her son. The three women smiled at each other. Two Bonnet's smile was slow to come, but it was broad when it got there.

"Crosses-the-River need one more baby," she said in halting white lingo to Many Stones, "and then we be alike."

Her sisters-in-law both laughed aloud. They were ahead of her in child production, if nothing else.

Inside the hut, Billy Cheyenne solemnly reported what he had learned from Harley Wilson about the official charge against Joe. Few whites would talk to Indians about such things, but Harley would.

It appeared that Delma Sue Raven Rock had seen Joe leave the hotel through Buck Failey's window that night. She always slept in a lean-to attached to the kitchen, and she heard the thud when Failey hit the floor. From the small window beside her bed she watched Joe drop to the ground, rub his ankles for a while, and then run away. She told her brothers about it and they told two Delawares they fished with. The Delawares told Old Tonk who, in turn, told Three Toe. And Three Toe, unknown to any of his friends until now, still considered Crosses-the-River his woman.

"He came to get her," said Killer Cross, "but you had took her with you, so he wanted his horses back. He couldn't have them, either, because I had already traded them for this team of mules."

"He said he'd turn you in for murder, and then he could have her," Billy added, "and that's what that goddamn Arapaho done."

They further explained that Dutchy Gilmore was telling in town that he would go after Joe himself unless T. Rowley brought him in within a week. It was common knowledge that Joe had gone Indian and fled into the woods . . . or maybe into the mountains above Fort Sill.

"Is that big rich white man named Roscoe still at the hotel?" Joe asked.

Billy nodded. "Dutchy Gilmore eats with him and his men every night, while they're waiting for T. Rowley to bring you back. Corinne Raven Rock—that is Delma Sue's young sister —serves the dining room tables there now, because they are holding Delma Sue in jail to testify what she heard and saw. They've scared her pretty bad."

"T. Rowley won't bring me back," Joe assured them. "Lives-in-a-Tree shot his finger off with her old carbine."

"Me and Joe captured him," said Long with a proud grin. "He has now quit marshaling."

Billy Cheyenne and his father were stunned with admiration. Killer Cross asked, "Do you mean that you boys has got T. Rowley now?"

"We're holding him in Medicine Water's tipi until we decide what to do with him."

"Then maybe we can keep old Three Toe there, too," said Billy Cheyenne. "We brought him to you."

"You brought Three Toe here?"

"Yes," said Killer Cross with satisfaction. "He's out there in my wagon right now, tied up in a cotton sack."

With Joe in the lead, the men ran outside, past the women, and down the incline. Among the supplies in the wagon bed lay the sullen Arapaho, tied inside the sack, up to his chin, and well tied, it appeared, for there was no evidence that he had continued struggling to free himself.

Joe climbed into the wagon. "They say you turned me in."

"You have got my wife and I want her."

With his foot, Joe contemptuously rolled Three Toe over onto his face. "We'll have our supper and decide what to do with a man like you."

"You are a dog," said Long. "We may just bury you in that sack."

They gathered the supplies Killer and Billy had brought and went back up to eat.

36

THEY held a strategy session that lasted through supper and into the night. Warmed by the new friendship, Long gave Billy his own knife and suggested that the Crosses stay a few days until Dutchy Gilmore made his move. Billy accepted Long's knife with great feeling and agreed to stay. He offered to make trips to town alternately with his father to find out what was going on.

"They won't pay no attention to me," he said, "because they don't know that you and me has made friends."

There were now ten adults and five babies in the hut. Sara begged Joe, privately, to go with her to their own tipi. She only made him angry. Friends should be together, he insisted; to go off alone would be an insult.

The babies went to sleep first, lined up beside each other on a blanket in one ledge corner of the hut. Rabbit Hand soon lay down with them. Lamb Woman and Sara slept in his bed with Lives-in-a-Tree. Many Stones slept in Long's bed with Two Bonnet. Tired at last, Killer Cross crawled over and curled up on the other side of the babies. Joe slept on the floor near the door, wrapped in Sky-Walker's old coat. Billy and Long were the last to feel sleepy.

They sat before the fire together, feeding it slowly, absorbing with its warmth the glow of new friendship. They told each other stories that had come down from the glory days, believing finally that, had they lived a few generations earlier, they might have established peace between the Kiowa and the Cheyenne in time to unite all the Plains Tribes against the U.S. Cavalry. History might have been changed by the power of two good friends . . . if only that power could have been applied in the right place, in the right way, at the right time.

Rain began falling as they talked. Long remembered Three Toe out in the wagon. They would turn him over to Medicine Water tomorrow for safekeeping until Joe's problems with the law were settled, making certain that if Joe went on trial, Three Toe would not be available to testify. For tonight, of course, lying out there in the rain was good enough for him.

Reconnaissance trips to town during the next three days invariably brought the same information: Dutchy Gilmore, always at Mr. Roscoe's side, was waiting to hear from T. Rowley Duggan.

The Indians in town were tight-lipped, even to each other, since word had got around that Three Toe had informed on Joe. They all knew that T. Rowley had been captured and was in Medicine Water's tipi on Owl Creek. It amused them to hear the whites making bets on when T. Rowley would bring Joe in.

On trips to town, Billy wore store clothes, but here among his family and in-laws he wore a breechclout and leggings. One morning Killer tried wearing a clout. When Lamb Woman laughed at him, he slapped her twice. She continued laughing, however, so he took it off.

Each day, while Joe was alone in the woods, his family and Sara's volubly discussed his search for honor. Each time he returned they were disappointed that he had not found it. Everyone but Sara accepted his presentiment of death. Some of them even felt that his meditations might reveal why he had to die as well as how he should do it.

Sara tried to stop their morbid talk. She screamed and shouted and once shook her fist at them, but she silenced them only momentarily. On the third day, more depressed than angry, she said to Many Stones, "Everybody already considers him dead. He's not dead. He'll decide how to handle this thing to the benefit of our people and he'll become a great leader."

Many Stones refused to answer. Sadness for her sister-in-law paraded in her eyes.

"Many Stones!" Sara cried. "I want you to use power on Billy Cheyenne. If he stops this talk, the others will."

Many Stones shook her head. "I don't use power on him no more. He agreed to let me go white if I would not poison him again. If my husband wanted to die with honor," she added severely, "I would help him do it."

Sara whirled in exasperation and went down to her tipi to wait for Joe.

She stood by the flap in agony, beginning to understand that overwhelming forces were in motion. Joe was in a tangle of dishonesty, made worse now by his search for honor where honor did not exist. She ran up the incline, snatched up her son, ran back down and into her tipi . . . to be alone with Running Stone, to hold him closely, and to cry.

But she did not cry. She lay beside her sleeping child, face down in the bedding, to wait until something moved her; it was impossible to believe that she would ever be able to move again of her own volition.

She heard her name spoken outside. Whose voice was it? She had heard it before . . . many times.

"Sara, are you in there?"

It was Joe. Calling her Sara instead of Crosses-the-River. She sprang up as he entered.

"It came to me today," he said. His face was alive. Resolution lived in him at last, sustaining him, propelling him. He looked magnificent. "I have traveled to the end of agony, Sara, and now I know what I'm going to do. I'll let T. Rowley take me in."

"Joe, I'd go away with you. To Mexico. Anywhere."

He shook his head. "I've injured my people. Roscoe wants me out of the way before his oil activities are investigated. Dutchy Gilmore is itching to shoot me down for him. The only chance I have to tell what happened is to stand trial for killing Failey. They can't try me unless I'm alive, and present."

"They'll convict you of murder, Joe. You didn't murder him. His death was accidental."

"I've just talked to T. Rowley. He's promised to testify that it was an accident, in his opinion. Whatever happens, I want to put the story on record. The white man's greed got into me. Roscoe knew that, and used it as bait to swindle everybody who looked up to me. I'm going to take a chance that letting T. Rowley save face, by bringing me in, will keep me alive until I go before the court. T. Rowley won't quit marshaling until he has me safely in jail."

"Can you trust him, Joe? He can't testify for you without giving evidence against Mr. Roscoe."

"Don't forget that Roscoe dug up dirt on him. He seems to hate that man as much as I do."

"Would you be willing to talk to Wills first?"

Joe's expression did not change and she knew he was dissembling. "I don't care to hear anything he might say. Sara, if they kill me, you must never marry him. Marry another Indian, or live alone."

"Joe, don't talk like that."

"Don't be such a white woman that we can't say honest things to each other."

"All this talk of honesty and honor!" she cried. "Joe, there's no honesty. There's no honor. Most whites are greedy and so are most Indians. Don't say we're any better than they are. All our tribes raided each other . . . took land, stole horses and women, made slaves of others . . . long before the white man came. Our prophets and medicine men were as phony and ignorant as the Jesus Road preachers. There *is* no honor, Joe. There are only families of people, and we're a family. We could live somewhere else without any trouble. If we disappear from here, they'll simply forget about us."

His face turned to stone. "I don't have time to listen to the shortcomings of my people. Promise me that you'll never marry a white man."

The baby stirred. She picked him up. And said, "If I promise, will you talk to Wills before putting yourself into T. Rowley's hands?"

"No."

She sensed sublime confidence buried beneath his anger and

knew that his decision had brought him as close to peace as he could come without her cooperation. Fighting back tears, she finally said, "I promise, Joe."

37

WITH his left hand, T. Rowley Duggan took his badge out of his shirt pocket and pinned it back onto his chest. "If I'm to put you safely into jail," he told Joe, "I have to make it look like I brought you in even though I got wounded doing it."

Killer Cross, Billy Cheyenne, and Long Neck wanted to accompany them to town, but T. Rowley objected. "Dutchy Gilmore's lizardy eyes is keen for things that ain't what they look like."

"As long as you jail me," Joe asked, "what difference does it make?"

"I'm going to testify that Failey's death was accidental, in my opinion. My testimony will carry more weight if I still have the prestige of always bringing in my man. I can give up marshaling in a blaze of glory and the jury will listen to me."

Joe grinned. "But you'll know you didn't bring me in, T. Rowley. Where's the glory in that?"

"To us whites," T. Rowley said incredibly, "glory is in what other people think. We always scheme harder for what others think than for what we think of ourselves. If you folks had of knowed that about us, we might not of took your land so easily. Not that it was real easy, at that. There ain't no reason for us not to talk honestly to each other, is there, Joe? You saved my life and now I would like to help you ruin that son of a bitch Roscoe, because he dug up dirt on me, and I have hated Dutchy Gilmore for about twenty-two years, come next March the sixth."

Joe saddled two of Long's ponies for the ride to town, but T. Rowley said it might look better if Joe rode barebacked because many of the men who would eventually sit on his jury were bound to see him arrive. The picture he needed to draw against Roscoe was of a simple Indian, still deep in the ways of his ancestors even though he had been away to school.

"I aim to tell the court," the marshal said, "that I tracked you out into the woods where you was asking your sacred bird, the owl, for prophecy and guidance in how to kill me before I closed in on you. I will tell them that I got the drop on you only because of my knowledge of Indian superstitions. And that will prove to them that I know what I'm talking about when I say you're a good Indian and did not mean to kill Failey."

Fascinated, Joe asked, "How will you explain your hand?"

T. Rowley shrugged. "We shot it out and you nicked me before I managed to take you alive. You'll be the twenty-eighth outlaw that I have took alive."

"Will the jury believe that Doc Freeland came out and operated on you while you were holding me captive?"

"I tied you up and operated on myself with my left hand. It's the sort of thing folks believe I could do. And Doc will keep quiet, because he could be prosecuted for not reporting the deadly assault on a U.S. marshal."

Joe threw a blanket over his pony and led the way from Owl Creek. T. Rowley, pistols once more on his belt, rode behind him. The Crosses and the Standings remained at the corral gate for a long time, watching the two men approach the shelf above the creek and disappear into the grass. Sara, carrying her son close to her bosom, turned from the corral, needing to be alone to weep, if possible . . . or perhaps to die of despair. She went to her tipi and hated it. She had gone to Carlisle to learn the ways of enlightenment, had been a successful student, had married the most successful boy in her class, and had lived in nothing but a tipi ever since.

Many Stones and Lamb Woman came down to comfort her, but comfort was not what she needed. When they left she fell into melancholia, for how long she had no idea. The sudden arrival of Maude Wilson, screaming her name at the bottom of the incline, startled her out of it.

The gangling girl, bare-legged even in November, had run all the way from Cloud Chief.

"Is Papa here, Crosses-the-River?" she gasped when Sara went to meet her.

"No, Maude. Get your breath for a minute and then tell me."

As Maude struggled to regain control of her voice, Long Neck, followed by Billy Cheyenne and Killer, ran down the incline.

"Dutchy Gilmore is coming to kill Joe," the girl finally said. "They found out in town that T. Rowley is a captive in Medicine Water's tipi."

"Who told them?"

"Papa doesn't know. He's coming across the grass to warn Joe. He sent me on the road to warn you if I got here first." Now Maude was crying hysterically.

Long and Billy rushed to the corral without waiting to hear any more. They threw bridles on two ponies. Killer met them at the gate with two rifles—Tree Standing's old carbine and the Winchester Long had borrowed from Medicine Water.

"I'll find another gun in the village and follow you," Killer said.

Rifles in hand, Long and Billy dug heels into their ponies and rode fast out onto the grass.

"Come inside and sit down, Maude," Sara said, "and tell me everything."

"That's all I know. Papa told me to hurry. . . ."

With T. Rowley following silently, Joe rode toward Cloud Chief, not looking back. At times he could almost believe no one was behind him. Had the marshal decided, when they reached the grass, that nobody would believe his story? That his career would end not with a blaze of glory but with the stigma of having been mutilated by a noseless woman? Had he purposely dropped back and then ridden away, to disappear from the blackmailing clutches of Dutchy Gilmore, leaving Joe to proceed toward his destiny alone?

No, he was back there. Joe heard his pony snort . . . and then heard the metallic click of a pistol hammer.

"I guess you had better stop now, boy."

Joe drew up and looked back over his shoulder. The marshal held a cocked pistol in his left hand. The bridle reins, looped over his bandaged right hand, were snugged up against his chest. His face, so often emotionless, now showed the hatred Joe should have known was in him, at bottom, all along.

"The thing that happened, boy, when I was bringing you in alive, was that you tried to make a break for it and I had to kill you. The reason you was so shot up was that my first shot didn't bring you down as it ought to, because I'm as good with my left hand as I ever was with my right, but I was riding a pony that was not familiar with the quick action required of a lawman. It shied when I reached, and that's how come I only wounded you with my first shot."

"What are you saying to me, T. Rowley?"

"That when I bring you in, not alive, but the deadest god-damn Indian that ever lived, you was so shot up they wouldn't believe it except for my wounded condition and a strange pony which got skittish on me."

Joe said nothing. He sat still on his pony. T. Rowley told him to turn the pony around. He did and faced the man directly.

"Before I start shooting you, boy, I'm going to explain you something about the white man that you don't know or you wouldn't be sitting there looking down the muzzle of a pistol that is just about to explode all over you. The white man don't ever stop using his brain. The Indian, on the other hand, ain't got one. You have some cunning left over from your pagan instincts and you don't scare easy, but you ain't got brains."

T. Rowley's fury made his voice tremble, but not the left hand holding the pistol. Joe said softly, "You fooled me, Marshal. I believed your promise to take me to jail."

"If you had any brains, you wouldn't have believed me. Because I told you I was caught up in fear acts. If you had any brains you'd know that folks in town would never swallow that cock-and-bull story that I operated on myself. How could I sew up that hole in my hand, anyway?"

To his dismay, Joe found himself grinning. "You got an old Indian woman that does beadwork to sew it up for you, T. Rowley. It's the sort of thing folks believe you could do."

"You arrogant son of a bitch, I'm going to shoot that grin off your face. If you folks wasn't so arrogant, you'd never have took to that stuff I told you about a white man getting his glory from what other people think. It's you Indians that always count coup." The pistol came up higher. T. Rowley aimed it at Joe and said, "Now, don't think you're dead when I pull this trigger. I'm going to shoot you in the ham of your right leg and knock you off that pony . . . and then I'll tell you something else that you don't know."

The gun exploded. The bullet hit Joe's leg with the impact of a granite boulder out of a cannon. He crashed to the ground but did not feel pain instantly.

He lay still, his leg numbed by the slug, and realized that his eyes were not closed. They were open, looking up at the crazed marshal. He watched the marshal's face, not the gun muzzle, and wondered if he could possibly still be grinning. He wasn't sure, for he seemed to have no control of his expression. But he could talk. He said, "What else were you going to tell me, Marshal?"

"That I have never took more than two outlaws alive in my life. I don't believe in live outlaws. It saves the government money when a lawman brings his man in dead. Now, I'm going to shoot you in the shoulder and then tell you something else."

Again the pistol exploded. The bullet smashed through his upper left arm, as though driving him into the ground. He still felt little pain. But he felt sicker than a man should, he thought, without pain.

The blow had partially turned him over. His face was in the grass. He could not see T. Rowley, but he managed to say, "What else were you going to tell me?"

"I gave you a chance to turn yourself in before you put on that Kiowa suit and hid out. If you had brains enough to know that I am a man of my word, you'd now be safely in jail waiting for a hearing on accidental homicide, which I would testify to. Roscoe would not have dug up dirt on me, Dutchy Gilmore would be in Topeka instead of here kissing Roscoe's ass, and I'd be looked up to by the courts for persuading a Kiowa to do the right thing instead of losing my principal trigger finger because a noseless witch with a rusty old carbine got off a lucky shot. She is going to lose more than her nose before I'm through. That is all I aim to tell you, boy, but you ain't dead for a while yet. I am having a good time, which I have not had the past few days."

T. Rowley pulled the trigger again and this shot went through the calf of Joe's right leg. It was the loudest shot he'd ever heard in his life. To the extent of his awareness, he attributed the incredible reverberation to his half-dazed condition and thought that he might have been chewing peyote or drinking mescal.

Blades of grass brushed his cheek. He waited for the next shot. Or for T. Rowley's next verbal onslaught. He heard nothing and wondered if his eardrums had burst. Perhaps the marshal was talking to him right now, cursing the loss of his trigger finger, for that was his outrage, that was what had generated the savagery. The mutilation. Whatever he is telling me now, Joe thought, I can't hear it. I wonder if I am still grinning at him. There would be honor in that.

He considered attempting to open his eyes. Just to find out if he could see. Perhaps he'd been blinded, too. He decided to try, but there seemed to be no hurry. He had the rest of his life to open his eyes, didn't he? Was T. Rowley waiting for him to open them? Must he see as well as feel the next muzzle discharge? Was there honor in waiting any longer?

Without moving, or even trying to move, he lifted his eyelids and could see. What he saw—three feet from him in the grass, toes up, he could tell by the boots—was T. Rowley Duggan. Perfectly still. Incredibly silent.

Joe stared at the boots for a time that seemed like a year while deciding to find out if he could move. He tried to and couldn't—and decided to try again. This time he made it. He moved his right hand, sliding his fingers through the grass until his wrist was near his face. He would be more comfortable, he thought, if he could rest his cheek on the back of his hand. The grass-blades touching him were painful. Three bullet wounds were not as painful as the grass against his face.

Perhaps he had not even been shot. Perhaps T. Rowley, lying about the accuracy of his left hand, had missed. Or had missed intentionally, believing Indians could be scared to death. *One thing about you, boy, is that you are easy to hoodwink. If you had any brains, you would never in this world believe anything a white man says. . . .* He listened, imagining he could hear T. Rowley's voice even as he looked at the boots beside him with their toes pointing up.

But there was sound, real sound, nearby. Of hoofbeats on prairie ground. Of a horse drawing up. Of a man dismounting. Of footsteps approaching. There was also more to see. Two more shoes beside T. Rowley's pointing-up boots. Two brogans, at the bottoms of blue overall legs. And there was more to hear. Harley Wilson's unmistakable voice.

"Joe, I got him. He shot you up, didn't he? Joe, can you hear me?"

Now he was being rolled over. Very gently . . . and the pain came raging. He tried to grasp his senses, to force himself into clarity, to test his strength against the pain, if any strength was left in him. And he tried to grin.

"Harley," he said.

"Joe . . . let me see how you are."

"You got him, didn't you?"

"With my rifle, just as he shot you the last time. I was too far away to hit him any sooner."

Joe tried to lift himself to an elbow but the prairie tilted and he began to fall. He feared that the grass, when his face reached it, was going to hurt. It didn't, for he was no longer conscious.

But he came to quickly. It was Harley, all right. And T. Rowley Duggan was not dead. He'd been shot in the chest, was still breathing, but unconscious.

"If I can pull myself up, Harley, I'll finish him off."

"Don't try it. He ain't dangerous now. I have his guns."

"He isn't going to live if I do."

"I shot to kill him, Joe, because he didn't have a right to shoot a defenseless man. You ain't got the right, either."

"You're the first white man that ever did anything for me," Joe said.

"That ain't true and you know it."

"Who else ever did?"

"Doc, for one. Dutchy followed him around until he caught on that Doc had a patient hiding out somewhere and arrested him, but Doc wouldn't talk. Etta Jenkins miscarried this afternoon and bled so much they had to let him out of jail to take care of her. Him and me and some other white men are better friends of yours than some of the wild-ass Indians around here."

"How bad am I shot, Harley?"

"I ain't got no way of knowing. We must get you to Doc somehow, but Dutchy is on his way after you and Doc may even be back in jail. You know, all three of them shots went clean through you."

Lying in the grass with his face near the ground, Joe heard hoofbeats again, felt the pounding even before he heard it. From the sound, unless he was still dazed, there was more than one horse coming. "Is Dutchy alone?"

"Far as I know. I hear something now." Harley sprang into

the grass, cocking his rifle as he stretched out on his belly. "Joe, it ain't Dutchy. I can see them. Two of your folks. Acting wild, from the looks of them."

Long and Billy rode up, leaped from their ponies, cursed and kicked T. Rowley even before paying attention to Joe.

"Leave him alone," Harley told them.

Long pulled his knife. "I'm going to take his hair."

"You ain't got time. Dutchy is coming this way right now."

"Let us handle Dutchy," Joe said to Harley Wilson. "Take T. Rowley to Medicine Water. He probably doesn't know who shot him because he was pretty busy shooting me up when you fired. Go on, Harley."

"Now, you listen to me. Don't kill Dutchy unless you have to. Killing ain't going to make things any better."

"Harley, go on!"

Long and Billy lifted the marshal onto Harley's horse, draping him over the saddle. "He's still alive," Long said. "I can feel his heart. He's a little bugger to act so mean, ain't he?" Again he eyed the marshal's hair, which was hanging loose, toward the ground.

Harley grabbed the reins and led the animal out of Long's reach. "I'll turn him over to Medicine Water if he ain't dead by the time I get there. If he is, I'm just going to leave him in the creek for somebody else to find. Did Maude come?"

"She's with Crosses-the-River," Billy said.

Harley climbed up behind T. Rowley and disappeared toward Owl Creek.

Joe told himself to get up. He tried and couldn't. He told himself again; and with effort he didn't know he possessed, he turned over and rose into a curious position—resting himself, face downward, on his right forearm and his left knee.

"Bring my pony, Long, and help me on him."

Long brought the pony. He took Joe's right arm, Billy took his left, and they tried to lift him. But agony convulsed him and he fell back into the grass.

"That arm is bad, Billy."

"I'll reach around you, Joe."

They tried again, succeeded in putting him astraddle his pony, but had to hold him upright until his senses cleared. At last he took the bridle reins and said, "Like T. Rowley said, I'm not dead yet."

"Can you ride?" Long asked.

"I've been knocked dizzier than this playing football. Now

I'm going to wait here for a few minutes. You and Billy ride toward Cloud Chief to meet Dutchy Gilmore. Make sure he sees you and then head for the gyp bluffs. If he thinks you're running from him, he'll follow you, and I'll have a chance."

"What're you going to do?"

"Find Doc if I can. I'm still bleeding a lot."

"Joe, it ain't safe for you in town."

"It will be if you can toll Dutchy Gilmore away."

38

JOE sat on the pony, giving them time. He cupped his good hand over the shoulder wound but the blood continued to ooze and the air chilled him.

He felt sick, but not entirely because he had been shot. His resolution, worked out in the woods of his ancestors, was now impossible. Honor, if he had been on its trail, seemed about to elude him. For it was clear that neither T. Rowley nor Dutchy Gilmore intended to let him reach the courtroom.

He dug his left heel into the pony, moved forward, and saw nobody until he neared the town. There, standing beside their ponies on the prairie trail, were Long and Billy. They had been arguing with each other—as friends, not enemies—and they were angry and confused. They had not met Dutchy because he had not come that way. Big Oak had come along and told them why.

It appeared that Dutchy had been onto the idea that the Wilsons were friends of Joe's in-laws since his first day in Cloud Chief. Hobart Jenkins had supplied him that information and a lot more. Being every bit as smart as T. Rowley—Dutchy had admitted this to everybody in town—he had planted the word for Harley's big ears that he was going after Joe that afternoon. Everybody in the hotel had watched him do it and nobody especially resented it because the Wilsons were not much better than Indians, living out there in the cotton fields among them and eating with them and, for all

anybody knew, sleeping with them, too. Now, Dutchy had
explained to his audience in the Iron Hotel dining room,
Harley Wilson probably considered himself as shrewd as an
Indian. He would set out in a wrong direction, falsely pretending to warn his friend, hoping the marshal would follow
him. But this marshal, you could bet, would follow that long-
legged girl instead. She's the one the family would send, hair
flying, arms churning, to warn their Indian friends. And that's
what he had done. Big Oak and many others had seen him
ride out on the road to Owl Creek just keeping out of sight
of the running girl.

"Then he must be there now," Joe said.

"We didn't know what to do," Long replied.

"Where's Killer?"

"Following us, if he found a gun he could borrow."

"Tree Standing can't shoot Dutchy," said Billy, "because
I have her carbine."

While Long and Billy told each other what they would do
if Dutchy harmed their women, Joe found himself convulsed
more with torment than with pain. For it was suddenly clear
that a terrible opportunity lay before him. Appalling, hor-
rendous, hideous . . . and sweet. Incomparably sweet. Opportunity looming in the form of a townful of people whose
principal entertainment derived from the misery of Indians,
whose marshals were away on the business of hunting Indians
down. You could go into that white-man town in search of
medical help and probably find its only doctor in jail for
having befriended your people . . . or you could go with other
motives and find its impressive and wealthy visitor from the
East momentarily unguarded.

As he thought about it, whatever was weak seemed to go
out of him. He knew that the white man had departed his
Kiowa soul at last and that whatever was left was strong. His
own Kiowa self remained, and so did his honor.

Here he was, on his horse, everybody's example of an educated Indian whose very purpose was to whitewash his people.
The U.S. government had created that creature and a U.S.
marshal had joyously shot it up. "Don't think you're dead
yet, boy," T. Rowley had said, squeezing with his left-hand
trigger finger because he didn't have a right-hand one anymore, even to point with.

Here he was, indeed, on an Indian horse, Running Standing—the true grandson of Spotted Foot, poised to achieve honor at last, in the glory way.

"Long," he said, in hopeless thrall to the bloodlust of his ancestors, "you and Billy know where the back door to the hotel dining room is, don't you?"

"Yes, we do. The lean-to where Delma Sue sleeps is beside it."

"I want you to slip up the alley, burst through that door, war-whoop as loud as you can, wave your knives and rifles. Everybody in there will think it's a massacre. Chase Roscoe out to me."

"Chase him?" Long asked.

"Don't kill him. If he's not in the dining room or the lobby, make Hobart tell you where he is. Don't stop war-whooping until you see him run into the street."

A wicked smile touched Long's face, caught there, and burst into flames of happiness. In all his life he had never known such exultation. "You're going to get him, ain't you?"

"Just like Spotted Foot would have got him."

"I'd like to get him for you, Joe."

"I'm strong enough. Look." Joe held the bridle reins in the hand of his wounded arm. He was not surprised that he could. There was no feeling in the hand, but it obeyed him. "When you're sure that Roscoe is outside, you and Billy head for the gyp bluffs."

"Will you come there, Joe?"

"As soon as I can."

Long and Billy wheeled their ponies toward town. Before reaching the wagonyard, they turned into the hotel alley. From his own horse, Joe could see them make the turn.

He moved slowly toward the south side of Main Street. People would soon come flying out of the hotel in hysteria. The question was: Would Roscoe be among the first to rush for the door? Or would he stay inside until he was flushed into the open?

Before deciding what Roscoe was likely to do, Joe saw people pour into the street—and heard screaming. The antic bragging of T. Rowley Duggan and Dutchy Gilmore during the past few days had built an atmosphere of tension and now it burst. Joe dug heels into his pony and went toward the fleeing people.

And he saw the man, Roscoe, in panic, running from the

front door of the little iron building, shaggy hair flying with
each lumbering step. It was probably the first time Roscoe
had run since he was a child, Joe thought with a very small
part of his mind. The rest of his mind rushed on satanically
. . . as he swooped toward Roscoe, leaning far over, drawing
his knife as he leaned. He grabbed a handful of hair in his
injured hand. He couldn't know how much he had grabbed,
for there was no feeling in the hand. He only knew that once
more it had obeyed him. With the knife in his good hand
he hacked at the base of the hair and came away with the
scalp lock he had coveted, without leaving his horse. He had
dragged Roscoe twenty feet in the process, and had dropped
him, separated from his hair. No Kiowa had ever done it
better.

He held the scalp lock high and dripping for everyone to
see as he charged down the street. The whites were not grinning now, he thought. Shots rang out and he knew he'd been
hit again.

He leaned forward, hugging the pony's neck, and rode west
toward the bluffs on the river . . . hanging on, hearing more
shots, feeling nothing, feeling everything, wondering about
Long and Billy, trying to remember the death chant his elders
used to sing for the youngsters on summer nights to demonstrate the old Kiowa manner of dying with honor from the
wounds of battle.

Dutchy Gilmore arrested all the women in Tree Standing's
hut and arrived in town with them in Killer Cross's wagon ten
minutes after Joe's attack. Maude Wilson was driving. Dutchy
was following on his horse.

Hobart Jenkins saw them coming and ran from the hotel
porch to meet them.

"He scalped Mr. Roscoe," Hobart shouted. "That goddamn
Kiowa scalped Roscoe alive. Sending him to school didn't do
no good, did it?"

Maude drew up the team of mules alongside the wagonyard
entrance. The women listened to Hobart tell the marshal what
he knew.

"I seen Long and Billy talking to Big Oak—he's that Arapaho—after I had saw you follow Maude Wilson out on
the Owl Creek road," Hobart said. "I knowed something was
wrong, and I was right. They come in the back way, naked
to the waist, and it's a wonder we wasn't all killed."

"Where is Mr. Roscoe?" Dutchy Gilmore asked.

"Over in Finlater's, but he ain't dead yet. Doc Freeland is working on him now. Doc says it's bad. I have already went over and saw him, and I can tell you, Marshal, that Doc is right."

"Take care of my horse," said the marshal. "Leave him in front of the hotel, I might need him again pretty soon."

Dutchy ran toward Finlater's, where a crowd of onlookers filled the doorway and flowed out into the street.

Sara said, "Maude, are you all right, honey?"

The girl's eyes were wide, her face tear-streaked. "I'm scared, Crosses-the-River, but I ain't a coward. What do you want me to do?"

"Your mother is at home, isn't she?"

"She ought to be."

"Drive there, and all of you stay with her until you hear from me."

"Are we still under arrest?"

"I suppose so. Now, hurry, Maude, while the marshal is out of sight."

"Where are you going?"

"To find my husband," Sara said, climbing out of the wagon.

"Me, too," said Many Stones, climbing out with her.

"Me, too," said Two Bonnet, following Many Stones.

Sara looked at her sisters-in-law, then said to Maude, "Take Lamb Woman and Tree Standing. And the babies. We'll come to your house as soon as we can."

Sara ran toward Finlater's store. Many Stones and Two Bonnet ran after her. Realizing that she would only subject herself to arrest again if she got in Dutchy Gilmore's way, she veered suddenly across the street and into the hotel. Many Stones and Two Bonnet veered into the hotel with her.

She found Delma Sue Raven Rock in the kitchen with two of her brothers.

"Sara," the girl cried, "they'll kill Joe if they find him."

"Delma Sue—did he scalp Mr. Roscoe?"

"Yes, I saw it. I don't blame him. He was all shot up and bleeding. Big Oak told us that T. Rowley double-crossed him."

"Where is he?"

One of her brothers silenced her and asked in Arapaho, "Who is this woman?"

Sara understood him but could not reply in his language. Delma Sue answered for her.

Satisfied, he said, "Running Standing, Long Neck, and Billy Cheyenne are on the bluffs above the river bend. Don't go there. Running Standing is doing his death chant. His half brother and his brother-in-law are guarding him."

Delma Sue translated and Sara whirled from the kitchen. It was a mile on the river road to the bluffs. She ran all the way, and again Many Stones and Two Bonnet followed. Many Stones, awkward in her fancy slippers, kicked them off and ran barefooted.

A crowd had gathered to watch. On a gyp rock ledge, high above the river, Joe chanted and danced. His step was halting, but he danced.

When Sara saw him, he seemed to be bleeding from every pore. She knifed her way through the crowd that Billy Cheyenne and Long Neck were holding at bay with their rifles. The crowd did not appear especially eager to go past the rifles. The people were spectators, curious to watch an Indian die in his own way, but that was all.

Long Neck held her back. "Leave him alone, Crosses-the-River."

"I'm going to him!"

"He wants to die with honor."

"Turn me loose!"

"He told me, if you came, to hold you back—or he'll jump from the bluff."

"Long!" she cried. Billy Cheyenne came to help hold her. She flung herself fiercely against them but could not pull free. She heard the crowd gasp and stopped struggling in time to see Joe sink to his knees on the white gyp rock. His death chant ceased, and he died. She always remembered that both Many Stones and Two Bonnet reached him before she did. She remembered, too, the way his blood glistened obscenely red on the white rocks in the cool afternoon sun.

39

Petroleum in great commercial quantities was never found in the areas C. J. Roscoe originally searched for it. The few surface seepings, such as Lives-in-a-Tree's medicine oil spring, proved to be no more than minor geological freaks, and the old Kiowa-Comanche, Cheyenne-Arapaho lands remained essentially unpolluted by the financial and social pressures of oil. The endless prairies and lush river bottoms became a prosperous agricultural area, with Indian ranchers and farmers scattered throughout the white community, maintaining their tribal identities fraternally but walking the Jesus Road.

Petroleum in incredible quantities was, of course, found elsewhere in the Twin Territories that became the State of Oklahoma that very month, November 1907. The Osage land to the northeast was the site of one of the first great oil booms. And because the Osage mineral interests remained corporate, each member of the tribe having a headright share of the total, there was soon no such thing on earth as a poor Osage.

Among the other Indian lands that produced oil, the Seminole, Cherokee, Creek, Chickasaw, and Choctaw sectors of the state made many individual Indians wealthy far beyond their ability to comprehend, much less to cope with, the strange new American status of being an innocent millionaire whom everyone envies, laughs at, and tries to fleece.

The whites got most of the money, just as they got most of the land, but there were ironies in the final Indian-white confrontation in Oklahoma that sent socially significant tremors into the future. Because the land was known to be valuable, it was all allotted—in severalty, they called it—to individual Indians. By what other mechanism could the whites ever have been able to get it?

The by-product of allotment was the abolition of all the Indian reservations in the new state. Perhaps allotment was not too high a price to pay for that deliverance.

Sara Standing was one of the Indians along the Washita capable of understanding those ironies. Wills Freeland helped her, and his help began the day following Joe's death on the gyp rock prominence above the river.

Joe's body had been carried to Otto Finlater's back room, where a box was made for it. Sara, at home in the tipi behind her father's house, listened all day to the members of her family and Joe's talk about heroism. She stayed in the tipi alone with her son. Early that morning Long Neck and Billy Cheyenne had gone after Rabbit Hand, whom Dutchy Gilmore had not bothered to arrest the previous day, and when they returned, they sat on the whittling log listening to him and Killer Cross describe heroic episodes from the Kiowa and Cheyenne past.

As the men talked of Little Robe and Powder Face of the Cheyenne, White Bear and Big Tree of the Kiowa, the women slaughtered a calf and worked it up in the yard near the tipi; they would feast after the burial of their hero. And they raised their voices, as they worked, to reassure Crosses-the-River of their respect.

"Running Standing was good," said Lamb Woman. "My daughter can be proud that the Jesus Road could not make him white. Now her son will always know that he has the blood of a hero inside him and he can be brave."

"Running Standing always treated me with kindness," said Lives-in-a-Tree. "When I lost my nose, he wept. Long Neck told me."

"He was very smart," said Many Stones. "He knew I was not part wolf the first time he ever saw me."

"He made a good Indian when he tried," said Two Bonnet. "When he put on Indian clothes, he looked like a man ought to look, and not many do anymore."

"I do not believe," said Lives-in-a-Tree, "that my son should be buried in the cemetery. Too many white men are there."

"He ought to be buried in Indian ground," said Lamb Woman. "Killer Cross would not mind if Running Standing used his grave."

At this point the men joined the women's conversation and it was quickly agreed that their hero should be brought here for burial. "I would like to steal the body," said Killer Cross, "and leave Otto Finlater's pine box filled with dirt."

"We could do it," said Billy Cheyenne. "The whites in town

are nervous. If we walk up and down the street about dark
tonight, they will all come out to watch us. While they are
in the street, the women can enter through the back door and
steal him. We can park the wagon near the door."

Long Neck said, "We will need some bags of dirt."

Rabbit Hand said, "I am old, but I would like to dig the
dirt for them to bury."

"I'll go with you," said Killer Cross. "While you dig dirt,
I'll clean out the grave. It hasn't been cleaned out in quite
some time."

Sara decided to let them do as they pleased. After making
their plans, they waited for her to object if she cared to.
When she said nothing, the men harnessed the team, drove
into the bottomland for the dirt, and returned for the women.

"I'll leave my sons with the two old aunts in the cottonwood
house," said Two Bonnet.

"And I'll leave my daughters with them," said Many Stones.
"Crosses-the-River should not have to interrupt her silent
thoughts at this sad time."

"I have something to put into that pine box with the dirt,"
said Lives-in-a-Tree.

"What do you have?" asked Lamb Woman.

"T. Rowley's trigger finger. I cleaned up after Doc's operation and I kept it. But I don't want it no more."

"Then let's throw it in with the dirt," said Many Stones.

They all loaded into the wagon and went to town.

Wills Freeland came at dusk. He appeared at her tipi flap
and said, "Sara, it's me. May I come in?"

"Yes," she said.

"I saw your folks in Cloud Chief and couldn't resist the
chance to visit you alone. Sara, you know how sorry I am."

"You don't need to say anything. I am consoled. Joe died
the way he wanted to. He knew he'd die, and I knew it, too.
I gave him my promise, Wills, never to marry a white man.
You should know that now."

"Yes, I suppose I should."

"How is Roscoe?"

"He's going to live. He won't be the first man to survive
a scalping."

"Perhaps he'll be the last," she said.

"Will you stay here now, Sara?"

"Yes. I'll make this ranch into a monument to Joe."

"I'm going to help you in every way I can."

"I won't need help."

"But you'll need water," he said. "If you go to Winding Creek, you may find me there, Sara. I'm going to begin painting again. I haven't done much painting lately, and I haven't been happy. The light along Winding Creek is excellent. Good-bye, Sara."

"Good-bye, Wills," she said.

The water at Winding Creek was good, too, she thought; and now she would have to decide whether to go there ever again.